# MasterGardener

*To Joanne*
*on her gardening journey*
*Claire Sullivan*

Claire A. Sullivan

Published by Parnassus Publishing

PEI@parnassusenterprisesink.ca

ISBN:  **10: 1463759231**

ISBN-**13: 978-1463759230**

Author's Note

Throughout the book, readers will find various quotes gathered from myriad sources over many years. These sources have been credited where known, but there are many that remain unidentified, having come to the author through word of mouth. Gardening lore, and specifically, herbal lore, travels and mutates extensively.

Interested readers will discover much literature on herbs, their history, lore, cures, and culinary uses.

Ontario Horticultural Societies often stock lending libraries for members' use and some distribute newsletters as well.

Ontario Horticultural Association website: www.gardenontario.org

Peterborough Horticultural Society website: www.peterboroughgardens.ca

Mary's 'bible' is: A Modern Herbal by Mrs. M. Grieve F.R.H.S.

Edited and introduced by Mrs. C.F. Leyel

# Prayer of St. Francis

Lord, make me an instrument of PEACE – Lily of the valley

Where there is hatred, let me sow LOVE – Rose

Where there is injury, PARDON – Hyssop

Where there is doubt, FAITH – Violet

Where there is despair, HOPE – Daisy

Where there is darkness, LIGHT – Rue

Where there is sadness, JOY - Marjoram

# Chapter 1

**A robin looking in your window is said to be an omen of good luck.**

Stella braked too late, wedging her wheelchair and Mary's between the bed and the dresser. "I drive too fast eh? Good thing we don't have to get a license for these things. I'd never pass. Are you crying?"

"You wouldn't understand." Mary muscled her feet against the floor to move away, but the two chairs stayed stuck tightly against each other. "Geez! Now we'll have to sit here until someone comes. What did you want anyway?"

"I came to tell you the latest," Stella said. "There's a new inmate in Libby Long Legs' room."

"Didn't take long to find her replacement. She only died Monday."

"What's today? Thursday? They're quick here. Move 'em out. Move 'em in."

"Yeah, that's for sure."

"It's Jean somebody," Stella said. "Deaf Art told me she's crazy as a loon."

"Deaf Art's crazy as a loon."

"Least he's quiet. Art says this new one, she hollered all night. No one got a speck of sleep. Lucky we're not in that wing."

"How would Art hear? He's deaf!"

Stella shrugged. "Well, she'll fit right in with all the loonies here. And Irwin had his third Code Two clean-up last night so he's wearing diapers now."

"Diapers, eh? Promise you'll feed me some arsenic if you catch me needing them, would you?" Mary rocked her wheelchair back and forth until she worked her chair loose from Stella's. "I don't want to watch these murderers." She pointed out the window at three men working outside. "They cut down my robin's nest while I was at breakfast."

Last spring, two plump robins had made a nest in the spruce tree outside the window and Mary watched the mother incubate her eggs day after day until they hatched. This spring the parents returned to nest in the same tree, and Mary watched the robins fret about the daily tasks of nest building, egg setting, hatching, and delivering food. They watched her too, Mary knew, through the window, as she combed her hair, put in her teeth, and searched for her glasses. It pleased her to imagine the parent birds explaining to their young: "See. That's a female human in there. See. She's talking on the phone." Mary sometimes picked up the phone and pretended to talk so the robins would see activity.

"Life isn't fair," Stella commiserated. "It's what my mother always said."

Mary frowned. "Don't let's talk about life not being fair. I could tell you a thing or two about that."

"You want to sit out in the garden?" Stella offered.

The two companions, hands on the armrests of their chairs, leaned forward, and walked their feet on the floor, to roll down the hallway and through the open door into the paved, fenced courtyard where three other residents sat dozing in the late morning warmth.

"You two girls need sunscreen and hats," Cathy, the health care worker said, producing a tube from the pocket of her sage green uniform and smoothing white cream onto Mary's cheeks. "Don't want your soft-as-a-baby's-bum skin to get sun-burned, do we?" Cathy turned to Stella and gently rubbed cream onto Stella's pale cheeks too, then gave each woman a kiss. Cathy chose two hats from a lidded bench and snugged them onto Mary and Stella's heads. "Isn't it a beautiful day out here?"

Two sets of aged blue eyes peered at her from underneath the wide brims. "And did you hear the news?"

Stella raised her eyebrows.

Mary gazed toward the rose bush that grew in front of the eight-foot high wooden fence. "Is that a blue moth on the bud? He's a small one. Come to me. Come here."

"They've hired a new staff person to run a gardening programme for the residents," Cathy said. "A horticultural therapist. The greenhouse is on its way and you ladies will be able to have your own plants and planting areas. There will be pots of different sizes for things like African violets and geraniums and such. And they're having three larger plots that will hang from overhead bars by chains so they can be moved and adjusted. For residents that want bigger gardens. Won't that be great, Mary? Just like when you were at home on the farm. I think it's wonderful that we can provide this opportunity for our residents."

Mary squinted at her and burped. "A garden."

Cathy spotted another resident in need of a hat and sunscreen and moved on.

Stella tugged Mary's arm. "You'd think she came up with the idea all on her own. Did you notice her earrings?"

Mary grinned. "Big fat Bs hanging from her ears. Must be bingo day!"

"Yes, so it is," Stella said. "Nice. Did you hear her say we get to have our own gardens? The first thing I want is tomatoes. Nothing like a fresh tomato, warm from the sun, eh, Mary?"

"Tomatoes. And Cathy can buy herself a whole new jewelry box full of earrings. Ones with tomatoes and sunflowers and pansies and goodness knows what else on them."

"Nothing better to spend her pay cheque on, I guess."

Mary didn't answer. She picked at a scab on her cheek. Sunscreen always made it itch. She wondered how deep the gardens would be. Would each resident have one of her own? Would a person be able to protect her garden from the other residents? She rubbed her hands together, aware that they hadn't felt black earth in many years. She sniffed her palms, remembered the scent of herbs she'd tended in past gardens.

Soil warmed by May sunshine had a musty scent and the worms were fat and juicy and cold, spitting water as they wriggled from one hand to the other. There were no clean fingernails in those days; she examined her polished, manicured nails. Pink nail polish. City nails. And the birds. The finches would be chirping away. The red-winged blackbirds would search for a spot to build a nest. Well. Not in a greenhouse. "Humph! They cut down my tree." She looked directly at Stella as she said it.

"I'd think you of all people would be happy about the greenhouse," Stella said.

"I'll believe it when I see it." Mary closed her eyes and feigned sleep; Stella followed her lead and in minutes was dozing under the warm sun, leaving Mary free to consider gardening possibilities she'd thought she'd left behind forever.

Mary imagined the staff and management of Sunny Acres Long Term Care Residence For Seniors gathered, behind closed doors, to decide exactly what type of trowel would be suitable for residents' use and the ideal height of a potting table. They would consider the logistics of watering and pruning for the wheelchair bound residents. Wheelchair. Wheelbarrow. Can a person wield one while travelling in the other? The nursing home staff would be careful that the residents not feel frustrated by such concerns, because the staff of Sunny Acres did a very good job at making life easy for the residents. They would likely decide on no wheelbarrows at all.

Everything in the new horticulture therapy programme would be planned and plotted with the safety and well-being of each resident in mind. Careful studies would be done. The best laid plans of mice …. and birds …

Where did the robins go after finding their home cut down and their whole neighbourhood gone? Poor mother robin must be bereft after those many hours of egg setting.

Mary's mother's voice rang clearly from the past. "Busy people are happy people." She had always been one to draw plans and write lists, as she sat by the fire knitting and stitching, repairing and quilting. Had Mother been happy? Mary had early memories of Mother lying on the couch, eyes covered against bright lights, shades drawn, a fearsome headache etching wrinkles of pain around her mouth, drawing her lips pale and her skin paler, her senses heightened and magnified, so the slightest of noises grated against her nerves. She said it felt like a carpenter's rasp scraped her sinuses, leaving them raw and braced for the next pain-ridden, torturous pass.

It seemed impossible that industrious capable Mother could be stricken so ill, so quickly, and Mary supposed that frightening debilitation was what inspired her to learn natural techniques for healing. The healing earth, the magnetic force, surely called to Mother first, and next to her daughter. Mother's green thumb, well-known in the neighbourhood, instilled in Mary all the gardening wisdom at her fingertips. From that base Mary had turned to books to learn more techniques and knowledge, adding wisdom to Mother's legacy by studying about native shamans, and herbalists of medieval monasteries. Books, with theories to be read and collected, studied and tested, took their place beside the books Mother had gathered over the years, containing recipes, teas to stop a pregnancy, salves to soothe a bee sting, remedies to knit a broken bone and so much more.

The documentation of herbal knowledge was important to Mother as a historical and technical resource of which plant worked to cure which ailment. Mary's fascination was with the plants themselves; their characters, their folklore, and their healing abilities enthralled her.

Beside her, Stella coughed in her sleep. Mary's fingers plucked at the red quilt laid over her knees. The quilt Mother made. The quilt she'd used to signal Arnie …

Arnie's face flickered through the haze of memories. The quilt is my memory too, he reminded her. Mine and Claude's and Stella's. Mary sat, waited, knew he'd come through more clearly. Resisted the urge to try not to remember. She surrendered and fell into warm thoughts of Arnie, and of her and Stella promising each other to live lives they could relish looking back on. They had done that. Mary let tears roll from her eyes to trace the wrinkles earned in her eighty-five years.

Stella coughed again.

Mary and Stella came back to Mary's room after lunch. "We've got a few minutes before bingo starts. I want to dig out some pictures from the garden at the farm." Mary handed a plastic-wrapped photograph to Stella. "There's my boy. My Edward. He's just three in that one. Here." She plucked another photo from the box on her lap. "Here's a better one. Looks exactly like his dad. The spring before he died. Remember?"

Stella grunted.

Mary pulled out a packet of photographs wrapped in an elastic band. "Here's what I'm looking for. The seasonal pictures. The Mothers called it a waste of time and money, but I did it anyway." She fanned them in her hands. A deck of memories. "You go on, Stella. Go down to the bingo. I want to sort through these here pictures."

She waited until Stella rolled out before removing the elastic band. It crumbled in her hands. No use bringing all the old memories back. Stella didn't much care for the old memories.

Mary turned the first picture over. 1964. The year Edward should have turned fourteen. The black and white picture drew Mary into the day – hot and sunny – a mass of blue and pink borage in full bloom against a background of tall green stalks of lovage. The lovage grew taller every year until it stood well over six feet high and towered over every other plant in the herb bed, just like family tradition towered over their home. It hadn't done the other plants any harm but it was always there, a plant to be considered when making any plans at all. Lovage claimed its own place in the garden and she'd been glad of its pungent celery flavour in salads and in soups. She'd learned to respect the tall strong plant.

The borage, different altogether, grew happily, and seeded itself each spring, a well-behaved plant, pleasant to look upon, Mary's favourite really, but of course she was biased.

She frowned at the few stalks of lily of the valley in the left corner of the picture, and wished she could dig it out and stomp the life out of it. Even now. I should never have allowed that plant into my garden. She pursed her lips. How foolish to dislike it so. Mary chose the plant for her herb garden while reading the book Stella gave her – her bible: A Modern Herbal by Mrs. M. Grieve F.R.H.S.

Lily of the valley had seemed the perfect addition to the herb garden, being a perennial and easy to grow, with sweetly-scented spring flowers. Well-rooted. Invasive. Almost impossible to oust from the garden once established. At first it was lovely, a novelty, a fresh, green, pencil-thin, curled leaf in the spring, opening to six inches long, with delicate scapes of tiny, white, lightly frilled, bell flowers. Hardly a plant to worry about, she'd thought, until she discovered the pale ropey roots spread underground in a tangled maze, like a den of albino snakes. They choked the nearby plants, threatened to take over the whole bed, forcing Mary to dig and hack all one summer, succeeding only in slowing its spread.

As she dug and whacked to kill the plant she'd put into the herb bed, Claude's mother Liz, had "Taken a turn for the worse." She had two bad falls, breaking first her shoulder, and next her hip and she began spending her days on the porch, sitting, watching, hovering. Judging.

"I've got no ambition," Mother Liz said to Mary, who quit working in the garden to take over more of the household chores. "My legs ache all the time."

11

Guilt welled in Mary's throat, worsening each time she noticed the pile of lily of the valley roots lying on the driveway where she had thrown them to be run over by any and all who passed. Placing them there, she hoped to kill the pariah of her garden, but finally sought Stella's help to save them instead. They gathered the roots into her wheelbarrow, carted them past the barn, and planted them along the edge of the gate going in to the west forty acres. They would do no harm there, she thought, and it tidied the driveway too.

Was it only coincidence that soon, Liz's health improved and Mary could return to her regular routines, quite forgetting her vow to eliminate the lily of the valley from the herb garden? Three years later, Liz started falling again and was back to sitting on the porch, not eating, leaving Mary to care for Liz, and to keep up with the housework and the gardens mostly all on her own, though Sadie, Mary's mother, did what she could to help. She wondered why she hadn't been more appreciative of Mother Liz's contribution to the housework.

When the church ladies held their annual bake sale, Mary bought pies and cookies and brownies, explaining, as the sellers bagged her purchased goodies, that since she hadn't time to bake for the sale, she would show her support on the buying side of the sale table. The church women's nods were full of the knowledge that it was Mary's inability to keep up with everything in and around the house, especially the baking, that prompted her purchases.

Claude's complaint of a new type of weed not responding to being ploughed under joined his litany that spring, and when he said he'd have to dig it out by hand and burn it she hadn't given his predicament much thought.

Mary didn't feel it right to voice her relief at Mother Liz's death.

Stella Jenkins, had no qualms about saying it aloud, even in front of other people. "Maybe now you and Claude'll have a chance at some time to yourselves. A private conversation over dinner, just the two of you."

Funny how it turned out that their first private conversation without Liz concerned that 'Christly' weed Claude had finally eradicated from the gate at the west forty acres. "I've been digging away at the old bitch since last fall and it's taken me all this time to clear it out. I thought I'd need to use some stronger weed killer on her. I won't let that one back on the land. I left them roots out to bake in the sun and when they got good and dry I made a big bonfire. Threw them all in. The day mum passed is the day that weed met its just end and good riddance."

Mary nodded. "You got rid of the lily of the valley."

Now, sitting in her wheelchair at Sunny Acres, Mary's arms felt goose bumpy. Do I really want to garden again? Yet her hands, especially her fingers, strained to feel warm soil. She longed to plant a seed, yearned to nurse it through its stages, to train it on a trellis or prune it into a particular shape. Maybe she'd try her hand at bonsai.

Despite the sun coming in her window Mary found the day chilly, and she rubbed her arms and pulled her sweater closed over her chest. She smoothed the red quilt on her lap.

She put her picture box onto the closet floor, shoved it to the back under the stack of sweaters, and rolled down the hall to the bingo room where Stella had saved her a place.

"B. Eight," said the caller.

B is for borage, Mary thought.

"O. Seventy-two."

O is for oregano.

Borage and oregano and lily of the valley. They won't be suited for growing in containers. Sage should do well. And johnny jump ups. Although why would I bring him back into my garden after all this time has gone by?

"Mary." Stella patted her hand. "He called B-eleven. You've got one."

Mary stuck a piece of bright pink plasticine onto B-eleven.

"N. Forty-two," said the caller.

Mary checked her cards. No forty-two.

N is for nasturtium and those I can grow from seed. It will be fun to see old plant friends again and the ones who weren't friends … well… Mary knew how to manage them. Pretend they didn't exist. Put their pictures under a pile of sweaters so their accusing eyes couldn't follow her around the room. And as for meeting up with them in the afterlife, Mary had no intentions of dying – not for a good long time – so she didn't need to even think about Claude and his accusing eyes.

"I. Nineteen."

Two of those. This might be my lucky day.

# Chapter 2

**Feverfew** – **Chrysanthemum parthenium** – **Sedative, abortifactant, a tonic.**

**Recent studies confirm that feverfew is remarkably effective at relieving and preventing migraines. Chew three feverfew leaves daily to stop migraines. Feverfew may also inhibit blood clotting, but those taking blood-thinning, anticoagulant medications should use feverfew only on the advice of a physician.**

On her tenth birthday Mary lay in bed listening to the robins discuss their building project. Someone must have got too close to their tree. Squawk! Watch out! Danger! Danger! Hide in the branches. Don't let him see you! Squawk!

It must be Daddy on his way to feed the pigs. She hoped he'd hurry up with the chores. Today, just in time for her tenth birthday, Daddy'd promised, the strawberries would be ripe, and he'd said that he and Mary would pick a big bowlful after chores, so they could have them at lunch with yummy chocolate cake and clouds of whipped cream.

Mary had been on her best behaviour for days, since Daddy began giving them daily progress reports on the ripening of the berries. Mom would say, "Tut tut. God won't send the rain to plump those berries if He sees you lying in bed in the mornings. Early to bed and early to rise."

The way she said it made Mary sure that there was more to the saying, but Mom would frown at Daddy, and he'd agree right away. "That's true, Mary. There are jobs to be done in the morning. When Jacob and I are feeding the beasts, your place is in the house helping Mother with the washing and cleaning."

Mary sat straight up in bed. "Get up, lazy bones," she whispered. She dressed, made her bed and hurried downstairs to use the toilet before the men tramped in for breakfast.

Mary and Mother worked quietly together, cooking bacon, heating water for tea, timing their preparations in order to have the food ready for the men to dig into as soon as they sat at the table. She heard their voices at the door and filled the plates.

Daddy smelled of the hay mow and corn silage as he gave Mary a one-armed hug; she placed his plate of two poached eggs with bacon in front of him. "How's my birthday girl?" he asked. He winked at Mary as he spoke to his wife. "Mrs. Murphy! Could we borrow your largest mixing bowl this morning please?"

Mary held her breath, awaiting the answer.

"What would you need a mixing bowl for, Mr. Murphy? Making a cake, are you?"

"There's ripe strawberries, Mrs. Murphy. I thought you might allow young Mary here to help me with picking them this morning."

All eyes watched Mother who paused, set the juice pitcher on the counter, and stood with her hands on her hips as she considered the request. Mary imagined that Mother's pursed lips were a sign of the many tasks that needed to be done this morning.

"And I would be expected to provide cake for the berries?" Mother said.

"Cake – one of your fine chocolate cakes – would be much appreciated, Mrs. Murphy."

Mother smiled at that. "I suppose it would save me picking the berries myself, wouldn't it? Although I don't mind picking berries. Out in the warm sunshine."

Mary felt Daddy's large hand on her back, propelling her forward. She put her arms around Mum's waist and rested her head against the bony frame, inhaling the fragrances of baked bread, bacon and oatmeal raisin cookies that clung to her apron. Mum patted her on the head and wiped Mary's arms from her waist, as she stepped back from her daughter and picked up the juice pitcher. "Eat up your breakfast and then off with you both. I set the metal cooking pot on the back stoop for you to use," she said.

"You give your mother a hand with the breakfast dishes," Father directed Jacob.

Jacob and Mary studied each other's eyes a long moment, until Mary high-stepped to the kitchen door, almost afraid to dare believe that her brother would work beside Mother at the kitchen chores. What would they talk about over the steaming tub full of dirty china?

"It's just you and me left to straighten up this kitchen while they gallivant about the garden," Mother might say, before beginning to hum a church song that couldn't quite be identified. Jacob's conversation was never much more than grunts. Of course Mother didn't much go for a lot of talking either, but she could when she wanted to. She knew good big words that Mary would look up afterwards in the dictionary. Gallivant was one such word, but more often Mother worked in silence and Mary kept her thoughts of unusual words to herself.

"I worried we wouldn't be allowed to go," Father said, as they walked between the rows of carrots and onions, through Mother's vegetable garden on their way to the berry patch.

Mother disdained the customary four-year rotation pattern suggested by the Ministry of Agriculture and had developed her own five-year system for her annual vegetables, to keep weeds and insect pests at bay. Each year she grew her five groups of crops in five tidily planted sections, running east to west. Where potatoes were planted in year one, carrots, peas and onions were grown the next, to be followed by beans, turnips and tomatoes the third year; the cucumber and squash vines were planted in the section on the fourth year, and on the fifth, corn took its place. The rotation was complete then and in year six, potatoes were planted in section one, where they'd grown in year one, with the carrots and peas, and onions in the section next to the potatoes, and so on, to begin again the cycle of uniform, tidy rows with twenty-two inch paths between each.

Mary's usual job, after the breakfast dishes were washed every morning, except Sunday, was to hoe one row, leaving no place for weeds to gain an advantage. The standard useful kitchen herbs grew in a separate section: lovage, sage, feverfew, savory, and sorrel, with annual basil and parsley and lettuce lining the outer edges of the perennial herb patch. Beebalm's vibrant red flowers competed with lovage to grow taller than all the others, its leaves useful in making Oswego tea. The walking onion insisted on growing free, seeding wherever it chose, and Mother, unable to control it, allowed the onions their own, special, four-foot square plot, where tangled masses of leaning green stems and purple bulbs criss-crossed each other, making Mary think of the onions as dancers.

"Your mom sure keeps the garden tidy, don't she, Mary? She's a hard-working woman."

Mary thought Daddy didn't mean for her to answer, so she kept walking in silence, while in her head, she thought of what answer she might give. Mother keeps everybody working hard.

She recaptured her special daydream, which consisted of dancing around and around under a high-domed ceiling where a hundred chandeliers' reflections shone in the glossy polish of a white marble floor. Her partner was the prince from her well-worn copy of Cinderella, handsome in his powder blue jacket and trousers and his carefully combed, slick, black hair. Fun and dancing and laughing too. Mary squared her shoulders, aware that many things would have to change before her daydream came true. First, she'd have to find herself a frog to kiss like the princess in her other storybook. Mary giggled.

Daddy knelt among the calf-high plants, his gigantic fingers fumbling to free a strawberry. The leaves rustled and scraped against each other like sandpaper as Mary reached for a fat, juicy berry. They treated themselves, picking and savouring and filling the bowl and their stomachs with handfuls of red, plump, delicious berries, while the layers rose in the bowl, and their stomachs expanded. Robins chirped and sky-blue butterflies flitted while they picked and Mary knew of no place better than the garden.

Daddy's hand fell warm and heavy on Mary's shoulder. "Let's sit a minute and catch our breath," he said. "That's what God made apple trees for, you know. For shade to sit in." They sat side by side under the apple tree, and Mary knew that when she chose a husband he would be kind and strong and gentle – exactly like Daddy. Almost.

"A man gets weary working. Make sure when you get yourself a husband, Mary, that you leave time each day to thank God for the fields, trees and sky and all this beauty."

"I will, Daddy." Mary admired a blue butterfly as it flitted along a row of strawberry plants. My husband will be just like Daddy. Except he'll know how to read and figure too. But that's not Daddy's fault. He doesn't have time for school what with working so hard to keep the farm going and food on the table.


The sweet scent of chocolate cake baking greeted Mary, as she rounded the hedge that separated barnyard from backyard. Daddy had sent her on ahead with the metal, berry-filled pot, saying that Mother would be looking for her to help in the kitchen by now.

She stopped at the pump west of the doorway and, setting the pot underneath its spout, gave the worn wooden handle three full pumps. Mother painted the handle fresh white every spring. Water splashed onto the berries, and Mary plunged her hands into its cool depths. She rescued two small beetles from drowning, and satisfied that the berries were clean, she drained the water onto the base of the bleeding heart shrub that flourished beside the well. Mary picked one pink and white flower from its green stem releasing the scent distinctive to the plant. Mary thought no other plant smelled like it – except maybe green apples. She pulled back the two edges of the sturdy flower to reveal the delicate 'lady in the bathtub', hidden inside.

She would have liked to check for frogs or toads in the low, soggy spot where, later in the summer, the cattails grew high. Once, she had leaned against the sugar maple and almost squished a perfectly camouflaged tree frog who clung there like a knob of bark. He hadn't moved, and she thought she'd killed him, but Daddy explained later that the frogs hide by keeping still.

Mother called and Mary hurried to deliver the berries.

"They're ripening fast from the looks of that bowlful," Mother said. "I have everything we'll need for making jam. Sugar, pectin, jars, lids. You be a good girl and stem those berries now, would you?"

"Yes, Mum."

"You were out there a long time. What did you talk about?" Mother asked.

"Just about the berries, and about how good they will taste with warm chocolate cake."

"Well now, you sound exactly like your dad. He's always trying to butter me up too."

Mary didn't mention that she and Daddy sat in the shade of the apple tree or that they'd eaten strawberries until they could eat no more. "The toads were jumping in the berry patch," Mary said. "I counted fifteen."

"They come to see you," Mother said. "You were born in the strawberry patch. June twenty-fifth, 1921. Six months after Jesus' birthday. Your dad and I had taken Jacob and gone to the patch to pick, with no inkling you were on your way that exact day. Must have been the stooping and walking that brought on the birthing." Mother paused.

"Quick, you were. Nothing like the time I went through to get your brother birthed. I worried about that all the while I carried you. Would it be a difficult birth? Wondered if I should bring in the midwife. It's why I waited until Jacob turned three before having another baby." Mother shook her head, looked at Mary in silence a moment before continuing. "But you popped out as easy as pie. No question of walking back to the house. I said to your father that I would sit down awhile and he could keep on filling the berry bowl."

"Was I born right there in the straw?" Mary asked, though she knew by heart what Mother would say next.

"Yes. In the straw. I wiped you off with my apron, gave you a little drink and we sat there in the patch under the tree, you and I, for a good long while. We napped and woke and napped some more, with the robins squawking over where to build their nest and the sky as clear as a person could ever wish for. A perfect day to birth a beautiful healthy baby." She stroked Mary's blonde hair. "I thanked God for sending me my own little girl who would work by my side."

"Was Jacob born in the strawberry patch?"

"Your brother was an altogether different case." Mother didn't offer more information. "We'd better get at these berries now." She closed her thin pale lips to hum.

When Mother recounted the story of Mary's birth she used simple words to describe the patch, the birds, and the sky, and always she told how quickly and easily Mary entered the world. "Not like Jacob," she would say.

Mary liked to hear that. And she liked to know that she'd come to earth on a beautiful sun-shiny day when the berries were ripe and the robins nesting. And she liked that Mother had no inkling, though she'd have to find inkling in the dictionary.

When Mary thought about it later, when she'd moved away from home and heard birthing stories from other women, she realized that Mother cleaned the telling. Things were always clean and neat in Mother's world. The birth had been expected but she mentioned no pains, no sudden gush of water, none of the signs a woman would watch for, just an urge to visit the strawberry patch, to squat beneath the apple tree, to push. And in what seemed like no time, the steaming girl-child lay at her mother's feet on the straw, and Mother used her apron to wipe her baby's eyes and nose. She'd felt no need to spank her, to make her cry, and force her lungs to work, because the baby's breathing expanded and shrank her miniature chest with quiet strong rhythm. Mother watched, fascinated, as the perfect fingers, each with its own perfect nail, dried under the warm June sun.

That was the version of Mary's birth that Sadie told her daughter.

"You belong to that place," Mother would say, and Mary would imagine Mother following a small toad to the patch, his short hops calculated to lead her on. He'd stop long enough for Mother to get the spade that leaned against the pole cattle shed, so she'd have something on which to rest when her legs tired.

She called to her husband. "Edward."

When he hurried to her she showed him the fine wee girl who had just arrived and he exclaimed as he saw the birthmark displayed on her tiny neck. "Just like your mother's, Sadie."

Later, after reading a book about native birthing, Mary embellished the story further and had Mother use the shovel to dig a hole in the middle of the strawberry patch, into which she laid the afterbirth and covered it with rich, dark soil. She wrapped the new-born child in her shawl and laid her on top of where she'd buried the afterbirth. The baby slept peacefully with her face puckered as only the new-born and the very old do.

Mary imagined Mother watching over the new baby, while Father kept an eye on Jacob and harvested the ripening berries, and soon a brown rough toad hopped along to pay his respects to the youngster. Other creatures of the garden came forward until the baby was surrounded by sky blue moths, green and white and black striped caterpillars, and a furry yellow and black bee, which bumbled over her cover, stumbling in and out of its folds. A fat robin let go of the straw he carried, to land on a strawberry plant beside the new-born, and a slim, short, grass snake, in his new spring green skin, slithered along the outside of the shawl.

"She is one of the old people," Mary thought Mum would have whispered, more to herself than to her husband. With their bowls brimming full of the rich berries, and the sun shining brightly on their few rocky acres, they dedicated their daughter to the land.

Stabbing her thumb into the warm damp earth, Sadie formed a gritty circle on the baby's forehead, and sprinkled drops of water from a strawberry leaf into the circle. With scissors from the leather tool carrier around her waist, she cut a lock of wispy blonde hair from the baby's head and holding her hand up high in the air she let the hair waft away on the soft breeze, while she turned a full circle.

"Earth, wind, water, fire."

Sadie's hair streamed around her head as she lifted the child and circled again offering her to the four directions. "North, east, south, west," she chanted. She crushed the leaves of a sprig of sage. "Her name is Mary," she announced and she kissed the baby's forehead.

"Mary," repeated her husband, lifting his arms high to offer thanks to the Universe for the perfect child bestowed upon them.

Mary's story of her birth grew more detailed and less like Mother's version with each birthday, but both stories were set in the same patch and Mary knew that every spring, on her birthday, strawberries ripened in Mother's garden, where nature reigned kind, and orderly, except in the section where the walking onions grew. For one had no inkling where a walking onion might plant itself next.

At noon, before clomping in to the kitchen, Father and Jacob washed at the pump, their wordless language of grunts and hand signals sounding to Mary as if some of the cattle had broken free of the pasture and were roaming about the yard. Or a couple of pigs. The thought made her grin. She sneaked a peak at Mother to see if she'd noticed, but Mother had no flights of fancy as she worked, straight-backed, reaching into the oven to lift out the pan of breaded chicken, and carefully placing it on the wooden counter next to the stove. Mother took off the quilted oven mitts she'd made last winter, and hung them on the nail hook away from the heat of the stove.

Jacob sat at his place at the table. He and Daddy didn't ever seem to talk like Mary and Daddy did, in the little bits of time they were allowed together. Mary heard Mother tell the priest one time, that Mary and Jacob inherited wavy thick hair and sturdy physiques from Father, but there the similarities ended, especially where personality was concerned.

Mary knew that she and Daddy could get the work done, and have fun too. He knew about things like tree frogs, and he got her up out of bed to show her the northern lights. Jacob didn't appreciate that sort of thing; he'd rather work away at his chores, just like Mother. Exactly like Mother. I should be the one to work with Daddy, to set out each morning beside him, slop pail in one arm and milk jug in the other. Jacob and Mother are the ones who should spend their mornings in the kitchen, baking bread and canning, while me and Daddy tend the animals and grow the crops.

Mother smiled as Jacob swiped a warm cookie from the cooling rack and popped it whole into his mouth. He didn't close his mouth around it right away, kept it open to let the heat escape.

"Sure smells good in here." Daddy winked at Mary.

"It's all ready. Sit yourselves down," Mother directed with raised eyebrows. A slight tilt of her head instructed Father to pray over the food. Another nod of Mother's head indicated that Mary should begin serving the chicken to the men.

As she served, Mary imagined herself sitting up close to the table and biting into the salty, crisp skin of the warm chicken while Jacob stood behind her ready to offer more meat or to put the plate of white, crusty bread within her reach.

"Thought we'd fix that last line of fence this afternoon," Father said to Jacob between mouthfuls.

Jacob grabbed his fourth piece of chicken and Mary refilled the serving platter with the last four pieces. Maybe there wouldn't be any left for her and Mother, not at the rate Jacob shoved it down. She offered the platter to Daddy, who took his third piece.

Jacob mumbled something. A bit of chicken stuck to his lip and grease glistened on his round red chin.

I'm smarter than Jacob. Jacob can't even talk right. Daddy winked at me. He knows what I'm thinking. He wants me with him, Mary thought. "I could help Daddy build the fence," she said aloud.

Jacob shoved a whole slice of buttered bread into his mouth, staring at Mary as he did. Mother surveyed the table as she took up the pie lifter to serve the cake, and motioned for Mary to spoon strawberries over the top. Father picked at a scab on his upper arm.

Maybe they didn't hear me. Maybe I didn't say it out loud. "I could help Daddy build the fence," Mary braved again.

"Two spoonfuls of berries." Mother spoke quietly, in the voice that meant something was wrong or soon to be.

Mary checked to see what was burned or broke, but all seemed fine. She decorated the desserts with a sprig of fresh mint as they'd planned, and served one dish to her father who kept his eyes down. Had Mother noticed the winking?

After Mary served Jacob his dessert, she scraped the plates from the men's main course into the scrap pail under the sink. If Mother was getting a fearsome headache, Mary knew that quiet would reign in the household until the headache ended.

Mary wished she could lay on her stomach on the fresh green grass, warm summer sunshine heating her back. It would be too hot, and the mosquitoes would eat me alive. It's better inside. She kicked her foot uselessly, as Father and Jacob pushed their chairs away from the table and stood to leave.

"Thank you, ladies," Father said, "for the delicious birthday lunch, especially the cake and the berries."

Jacob used his sleeve to wipe his face, grunted his thanks, and the two men left.

Mary doled out the two leftover pieces of chicken and the potatoes and set them at her place and Mum's place on the table. Mum continued working silently as Mary poured the tea.

"The tea is still warm. Your headache will feel better once you've eaten some food. I can wash up the dishes after."

"Yes, Mary. Thank you. You're so good to me, your old Mum. You look after me well. There's a new dress for you laid out on your bed. You can try it on after lunch. The blue will be nice with your eyes." Mum patted Mary's head.

Mary wondered how long it would be this time until Mother's toneless humming signalled happy times again. She didn't mind really, since a fearsome headache meant she could spend most of her day outside in the garden, hoeing, picking strawberries and spring onions. The silence Mary would welcome too, as she entertained herself by embellishing familiar stories. How did Cinderella ever dare get into that pumpkin-turned-coach?

"I'll lie on the couch this afternoon while you do the dishes. We'll make the jam while supper cooks. Bring in some fresh mint and feverfew leaves and brew them into a pot of tea, there's a good girl."

Mary thought she would bring in some extra feverfew leaves for Mum to chew as the tea steeped. They always helped with the headaches.

"You can spend the rest of the afternoon in the garden. A good place to be on your tenth birthday. And mind you don't bother the men. They've work to do!"

# Chapter 3

Mary tucked the red quilt around her sore knees then rolled down the hall using her feet and her hands to keep the wheels moving. Today, June 15th, they would celebrate the birthdays of all the residents born in June. Right smack in the middle of the month. There'd be balloons, and a choice of chocolate cake or white cake, and the staff would all stand at the front of the dining room to lead them in singing happy birthday.

"Hello, Mum." MaryArlene carried a box wrapped in blue foil with a big bow on top. "Happy birthday."

What did she bring? MaryArlene always chose thoughtful gifts. Mary held out her hands to accept the present and offered her cheek for a kiss. "For me? Thank you, sweetie."

MaryArlene wore her navy blue suit with a cream-coloured blouse and a large sparkly brooch. Her one-inch heels showed off her toned, tanned legs, and looked comfortable enough to wear and to walk in all day. Such a sensible girl, my MaryArlene.

"No opening gifts until after lunch." MaryArlene pushed the wheelchair, leaving Mary's hands free to pluck eagerly at the wrap. "I hope you'll like it."

"I should open it now," Mary said. "So we'll know if I like it."

"Very sly, but no. After lunch."

Eleven residents celebrated birthdays in June and staff helped each of the eleven to don a shiny foil and cardboard hat to wear during the meal. At the table next to Mary's, Tom Howe's shiny hat slipped across his glistening bald head to rest on his bushy eyebrows.

Mary reached up to check that her hat sat straight. She wondered if all the other residents were watching her, wishing they could have hats too. Across the table Stella and MaryArlene talked about the movie, The Rock, that had been shown last night in the activities room.

"I've seen it at least ten times. Sean Connery looks better every time," Stella said.

"How did you like the movie last night, Mum?"

Mary could catch only one piece of pasta on her spoon at a time. "We need bigger spoons," she said, conscious of the weight of the hat perched atop her fresh perm. The blue foil, gift-wrapped box glinted under the bright fluorescent lights.

"How old are we this year, Mary?" Cathy kissed Mary's cheek and put a dinner roll onto each plate at the table. Her dangly, birthday-cake earrings tinkled as she moved her head.

"I can butter the rolls today," MaryArlene offered.

Such a helpful child. I always felt lucky to have her, Mary thought. "Did you wash your hands before eating?" Mary asked. "It's important, especially after you've been in the barn."

"Oh, Mum. I haven't been in the barn. I've just come from the office to have lunch with you on your birthday." MaryArlene rubbed Mary's back and straightened her hat. "Do you want butter on your bun?" She broke the bun open and buttered it, not waiting for her mother's answer.

Mary remembered now, the barn had been sold along with the house to those people from the city, who renovated the barn into what was now the site of a popular dinner theatre. MaryArlene had called it 'eclectic', a nice word, Mary thought, though it didn't seem quite right to have a restaurant in a barn – regardless of its eclecticity. They'd driven past once, on a wintry Sunday, and stopped at the new stone and wrought iron gate. MaryArlene pointed out the two, twenty-foot tall yew trees, their branches dancing wildly in the wind.

"You planted those two trees, remember?"

They'd been shrubs, barely two feet high at the time Mary and Stella each brought home yews from the nursery to plant at their front gates. She'd asked  MaryArlene could they drive by to see Stella's trees too and so they had.

The yews survived. What was it about yews? In the herbal, Mrs. Grieves described the yew tree as sacred and favoured by the Druids, who built their temples near ancient yews.

"Taxus baccata," Mary said.

"Pardon me?" MaryArlene said.

"Greek to me," Stella said.

"Not Greek. Latin," Mary said. "It's the Latin name for yew. I cannot fit a yew tree into the garden I plant here. I think not." She shook her head dislodging the shiny hat, so that it fell into her soup, splashing red broth onto her terrycloth bib. Will yew work as a bonsai? Could I do it?

Mary eyed the gift box. Chocolates? Perfume? A scarf maybe. A blue scarf to highlight her eyes. I hope it's a scarf.

# Chapter 4

**Sage** - Associated with longevity. Restores failing memory and increases brain power.

**Where sage grows vigorously the wife rules. The plant will thrive or wilt where the owner's business prospers or fails. Smelt for some time, sage causes intoxication and giddiness. Dried leaves when smoked will lighten the brain.**

Mary began her seventeenth birthday picking strawberries in the garden with Father. As on her last ten birthdays, she sat on the stoop at the pump, stemming the berries, and then she bustled about in Mother's tidy kitchen, washing the jam jars and lifting the canning kettle down from its hook by the window. At the table Mother hummed as she leafed through her cookbooks in search of a recipe she remembered clipping from Hoard's Dairyman Magazine.

They worked quietly together, last night's words on both their minds. Mary had told her parents of her plan to enrol in the school in town to study business for women, a new course that would start in the fall. Father had sat in his chair by the fire, nodding as Mary spoke.

"I'll move into town," Mary said. "Into the boarding house with Stella. I can share the rent with her and come home on weekends to help you with the gardening and the housework."

"Stella Perkins," Mother said.

Stella and Mary had been friends all their lives and they'd planned since childhood to be friends forever. They'd also planned to live together in town until they fell in love and married the men of their dreams.

"You should get married," Mother said. Only Mary noticed Jacob smirking beside the fireplace. On Saturday nights, Jacob stepped out with Amy Perkins, Stella's older sister, and everyone knew that they'd soon be married. And everyone knew how that would turn out. Amy would move into this house; Jacob would farm with Father, until eventually the parents would die, leaving Jacob and Amy to carry on.

"What about Claude Johnston down the road? He'll be taking over his parents' farm," Mother said.

Marry Claude Johnston down the road, and move in with his parents for more of the same drudgery. Not on your life, Mary thought. "I could join the convent," Mary said out loud.

Or get myself a trade and move into town. That would leave you and Father with Jacob and Amy, Mary thought. "I could study to be a teacher or a nurse," she said. "Maybe a missionary. Travel to Northern Ontario to teach in the native schools up there."

Father said, "You want to have a pot full of money to bring with you to the convent or you'll end up being kitchen staff for the rest of your days."

Mother said, "Studying is a complete waste. And altogether unnecessary, because once you're married you'll stay home to keep house." She laid her hand full on her forehead glancing at Mary as she did.

Even Stella expected to marry and become a housewife. But not until they'd both been to school, away from home and explored for themselves all the possibilities that life offered.

Mary used tongs to set the jam jars into the boiling water to sterilize. She thought that probably her parents found her lacking because she didn't feel more attached to the land and the farm and the house. She loved it, and especially the creatures that lived on it, but it didn't hold her. Not like it held her parents. Or Jacob.

Mary wished she could explain to Mother her feeling that the land, and the farm knew there was more to her life than this, but how could Mother ever understand? She came from a whole different generation, and likely had never wondered what lay beyond the bend in the road or over the next hill. Mother and Father barely saw past their own property, but for Mary, the whole world called her name.

"Here it is." Mother waved a page triumphantly. "It has a quilting pattern on the back. Lucky I even noticed the recipe."

"Hope it calls for plenty of berries," Mary said, and dunked her hands in the sink full of the ripe red crop waiting to be stemmed. "I've got two tons of strawberries, I swear."

"It's a good one," Mother said. "Anyway, we'll need to make some extra this year, of everything, with Jacob's wedding coming up, and I'm sure you and Stella will like to have home-made jam for your breakfasts."

In silence Mary considered her answer.

"I won't go if it's not all right with you and Father."

"Your father and I talked it over last night after you'd gone to bed. There's the money we set aside to send Jacob to school, but he'll never go, so you will go instead. Have a chance to better yourself."

"Thank you, Mother. I'll work hard. I'll make you both proud of me."

"We're already proud of you. It's a shock to us, is all. We didn't realize you were thinking of leaving home."

"I know. I didn't quite know how to tell you."

"There's big changes coming. We can't stay the same even if we wish we could. Best to have our eyes wide open."

Mary dared a look at Mother. She had her chin resting on both hands.

"I wonder how it will be," Mother said. "You and Stella in a little apartment. We can make it cozy. I'll sew a quilt. And you'll meet new friends in your classes. You'll need some new dresses. And a decent handbag. That old one has seen better days. I saw some blue cotton at Town's Store that will make a nice summer dress. We'll take the little white collar from your old yellow one." She stared out the window. "It won't be the same without you here, Mary."

"No. It won't. But soon you'll have Amy to help you."

"She couldn't take your place, ever."

"No. Stella says..." Mary stopped herself.

Mother looked up.

"Stella says I look good in blue."

"We'll have to divvy up the work – Amy and me."

"Yes, that's right. And I plan to come home every second weekend to help with things too."

"Your dad won't likely get into town regular like that to pick you up. He's not much for town driving."

"That's all arranged. Claude Johnston goes to market on Saturday mornings so I can drive home with him when he's done at the market, and back again on Monday mornings when he makes his deliveries. So there's my ride all looked after."

"Oh. Claude Johnston. That's settled then. Maybe you and Claude ..." Mother raised her eyebrows.

Mary shook her head. "Don't get your hopes up about Claude Johnston. He's just a friend." She emptied the stemmed berries into the black kettle and measured eight cups of white sugar over the mass of red. Art in a bowl.

Mary rummaged in the utensil drawer for Mother's wooden ladle. "And if there's a war, he'll be gone overseas."

Mother wasn't the only one questioning Claude's intentions. Stella insisted that Claude sought more than a bit of company on the long drive. "He's got an eye out for you," she'd said, more than once.

"He'd better have an eye for adventure too then. Mother and Father think Claude Johnston will settle me down. They don't know I have every intention of making my own living even after I'm married. If there ever is a wedding. They just don't understand."

But Claude had dreamy, rich, chocolate-brown eyes that lit up when he talked about his plans to open a welding shop in Peterborough. Mary encouraged his dreams about the future.

"I think he's smart," Stella said. "Too smart to stay home on the farm. I can see him in town, making a good living in his own shop. You and him both. You could do worse than Claude Johnston."

Now, Mother said, "Claude Johnston is a good boy. He's always been reliable. Looks after his parents. And that's a good farm there. Never run out of water – even in a dry summer."

"I'm not marrying Claude Johnston and I'm not living on that farm!" Mary's foot itched to stamp on the wood floor but she stood still instead, and stirred the berries hard as they roiled over the high heat. A bubble popped and landed a hot speck of red juice on Mary's cheek where it burned a moment until it cooled.

"Your classes..." Mother said.

"I'll enrol in the new School of Business for Women. In two years I'll have my secretarial diploma and I'll be able to study herbs on my own time and maybe get taken on at Fynch's Apothecary."

"Don't get so caught up in your studies that you miss your chance at meeting your future husband."

Stella and Mary had already decided they'd be joining the ever increasing group of young people that met at the Knights of Columbus sponsored dance every Thursday evening.

"Don't worry. I'll take some time off from my studies to look for a husband," Mary said now to Mother.

"Not too much time, I hope," Mother said, and wiped the red spot from Mary's cheek.

Mary and Stella soon settled into a routine of living together, tidying their rooms on alternating Saturday mornings, shopping for groceries at the Saturday market, and studying on Sundays, after they attended mass in the college chapel. Every second weekend Claude drove Mary home to visit and to help Mother, and Mary found herself at ease with his quick humour and pleasant conversations. She told him about the Thursday dances at the Knights' Hall and suggested Claude might like to come.

"There's lots of girls there. You could meet your future bride," she teased, aware of his aspirations toward her. "You and Stella might find you've plenty in common."

"Stella. I've known her since I wore knee socks," Claude held his hand at knee height.

"Plenty of folk marry the girl next door," Mary said, amused at his discomfort. Would Claude and Stella ever make a couple? "It seems to be a place for boys who've enlisted and are waiting for their instructions to leave. Lots of dance partners."

"Maybe I will come in next time I have a delivery on a Thursday. Are you there every time?"

"Every Thursday. Like clockwork, as they say," Mary assured him. "You're welcome to join the gang and you could even bring a friend. There's no shortage of single females."

"You've got a mischievous smile on your face today, Mary." Cathy's perky voice brought Mary away from her seat beside Claude on his parents' wagon into the present where she sat, in her wheelchair, red quilt covering her aching knees.

"Have you been up to some more of your tricks?" Cathy's sunflower earrings glinted in the fluorescent light.

Mary smoothed the quilt; its worn softness helped her stay beside Claude, bouncing along behind the horses, their muscular flanks rhythmic in the fresh fall air. Claude's scent was of hay and soap and Mary wished she could reach out to touch that Claude now. Smell once more, the Claude she'd fallen in love with.

"No tricks today, Cathy," Mary said. "My knees are aching so bad I wonder how I ever danced."

"You poor dear. Let me rub some of your ointment on." Cathy reached for the tin of Rawleigh's that Mary kept in her bedside table drawer.

"That feels good, Cathy. Thank you. I guess I wore out my joints with all my gardening and dancing over the years."

Mary and Stella were standing at the back of the room on the Thursday night that Claude and his friend Arnie first made their appearance at the Knights of Columbus Hall. It was a large room, smoky, and dimly lit with a candle on each of the tables that ringed the perimeter. In the center, couples, in varying stages of inebriation, filled the dance floor. Many made no pretence of dancing and stood, talking and laughing. The two girls watched Claude and Arnie wend through the crowd to the bar. As the boys waited for the bartender to serve them they leaned on the bar, casually chatting and looking out into the room, drawing the attentions of the red-haired Brandon twins from the secretarial course – the self-appointed social conveners.

"So, do we rescue them?" Stella asked.

"We could. Course, the longer they talk to Tootie and Fruitie the better we'll look," Mary said, watching Claude search the room and hardly taking part in the current conversation.

"Who's the friend, I wonder?" Stella said. "Haven't seen him around before."

"That's Arnie Jenkins. You must remember him from grade school."

"Arnie Jenkins! I never would have picked him out. He sure has changed." Stella primped her black curly hair.

Mary knew they would have to make their way to the girls' room together, and that they would take the long way around the room. She straightened her skirt and turned away from the crowd to freshen her lipstick. She and Stella checked each other for stray eyelashes, twisted collars, and undone buttons before setting out, keeping themselves clearly in view of Claude and Arnie, while seeming not to notice the boys at all. Smiling, stopping for a quick word with classmates and acquaintances, Mary and Stella made a circuitous route toward the Ladies' Room. The two boys were still engaged in their dalliance with the twins and seemed not to have noticed Mary and Stella yet.

Stella tugged Mary's sleeve. "There's more uniforms here every week. Oh oh … Here comes trouble."

George headed toward the girls. "How's the two prettiest ladies in town?" he called over the heads of at least fifteen people. "I've been looking for you two ever since I got here."

"We were just going for a washroom break," Stella said, after George pushed his way to them. Mary noticed Claude watching and she caught his eye and smiled at him, pleased to see that he immediately jerked his head to signal to Arnie.

"So, George, tell me. You are late getting here tonight. I thought maybe you weren't coming."

Stella could sure purr when she wanted to. Mary watched Claude and Arnie make their way through the press of dancers. Claude didn't look half bad with a white dress-shirt tucked into his Sunday trousers. She grinned at him and gave a little wave.

"I signed up today. For the army," George said, stuffed his hands in his pockets. "Figure it's my ticket to see Europe."

"When do you leave?" Stella asked.

"Train pulls out Monday morning. I'll be on it."

George laid his hand on Mary's shoulder, waited for her to look at him. "I want to ask you, Mary, if you'd … you know … mind if I sent you a letter … if you'd write back to me?" His hand tightened on her shoulder.

Fierce. A fierce hand. An image of George and that same hand holding a gun, a rifle, pointing it... "George. I ... no ... I..."

His eyes were glittery, his lips wet, slick, as he licked them once, twice and then again. He ducked his head to hers, fast, wiped her lips with his wet mouth. His tongue flicked, then he pushed it into her mouth. Let it rest there, kept his cold wet lips pressed against hers.

Mary backed away, but was held; she looked up, past the face that loomed against hers and suddenly the kiss ended.

A hand closed over her elbow. Claude. He put his other hand onto George's shoulder, maneuvered himself in front of Mary. "Is everything OK here? Mary ...?"

She nodded.

"We'll find us a table." Claude held his hand out to Stella. "You girls remember Arnie? Arnie Jenkins ... Stella Perkins ... Mary Johnston.

Stella and Arnie shook hands. "Sure, I remember you. Spitballs. Mrs. Rodd's class."

Arnie feigned embarrassment. "It's a hard act to live down," he said. "I don't do spitballs these days."

"And what are you keeping busy at?" Stella asked.

George was almost forgotten and when Mary peeked behind Claude she saw that George had made his way to another group. "Poor guy. He needs a girlfriend," she said.

"Fellows like him find their own level," Claude said. "Let's get a table. And some drinks?"

Claude and Arnie gave Mary and Stella no time that night to talk to anyone else. The four stayed on the dance floor, stopping only for sips of their drinks, switching partners between dances. At the end of the night the four friends decided they'd meet again at the dance next Thursday evening.

"That was heaven," Stella said, when she and Mary were both wearing their pyjamas and safely ensconced in their beds. "I might be in love."

"Who with?"

"Both of them. They are the handsomest boys and the best dancers. I could live happily ever after with either of those two!"

"Mmmmm," Mary said. "The cat's pyjamas."

"The bees' knees," agreed Stella.

"We'll have to choose you know. But not tonight, I suppose." Mary could still feel Claude's arms around her as they waltzed the last dance. When she opened her eyes she'd looked straight into Arnie's baby blues staring back at her with … speculation or amusement as he and Stella swayed to *'Smoke Gets in Your Eyes!'*

"It's dangerous for both of us to like two guys equally well. How much did you drink tonight?"

"Hardly time to finish one before another arrived at the table."

"Yeah. Me too."

Stella hugged herself. "Those are two extremely attractive boys. I think I am in love with Clarnie!" She giggled and chatted to herself all the way to the bathroom. "Arnaude. I mean Claudnie! Oh dear."

"Who's in there with you?" Mary settled herself against the pillows, laughing as she waited for her friend to reappear.

Drying her hands on her pyjamas top, Stella stumbled out of the bathroom and pushed herself into the corner of the bedroom, hugging herself and running her hands up and down her back so that from Mary's position Stella looked to be in an intimate embrace.

"I swear, Stella, I saw you in that position already tonight, when I danced with Arnie. I'm pretty sure I saw you letting Claude Johnston play touchy-feely at one point."

"Couldn't be me," Stella slurred. "Though I wouldn't mind some touchy-feely with Claudie-waudie." Her hands moved faster; her hips wiggled against the wall. She groaned. "Oh, I've got to get me a boyfriend. Fast!"

"If Mother only knew the kind of girl I'm living with!" Mary fell onto her bed laughing. "I'd be dragged home by the ear ..."

At 2 AM Mary and Stella were still talking.

"It's settled." Stella summed up their discussion. "I'll try out Arnie and you stick with Claude. "If we're not happy down the road, we'll make a switch." Stella watched Mary's reaction in the mirror as she slathered face cream onto imaginary wrinkles.

"You are such a bad influence," Mary said. "But I'm not complaining. We'll switch if we need to. Or maybe even if we just want to. Heck, what do they say about variety?"

"Now who's the bad one?"

# Chapter 5

**Go often to the house of thy friend, for weeds choke the unused path. Unknown**

Mother pelted Mary with questions on her at-home weekends and wanted especially to know how the dating was proceeding. "They tell me the young people are snapping up partners quick these days – wanting to be married before they're called to war."

"We see plenty of uniforms at the dances," Mary said. "Stella and I go out every Thursday night to a dance – put on by the Knights of Columbus – and there's boys there. And dancing. We have fun."

"Make sure these boys are able to support a family. Can't have one who wastes his life dreaming."

"I'm not marrying them. Just having a look around to see who's available." Mary wondered how close to the truth that comment was. The thought of Claude or Arnie being shipped overseas was in her mind too often these days.

"Be careful. That's what I'm saying," Mother said. "You're a bit flippant sometimes and that might make a fellow who's shy give up before you even know he's interested."

"Flippant! Me? How about high-spirited? Or enthusiastic?"

"You're taking my meaning wrong," Mother insisted. "I want you to find a nice boy to settle down with, raise a family. I don't know what you're doing there in the big city."

"I'm fine, Mother. Just teasing you, that's all." Mary kissed Mother on the cheek, unwilling to start a disagreement.

"You do have some high-faluting ideas."

"High-faluting! Flippant! Jeez, Mother! That's not true!"

Mother's hand went to her forehead.


"She has been sick quite a lot since you've been away," Father said to Mary, as they set flakes of hay in the mangers for the cows' overnight meal.

"It's likely worry about the upcoming marriage," Mary said. "How does Amy seem to be with Mother?"

"I don't see so much, I guess," Father said, "being busy in the barn the way I am."

"Yes, it does take all your attention doesn't it? Has Jacob signed up yet?""

"He went in to find out about putting on the uniform but there were tests." Father shrugged. "Jacob doesn't get along with tests."


Back in the house, Mary suggested to Mother the time had come to invite Amy for dinner. "She can sit around the table with us, help with the dishes, that sort of thing, and get an idea of what it might be like living in this house for the rest of her life."

"Why would we do that?" Mother said, but didn't stop Mary putting on her coat and walking down the road to the Perkins' house to offer the invitation.

"Amy isn't exactly the sharpest knife in the drawer," Stella had said to Mary once when a late night conversation veered around to the marriage of Jacob and Amy. "Even if she is my sister. She hardly speaks."

As she walked, Mary pictured how life at home would change when Amy and Jacob married. Father's usual method of dealing with a difference of opinion was to stay at the barn, while Mother baked when distressed, or came down with a headache. Jacob knew only how to farm. He could cultivate a field into a masterpiece of straight even furrows, with headland cut close to the fences, so as not to waste an inch of arable land. His skills were animal husbandry and ploughing; the women in his life would be on their own to sow seeds of harmony and friendship. Or not.

It felt odd to Mary to approach the door of Stella's childhood home, not to call on the girl who had been and still was her best friend, but to invite Stella's sister Amy for supper, and extend the as yet unspoken invitation into their family.

Amy opened the door as Mary lifted her hand to knock. "I saw you coming up the road aways. Is something wrong with Jake?" She looked straight at Mary, motioning her into the house with a jerk of her head.

Jake? She called him Jake? The kitchen was tidy, Mary saw, noticing Amy's large, work worn hands. "There's nothing wrong at home. Jacob's fine,"

"I put the kettle on. Will you have a cup?"

"Yes. Please. Tea would be nice. I've come to invite you to supper on Sunday. Since you're coming into the family. And the home. We've waited too long already to have you over for a meal."

"I've made onion pies this morning. I'll bring one. I've never had a lot of girlfriends," Amy said, taking two teacups and two saucers from the cupboard. "I hope you and I will be friends."

"We'll have to be, won't we," Mary said. "Seeing as we'll be sisters-in law. That will be nice. Although I am living in town so I'm not often home." She paused. "Have you much to bring over to the house? When you and Jacob are married?"

Amy shook her head, and twisted the top button of her blouse as she looked around the kitchen at the one built in bank of cupboards and the bare walls. "We don't go in much for fancy trimmings. I have some tea towels I've made. Some family pictures and my grandmother's quilt frame. It's big. I've been wondering where I could set it up."

"I didn't know you quilted. Mother will be pleased."

Amy smiled at Mary, and Mary saw Stella in Amy's expression as if she was planning some naughty bit of trickery. But Amy's teeth were dirty with green bits lodged between them and small white cottage-cheesy particles. Mary wanted to tell her to brush her teeth. How can she stand to rub her lips against those teeth with that gunk on them? Mary ran her tongue along her own smooth, clean enamel. How can Jacob ever think of kissing that mouth? Do they kiss? Would he ask politely? Or just grunt? Does she bat her eyelashes at him? Or are they silent, except for pushing needful clutches like animals? Maybe they haven't kissed yet. Maybe Jacob doesn't even know the facts of life. He has to know. He knows about cows and pigs. His teeth are surely cleaner than Amy's. Someone should tell her. Mother will, if no one else does. Mary looked up as Amy leaned over to pour the tea.

"She's a bit quiet, your mom. Is she stern?" Amy set the tea pot on the bare table and twisted the blouse button between her full breasts.

Mary tried to imagine Mother from an incoming daughter-in-law's perspective. "She's got her own way, but deep down Mother is kind... hardworking, and expects the rest of us to be the same. And she dotes on Father. He needs that now more than ever."

Amy nodded. "I've noticed."

"Mother likes to garden," Mary said. "Keeps her rows straight and won't allow a weed in the plot."

"I'm not much of a gardener," Amy looked out her kitchen window. "Some of us have no way with growing things." She looked down at her hands. "I can milk a cow, and toss bales with the best of them, but the green ones pull away when they see me coming." She smiled ruefully. "Not like Stella. She's got the way. And you're studying herbs, isn't that what I heard?"

"I am. Yes. And business too." Do Jacob and Amy talk about me? And why not? Couples about to be married discuss many things, sisters probably being one of them.

"It's kind of you to drop in unexpectedly. I wish I'd had time to freshen up a little bit. We're in the middle of lambing and that takes over our whole household, I'm afraid. No time to even brush my hair some days. Look at the mess of me." Amy smiled gently at Mary.

"How rude of me," Mary said. "I didn't realize about the lambs. We bred them at one time. Such a joy to work with the little ones, I remember, but we didn't have enough hands for them so Father gave them up. Maybe he'll take on a few when you're settled in to home."

"I hope not," Amy said. "Maybe we'll come down here to help at lambing time. They are a lot of work. I suppose we'll see what the good Lord decides for us."

It won't be the good Lord. It'll be Mother deciding. Mary bit her tongue. Let Amy find that out for herself.

"Anyway, I mustn't keep you from your tasks. You'll come for dinner? We eat at 5 o'clock."

"Yes," Amy said. "The parents will have to get used to me being away. And I appreciate your invitation. Jake wouldn't ever think of it, you know."

"I know. He's mostly got room in his head for the farm. Eat, sleep, farm. Everyday."

"Yup. That's like my dad. A simple routine that takes a love of nature and of God's gifts to do well. Jake has a way with the animals."

"He does that," Mary said. "He learned that from our father."

"I think so too. I respect the boys that follow the old ways. Can't all set off for new and exciting lives, else who'll tend to what's gone before?"

Mary idled her way home, reviewing the visit. Maybe Stella underestimates her sister. Maybe I underestimate Jacob. "Jake." She tried the name out loud. Someone's got to stay home. Better him than me. I'll do what I can to make sure things run smooth. Make it easier on everyone. Amy will be a good fit into the family. And she'll learn to brush her teeth. Mother will make sure of it.


Mary smoothed the faded red quilt over her knees. The view out the window brought Jacob to mind. He'd liked the fall best of all the seasons because he could spend the chilly days outside ploughing the fields, followed by squawking wheeling seagulls in search of a meal of fat worms and left-over kernels of corn.

"Jake's at his mindless work," Amy would say. She always called him Jake, even though Mother made it clear his name was Jacob.

Mary thought it didn't matter awfully much since Jacob answered to most any name. And he answered especially well a call to a meal. He'd looked pretty good when he put on the suit to get married, Mary had to admit, if only to herself. He was her brother after all. The day he and Amy married at Saint Joseph's Church in Douro, most of the community attended. A sign of the times, Mother said, that so many boys came in uniform. Father said it was the right and proper thing to do, to sign up for the forces, and Mary noticed Father and Claude and Arnie a few times during the day standing together in serious conversation.

Claude and Arnie talked often of signing up, and Mary and Stella knew it was no longer a question of if they would enlist, but rather when. It was hardly a choice. Every week more uniforms showed on the streets, at the dances, at the train station. There'd been two local boys reported missing in action; and there was George, the first local casualty of the war. George sat at the back of the Knights of Columbus hall on Thursday nights – dance night – a glass of amber liquid in hand, tapping his left leg on the floor as if he'd still like to dance. Mary and Stella made a point to stop for a chat each time. Arnie and Claude nodded at George.

Now I know how he felt, Mary thought, fingering her red quilt. Stuck in a wheelchair all those years while around him people were walking and dancing. George had stayed thin, chain smoked, never married, but he'd taken a job after the war, with the telephone company.

"We were lucky not to lose anyone in the war," Mary said, startling Stella, who'd been deciding between rice pudding or cookie for her mid-morning snack. "Jacob didn't even get past the initial tests so he was home on the farm while the fighting went on. Lucky Amy never had to worry about her man making the ultimate sacrifice. But Claude and Arnie signed on. And got accepted, eh Stella? Shipped out and gone to war. Almost quicker than we could think about them leaving, they were gone."

"I think I'll have the rice pudding," Stella said. "Is there raisins in it, I wonder?"

"Arnie too, but he was a Navy man," Mary said. "He made it sound like a grand adventure, didn't he? Working out on the ocean. The Atlantic. And they'd sail over to Europe or down the coast escorting merchant ships."

"My Arnie was a Navy man," Stella said. "You having a chocolate chip cookie, Mary?"

"Mother got in a snit the day Amy decided she was going to make chocolate chip cookies. I'll never forget it. The sugar and the chocolate were rationed, and Amy never gave it a thought. She went ahead and used up every last bit in the cupboard for her cookies. Mother phoned to tell me what she'd done. Oh, she was mad."

"You want one now, Mary? Whyn't you just give her one?" Stella said to the snack lady. "Mary's gone off somewhere in the war years. We mightn't see her 'til suppertime."

"There you are, Mary." The snack lady put Mary's tray on the table beside Stella's.

"Yup, Mother phoned to complain about Amy and the chocolate chips. Those were long years. I was glad me and Claude got married before he went away. And rented the little house. I was always hopeful that he'd change his mind. Decide not to go to war."

Mary bit into her cookie. "Kept us on edge. We were never sure who would be the next of us to get a knock on the door with bad news. We survived though, most of us. Some of the girls went to work at the factories. And we all gathered Tuesday evenings to package parcels of knitted socks, letters and chocolate bars for the troops."

"Stop the Germans. Stop the Nazis. It's all we heard. And reports of ships sunk and men lost. And every week it seemed there was another of our boys reported missing. Or wounded. Like George. I get confused though, sometimes thinking about it all. What happened when, Stella. About when we were in school, when Jacob and Amy were married. That was before our men left for duty. That's right. I remember now, because Jacob was the first one of our men folk to go register and he came home saying they couldn't be that much in need of warm bodies if they didn't take him. Course we knew it was because Jacob wasn't all that smart, but I guess we got some comfort from it too.

"Glad you got that all figured out," Stella said. "How's your cookie?"

Mary looked down at the cookie in her hand. "Oh." She took another bite. "How'd you end up with rice pudding?"

"Luck of the draw," Stella said. "Early bird gets the worm. I'd forgotten about George."

"George? Came home in a wheelchair. Jeez! I didn't much care for George but he sure didn't deserve that."

"Changed people's lives in the blink of an eye." Stella pointed at her rice pudding. "This is delicious. I wonder if there's anymore. Let's ask if we could have another dish."

"Yes. Rice pudding, please. Mother always served a nice rice pudding."

# Chapter 6

**1899 – Aspirin introduced by Bayer Co. from Germany, to Europe and North America.**

"It's time I go home for a while, Stella. Mother needs help with her fall work."

"Oh no, Mary." Stella grabbed her by the shoulders. "It's a mistake. I know it."

"I can't refuse my father. He's not …. On the weekend when I was home, Stella, he spent the whole time out in the barn. Hiding, I'd say. Mother and Amy bicker all the time. About everything."

"But your courses, Mary." Stella shook her head. "You remember Christy? She intended to take a short leave from school when her sister needed help with the new baby, but she didn't ever come back."

"Yet," Mary said.

"It's hard to come back. I don't think it's a good idea for you to go home right now."

"It'll be good to be with Mother again. Or maybe it's more selfish than that. Maybe I can smooth the way for her and Amy. They have a lot of years together ahead of them. One hopes. It's to my benefit to be sure they get along. I feel obligated to be the peacemaker. Otherwise, I may have to live there forever."

"It's too easy to quit school. Not so easy to get back. You'll get behind."

"I know. I don't know what else to do. I suppose we could bring Mother here to our rooms to live with us."

"Not on your life!" Stella flopped onto her bed. "And the dances, Mary. They won't be the same if you're not here."

"Maybe I could come in with Claude and Arnie? And you'll be home at Christmas. I've told the dean I'll start back after the Christmas holidays. He said no later."


Mary re-packed her bags to move home again, bringing with her all the textbooks and papers she'd collected from her classes. Claude picked her up in his horse and buggy. "There's not many like you, Mary. Coming home to be with your mother."

"It's best if Mother is settled though there is nothing I'd like more than to stay in town with Stella. I hope in a few months things will be better at home. Mother has headaches ..."

"So does mine." Claude's voice held sympathy. "Growing up I always knew when to be quiet, to stay out of the way."

"That's it exactly. I suppose part of the problem is that Amy has no experience. And Mother couldn't explain to Amy," Mary said. "Or wouldn't."

"My mother would lie on the couch for a whole day sometimes," Claude said. They both sat silent.

"There's a few ways I know to bring some relief. Feverfew leaves, or peppermint tea – they work – but it's mostly a matter of tiptoeing and whispering until she feels better."

"I always felt lucky not to have them myself," Claude said. "Do you get them? The headaches?"

"No. I don't. Although they can run in families," Mary said. "I try not to think about it, but I read a case study of a woman who was fine until her second child was born. After the birth she suffered blinding pain, off and on, the rest of her life."

"Hits women mostly? These headaches?"

Was his voice hopeful? "Seems so," Mary said. "But there are some cases of men having them too. And there's more research being done. I'd like to study it further. Herbal cures. Testing the results. The Germans have done a lot to that end."

"The Germans," Claude said. "Hmph."

"Yes. Well, they encourage experimentation in the medical field, and that's how discoveries are made."

"They're the enemy, Mary. They're killing people all across Europe. You've no idea."

"I do know. It's always on my mind."

"Mine too. Lots of the guys are signing up."

"It's hard to concentrate on my studies with all the talk of war."

"You'd do well to forget about the German studies anyway. I took you for a home girl, Mary Murphy. It's a pleasant surprise to realize that there's been a woman who's a healer living right close by. And studying business too."

"Not for a while, Claude. I'll be staying close to home to help Mother I'm afraid."

He regarded her appreciatively. "You're right welcome to drive to town with me any day you like."


Amy and Mother's loud voices carried to Mary as she travelled the path from the garden to the kitchen. Mother slammed the door and stomped past Mary. "That girl. Ooo! She'd try the patience of a saint."

Inside the kitchen, Amy stood with her arms folded across her chest. "I can't do anything right it seems, Mary. I bake bread; she says she wants scones. I sweep the floor; she says I should have washed it. But, if I wash it, she says I should have just swept it. I want to fit in here but she won't let me. I ask her what she wants and I get the silent treatment – she won't explain things. And I'm not a mind-reader. Jake is no help at all. Just keeps saying to work it out between us."

Mary nodded, recognizing Mother's ways in Amy's description.

"I don't know what to do," Amy continued, twisting her button as she spoke. "He scoots out the door first thing in the morning quicker than a dog after a rabbit. It can't be easy for her having another female living here but she surely can't expect it all to go on as it did before. Can she? Can she truly think she'll continue running everything?"

Mary opened her mouth, shut it again as Amy drummed her fist on the table.

"I've a mind … let me tell you … I've a mind… Oh it's not your concern is it? But can you tell me anything, Mary, that could help? I'm desperate. I am. I can't think what to do."

"I can try talking to her," Mary said. "But what exactly do I want to be telling her? What about the quilt frame? Have you been doing any quilting? Or what about some project for the house? Could you make some project together? Something new for both of you?"

Amy plucked at her blouse button. "We need to agree on something. I guess. Jake's no help. He won't or he can't. So now what? I have to fix the mess or live with it. That's not fair. Even if I can fix it, then what? Does he just carry on as if it's all fine? He'll have done nothing. He'll expect to get his house cleaned and his meals cooked and that's the way of it?"

"It might be. Jacob doesn't have much more depth than that. He's a good worker, good with the animals, good with the plough."

"Oh dear. What have I set myself up for?" Amy thumped the table. "I knew it. It's my fault. I should have seen it. It'll be just like living at home – never ending work – and eventually …" She sighed. "I thought we'd be different, Jake and me. That we'd make our own lives." She shook her head and smiled sadly at Mary. "Aren't I about the biggest fool ever?"

"No," Mary murmured. "There are bigger fools than you. No. It's why we read romance stories and daydream. Cause life is just too darn hard by times. And there's problems that aren't ever going away. How have Mother's headaches been this while?"

"Sadie has headaches, that's sure. And no one ever mentioned them to me before – just left me to find out for myself. I've been around here for well over a year. What else is hidden?"

Mary worried that Amy would twist her button right off.

"Forget I asked that. I think I don't want to know any more for right now."

On Mondays and Thursdays, Mary met Claude at the end of the lane-way and he drove her into town on his way to the market. "Sure is good of you to come back home and help your folks, Mary."

"It's the only right thing to do, Claude. I could just see her there. Jacob and Father hardly know how to light the fire. Leaves Mother with too much work to do."

"I'd think Jacob's new wife would pitch in. Do some of the housework."

"And she does some but she goes back home to help her own parents with their chores too. Me coming home every second weekend to do housework wasn't enough. Mother seems weaker than I remember. And her and Amy are having troubles. Two women in one house."

"Seems that would be a good thing."

"You'd think so but neither is giving an inch. They need to do some adjusting. Like last night …"

Mary stopped herself. How much should she tell Claude about what went on at home? Maybe they didn't know each other well enough. Yet.

"Oh, Mary," Mother had said, when Amy left the kettle to boil dry on the wood stove again.

"Now, Mother. It won't take her long to learn the ways. Be patient. She'll come around."

"Did they not use wood in her parent's home? And, Mary, she frightens the chickens with her booming voice. She makes my head ache."

"Yes, Mother. She's a loud one. She'll never sneak up on you, though, will she?"

Father spoke from his chair near the fire. "Aren't you a wise one, Lass? You'll make a fine wife someday. Soon, I hope. Make a good home for your mother to enjoy her old age in."

"That won't be for a long time yet, Father. I'll take Mother in when the time comes." Mary hoped that by then she'd be working and would have a good place, but for now they needed to get Mother's health improved, and Mary was hopeful that with plenty of gentle coaxing, Mother and Amy would find ways to accommodate each other.

"That's my girl, Mary. I know I can count on you."

Mother looked up from her needlework. "I don't know why you're making plans for me as if I wasn't here. The two of you are always having secrets with each other."

Mary and Father exchanged a quick glance. What brought that on? Can she truly think that? Or is she just unsettled by this new living arrangement …

Claude reached over and placed his hand on Mary's knee, and she realized she'd been silent too long, thinking and remembering. She knew she should say something but the heat of his hand distracted her from forming words. The warmth radiated along her leg.

Claude didn't speak, just looked ahead at the road and the horses.

"Mother said she never appreciated me enough when I lived at home," Mary said. "And Amy says Mother's forever comparing Amy's work habits to mine. I hate being put in the middle of those two." Mary wished she dared to put her hand on top of Claude's.

"What does your father have to say, Mary?" Claude brought his hand back to hold the reins.

"Father just hopes everyone gets along. But I know he's worried. He says there's something not right with Mother. I wonder if it's just old age. It could be some medical problem I suppose. Senility? I don't like to even say the word. Father's in the barn most of the time. Stays out of the way."

Father had become even quieter than usual, Mary noticed, and she strove for a pleasant routine trying not to feed Mother's worry that they were planning things without her knowledge.

On Tuesday and Wednesday each week, Mary made a point of spending time in the garden with Mother.

"I'm not able to keep it up, Mary. I'm slowing."

"Oh, Mother. I'll help you." Mary surveyed the long straight rows. Where the asparagus grew, dandelions had positioned themselves between stalks.

"Would you look at that. They are the toughest ones to get out."

Mother shoved her dandelion picker deep beside one of the culprits. "They're hard ones to control, that's sure. We'll dig out what we can though. And pick off their heads so they don't go to seed. Next year this patch'll need dug up and transplanted."

"Mother seems more herself in the garden," Mary told Claude now, the smell of the horses mixing pleasantly with Claude's clean soap scent. "She's less confused. And of course she's happier."

The thick white roots of the asparagus were sometimes exposed as the women searched for and dug out the weeds.

"How was the crop this spring? Did you get any of these put into jars?" Mary asked Mother.

"Just a few. I got waylaid with having Amy here all the time. And not having you here to keep me straight didn't help."

"I wished I could have been here more but there were the exams … and … "

"There's always a reason, Mary."

Mary didn't answer. She pulled another dandelion.

"I sure like driving into town with you like this," Claude said.

"Father has asked me to stay on at home for a while longer. My plan was to return to school right after the Christmas holidays but that isn't going to happen for another few months anyway." Mary sighed, then she smiled up at Claude. "Driving with you is certainly a benefit. I told Father I'll stay on as long as he needs me to."

"Right." Claude ran a hand through his trim brown hair. "It'll give you and I a chance to find out all the things we have in common." He concentrated on his driving, frowning as he watched the road and the horses. "My dad would like me to stay on at home too." His hair moved in the breeze as he and Mary bounced along. "Keep the farm going."

"It's a good farm." Mary repeated what Father had said again just last night.

"It's a living," Claude said. "But, I've got a hankering for something different. A place of my own. Maybe I could work at shoeing horses or trimming cows' hooves. A firewood business on the side would help in the slow months."

An image of Claude in a canvas apron standing in the doorway of a shop jumped to Mary's mind. Overhead the sign read, 'Claude Johnston – Shoeing and Forging.' She saw herself in the back room with a baby sleeping in a basket that she rocked with her feet, while she tallied an invoice for a customer.

"Maybe you could produce maple syrup in the spring – a sideline," Mary said, thinking of what the teacher had explained to the class last term: how to diversify a business so you wouldn't be relying on just one enterprise.

"Maple syrup?" Claude asked.

"Maple syrup. Diversification," Mary said. She sensed Claude staring at her.

"In fact," he said, "I've been thinking along that line myself. No sense trying to raise cows for a living. Sure, every house on every road has got a milking cow and a couple of beef cattle. They're not going to buy from me what they can produce for themselves, but there's work people can't do or won't do because they aren't set up for it. I could do it for them. And make good money at it too."

For the next six months, Mary and Claude made twice-weekly trips to and from town.

"Mother hasn't complained of a headache in three months," Mary told Claude on one trip. "I'm sure it's our time in the garden and doing the kitchen work together that has helped the headaches subside. And she has so much knowledge. I never realized before how much she knows."

Claude nodded, clucked at the horses and rubbed Mary's knee, knowing she'd be off on a reverie which she might or might not share with him.

"This has been my growing place for twenty-six seasons," Mother had told Mary as they stood surveying the garden. "I've come here to weed and grow and plant all of my married life."

"Twenty-six vegetable gardens in the same place," Mary said. "That's a lot of seeds."

"You get to know the characters of the plants the more time you spend with them," Mother said. "Take that walking onion for instance." She pointed her spade at a lone onion plant. "That one I'm sure is the same plant that gets out time after time. I dig him up and plant him back where he belongs but every year he gets himself a new spot and settles himself in pleased as can be. I've tried reasoning with him. Once, I tried to trick him and I didn't transplant him back to the onion patch. Instead I threw him on the compost heap, and lo and behold if he didn't set himself up right there, King of the Heap, and it wasn't no time at all 'til he'd grew himself a nice little family of spring onions. It sounds impossible, I know, but I think they tasted better than the ones in the patch."

Mary considered the unruly group of Walking Egyptian onions that were expected to grow within the confines of the four by four foot patch laid out in a raised bed, with a boundary of wooden planks and a wide path of straw mulch. How had this onion walked all the way from the onion patch to the end of the carrot row? "That's at least thirty feet away! How'd he get that far?" Mary wondered aloud.

"That's my question too," Mother said, lifting the onion's small purple bulblets to examine the green shoots ready to grow when the bulbs took root. "It's you, I think." She spoke sternly to a group of goldfinches gathered to harvest sunflower seeds. "Getting up to mischief and thinking I won't notice. I'm not so old that I'll miss your trickery. You always have enjoyed a joke on old Sadie haven't you?"

"Mother! You're talking as if they'll understand you."

"Of course they will. I knew their grandparents!" Mother laughed a little too wildly, and turned back to her weeding.

"I'd forgotten how much Mother talks to herself." Mary said to Claude as he turned to her in the wagon seat. "I wonder if it has gotten worse or do I just notice it more now? And is it a problem?"

"A little imagination is certainly a good thing, Mary," Claude assured her. "How much talking does she do? Maybe she spends too much time alone."

"It's possible. Jacob has coffee with his cronies at the feed mill every day. Father has the cows and the pigs and the horses. Amy has her parents up the road to visit. And I keep my nose in my books as much as possible. It's reasonable that Mother have her own group of friends. And she's found them out in the garden. Are they friends?" Mary laughed. "Now who's acting crazy?"

Claude laughed with her. "It's a fine line, Mary. We all have a trace of crazy in us."

"Truth be told, Mother has always talked to the plants. And I do too. And the toads and the bees and the sweet wee hummingbirds. Not so crazy when I do it." She looked up to see if Claude was still in agreement.

It was natural to talk to the plants sometimes. Mother got engrossed in her own thoughts, her lips pursed, and Mary imagined her working out some silent argument with Amy over what to eat or which room to clean first. The garden was looking orderly again and that felt right.

This morning in the garden Mary had smiled at the walking onion, at his innocent stalks heavy with bulblets like a crown round the larger middle bulb.

"Happy there, aren't you, little guy? Make yourself at home, my friend." She broke off a short bit of onion shoot to chew, and got an instant picture of Arnie's face close to hers, on his breath the faint scent of onions. He'd been going to kiss her, the last time they'd been on the dance floor together. Of that Mary was sure and that was ... that was ... confusing, interesting, unsettling, complimentary. Why had Arnie sprung to mind? Ah. The walking onion. Putting itself in a new place with a calm assurance that he'd be accepted and successful.

No need for worried contemplation. No should I or shouldn't I. No sir. Arnie saw what he wanted and went after it. That was ... nice. Nice. Easy. Not planned and plotted like Claude who needed everything laid out perfectly in a row to be sure there was no mistake, no hidden glitch to set a man back. That was an unwelcome thought. What brought that on?

Claude. Clod. Plod. I like Claude's methodical way. It is good to plot and to plan and be prepared. The lone onion seemed to nod its heavy ring of bulblets at her.

Claude. Plod. Flawed.

Now this is crazy thinking.

Claude. Odd. Broad.

He had broad shoulders. And big plans. That they'd gone over and over for long enough. Maybe the walking onion was on to something. Time to take the next step. Turn the plan into reality. Enough talk. Now action.

That must be it.

"Sometimes though, Claude, I worry that the heat and the sunshine in the garden is addling my brain."

"You're not addled yet, Mary. You're the smartest girl in these parts."

Mary's throat was dry. The time was getting to where she knew Claude would be asking to marry her. And what if they got married? And what if he signed up to go to war? He would; Mary knew it. If she didn't marry him ... if she didn't think about it ... would he maybe not go away? Would he and Arnie stay home? Could they? Was she ready to say yes? Was there any other answer? Would Arnie ever ... try to kiss her again?

Mother's health was much improved; she and Amy had a peaceable working arrangement, and Claude had mentioned a number of times that his bank account held a sizable sum from his egg and firewood sales. It was the right time and they both knew it.

As if he'd had the same thoughts Claude came by the house after dinner and he and Mary, and Mother and Father, and Jacob and Amy, all sat in the front room with cups of tea and cake that Mother had baked in the afternoon. When they'd made sufficient small talk with the family Mary and Claude sat out alone on the porch swing.

"Let's get married, Mary. Throw our luck in together, move into town and have a go at being on our own. It's hardly fair to you, because I know me and Arnie are going to sign up right away, but it seems, we'd be better being married before I go. Settled into town. Then when I come back …"

"If you come back. Arnie too?"

"We have to go, Mary."

"I know. I want you to go. Just not so soon."

"I know. We'll be back. You must count on that. You'll be my reason for making sure of that."

That's no plodder speaking now. Strange that he'd come so quickly to propose after she'd been thinking of exactly this conversation earlier in the day.

"We're made for each other – that's sure. Both business people and we both plan to live in town, away from our parents but still family is important too."

"Well, yes," Mary said.

"You mean you will?" He held her hand in his. "You'll marry me? And live with me? And …" His voice trailed away as he thought of it all.

"Oh yes. I most certainly will!" Mary reached up to kiss his dear dear lips. "And we'll live on our own in the town." She needed to hear him say it.

"That's sure, Mary. Somewhere not too far, but far enough that we'll be away from the day to day of our parents' lives."

How will Mother manage? Will she take sick again when I leave?

"There's not much for sale hereabouts," she said. "Except maybe the old Timmerman's farm in a few years." They'd already talked about Timmerman's farm.

"Too rocky," Claude said. "Be picking stones for months before you'd ever get a house built or a crop planted. Over Peterborough way we might stand a chance with so many people wanting homes in town. If we got a place on the edge of town, it would be handy for bringing our goods to market on Saturdays. Firewood, maple syrup, eggs." Claude stopped to catch his breath.

"Butter tarts. Herbal creams. Bee sting ointment," Mary said. "We'll need about eight children to help us with all the work." She blushed at her forwardness, and Claude lost his train of thought, as the logistics of fathering eight children overwhelmed him.

"I hadn't thought about children," he said. "But they will happen."

"I didn't... I shouldn't..." Mary's sweater felt unseasonably warm though they were stopped in the deep dark shade of the wooden verandah. They both fell silent and Claude reached his large hands to her shoulders and rested them there.

He pulled in a huge breath and eased her toward him until their faces were six inches apart. "Shucks, Mary. Would it be all right if I kissed you? I mean really kissed you?" One finger traced the outline of her lips, then with a hand on each of her cheeks, he held her face still and brought his mouth to hers. His warm welcome mouth.

Mary opened her mouth to answer and let out a happy sigh instead.

"Let's talk about children another time," he promised.


"Amy's not all that smart," Stella tried to reassure Mary. She was home for Christmas break and the two friends visited back and forth in the mornings for tea.

"I feel sorry for her. And all the while we're talking I'm thinking of how I'm so glad it's her and not me. I sure won't get the charity award this year will I?"

"You won't get caught in a set up like that either."

"But I already promised Father I'll look after Mother when it comes time."

"And you will, but not for ages yet. Get Amy and your mom all settled in together and Sadie might be happy to stay there forever. After all it is her house."

"It is her house," Mary said. "And I do hope she'll be happy there a long while. Give me and Claude a chance on our own."

"Mary!" Stella grabbed Mary's left hand, checked her ring finger. "Claude's popped the question, hasn't he?"

Mary grinned.

"Tell me everything! Are you moving in with Claude's parents? Are you?"

"No. I'm not. We're not. We're going to live in town. After we're married. And no one but you knows yet."

"I knew it!" Stella said. "I could just tell you two were meant for each other. You'll be so happy. When? Did he kiss you yet? Of course he did. How did he do it? Did he say he loved you? Did he get down on his knees? Or just the one knee? This is so exciting." Her voice rose to a squeak. "Not even your parents? What about Claude? Do his parents know?"

"No. Not yet. You're the first."

"Let's go out. You and me and Arnie and Claude. Let's celebrate just the four of us and …"

"What about you and Arnie? Any news on that front?"

"He's getting there but nothing yet. Maybe Claude'll prod him into taking the next step."

"Seems like it should be his idea," Mary said. "Is he a romantic? Does he hold your hand? Does he talk about your future together?"

"He's a bit quiet," Stella said. "He's so slow."

"Let's the four of us ride into the dance on Thursday night. We could ask Jacob and Amy to join us."

"Let's," Stella said. "We could all end up being neighbours, couldn't we?"

"We're going to live in town," Mary said. "That's the one thing I am sure of – Claude and I having our own place in town. He'll have some sort of shop for welding and fixing and I plan to work too. Now, your turn. Tell me about you and Arnie. Is Arnie going to farm?"

"He wants to. Says he'll build a house on the property."

"A brand new house, Stella. That sounds promising."

"He hasn't asked me to share it with him. Yet."

"Sounds like we've got work to do while you're home for the holidays. Thursday night we sow the seeds of marriage with Arnie. Let him think it's his idea of course."

"The seeds of marriage," Stella repeated.

In Mary's mind a solitary walking onion bowed its bulblets at the end of the row of carrots. "I just hope Claude's parents won't be too obstinate about our moving so far away. And what happens when they can't look after themselves? Then what?"

"Will they move in with the two of you?

"I guess they'd have to. I can't say no. They'd have to come to us. Claude's their only child. At least it'll be our house. And we'd have the say about how things are run."

"That's right. Did you and Claude talk about this?"

"He's firm about us moving to town."

"So you're set. No worries right?"

"That's right. No worries." Mary frowned. "Well … one worry."

"Is he talking about enlisting?"

"Yes." Mary's throat closed and she couldn't continue.

"I'm sorry." Stella hugged Mary tightly. "Arnie will follow Claude. I know. We'll be war widows before we're even married."

"Don't say it, Stella."

# Chapter 7

**Angelica** – Angelica archangelica – Likes a rich, damp, shady, position. Keeps witches out of the garden.

It has been claimed ... I cannot say with what truth, that if taken regularly ... the herb will cause an aversion to alcohol and bring about a cure of even the most confirmed dipsomaniacs.

Pour a pint of boiling water over an ounce of the bruised root. Drink a wineglassful after every meal to relieve flatulence. The same infusion, if taken hot, is said to give help in cases of delayed menstruation.

"Amy and Stella get along pretty good, considering they're sisters and all," Arnie said, as he bounced beside Mary in the wagon. Stella insisted on sitting up front beside Claude, who was driving the horses, and Jacob and Amy stayed so close to each other as the three couples were getting on that there was no chance of them being separated. Mary looked at the two of them. It seemed such a short time ago that she and Jacob were youngsters vying for their parents' attentions, and now suddenly, though she knew it wasn't sudden at all, they were all grown up and driving to the dance together.

"They sure do," Mary said. "And it makes me so glad that my brother and Stella's sister are married. It makes Stella and I sisters of a sort too." She turned to smile happily at Arnie. Between them Mary's hand on the seat kept her balanced. Arnie reached down to pat her hand and kept his there atop hers. The warmth of it travelled quickly up her arm like a lick of flame and was reflected in his eyes.

"It's nice sitting here beside you like this," Arnie said. "We should spend more time together."

"We do spend plenty of times together, Arnie. Almost every Thursday night." Mary felt a guilty tingle of excitement. Ahead of them, Stella rubbed her hand on Claude's knee as she made a point. Well.

"I'd like it to be just you and me. We should get to know each other better."

Mary laughed. "We have a whole lifetime ahead of us, Arnie, to get to know each other. We'll always be friends like this."

He squeezed her hand. "That's what I want to hear, Mary. I want us always to be friends. You know you can tell me anything don't you?" There was the fragrance of onion on his breath.

"I know it, Arnie."

Arnie reached his other hand to her neck, ran his smooth finger from the indent in her breastbone up, up slowly along her neck bringing all fingers into the touch, so large tendrils of heat coursed toward her scalp; her cheeks heated; her breath caught. Arnie is going to kiss me!

"Arnie! I …."

"Hey! What are you doing?"

They jumped away from each other as the wagon lurched. Neighing horses, splintering wood, and shouts filled the ensuing dusk.

Mary, Stella, and Amy stood at the side of the road as the men examined the damage. "Oh! My heart is thumping!" Mary couldn't keep herself still, worried that the loud voices might turn into something more physical.

Arnie was going to kiss me.

"It doesn't look too bad from here," Amy said. "Probably just need to settle the horses and we can get on our way. A drink might help the negotiations. Lucky for us, Jake's got a flask with him."

Stella eyed her sister. "A flask? Isn't that handy?"

Mary didn't recognize her tone.

Amy shrugged. "He likes to take a drink. And so do I." She twisted her coat button.

They could see that the flask was certainly being handed around the circle of men and after they'd all sipped, they shook hands and the two lone fellows from the other wagon raised their hands to the three girls, jumped into their wagon and disappeared into the darkening evening.

"Navy men," Claude sneered. "Sailors. They're making a bad name for themselves."

"No harm done," Arnie said, grasping Stella and Mary's elbows and escorting them back to their wagon too. "Gave me a bit of a start though. They'd been drinking from the sounds of them. And going too fast of course."

"Too fast." Mary heard herself laugh a little too loudly. Maybe Arnie should rethink his speed. She took her arm from Arnie's hold and moved quickly to claim the seat up front beside Claude.


"It's happened, hasn't it?" Sadie frowned at the needlework in her lap. She and Mary and Amy had spent the past weeks in a flurry of baking and sewing in preparation for Mary and Claude's upcoming wedding. They'd been able to agree on the dresses, the men's suits, and the menu for the dinner that would be served at the church hall after the wedding ceremony.

"It's happened," Mother repeated. "I see it in your face, the worry, the fear, wondering if you've made a mistake. It's too late to change your mind – to stay home with Mr. Murphy and me where you know you're safe. Don't get scairt now, girl." Mother jabbed her needle into the fabric, making neat, tiny stitches of sky blue against the cream-coloured broad cloth. "Claude Johnston's a good man. He reminds me of your father when we were young, and he was eager to make a life for his wife and family.

"You'll have a far easier life than we ever knew. When we first got married there was no indoor plumbing." Mrs. Murphy shivered at the memory. "There was no electricity. Young people, these days, just expect that sort of luxury as their right. You'll not be making a mistake marrying that man." Mrs. Murphy's Irish accent become noticeable as it did so often these days.

Mary wondered again if it was old age creeping up or worries. "Oh, Mother, you're right," she whispered, and rose from her chair to kneel on the wooden floorboards in front of Mother's rocker. She put her arms around Mother's waist and laid her head on the bony comfort of the checkered, gingham dress that today smelled of cinnamon and apple pie.

"But I sure won't ever understand why you're finding it so important to move off into town. It's like you're trying to get away from us. Especially when Claude enlists. You'll be all alone in a strange place."

"It's not to get away from you, Mother. There's more opportunity in town."

"Opportunities enough here at home. You'd never want for anything if you stayed local. Seems foolish to be upsetting the whole apple cart for some unknown adventure."

"Claude says it's better now while we're just starting out. We're still young and there's no children to uproot. And the war won't last forever."

"Yes. I suppose so. If that's what Claude says."

Mary knew Mother was more inclined to agree with Claude's logic than with any arguments Mary might use.

Mary thought this feeling must be what was meant by the word. She tried it out loud in her bedroom. "Glee." With a grand exhalation she emptied her lungs into the word and laughed aloud at herself staring into the smiling happy face reflected in the small mirror.

"Glee! Soon the only house work I'll be doing will be my own – in my own house for my own family. Glee." Mary twirled lightly in the wee space. "Our own house – mine and Claude's. We'll have evenings by the fire. We'll think up names for our children. Glee. We'll live close to the town. We'll go to dances on Saturday nights. Meet up with Stella and Arnie. Maybe we'll have a creek running through our place – for fishing in the spring and skating in the winters."

Through her window Mary spied Father limping to the barn. From this distance, his age was apparent – the rounded shoulders, the hitch in his giddy-up. From beyond the barn, Mother appeared, wearing her apron, and carrying the kettle filled with red strawberries. They were ripening early this June. Her white hair was like … When had Mother's hair turned so completely white? It was like a white wool hat. Her back was as straight as ever, but her steps had slowed, as if she was taking care not to fall.

Mary remembered hearing that they had married late. Hadn't Father been thirty-five and Mother thirty-three? Jacob's birth was registered nine months to the day after the wedding, and Mary's three years later. I'll be twenty-three next week. So Father is sixty-one and Mother fifty-nine. They're bound to be showing their age. Still, Claude and I should have a good long time alone together before our parents come to live with us.

At the barn Mother and Father stood side by side, eating berries and laughing. They'll get along just fine without me. Claude and I must be sure to plant some strawberries in the fall or is it in the spring? I'll ask Mother. We surely must have strawberries. And a creek in the yard.

As she gazed at her parents she felt a chill, and unbidden, she whispered, "Be careful what you wish for."

# Chapter 8

"Mother! Mother! Can you hear me?"

Mary pushed at the hands touching her face, her arms. What do they want with me now?

She turned back to search the crowd, all those beautiful hats bobbing in the sunshine. A garden of hats it was. All the lovely ladies and the handsome men and the handsomest by far were Claude and Arnie who stood to the right of the altar. Was there ever anything so appealing as a man in a suit? Claude's large frame looked well, clothed in the dark blue suit she'd helped him choose. Was it just a few weeks ago?

Surely it was, and yet, other images of the suit, the hats, the sunshine, the bobbing heads, filtered over and through her memory like those clear plastic sheet covers that MaryArlene used to plan her gardens. Mary liked how another layer of the garden was added to the picture as she turned each clear sheet. Mother hadn't ever drawn plans of her garden that Mary could recall, although she realized it was quite possible, even probable that there existed an original plan, just to get the complicated rotation system worked out. In Mary's experience, gardens never did turn out looking like those neat drawings with the shrubs placed uniformly along the edge, the perennials drawn onto the clean white sheets in lime greens and deep dark greens.

"Just the outline," Stella used to say when they'd sat at their plans. "We need just the idea of the shape of the plant not each individual leaf of the thing." And she would sketch in spiky yucca shapes, and round smiling faces to denote the pansies.

The suit fit Claude perfectly on their wedding day, and when Arnie and Stella were married the same year, the same suit reappeared from the back of the closet again. And for the funeral. Again. He'd worn it for them all.

At Fynch's Apothecary there'd been an understanding that a man wearing a suit had been to a funeral, or to the bank to apply for a loan, but most likely a funeral.

Mary forced her mind back to her wedding. The first wearing. The first time she'd seen him wearing the suit was for their wedding. And the last time … She wouldn't think right now about the last time.

After the wedding, they'd come to the house to have their pictures taken in Mother's garden before going back to the church hall for dinner. Father slipped out to the barn to check on the one cow that chose Mary's and Claude's wedding day to calve, pulling coveralls on over top of his grey suit normally stored in the upstairs closet in a garment bag and pulled out for occasions such as this. Weddings and funerals. Funerals and weddings. Jacob of course made his way to the barn saying he needed to check on Father. Well, that's the way it was. They'd come back smelling faintly of the barn and of the whiskey sipped from the brown bottle stored over the feed room window. Everyone knew it, expected it. It was comforting, to know that life in the barn continued on despite the weddings. And the funerals. And the headaches. Had Mother's head ached that day? Was Liz plagued with a headache? So difficult now to bring the memory clearly to mind.

Mary watched the crowd as they turned in their pews to catch a first glimpse of her white lace and satin splendor. She'd been a lovely and radiant bride. They'd all said so. Stella and Claude and Mother and Amy. And Arnie. His expression told Mary he found her beautiful without a word being exchanged. She'd known it too as she watched herself in the mirror. Stella offered to 'do' her makeup though Mary insisted that there was no need. It would all just smear in the muggy heat of July, Mary said, but Stella said it just wouldn't be right to not have a hint of rouge on Mary's cheeks and she might as well lengthen Mary's eyelashes with a touch of mascara while she was at it.

Stella had spent the whole morning washing Mary's long blond hair, combing it dry, to straighten the pieces that wanted to curl.

From the back of the church where she'd stood waiting with Father and Stella and Amy for the organist to begin the Wedding March, Mary thought how like a garden all those bobbing hats were. Some, adorned with flowers and feathers, could easily have been the birds and the nodding cosmos and the pansies she so loved. Which was why she chose the pansy as Claude's flower when she'd gotten round to planting her herb garden.

Why was the memory of the herb garden intruding on her wedding? The garden wasn't even a spark in her eye yet, but here she was knowing all about it as she waited in back of the church to begin her march up the aisle to be wed for better or for worse to her beloved Claude. But if the herb garden was already a known entity … well, that hadn't come to be until after … after other heads bobbed.

A wave of remembering grieved over Mary and there she stood in the upper hallway of the home that she and Claude and Edward shared with Mother and with Liz, her mother-in-law. The mothers.

Edward and Nelson discussed what they should bring with them, preparing for the trek out into the cool, rainy October day. "Stay inside," she yearned to call to them. "Play with your puzzle this afternoon." The wooden floor creaked under her feet as she swayed toward their precious voices but her legs, motionless, refused to hasten to the boys. She couldn't move though she knew she should. Stop them. Knew it, as well as she knew there was no way to stop them. They were determined to be outside on that gloomy dreary day which was unfit for life. Mary stayed in her reading chair, lifted her head intermittently from her book to watch the two playing lads from her window,

What book kept her so enthralled that day? Was it some silly romance novel? Or some unrecalled ailment she studied to cure with a herbal remedy? So many of the day's details were clear, but the book she'd read slipped from her memory as easily as it slipped from her lap when she stood to see the boys whose shouts she could no longer hear. There they were in the ditch – she'd told Claude he'd made it too deep – bobbing, faces down, in the rushing water. It wasn't right.

"The boys! The boys!" Mary's legs moved now. Raced down the stairs. Pumped her to the door.

Sadie and Liz stared up from their cookies and tea at her.

"The boys! They're in the ditch!" She ran out the door. Didn't care that the door stayed open, cooling the kitchen behind her. Was this the last time caring about anything kept her attention?

No. There were the bobbing heads of the onions in her garden. And the borage with its sweet blue and pink flowers. She cared about those.

There was Arnie standing beside Claude on the steps of the altar as they waited for Mary and her attendants to make the long walk down the aisle on Mary and Claude's wedding day. Arnie, with his clear blue eyes. Finally the organist played the familiar three bars and Mary watched as Amy stepped out into the center aisle of the church. One step, pause. Step, pause. When Amy reached the fourth pew, Stella kissed Mary's cheek, then stepped out. One step. Pause. Step. Pause.

Mary and Father watched the progress. She felt his arm muscles tense. He leaned to her, whispered into her hair, sending out the fragrance Stella had insisted she wear for her wedding day – Heaven Scent. "I love you, daughter. I love you so much." They began their march up the aisle. Step. Pause. Toward Claude and their long life together. Past the bobbing hats of the congregation, past Mother's bobbing hat as she wept joyfully into her monogrammed, white lace, handkerchief, watching her only daughter walk with Father, to the altar, to Claude.

At the altar were the flowers from Mary's garden, but that couldn't be right. She didn't have a garden yet. But there were the shroud-covered caskets of Edward and Nelson, side by side, and in the congregation, the bobbing black hats of all the ladies. The men, bareheaded, the children, playmates of the two dead boys, weeping some of them, but mostly just there, standing in shocked disbelief, as they took part in the funeral prayers. Mary and Stella and Claude and Arnie sat together in the front pews surrounded by family and friends.

How often had this church witnessed their lives? How many times were these same suits pulled from closets, amid tears of joy or happiness or grief?

Mary shoved at the hands that reached out to her. "She's having an episode. It's not unusual. At her age. We must expect it. Prepare ourselves." Mary heard them talking over her. Knew they couldn't see the wedding, the garden, the ditch, the funeral, Arnie. The bobbing. Knew she couldn't not see it all happening over and over.

She opened her eyes.

MaryArlene knelt in front of her, brilliant green foil hat lopsided on her head, a giant shamrock nametag announcing, "Hello! My name is MaryArlene." Around the room, green foil hats bobbed, glinting in the fluorescent lighting of the Sunny Acres' dining room and at the piano, a lively green leprechaun sang, When Irish Eyes are Smiling.

"We didn't wear hats to the dances," Mary said. "That's the one place I liked to go where there were no hats."

"Are you alright, Mother?" MaryArlene's concern and relief softened her sometimes strident voice. "I was worried about you. You worried us."

"It's just the hats. They're so…"

"Green," said Stella.

Mary nodded her head, felt her hat slip sideways.

"You'd not know Mother's head ached to bursting from that smile on her face, would you?" Mary, MaryArlene and Stella were in Mary's room going through the photograph box in search of wedding pictures. "She got them awful bad. And you never suffered them?"

MaryArlene shook her head. "Lucky, I guess."

"Lucky you were. Funny though, with the headaches on both sides, your father's and mine, that you missed inheriting that plague. But then, I didn't have the headaches too much either. Not like Mother's anyway." Mary recalled just a few headache episodes after MaryArlene's birth. Almost as if she was being punished, Mary thought. Divine retribution, Father Byers might have said.

"So there's the wedding pictures. I never liked this one too much." Mary showed them a black and white photograph of her and Claude standing on the steps of Saint Joseph's Church. "Feels like his eyes follow you around. I never liked that."

"And Stella. Your best friend, right, Mother?"

Mary nodded.

"What a beauty! Look at that curly mop of hair."

"That's what you called it too."

Stella nodded. "A curly black mop, fit only for cleaning floors."

"Stella would get so frustrated with her curls, and mine was always quite straight – straggly."

"And Arnie, Dad's best man. He's good looking. He and Stella got married  that summer too, right, Mother? How romantic. Your bridesmaid and dad's best man."

"The same summer." Mary squinted at the picture. Nobody but her would ever know that Arnie's hand rested warm and heavy on her lower back as the photographer snapped the picture. That day Arnie had told her of his regret over not being the one making promises to her, 'to have and to hold until death do us part'.

"Arnie! You can't mean that!" Mary had said. "Why didn't you say? Why now? Why are you telling me this now?"

He'd stood quiet a moment, then said, "I'm not good enough for you. You deserve a man like Claude who's smart and steady. I want you to have the best, Mary."

"And then they were gone," Mary said, to MaryArlene. "Arnie to the navy. Claude to the army. There's the picture of Claude in his uniform. So young. We went to Roy Studio … they all did … the ones that enlisted, to get a picture in their new uniform."

Mary stroked the picture. "Arnie and Stella came too. We did everything together, we four. Always together in church for the different reasons – weddings, baptisms – all you kids were baptized in that church – funerals. We spent a lot of time there. Crying."

"And laughing too, Mother. Right?"

"Laughing too. Arnie could make us laugh like crazy. Always playing the fool."

Mary stared into MaryArlene's familiar deep blue eyes. "You were …"

MaryArlene waited a minute then asked, "I was what, Mother?"

"You were a lot like your Uncle Arnie."

"I liked him a lot too," MaryArlene said. "He wasn't so serious as you and Dad. He taught me wood carving. And he made me laugh too."

"Laughing," Stella said. "What's underneath the laughing sometimes isn't so funny."

"Aren't you just a ray of sunshine?" MaryArlene rubbed Stella's shoulder. "Come on. Anyone up for a trip to the greenhouse?"

# Chapter 9

**Jewelweed** – Impatiens birlora – North American woodland plant with distinctive orange-yellow pendant-like flowers. Juice of freshly crushed leaves are effective for the treatment of poison ivy. When applied liberally to affected skin, it works almost immediately to soothe and help to reduce the itchy rash caused by poison ivy's irritant oils. Juice of plant can be added to soaps to make an effective poison ivy-fighting soap. Often grows in the same area as poison ivy, but it's handy to grow a patch of jewelweed just to be sure.

The apothecary shop on the main street in Peterborough needed a girl to 'mark the books', and Mr. Fynch, the proprietor, hired Mary to work three half days each week. She and Claude found a rental house for thirty dollars a month on Water Street, on the west side of the Otonabee River, with room for a garden and an empty stone building on site for Claude to set up his welding shop. The owner of the property promised they could buy the place when they'd come up with fifty-five hundred dollars.

"At twenty-five cents a dozen we'll need to sell twenty-two thousand cartons of eggs." Claude was calculating their bills at the kitchen table. "We'll never have enough. Maybe I should go back farming," he said again. "It's not right you working so hard."

"I love being at the shop. It's what I've always wanted to do and imagine! Mr. Fynch pays me for it. I learn something new from him everyday."

It was a fifteen-minute walk to work and the fifteen dollars she brought home every week added nicely to their savings. Mary had never considered how many ailments the people of a town could have, but she soon found that they trusted Mr. Fynch with their goiters, their carbuncles and their bunions. Mrs. McKinley needed a cure for warts and Mr. Nelson's rupture could hardly be contained much longer. If Mr. Fynch was busy, the customers were glad of Mary's sympathetic ear and often told her more than she wanted to know.

"Oh, dearie, you don't want to see this," Mr. Craig confided, as he pulled up his shirt, to expose a midriff covered with oozing pus, now in dire need of treatment, having been left without for too many days. "It came on suddenly, about Monday." Mr. Craig looked up to heaven to confirm the day. "Yup, Monday. We got at the hay and bin steady at it ever since. This is the first I've been in town to get this mess looked at." He scratched the sores, using his shirt to rub over them. "The Missus' says I shouldn't touch 'em," he explained to Mary, as she stared at the red and festering, ulcerated chest.

Mary identified the eruptions as poison ivy. "If you don't quit scratching, you'll have it spread from head to toe." As she watched Mr. Craig rub his backside against the counter, she envisioned just how far it may already have spread.

"Does your Missus have any of the rash on her?" Mary asked, taking down the bottle of Carbonate of Soda from the shelf. Poison ivy had been bad this season with so many of the farmers brushing fence lines or clearing an extra patch for planting.

"Always a rash of poison ivy this time of year," Mr. Fynch had told her. "Expect plenty of it."

"You'll have to stop scratching it," she cautioned. "Instead of scratching, put on a coating of this bicarbonate. You can't put on too much, so apply it up to ten times a day. Make sure you wash any clothing that has touched the rash, such as blankets and underwear, in hot soapy water. Poison ivy is a menace." As she spoke, she dabbed the thick liquid on Mr. Craig's chest with a cotton ball.

"You're an angel, Mary." He sighed with relief, his breath carrying stale evidence of his own attempt at medicating the rash.

"Use a fresh cotton ball every time so you don't contaminate the bottle," Mary said.

Mr. Fynch bid her to remind all their customers of this, concerned that their frugal natures might cause them to skimp on the cotton balls, 'and there's no sense in that' Mr. Fynch said. 'Tell them they'll waste more than they'll save in the end. That'll convince them.'

Mary was glad to be learning so much from Mr. Fynch and shared it with Claude as they sat on their front porch in the evenings. "Mary, Mary, Mary," he laughed, "you'll have me afraid to lift a hand or foot with your tales of poison ivy, snake bites, and rusty nail punctures. You sound like my mother, and I'll say to you what my father would say to her when she got on at him. 'It's far from the heart, woman.' "

"So it's getting on at you, I am, is it? You'll watch your tongue, Mr. Johnston." Her heart made itself known in her chest as she watched a flush of colour begin at Claude's neck and work upwards. He so easily became flustered when they talked of his parents. She forced her voice to be stern. "I don't allow that sort of talk in my house. What do you think should be done about it?"

She was in the rocker and Claude crouched in front of her. "I shouldn't have ever compared you to my mother," he said, resting his chin on her knee. "Nor should I have answered you in my father's words. If there are two people in the world that I don't want us to be like, it is my mom and dad. Dad sits with the bible on his knee every night, giving us lessons from the good book, but he's the worst one for judging his neighbour or giving himself an extra measure at the expense of someone who can ill afford it.

"Our motto in this house will be that if we can't decide what to do in a certain situation, we'll ask ourselves, 'now, what would Claude's parents do,' and we'll do the exact opposite," Claude said.

Mary ran her fingers through his hair. It was thick and black and begged to be gently tugged. She grabbed two big handfuls at the

80

top of his head and rocked his scalp forward and back, laughing at the expressions his eyes made as his eyebrows moved up and down at her bidding.

"Here, I'm trying to be serious." His acrobatic eyebrows made her snicker, and he crawled his way up, past her knees, blowing breath against her stomach, her breasts, her neck, until he reached her chin. Her hands let go his hair, moved to his neck and the newlyweds became solemn as their lips met.

The kiss almost instantly had them both aroused. "Again?" she asked.

"Can't do it too often," Claude said. "Don't worry so much. I've been waiting for you to get home since noon when I sat alone at the lunch you left me. I imagined you there in the kitchen with me." They kissed, their breath and their tongues hot and wet. The scent of wood smoke on his clothing ingrained itself into her memory, mixed with the feel of his hands and the clinks of their teeth meeting.

How would she ever survive when he got his call to go to war?


Mr. Fynch insisted she have the whole week of Christmas off. "We'll close the shop," he said. "Let everyone know well in advance, so they can stock up, but there'll still be the regulars who come to my door for their emergencies." Mr. Fynch and Mary wrote a list of those they knew would have an emergency as soon as the closed sign was hung.

"Witch-hazel and cotton balls for Arthur's haemorrhoids. Remind him to keep the bottle in a snow bank so it will stay cool. More relief when it's cold," Mr. Fynch explained. They spent the last morning, before they closed on Christmas Eve at noon, preparing what they could.

It had snowed lightly overnight and most of the morning. By the time Mary arrived home, Claude had the wagon loaded for the trip to visit their parents.

"Four days we'll spend with them and then we'll be back home. We'll tell them you have to be back to work so there'll be no trying to convince us to stay," Claude said. Mary agreed. They planned to spend one night together with Mary's parents, then Claude would travel to spend two nights with his parents.

"Before we leave there's one thing we must do." Claude clasped her in his arms. "I don't want to be four nights away from you." He nuzzled into her warm hair and they leaned against each other there in the kitchen.

"Four days is a long time," she acknowledged. "But it's only two nights apart." At his insistence she sat in the wooden chair he'd finished making that day.

"It's the one piece of furniture in the kitchen we haven't tried yet. Shall we christen it?"

Mary blushed. How had she become so wanton in just five short months?

Claude grinned. "We've plenty of years ahead of us to be responsible and boring married folk. For now let's do it every place possible." He ran his tongue lightly around the outline of her lips, held her against him, pressed his hands and arms along her length, moulded her body to fit tightly into his.

How many more times would they be free to make love? How many more times before Claude left for the war?

Claude helped Mary to her feet, his large fingers fumbling to button the bodice he'd so recently undone. "We'd best be going." He was tender as usual but Mary noticed his over-quick movements.

"Are you sure you've packed everything, Claude? I know you won't want to turn the wagon around once we get on our way."

"Everything we talked about last night. I made a list."

"You made a list?" Mary smiled. As they made their way through the town, travelling south and east they received greetings and waves from the town's folk. Mary knew many of the women, and a few of the men too because of her position at the apothecary.

Claude also was beginning to see familiar faces among those they passed, and they identified for each other the ones the other did not recognize.

"That's Elwood Dickens. He came in this morning, asking if I'd cut some wood for him once freeze up comes. Said usually the missus does it, but she's pregnant and the doctor suggested she lay off the wood splitting. She's lost two of his babies in the last two winters," Claude said.

Mary registered the information. "That's probably who Mr. Fynch was talking about earlier this week. Two miscarriages. Poor woman. Mr. Fynch said the husband was in boasting about their five healthy children. Which would be the misfortune – another child to feed and clothe, or a miscarriage? Four of the children are boys. I know that much. Surely four boys are enough to help with the farm work. Why not have them cut the wood?"

"Does Mr. Fynch think that way?"

"What way?"

"Managing how many children a man and a woman should have. That's up to the Good Lord."

Mary looked to see if he was teasing, but his face was serious. She and Claude had talked about starting a family, but so far there'd been no discussion on exactly how many children they would have. "As many as the Good Lord sends us," was Claude's standard answer. Of course, Mary thought, that is never something Claude and his parents would have discussed around the dinner table or anyplace else. Not something many would discuss if you got right down to it. Planning the size of a family was one of those subjects you'd hear about, whispered quick, when there were no men around – certain herbs recommended to be taken monthly to ward off pregnancy and bring on the monthly flow. Bedstraw, vervain and certain ferns found growing along the road. Mary listened hard when the subject was raised at the apothecary and she read all the information available.

Mother's wooden herb box, presented to Mary shortly before her marriage to Claude contained various herbal remedies for sore throat, stomach ache, tooth ache, and one package wrapped in yellow ribbon that Mother said should be made into a tea to be drunk every fourth week for seven days.

"When you're ready to have a baby, you stop the tea, and in a few months you'll be pregnant. Mind you remember to start up with the tea as soon as your monthly flow starts again after the baby is born."

Mother had written the recipe for the tea in large perfect letters, along with specific instructions on when to drink it, and when not to drink it. The mixture wasn't sold from Fynch's Apothecary though all the ingredients were commonly in stock.

"It's the recipe my mother gave to me when I married your father. Be sure to pass it on to your own." Mother had been much more talkative than usual in the weeks before Mary and Claude's wedding. She'd instructed Mary to write out some of the family recipes – the Christmas pudding and the chocolate brownies and the red tomato chili.

Now, Mary thought, it's five months later, and I am returning as a married woman to my parents' home. Will they treat me differently? And how are things with Amy and Jacob I wonder? Is she pregnant yet?

Mary and Claude traveled on. "We've sure spent a lot of our times together in a horse and wagon, Mary. Now here we are at it again – travelling together." Claude rubbed his hand over Mary's knee, and she snuggled in closer to him. As the miles passed, they talked of her customers at the apothecary and ways Claude could build more trade for his shop in town.

This time, when the topic of children came around, Claude wondered how many, and when, and whether they'd be boys or girls. They decided they'd like to have three children – two boys for Claude and one girl for Mary. The names, Claude declared, weren't important, as long as they named one after his father and if the girl could have MaryArlene in her name, after his maternal grandmother, that'd be just fine.

Neither wondered aloud if their children would turn out like Jacob.

"I'm not especially looking forward to sleeping in my boyhood bed again," Claude said. "Alone. It'll be the same I suppose, as when I lived at home, and I was driving you into town those days for your lessons. I'd lie in bed at night and think about what we'd talk about."

"I thought sometimes you seemed to be reciting lines," Mary said.

"Mostly I was just hoping I'd get a chance to kiss you."

"You won't have to think about that tonight," she said. "My parents will let us sleep in my old bed together."

"We'll have to be very quiet," he said.

Not in my parents' house, she thought, and wondered again, a recurring self-examination in their months together, if they were normal. Who did one ask about this sort of thing? Stella? Claude seemed very ready to make love often, and she admitted to herself that she didn't need much encouragement to be ready for him. She wondered if she touched him now, would he stop the wagon? Just for a quick moment – a hug, a kiss, maybe a little more to bolster their confidence before arriving at Mom and Dad's. But Mother would surely know they'd been up to something. How would they get through the next four days – together tonight then apart for two nights? Mary's head ached at the thought. It would have been so much easier to stay home – just her and Claude. Well, they'd test the waters this time, and next time they'd visit each set of parents together.

She reached for his hand, which rested on her knee, and they squeezed hands awhile. She lifted her face to nuzzle his chin with her cold nose, and he tilted forward to kiss her.

"It's just four days, Mary," he said. "We'll get through it; do whatever we have to do to keep the peace, and then it'll be just you and me together again at home."

"She'll ask why I'm not pregnant. When she's going to be a grandmother."

"Tell her we haven't figured it out yet – how our parts go together, but we're practicing hard at it, sometimes three or four times a day. That'll quiet her."

"She wasn't very encouraging when Amy mentioned having children. Mother probably figured one Jacob in a family is enough." Mary wondered if Mother was ensuring it didn't happen with the tea she served each night after supper. Easy enough to slip in a sprig of Hedge Mustard or Bedstraw.

"My parents won't ask. They will be busy asking when I plan to take over the farm."

"Just promise me you won't change your mind and decide to go back."

"Not as long as I've got you," he answered. "You're the one who gave me the reason to get away. Although they will ask. What will become of the farm? They are getting older, Mary."

"We agreed. We said we'd make our own way in town and we're doing it."

"I know. I know. It's just … they always thought … me being the only child …"

"Claude Johnston! Don't you back up now! There's some things that aren't negotiable and moving to the farm with your parents is one of them!"

"What's wrong with my family? They've a right to expect some help from their son. Their only son."

Mary didn't answer. What was to be said? Claude as much as admitted himself that his dad was a religious hypocrite and that the further away from him they stayed, the better. She knew Claude didn't want to go back. It was the same situation with Mary and her parents. They'd need help as they aged but they'd have to understand that Mary and Claude were making their own life in town.

It was easier for Mary; she knew that. Once again she felt lucky to have a married brother who'd stayed home on the farm and kept the parents with him. For the present at least, Jacob could keep things going at home, and he got some help from the parents, but Claude was an only child. Maybe it was time to have a word with Stella. Stella Perkins' and Arnie Jenkins' newly built home was visible from Claude's mother's kitchen window. Stella and Mary had laughed on the phone about how the clotheslines' sightlines made them ideal for some sort of clandestine communications signal.

"We don't though," Stella said. "Of course. We hardly see our nearest neighbours. Too big an age difference."

It would be good to visit with Stella and get caught up on the news. Maybe she was pregnant by now. Mary looked again at Claude's serious face as he drove the wagon onward.

"Maybe Arnie would think about renting some land from your parents," she said.

"That's a thought." Claude's words steamed in the frosty air.

"I wonder if Stella is pregnant yet?"

"But Arnie doesn't like to pay." Claude slapped the horses' flanks a little too emphatically.

"I didn't know you'd any dealings with him."

Claude grunted, putting Mary in mind of Jacob.

"When was Arnie in to see you? Was Stella with him?"

"No. She doesn't often come."

"Why didn't you mention you'd seen him?"

Claude turned to look at her.

What was that expression?

He looked away quickly.

"Claude?" She put her hand on his leg. Felt him stop himself from pulling away. "Claude? What is it?"

He didn't answer.

"We'll go visit them when we're home. I've got a Christmas gift to bring to Stella and we'll catch up on the news."

"We'll see," Claude said.

They rode without talking past two concession road signs.

Maybe Claude was on edge thinking of being with his parents again. One of the things Mary admired about him was his general good temper, but he displayed an odd streak of obstinacy that Mary found frightening. Was obstinacy the right word? Judgmental? There was no changing his mind once he'd settled on an opinion. She'd have to tread carefully where his family was concerned. And Arnie. What was happening between the two of them? Maybe Stella could help. Then again, maybe she couldn't. Could it be that Arnie had changed his mind about enlisting?

# Chapter 10

**"The cure for an ill**

**Is not to sit still**

**Nor to sit with a book by the fire.**

**But to take out a hoe**

**And a shovel also**

**And dig 'til you gently perspire."**

**Rudyard Kipling**

Mary lay beside Claude between the white sheets she'd slept on every night of her childhood. The wallpaper was newly glued; careful blanket stitches were apparent where Mother'd re-sewn the binding of the blue and white border on the Sunbonnet Sue quilt on Mary's bed. Sunbonnet Sue was dressed in a different hue of blue in each square of the often-washed cover.

The whole house showed signs of Mother's busy hands: the wide-planked, wooden floors gleamed tawny brown in the golden glow of the setting sun. The windows sparkled, with no specks of the fly detritus that accumulated every autumn when the glass panes magnified the fall sunshine. Mary remembered how, in years past, the flies congregated for a last bask in the fading, Indian-summer warmth.

In the pantry Mary's throat tightened at the sight of Mother's preserves. Brilliant green mint jelly and sparkling red cherry jam sat next to golden honey, flesh-pink applesauce, and pepper-speckled mustard pickle, a testament to Mother's industriousness. And Amy's, Mary hoped, with an unexpected twinge of jealousy. Memories of the scents and the tastes and the days spent chopping, tasting, boiling and stirring together in the kitchen washed over Mary. Mother's home was orderly, clean, known, predictable. Mary had been so busy this fall, there'd not been time for preserving, but she hoped to trade some of the chickens Claude raised for jams and relishes to carry them through the winter. She hoped Mother wouldn't ask about Mary's preserves, though maybe she would offer them some.

"Your dad's showing his age," Claude whispered. "He forgot my name once at supper. Did you notice?"

Mary had. She'd also noticed that Mother cut his meal for him. His limp was causing obvious pain with each step; maybe the cold weather was the cause; she wished she had gone with him to the barn after supper, but Jacob and Claude moved to accompany him, and Mary knew she was expected to give Mother and Amy a hand with the dishes. Edith Chown's teachings on equal rights weren't common knowledge in the local homesteads yet, and not likely would be anytime soon.

The house quieted, and Mary heard Father's familiar snores coming from her parents bedroom; a new snore came from the room Jacob now shared with Amy. Mary resigned herself to stepping back into the role of her childhood for the next four days. Three now. She hoped Claude's visit with his parents would not be as guilt-ridden as he expected.

They had exchanged Christmas gifts after supper and would go to Mass in the morning, then Claude would leave to spend time with his parents.

"I want to visit Stella Perkins…Stella Jenkins … in the morning. Give her a gift. May I catch a lift with you when you're going to your parents? I can walk back."

Claude's hands stopped exploring the buttons on her new flannelette nightie. A gift from Mother and Father. "I'll drop you over there. Don't be too late. Your mom likes you here."

"You should come in for a visit too. We four used to have such good fun together."

Claude didn't answer.


When they finished eating breakfast, Claude stayed inside with the women and helped to clear the dishes. "I want to spend some time with my mother-in-law and my wife since I won't be seeing them again for two whole days," he explained.

"I'll be staying with my folks," he told Mrs. Murphy. "Dad will likely need a hand carrying in another load of wood to get them through the winter, and I imagine Mother will be looking for me to put in her winter windows if she hasn't already climbed the ladder herself to put them in place."

"You're a good boy." Mrs. Murphy bestowed her highest praise on him. "I hope Mary appreciates how lucky she is to have you."

Mary felt Mother's warning frown as Claude carried the stack of plates to the sink. Women's work. When he could catch Mary's eye in the sideboard mirror, he wagged his tongue and ran it back and forth over his upper lip, as he winked at her. Immediately Mary blushed, as certain covered parts of her body responded to him; she looked away, flustered.

"Enjoy your visit with Mary," Claude said, smiling at his mother-in-law. "Could you give Mary that secret ingredient now?"

"What do you mean?" Mrs. Murphy asked.

"The secret ingredient in your delicious chocolate brownies."

"Get away with you." Mrs. Murphy laughed. Mary wondered how he knew the exact right thing to say. She was sure he hadn't learned it from his parents.

At the Jenkins' place, Stella ran down the path to meet Mary and Claude's wagon.

"I was so hoping we'd see you both."

Mary noticed a small bulge under Stella's apron.

"I'm just done putting the potatoes on to cook and the kettle's hot so we can have a good visit."

Claude leaned over to kiss Mary. "I'll see you on Friday," he said.

"Oh, Claude. You must come in. Arnie would sure like a chance to talk to you. He wants to explain …"

"Sorry, Stella. Not this trip. I have to be getting to my parents. Merry Christmas to the both of you." Claude slapped the reins against the horses' backs and was gone.

"I don't know quite what's turned him into such a wet blanket. Maybe it's concern over his parents." Mary hated feeling the need to apologize for her husband's behaviour.

"We see them at church every Sunday," Stella said. "They're not getting any younger."

"Nor are my parents," Mary said. "Dad's really gone downhill."

"Yes. I've noticed." Stella put her arm around Mary's shoulders. "It's so good to see you, my friend. Have you lost weight? What's the news from you and Claude? Any announcements in the wind?"

"Nothing yet," Mary said, pointing at the firm lump bulging into view as Stella pulled back her apron. "What's this?"

"He's just little yet, but by the spring, May, we think, there'll be another Jenkins in the neighbourhood. Arnie is so pleased."

"Do you care if it's a boy or a girl?"

They walked into the house with their arms around each other, and discussing the new baby.

In the kitchen, Arnie pulled Mary to him in a bear hug.

Arnie smelled of aftershave and clean laundry.

"My second favourite girl," he said. "I suppose Stella's already convinced you over to her side on the baby names?" He kissed the top of Stella's head. "I guess the name won't much matter so long as he's healthy. Hey, where's that old sod, Claude?" He looked out the window. "Don't tell me he's not coming in."

Arnie and Stella exchanged raised eyebrows as Mary made more apologies for Claude. "He … His parents are anxious to see their only son."

"Claude's taking it as an insult that I've chosen the navy rather than the army," Arnie said.

Stella shrugged. "No matter. More Christmas goodies for us." She rubbed her tummy making them all laugh and soon the three of them were deep in conversation about babies and herbal remedies for backache and stretch marks and the war.


Claude and Arnie were called up to depart on January 14$^{th}$, 1940, with ten others from the area. Claude's first destination would be the training camp in Belleville while Arnie would go to York for his orientation and training. There wasn't much to be packed from home; uniforms had been supplied when they enlisted. After all the discussion around signing up, when they finally committed their names to paper it seemed the days had rushed by and now the time was come to leave. Tears, plans, promises, instructions on where to send letters and parcels, and what could be sent, were exchanged, and then on Monday, Claude and Mary set out for the train station on George Street.

"There's Stella and Arnie."

"Mmph. Him."

"You won't see Arnie for maybe years you know, Claude."

"Thank the Lord for small mercies."

"Aren't you a grouch. Come on. We'll have a word with them both and say good-bye like mature adults."

They met up with Arnie and Stella among a crowd of other fellows and their wives and girlfriends. "Sean Wilson, you old sot! I didn't know we'd be seeing you here."

"Yup. Off to York to win the war for the Allies," Sean said. "Me and Arnie'll keep the coasts clear of those pesky U-Boats for you girls."

Claude squeezed Mary's hand and Stella whispered into Mary's ear. "Sean and Debbie got married finally." She eyed Debbie's ring finger. "Wonder how many kids it took before they plunged into marriage."

Mary giggled. She held Claude's hand; didn't allow herself to remember she didn't know when she would see him again. Six months? Never? She wouldn't let herself even think that. At least she wasn't pregnant. They'd talked about that last night. How would Stella manage a new baby without Arnie?

"She'll manage fine," Claude had chided Mary. "Your mother will help her out plenty. And Amy. All the women love babies. Mine will be over there whenever she can be."

"I can hardly wait to have our own baby," Mary said now, as she noticed Arnie pat Stella's stomach. "A boy first, I hope. Then a girl. Or two."

"Whoa there, Mary Eileen Johnston. First let's get me off to war and back, and then we'll have the babies." Claude kissed her. "I'll miss this." He kissed her again.

"I'll miss you too," Mary said. "Me too." She murmured it against his lips.

"Stella tells me I have to write every day," Arnie announced.

"That's a lot of writing," Mary said.

"Probably have some time between watches to set down a line. You a writer, Claude?"

"I know how to write." Claude scowled, tightened his grip on Mary's hand.

"Let's say we make a pact to write. I can't promise daily but as often as I can. And I'll be sending notes to you too, Mary. So she can tell me your news, Claude, and you let Stella know where you are. We need to stay in touch – all of us. No telling what may happen over there. Or even over here."

As Arnie held Mary's eyes his smile faded. She would have liked to hug him, to say she'd miss him too. But Claude wouldn't understand. She held her hand out to clasp Arnie's.

"I'm glad we made ourselves some memories before we had to say goodbye for real. And you'll have a new baby to come home to." Mary held Arnie's hand as long as she dared.

"I'll be home before you know it." Claude said and squeezed her again, then picked up his bag. "Come on, Arnie. Time to go. I'll send you a card, Mary, as soon as we're at a post office."

Arnie ducked his head to kiss Mary's cheek and Claude scowled again.

Mary and Stella stood surrounded by the screech of steel wheel on steel track, waving and watching until the train carrying their husbands was no longer visible. The girls stood holding hands, staring down the empty railroad tracks until the ground-shaking rumble of the train faded into stillness.

"Oh, Mary." Stella's words waited in the cold winter air. "They're gone. For real."

"Mary? Stella?" Debbie Wilson stood in front of them, her clothing speckled with snow. She wore the colours of the British flag and a large V on each breast pocket. Mary too, had chosen carefully the clothing her husband would carry in his memory: a navy crepe dress with white embroidered trim; the fitted red wool jacket to which she'd added brass buttons.

The platform emptied until just Stella, Mary and Debbie were left in the silence of the absent train. Snowflakes fell faster. The Stationmaster came out to sweep the slush away from in front of his door, his office exhaling a roomful of pipe smoke. He stooped against the cold. "Sad to see our young men leaving," he said. "Everyday I watch 'em head out on the trains. Only be us old guys left pretty soon."

Mary and Stella unclasped their hands, each taking one of Debbie's and the three girls left the station, watched by the old man with his broom.

"We'll be on the phone often, you and I," Mary said to Stella. "And when you come in to deliver the baby, I'll be able to visit you right away. I can walk to the hospital from our place."

"You'll be my first phone call when the labour pains start." Stella sucked on a piece of hair.

Mary held back the urge to yank the hair from Stella's mouth. "You know I'll come right away as quick as I can. As Claude said, you'll have all the neighbourhood women at your door wanting to help with the baby."

"I've already had umpteen offers to baby-sit. And your mother gives me lots of advice about what to eat and especially what not to eat. I can hardly wait until you get pregnant so she'll leave me alone."

"That's a ways down the road yet," Mary said.

"The boys get the finest of training before they're sent overseas. That's what Sean told me," Debbie said.

"Arnie doesn't know what to expect exactly but he promised to write a lot. I wish him and Claude were staying together."

"Mr. Fynch has pledged dressings and syringes to the next load that goes out of Halifax. I hope this war is soon over."

"Not to wish the days away, but ... yes, me too. I want the war over right now," Stella said, her free hand resting on her round stomach.

"We'll keep ourselves busy. I've got my work at Fynch's. You've got the baby coming. You've family to care for." Mary nodded at

Debbie. "And the men have their work to do overseas while we've got ours here at home."

They walked on immersed in private thoughts.

# Chapter 11

## "The poet's eye encompasses the beauty of the whole world."

There was no way of knowing that it would be five years and nine months before Arnie and Claude would arrive back home again. Nor could they know that Debbie's husband, Sean, wouldn't return at all. Stacks of envelopes postmarked Europe, Halifax, and Scotland, from Claude and from Arnie, piled onto Mary's living room table where she kept the photograph of her husband, taken at Roy Studio before he'd left for training camp. Also on Mary's makeshift altar was the photograph of her and Claude and Stella and Arnie taken the day the men had left Peterborough for their training – all four of them, their arms around each other, smiling into the camera. She'd had copies made – one for each of them and often she held her copy as she read a letter from the front.

Claude's letters arrived regularly, usually every two weeks; Arnie's were not as often but treasured too. She could never be sure exactly where Claude was writing from as often times whole paragraphs had been blacked out by the censor. Her letters too were read before they left Canada to cross the ocean.

'Busy people are happy people,' Mother had said so often during Mary's childhood, and now Mary discovered that truth for herself. She looked forward to evenings spent with girlfriends, and wives of army men, laughter ringing out as often as tears were shed, while knitting needles clicked; giggles bubbled forth during stories told of weekend visits with husbands and boyfriends who'd not yet shipped out. Some of the women were girls; Mary noticed the new women joining their group grew younger each year that the war continued, and they all enjoyed hearing about dances with boys in uniform, love affairs made urgent by war. Some girls became pregnant and arranged hasty marriages. Mary thought they mightn't even recognize their husband when he arrived home after a few years, having only known the man for one night or maybe two. It seemed necessary to have a loving face to kiss and wave good bye to at the train station and the last-minute marriages continued.

Word of husbands missing in action was a reminder to all to make every minute count. The wives felt each death as a direct hit to their own family and Mary and Stella were no different than the others. They consoled Debbie when news of Sean's death reached home and made sure she came with them to the twice weekly gathering at the Red Cross, to pray together, to knit socks for the troops, and prepare parcels for the men.

When Claude's letters weren't coming regularly, Mary kept her hopes up with the stories of troops who'd found shelter in 'friendly' homes. She made sure to send greetings to Claude from Stella and included news from Arnie of places he'd been and his exploits on the seas between Halifax and Britain where he worked escorting merchant ships.

Each time a letter arrived to Mary or Stella they phoned each other, read them aloud and discussed the meaning of every word.

The baby, Arnie Junior arrived on time and seemed fully grown at 9 pounds and 3 ounces.

"How lucky," Mary said, "a beautiful baby with Arnie's eyes, to snuggle and love until your husband gets home."

"I wish you'd come stay with me a while," Stella said. "Help me get settled in with the baby," and Mary promised to visit whenever she could take a day off from the Apothecary and arrange a ride out to Stella's.

They didn't see each other often with the distance into town, so phone calls were the main venue of their friendship though they were always mindful that there'd be at least six neighbours listening in on the party line. It made Stella giggle when Mary delivered some juicy bit of gossip that might or might not be true just to prod Ruby or Fay to gasp.

"Did you hear that sound, Stella? I swear someone must be listening in to our call. Is anybody there?" Sometimes the culprit would hang up with a huff, but more often than not, there'd be no reaction, and they'd know their eavesdropper was still on the line.

"You're terrible," Stella would say. "And I love you for it. Thank you."

"I can't be too hard on them," Mary said. "Life is tough these days; people need to take their enjoyment wherever they find it."

Sitting at the War Services meetings she thought the milk of human kindness had been warmed by the war and was thankful for the camaraderie it fostered.

She'd arranged a ride to Stella's with a neighbour. "I can only stay until 6 o'clock, but that'll give us time to have an early supper and get caught up on our news," Mary said. "And, no one listening on the party line, so we don't have to be careful what we say."

"No husband to cook or clean for," Stella said. "Almost like being single again."

Mary and Stella hugged in the hallway.

"Arnie Junior! You've grown a foot I swear since I saw you last!"

"I think there's something in the water here makes him grow so fast. And me too. I'm not losing the extra pounds as I'd like to."

"You look wonderful," Mary said, holding out her arms to take Arnie Junior, who held tight to his mother's neck.

"That means you don't visit often enough," Stella said as she gentled his grip and set him into Mary's arms. "Arnie's written a poem for his baby boy. Come on. I'll read it to you."

Mary snuggled her face into A. J.'s soft neck folds and inhaled. "Oh, Stella. I can hardly wait for a baby of our own. I wish I'd gotten pregnant before Claude went away." She hadn't realized how close her tears were and wiped her cheek against Arnie Junior's chubby shoulder.

"You and Claude will be popping out babies soon enough. You're welcome to change A. J.'s bum," Stella said.

"I've never even changed a diaper." Mary felt the tears coming again. "I don't know why I'm so weepy today."

"Nerves probably. Here. You'll have a laugh over this. Stella took Arnie Junior back and handed Mary a note card. Inside was Arnie's familiar handwriting. "Read it out loud would you?"

"A fine wee boy. With all his parts. His pa's good looks, His mother's heart.

God made him healthy, He's sweet; he's strong.

I'm proud as a peacock after waiting so long.

I seek the black sky

Rest my eyes on the moon

I tell it a prayer

That this war's over soon.

I pray for your safety every night

That you and your mother

Are tucked in cozy and tight."

Love and Hugs, Arnie – Dad

Mary looked up from the card. "Oh, Stella. That is so sweet." Mary sniffled and dabbed at her eyes.

"Yeah. Easy to be all mushy-lovey-dovey when you're off at sea."

"Better than Claude. I'd rather have Arnie's lovey dovey than Claude's down and outs."

"I'm worried about Claude," Stella said. "He sounds unhappy."

"He sounds like a miserable grump," Mary said. "I wouldn't want to be stuck in a trench with him anywhere."

"What's happened to him," Stella wondered.

"It's terrible, how he sounds. He was down in the dumps before he left – worried how things would run at home without him, but I thought once he got into the routine, everything would fall into place."

"He doesn't seem to be doing well at all." Stella sniffed A. J.'s scalp and rubbed her nose along his cheek. "He smells so good, Mary. Good enough to eat." A. J. gripped his mother's ear and held tight, his eyes following Mary's every movement.

"He's so beautiful, Stella." Mary kissed his soft cheek. "Claude says his feet are freezing. He's always wet and hungry. Sounds like it's rained every minute since he got there." She stroked A. J.'s hair. "He complains every letter, Stella. Doesn't have one nice thing to say about anything. And I think he's getting worse. Listen to this." Mary pulled his most recent letter from her pocket. "I didn't read this over the phone to you."

"'Dear Mary,

I hope your hands and feet are warm and toasty not like my frost-bitten wet joints. It's still raining and cold cold cold. They tell us we aren't even into the wet season yet! I swear I don't' know how I'll stand this if it continues. The other fellows are sleeping now. It's my watch over this vast graveyard tonight. Always there's the sound of wounded men waiting to be moved to a medic tent and the rain.'"

She waved the letter at Stella. "There's five full pages of this stuff. I get a packet of pages every two weeks. On and on and on. I should be glad to get his letters; I know it, but they make me want to scream," Mary said. "Does he send you letters, Stella?"

Stella nodded. "I had one from him last week. He doesn't write often. He's sure not adjusting to life in the army. I thought it would be easier for him than for Arnie."

"I am worried about him. And then Arnie writes and his letters are so funny and cheerful. He sounds almost like he's having a good time. At least he's making the best of a bad situation."

"Too good of a time, do you think?" Stella asked. "In his last letter he seemed downright pleased with himself."

"And then Claude has the nerve to say the navy guys have it easier. Jeez! A whole ship load went down at Newfoundland there. Claude says … oh forget it. I'm sorry. Your husband's too happy. Mine's not happy enough. Never satisfied."

"We can only be patient and wait 'til the boys get home," Stella said. "And in the meantime try and send cheery thoughts to Claude. No use worrying over what we can't change is there?"

"You're right of course," Mary said. "At least I know he's still alive. Stiff upper lip." She shook her head. "I promised myself not to burden you with my worries today, and then I did just that." A. J. grabbed a handful of Mary's hair and she kissed him again. "Your mom's a lucky girl to have a charmer like you."

"You've got to talk to someone," Stella said. "When you're worried. I know."

"Are you worried, Stella?" Mary studied the eyes of the girl she'd been friends with all her life.

"I'm so worried. What if …"

"What if …," Mary said. She pulled Stella and Arnie Junior in to her and they stood hugging. "I don't know what if, Stella. We none of us do, do we?"

"No. Half the time I miss him so bad I can't think of anything else and then there's days when A. J.'s cranky and I'm tired and I'm so mad at him over there sailing the ocean with his mates and me stuck here at home."

"That's the feeling exactly. Keeping busy is the only thing I know to do. And phoning you. Teasing the people on the party line."

They both laughed, startling A. J. into yanking a handful of hair from each of their heads. "Jeepers! He's got a grip on him. You'll be a sailor like your father maybe."

"Gotta watch out for those." Mary laughed. "There's my ride. I'll have to run. Thanks for lunch. I didn't even tell you about my sewing. I've been making cushions out of some broadcloth I had stored away. Two cushions, I figure. And a runner for the dining table. Oh, and I've painted all around the dining room just over the chair rail. It's brown bulrushes with turquoise flower heads on them. Colourful if not realistic."

The friends parted after their afternoon of conversation and tea with promises to phone as soon as either received another letter.


Back at home, Mary read over the last letter she'd received from Arnie.

Dear Mary,

You'll be pleased to know that your favourite seaman (for we are men now, believe me!) has spent a wonderful weekend away from the sea. We landed at a small village (my foreign language skills are better than some but that is not saying much) for a necessary rest after two months of seasickness and wet mess decks. I swear there's nothing ever dry at sea.

On our weekend away, we got caught up on bathing, washed all our socks and underwear – both pairs of each!! And got them dry too. What luxury. And we slept for hours. Sleep, beer, and more sleep. Oh and you'd have been terribly proud, I say, tongue in cheek, to see yours truly speaking XXX. They tell me that I asked a young woman where I would find her underwear which would of course explain why she turned so red and flustered. I truly was asking where the market was but this is a risk I suppose in a new country.

We must return to some of these beautiful places when the war is over, you and Claude and Stella and I. I ache to have my woman back in my arms. I can hardly wait to take you two girls dancing, and

Mary, you'll enjoy the wonderful herb gardens. Everyone has one here it seems, on their balcony or tucked into a corner of the yard. They all grow gardens to keep themselves fed and keep livestock if they've any room at all. We stayed in a home that also housed two goats and a pen of chickens. Imagine! I figure it took our hosts minds off our stinky feet anyway!

Signing off now, I remain, your friend, and trust you and Stella are looking after each other and my son,

Love, Arnie

PS It's always a high point for me to get a letter from home.

Claude wrote in another letter:

Dear Mary,

We've had a long weekend in a small village away from the front to recuperate our spirits after suffering through heavy fighting. I'm not sure we should be off resting while our mates are embroiled in the war still, but we were ordered to go. It was a relief to have time away from the never ceasing gunfire. We're hosted by a family that doesn't speak our language so hand signals and smiling are our main communications modes. I find it tiring and retire to my bed at every possible opportunity. My mate is more adventurous and makes embarrassing mistakes sometimes in his attempts at seeking information. I can hardly wait to be quit of this country and this war but I know we must soldier on until we've finished with our mission. Pray that it is soon over.

Mary, I hope you're doing well and staying in touch with my parents as well as your own. I've had some letters from both; they sound busy and that's good.

Take care,

Love Claude

Arnie sent bits of poetry to Mary that he worked at between his long hours on watch, seeing beauty in the waves, whale sightings, a full moon. He often included a short note to Debbie, more often after Sean's Carly float was lost at sea. He wrote a poem about Sean's bravery and what an important part Sean's contribution had been to their mission, even as he explained that he couldn't give any details.

"How kind. How thoughtful he is," Mary said to Stella over the phone.

"Yes. He is," Stella agreed. "I wish … I wish he'd write me a poem sometime. About me."

# Chapter 12

**Culinary and medicinal herbs were the object of every head of a family; it became convenient to have them within reach, without seeking them at random in woods, meadows, or on mountains, as often as they were wanted. Separate enclosures for rearing herbs became expedient.**

**On Modern Gardening, 1770. HORACE WALPOLE**

Spring was early and dry in 1947 and Mary was able to till the garden and get a patch of salad crops in by the last week of April. Working outside in the spring sun gave her time to think and plan – maybe too much time, she thought – as once again her mind slipped to Christmas, and the scene in the barn, the last time she'd been alone with her father. He'd had tears in his eyes that night and the feeling that he wasn't long for this life stayed heavy in her heart all winter. Claude was worried about his parents too, and it seemed to Mary that since he'd returned from the war, their main topic of discussion was seeking solutions to their responsibilities. What would happen to Claude's parents when one was dead and the other left alone? And the Johnstons? Could Amy and Jacob manage now that the parents were old?

Mary insisted that they could come and live with her and Claude, but she knew realistically that couldn't or wouldn't happen. The house was too small and unfamiliar and ….

Mary arched backward. She'd been digging so long that stiffness had settled in, yet her thoughts kept her busy enough not to realize her soreness. It probably isn't fair to leave our parents as they are much longer. Sadness came over her again. It felt like she'd been sad since she and Claude returned from their Christmas visit. Mr. Fynch had alluded to it and she caught Claude's quizzical stares when he thought she wasn't noticing him watching her. He was jumpy lately too, and Mary figured it was due to worry over his mom and dad. As concerned as Mary was about her parents, at least Jacob and Amy were living with them and would react in an emergency. The Jenkins – Arnie and Stella – lived next door to Claude's parents and would act in a neighbourly manner should the Johnstons need help; Mary reassured herself with that, though a small voice argued, 'They're not family, and they're not close enough.'

But, she reasoned, she and Claude had every right to make their home here in Peterborough, where soon, she hoped, they could hand over their savings and have themselves a house of their very own. Still, doubts and guilt poked holes in her dreams. Claude had returned home physically healthy – in much better shape than many – but he wasn't the same man. He'd become quiet, cold, somber, and ... different.

"The strong, silent type," Stella said. "He takes life seriously."

"I don't know what's he's thinking the way I used to," Mary said. "I don't know who he is sometimes and that scares me."

"We got a heifer calf this year and two bulls," Father had boasted to Mary at Christmas. She'd come to the barn with him and Jacob after supper. "Exactly what we were hoping for. Jacob, you go look after the pigs. Mary and I will finish up in here." He slurred his words.

They worked without speaking as Mary searched for the right words to ask Father how long his left arm had been giving him trouble. "Signs of a stroke." Mary could hear Mr. Fynch's coaching voice. "Go ahead. Speak up. He needs to see a doctor."

Mary remained silent.

"I'm not doing so good, Mary," father said, as they fed hay to calves in the last pen. "I don't like to complain, but I'm worried about your mother. She says I'll outlive her, but we all know that ain't true. I won't likely see much past next spring's planting and it'll be a relief. My chest pains all the time, and I have to sit and rest between forkfuls of hay. I guess she'll be happy enough here on the farm, just like she's always been. So long as Jacob's here, and Amy. She'll have them to look after."

"Did you see the doctor?"

"What good's that gonna do me? My times up, Mary; I'm worn out. But yer Ma's got years ahead of her. Girl, you promise me, you'll keep an eye on her for me. If anything happens that she's here alone or unhappy, you promise me you'll look after her. Jacob's a good boy, and he'll do his best, but he's not smart, Mary. Not like you. You've done well for yourself, girl, and Claude's a lucky man to have you, so long as he appreciates what he's got. But I need to know you'll watch out for my Sadie. Please, Mary, promise me."

Tears rolled from his aged, blue eyes, catching in the many wrinkles that etched away across his cheeks. Mary pulled him into her arms.

"Of course I'll look after Mother. Claude and I will; you don't even have to ask." She'd squeezed him gently, carefully.

Now, home again in Peterborough, with Claude back from overseas, she'd thought things would run smoothly for a while. But, the garden work was tiring, and Mr. Fynch had remarked again yesterday that she looked peaked. Soon enough she'd be certain, but until two more weeks passed, Mary wanted to keep secret her suspicion that she was pregnant. When there was no doubt, when she'd completely missed her second period, she would tell Claude. Meanwhile she must consider what should be done about the problem of the parents. She hated to admit, even just to herself, but she knew that Claude was leaning toward moving back to Downers Corners, either in with his parents or near to them.

They could easily do it, Mary knew. And, there was talk in the township – predictions that their parents' farms would soon become part of the town of Peterborough so they'd be living in town anyway. The little house on Water Street was perfect for the two of them, but with a possible family increase they would need to add on, especially when it became necessary to bring one or more of the parents to live with them. Claude's parents' home was large enough already to house four or even six people comfortably.

Mary sat on the stone Claude had placed for her at the entrance to her garden and let tears mix with her sweat. The little house was her dream, their dream, and she'd fixed it up so nicely while Claude had been away. Though it had served them well, it was clear the time was come to reconsider their plans. She needed to be realistic, for all their sakes. If she wasn't pregnant now she surely would be soon, as she had stopped drinking Mother's special tea three months ago. When a good time presented, Mary promised herself, she would let Claude know she was willing to reconsider their living arrangements. Perhaps his dour mood would lighten if he wasn't worried about his parents.

Mary returned to her task of preparing the ground for the large vegetable garden she intended to plant over the next four weeks. Tears fell as she worked, water dripping from her eyes into the freshly hoed row where she would plant the carrots. The garden work was getting too far ahead of her. She should have heeded Mother's example and done a thorough clean-up of the garden in the fall, she scolded herself, and a fresh swell of tears overflowed. I'd better be pregnant. How was it that what they'd been so clear about – their dream of a new life away from their parents – was the one thing they could not in good conscience, give themselves? She sniffled, searched for her handkerchief and noticed Claude standing near her rock. How long had he been watching? What sort of mood was he in now?

He came to her; patted her shoulder. "How did you find out?" he asked.

Mary stared at him afraid of his next words. "Find out what, Claude?"

"Your father has died, Mary. I'm so sorry." Weeping, she held onto his hand as they walked to the house. "Your mother called. I came right away to find you."

"We'll have to let Mr. Fynch know," Mary said.

They packed the essentials and left for Downers Corners. There was no need to tell the neighbours; Mr. Fynch and the party line would spread the word.

Mother seemed strong through all the preparations, the wake and the funeral, explaining to Mary and to many others as they offered condolences, "He's not been well since late last fall. We both knew it was coming. Still we'd hoped ..." She gazed into his coffin, dry-eyed, as the line of neighbours and friends rearranged itself and the next mourner stepped forward to grasp her hand.

Mary's period arrived on the second day of Father's wake. She sat on the toilet in the funeral home washroom, crying for Father and for her non-existent baby.

"Mary, I saw you come in here and I followed you." Stella pushed open the door to the toilet.

The first of Stella that Mary saw was her ripening belly. "I'll never be pregnant," Mary cried.

"What's brought this on?" Stella let herself carefully down onto the bathroom floor before taking Mary's hand in hers.

"I thought I was pregnant," Mary confessed. "I thought I'd be telling everybody about the new baby coming and it's not. I'm not. And Father's died and we might have to move back home to look after Mother. It's so awful, Stella."

"It surely is, Mary." Stella pulled Mary's hand onto her stomach. "If it's any consolation to you, Arnie and I aren't making love these days. No sex in the last two months. He says he doesn't want to hurt the baby."

Mary felt the solid baby move inside Stella's abdomen. "Not for two months?" She remembered Claude's touch on her this morning. He'd pulled her against him as he did most mornings on first waking. "Oh. That's too bad."

Stella smiled and frowned at the same time. "Don't you dare tell me what you and Claude did last night! Or the night before! Don't make me have to kill you!"

Mary giggled for the first time in two days. "Thanks for that, Stella."

"It's what friends are for, isn't it?" Stella patted her bulge through Mary's hand. "I love the little guy, or girl, but it sure puts a crimp into things. And don't worry. You'll get your chance at motherhood, I'm sure. How long have you been trying?"

"A few months," Mary said. "Three."

"There. Be patient. No sense in rushing these things. This way you'll have me to give you advice when your body starts to change. I'll be an old hand at it with one baby spit out already and one in the oven. And you can borrow my maternity clothes when you're ready."

Mary fingered the loose white shirt Stella wore.

"You're probably thinking you won't get this big, but believe me, you will. And I'll be right there to laugh at you when you do as I prance around in my new crepe trousers, with my blouse tucked in and my belt cinched tight." Stella raised her eyebrows at Mary's neat slim figure.

"Ok. Ok. Enough. You've made your point," Mary said. "And you're right. I'm feeling sorry for myself. It's not a great time to be pregnant anyway I suppose."

"What's this talk about moving back to the farm? Do you mean it?" Stella looked hopeful.

"We've been talking about it." Mary sighed. "Claude's worried about his parents. And Mother might need to live with us too. This is my worst nightmare coming true. A houseful of parents and no babies."

"Oh, Mary. I'm sorry. We have things to talk about then. Time for us to get together over tea. I'll have Arnie bring me around. You're staying at your mother's?"

Mary nodded. Together they went back out to the room where Mr. Murphy lay in his coffin. Mary greeted the mourners with her mother for the rest of the wake, letting tears of sadness at her infertile state mingle with her tears of mourning so no one else, not Mother or Claude, realized there was any reason to cry other than Father's death.

"Mary, my girl, what would I do without you?" Mother lay on the living room sofa sniffing peppermint oil, a gift Mr. Fynch had sent home with Mary. He'd advised rubbing some drops on the temple at the first sign of a headache.

"You knew we would come to be with you."

"Father said I could always count on you. Not like that other one in there." Mother pointed to the kitchen where Amy sat reading the paper. "She as much as asked me to pack my bags when your father died. Oh, Mary, what ever am I to do?

Mary and Claude whispered late into the night. Was Amy as bad as Mother made out? Jacob seemed oblivious to any trouble; as long as his meals were set in front of him on time, all was well and life was good.

Mary shared with Claude the conclusions she had come to in the vegetable patch the day he'd come to tell her about Father's death, regretting as she did, that she couldn't tell him she was pregnant.

Each day she spent time in Mother's garden, amid the crooked rows of lettuce and radish, a sure sign of Mother's decline, if another sign was needed. On the day of the funeral Claude had gone to his parents' farm and driven them to the funeral home to pay their respects, since Mr. Johnston didn't feel able to handle the horses for the whole length of the drive.

The responsibilities Mary'd always considered a far off event suddenly were immediate and she could no longer pretend that caring for aging parents would happen in the future.

"Is this how dreams slip away? I've joined the ranks of adulthood," she blubbered to the radishes, "and it's not of my choosing." A blue moth fluttered between the plants. "You don't complain. You just take what you're given. Do as all your ancestors did. Why should I expect to be special or different?" Still, she knew that she was.

A tiny brown toad crossed in front of her and she thought of the birth story she kept tucked in her memory. She thought of Edward and Sadie, her parents, before they become parents. They'd been young once like she and Claude were now. She thought of them, in the strawberry patch on the day she was born, as the bees bumbled and a cool green snake slithered.

It seemed as if she'd already lived the future and now she was looking back at it. As if her life had compressed into a book that she knew the ending of. As if she and Claude were Sadie and Edward. And though she didn't know the exact path or the specific steps, she saw their lives happening in the present yet as part of the past at the same time. She knew that she and Claude were shaping their own destiny but it felt as if they followed a predetermined course to an outcome they'd already lived.

Stop thinking, Mary.

She watched two robins fuss over jutting spikes of straw in the manure pile. It would be so easy, she knew, to make one long straight furrow with her hoe, to mark it with two or four stakes and some string and transplant that crooked row of lettuce into a regimented line. Mother would be pleased. Tears welled again from Mary's eyes. Would they ever stop? I can do this one small thing, Mary thought, that will remind me every time I look, that one day I made order in one place and for now that is as much as I am able to do. She rolled her eyes at the robins who'd paused their discussion over the straw to watch Mary's internal debate.

Way too philosophical for a spring morning in May, aren't I? That's what happens when I get out in the garden by myself. The male robin snagged a worm and jerked hard to pull the creature from its dark, safe, underground hole.

"And you," Mary told the worm, "should know better than to stick your neck out. That's when a dang mean sharp-beaked hungry bird swoops in on you. As if life wasn't tough enough just getting by. So you might as well take the risk I suppose. Stick your neck out. See if I care." She watched, wondered if she should stop the carnage, figured the worm was likely already mortally wounded. Robins have to eat. It's the cycle of life. Things die, they change, and yet it all goes on as life is meant to do.

She had the stakes set out, the furrow opened and she was on her knees moving lettuce plants. "Might be a worm or two here for you," she promised the robins. "They're beautiful and fat this time of year."

Mary and Claude's late night discussions returned again and again to the parents, what to do, how to make sure they'd be safe and comfortable. "We have to move back to home, Mary, there's no two ways about it. I can't live with myself if I've not done the right thing, and my parents need me at home. You need to be close by your mother. Sadie's not getting any younger. We can keep an eye on her. See for ourselves what goes on with Amy and Jacob."

Mary murmured almost asleep. "It's not what I want but it's what's right and so we'll do it."

"Do you think Jacob can keep the farm afloat without your father's help?"

"I don't know."


The days at the little house on Water Street in Peterborough took on an aura of bittersweet leave taking as they prepared for their future.

It was best, they decided, to move in with Claude's parents, to use the money in their savings account to buy a car instead of the house. The account held almost one thousand dollars of their combined savings; a car cost eight hundred and fifty dollars, Claude said; he'd been asking around. He seemed better able to hide his disappointment at this change to their lifestyle, dreams, and plans, than Mary was. Life is full of lessons she counseled herself. This will teach me patience. Still, she found herself weeping as she dusted the second hand coffee table they'd bought from a neighbour who had moved away.

"Our first purchase as newlyweds. What about all our things? Will there be room in the house for them? For me?"

Claude said, "Don't worry. You will love my parents' home. You must learn to call them Mother and Father. They have furniture enough that these pieces can be sold." He saw Mary's face crumple and took her into his arms. "Not again, Mary? It'll be better. You'll see."

Claude could come up with long lists of reasons why leaving their independent life made sense; Mary knew he was right and searched for reasons of her own to be happy to be moving back to the community of her youth. She tried to think new thoughts and to keep herself busy packing and saying goodbye and tried not to resent Claude's eagerness to leave their cozy home.

"We'll store this furniture. Think of all the money we'll save every month by not paying rent. And you can have a huge grand garden. And visit your mother as often as you like. Or she could come to live with us. We both must learn to drive the new car. And you'll be near your chum, Stella. That will be nice."

"That will be nice. You and Arnie can chum up again too."

"I think it's wise to keep Arnie out of our conversation."

"What are you saying?"

"I know how things were with you two. Best to let that yahoo alone."

"I thought you and Arnie were best friends?"

Claude grunted.

"I don't like this, Claude. There's nothing on between Arnie and me. Never has been. It's only you. You know that!" Mary took his hand in hers.

"I know you're not looking at him, Mary, but he's a wanderer that Arnie. I've known him a long time. He likes the girls."

"And you don't?" Mary shoved Claude's shoulder, noticing as she did that he held himself stiff. "He's married for goodness sake! To my best girlfriend!"

"Then he should remember that instead of writing poems to his wife's best friend."

"We're wasting our words on this conversation." She waited for his apology.

Claude remained silent.

"One thing's sure. If I have to move and live with your parents I expect you, Claude Johnston, to make up with Arnie. I don't care how you do it but Stella and Arnie are going to be our neighbours and you and him are going to be friends. So you get to work on that."

"You're right, Mary. I know it. We've got to be on good terms with the neighbours. I'll do my part."

They decided to start off on the right foot by inviting the Jenkins for dinner. Claude's mother, Liz, wondered why they couldn't just come after dinner for cards or games. "Father wouldn't welcome card playing in the house," Claude said, and Liz agreed right away.

"It's a lot of fuss over a dinner," Mary said. "How much easier it would be to give up."

"We'll start as we mean to continue," Claude said. He turned to Liz. "Mother, what will we serve for dessert? Cake? Pie? I think Stella is not much of a cook. I'm sure Arnie will be pleased to learn the art of baking hasn't completely disappeared from the township." He winked at Mary. Maybe the old Claude would come back to life when they moved to the farm with his parents.

# Chapter 13

"Two months to the day," Mary said. "The doctor told us – me and Claude – that Mr. Johnston would have survived, that the injuries were minor, but his lungs filled with water and he was pinned down for too long. He drowned in a puddle."

"It'll take time I guess, 'til Claude adjusts to being the 'man of the house.' Too bad it happened so soon after you moved in."

"Once me and Claude got the tree lifted, we saw right away that Mr. Johnston was dead." Mary shivered. How quickly a life could be snuffed. It seemed careless somehow, yet there was no cure for it, nor blame. "He drowned. The doctor said his ribs would have healed completely, but he didn't get the chance. I don't understand. It was so quick. So unnecessary." Mary sipped at her tea. "And Claude is gone down in the dumps. Worse even than when he was overseas. Not good at all."

Mary watched Stella fill the kettle. "He's so short tempered these days," she said.

"Claude and his dad were planning on getting into the firewood business full time?"

Mary nodded.

"Will he set up on his own then?"

"We're not sure. He'd planned to open a welding shop too, similar to what we had in Peterborough. Before we moved. Before the accident. But now ... I'm afraid his mother won't let him. Too dangerous working on his own, she says."

"He could turn into his father if he listens to her."

"Not good," Mary said.

"Him and Arnie should talk about getting into business together. Friendship carried us through the hard times when the war was on. We can navigate another tragedy."

"Claude could use a friend right now. I need them to be friends again. Give him someone else to go to for advice besides Liz. I don't quite know what to do about her."

"Mr. Johnston's reputation wasn't wonderful. I've heard them say he's ... judgmental ... and ... overbearing ... and maybe not completely above board," Stella said.

Mary remembered her father telling them at home about Mr. Johnston's trouble getting along. Dad had always made it his habit to seek the good in anyone he met, yet even he had been careful in his dealings with Claude's father.

"'He was always on the shady side of honest,' is what my dad said about him," Mary said.

"The branch doesn't fall far from the tree. It'd be a shame if Claude carried on that tradition." Stella lifted her shoulders in a sort of question mark.

"Right." Mary didn't tell Stella about the cool reception she'd gotten when she tried charging some groceries on the Johnston family account at the store. "At church they have only good to say about the man. At home, Claude's mother talks as if her husband was a saint. But he wasn't perfect. No doubt of that."

Stella snorted. "He was no saint. The things he'd say about other people as if he was God's chosen judge. The self-appointed righteous are downright frightening. But we're not allowed to speak ill of the dead." She rubbed her arms. "Let's not talk about that cross coot right now. The baby's moving a lot today. Just four more months and he or she will be making his way into the wide world." She gave her unborn baby a hug.

"Oh, Stella."

"I'm not looking forward to the delivery, Mary, but people keep telling me it's too late to change my mind about having a baby now."

"And that is the truth, my friend. Are you up for taking a bit of a walk with me then?" Mary jerked her head toward the west. "I have something to share with my mother and I know you'll want to be privy to it."

"You're not!" Stella grinned. "How dare you sit here in my kitchen and not tell me first?"

"I haven't any idea what you're talking about." Mary pulled her coat on and made to leave. "You're coming, my friend?" She pulled open the door. "I'm not sure I should be walking alone … in my condition." Mary grinned at Stella.

"Do I have to beg? Are you or are you not, Mary Eileen Johnston, having a baby?"

"Since you've guessed, I'll tell you. Yes, we are. I am. But you have to act surprised when I break the news to Mother."

"Mum's the word." Stella promised. "Not a peep out of me."


Stella and Mary walked to Sadie's house to share the news.

"A baby." Mother hugged Mary. "A little grandbaby. I'm so happy."

"It's wonderful news," Amy said. She wore a man's shirt over her flannel pyjamas and her hair was still awaiting its turn with a comb this morning. "Jake and I have been trying too. Maybe …"

"A baby," Stella said. "What's Claude say about that?"

"Oh. I uh haven't found the right time yet to tell him. Tonight, I thought. After Liz goes to bed."

"When does she go?" Mother hugged Mary to her again, enveloping her in fragrant memories of cinnamon buns and apple pie.

"Some nights, I swear she's never going to bed. Claude says we have to give her time to adjust to Mr. Johnston being gone. He feels guilty."

"Trouble sleeping. Too bad."

"Yeah. She gets him up to sit with her."

Mother poured more tea into Stella's cup. She raised her eyebrows at Mary. "Have you changed your eating at all? You'll need to get more iron. Keep your blood strong as the baby develops."

Stella laughed. "One good thing. Now she'll have two of us to spread her worries onto." She reached over to pat Sadie's hand. "Eat lots of spinach and red meat, but not too much. And not too much coffee either. But tea's OK. I appreciate your help, Sadie. Just don't like that you make me feel guilty for eating peanut butter cookies."

"There is a place for peanut butter," Sadie laughed. "Just not baked with lard, sugar and chocolate chips, as a steady diet, my dear."

Mary groaned. "No cookies?"

"That can't be good for you. Giving up your favourite foods." Amy bit into a rice krispie square. "When I get pregnant...."

Mother broke in. "You two will be able to share maternity clothes. Stella has some nice ones."

Amy rolled her eyes. "I might be ready to share pretty soon too."

"I don't think so, dear. I'm not seeing a baby in your future anytime soon."

"Mother!" Mary looked at Stella wishing she would say something in support of her sister.

Amy pulled the button off her shirt sleeve, stared at it a moment. She carried her teacup and plate to the counter and turned on the water to fill the sink.

"So," Mary said. "We'll see how it goes. I'll be asking you both for advice. And, Amy, when you're pregnant we'll pass on what we've learned to you. And maternity clothes too. But for now, it's time to go. I'm telling Claude tonight. I wish Liz would go out somewhere."

"Or fall in the creek," Stella muttered.

Before they'd even gotten out of the yard, Stella turned to Mary. "Holy Cripes! Did you hear Sadie?"

"She was pretty tough on Amy wasn't she?"

"I'll say," Stella said. "Glad it's not me living there."

"Makes Claude's mother look better. That's not true. I'd still rather have my mother living with me than Claude's any day. I wonder if we could ever switch houses or something. Liz is so annoying."

"You were good smoothing things over with Sadie and Amy. Sounds like they're having serious disagreements about her getting pregnant."

"I feel guilty being so angry at Liz and her so newly a widow. You got any wise ideas?" Mary looked hopefully at Stella.

"I don't have any answers, but you surely should not feel guilty." Stella put her arm around Mary. "That's pretty strange, her getting Claude out of bed at nights."

"It is weird. She gives me the creeps. I wouldn't care if it was once in a while but it's every night or twice a night. She's moved into the bedroom next to ours to be closer to him."

"Maybe she'll die soon. Is she sick?"

"Stella!"

"Yeah. We're not allowed to say that kind of stuff out loud are we?"

"I wonder if Mother has any 'interesting' tea I could be mixing up for Mother Liz. Something for her depression maybe."

"It's a slippery slope, Mary."

"And I wish I could push her down it." They both laughed. "Seriously though, I have to tell Claude tonight that I'm pregnant. Help me figure out how to get my mother-in-law out of our hair for a little while so I can tell him in private."

"How about getting him into the bedroom?"

Mary wrinkled her nose. "Not real private since she knocks and walks in. Maybe after supper she'll go do something in the kitchen. That's my best hope."

"Your mom's real happy about the baby. Of course." They were at Stella's driveway. "I'll see you for tea tomorrow morning. Tell Claude tonight."

"I will."

Mother's joy and Stella's excitement stayed with Mary as she continued alone on her way home, but her steps slowed the nearer she got to the Johnston property. Her throat constricted and she choked on the words she would use to tell Claude she was expecting their baby. In the house that revolved around mourning the death of Claude Senior, feeling happy felt wrong.

"Claude," she said, after supper, when Liz had gone to the bathroom. "I've been sick to my stomach lately. Especially in the mornings."

He looked up from his newspaper. "Something going around maybe?" he said. His eyes were dull. "I hope Mother won't catch it. Whatever you've got. That would be all I'd need. To have her get sick."

"It's not contagious, Claude."

"Good. Good then." He scratched his head, looked back at his paper.

"Claude, I'm pregnant. We're having a baby."

He looked at her again. "We haven't...." He scratched his head again. "Are you sure?"

She nodded. "I'm sure." She waited for him to jump up, twirl her around the room. Smile. React.

He tilted his head. "When ... How ..."

"I'm eight weeks along at most. Must have happened almost as soon as we moved here. Before your father died." Of course.

Claude stood. "Mother!" he called. "Mother! We're going to have a baby! You'll be a grandmother."

Mary listened to her husband tell his mother her news. Their news.

Her stomach churned and she ran to the toilet and vomited.


"Stella, you must be so tired of hearing me complain about my husband and my mother-in-law. You're the only one I can talk to about this."

"I know. It's okay. You can tell me."

"I feel like such a traitor. Remember when Amy was fretting about my mom? Now here I am going through the same thing. Different, but the same."

"Liz is much worse than your mother from what I've seen. Although that was a nasty episode with Amy the other day. And Liz is using Mr. Johnston's death. Milking it way more than Sadie would ever dare. How can you fight that?"

"I feel so mean, but Stella, she gets that little trembly lip or the shaky voice and what can Claude do but exactly what she asks? She chooses which Mass we go to on Sunday. And she sits in the front seat of the car beside him. And ..." Mary clapped her hand over her mouth. "I'm going to go straight to hell," she said. "No doubt about it."

Stella patted Mary's hand. "You poor dear."

"I told him. Told him we're having a baby. And right away he ran to tell his mother. God help me! I don't know how I'll ever survive this mess without murdering someone. Him. Her. Me. One of us has got to go."

Mary tried to keep herself busy experimenting with new recipes.

"Oh. I couldn't eat salmon tonight," Liz remonstrated, when Mary presented the meal she spent all afternoon preparing. The fish flaked perfectly, the sauce bubbled to smooth white velvet, and fresh garden dill set off the steaming pink flesh.

"Salmon was your father's favourite," Liz could barely speak, and Mary was left to eat supper alone as Claude comforted his sorrowful, grief-filled Mother.

The baby fluttered next to Mary's heart for the first time that night as she picked at the salmon, alone in the kitchen, wistful for the comfortable hominess of Water Street. She placed her left palm on the gentle curve of her incubating baby, absorbing the first movement of life inside her.

Claude and Liz joined her after she'd cleaned up the dishes and moved into the fireplace room. He presided, sitting in his father's easy chair, his now, at Liz's insistence, and Mary watched her husband, with her hand on her stomach, in love with the baby's first movements, eager for tomorrow when she would share this development with Stella. Claude's left hand rested on the bible from which his father used to read aloud each night.

"Claude, read us a passage, please," Liz said, and Mary sat, listening to Claude's strong, clear voice, regret threatening to push salmon and baby from her stomach. Or was it anger? When had this begun? Could it be stopped?

Impending doom became Mary's companion, and fear for the future joined her happiness and hope for the growing baby. Evening routine came to include a bible reading for Liz by Claude while Mary found reasons to be out in her garden or visiting her mother or Stella, trying to deny the wedge forming between her and Claude.

Mary gravitated to the garden more and more often. She asked the robins what she should do, taking comfort in their steadfast busyness. Their work ethic assured her that life would go on. Sometimes she lay on the grass watching the clouds and the birds overhead, losing herself in the reliable sounds of squawking blue jays and screeching crows to the background chorus of tractor song.

Big skies in blue hues with puffs of white and grey clouds balmed Mary's soul, and fall ploughing and harrowing followed by the planting of winter wheat gave her hope. And so, Mary waited. Waited for the baby and waited for her husband. She waited for relief from grief and from heartache. In the garden she fancied herself like the fertile ground, carrying the seed.

"I'm feeling quite mother earthy these days," Mary said, watching Stella nod and try to understand while clearly not understanding. "Like if I wait long enough and for the right conditions, my life will renew itself." Mary spread her hands on the table. "Look at my hands. Brown spots. What's that from?"

"Being pregnant brings all kinds of changes," Stella commiserated. "Those brown spots are the sun's doing."

"You mean I can't work in the garden anymore?"

"You should do whatever feels right, I think," Stella said. "You'll get the brown spots no matter what, and you might as well do what makes you happy. Take care. No heavy lifting. Might be a chance to get Claude alone out in the garden. Use the pregnancy to get some time with your husband."

"You are one brilliant woman, Stella."

"Oh yes. Listen to me. I know it all." Stella laughed. "So what have you done? Have you got some diapers or any of those sweet little sleepers?"

"Liz dug some out of the attic that she'd saved from when Claude was a baby. She's getting excited about her grandchild. In her own way. Mostly she tells Claude things that she intends for him to pass on to me – like not to raise my hands over my head or …"

"Maybe this'll be the thing that gets her out of her self-absorption."

"We can only hope. It is possible that the baby will be the distraction she needs. Maybe let Claude and I get back to being married." Mary shook her head. "It's like she's watching us all the time. To see if we're being too happy. It's creepy."

"She needs something to do," Stella said. "Something useful. Does she quilt?"

Mary shook her head.

"Sew? Garden?"

Two more shakes of Mary's head. "No. She likes to bake. For her son. She doesn't have any friends. No other interests. Just her son. I can't stand it. Seems like it would be easier to contend with a girlfriend. How do I fight the mother?"

"It's a problem that's sure," Stella said. "What about…you know…sex. He is a man first, right? Do you think you could like … lure him away from her that way?"

"I've been trying," Mary said. "My 'attraction' doesn't seem to be working quite as well as it used to."

"Maybe a few little changes…?" Stella suggested. "His favourite perfume? Or, I know … what would remind him of when you were first dating?"

"You mean I should get him out in the wagon and put the make on him? It seems too schoolgirlish but it could work."

"Yeah. Well. In times of desperation we use all means at our disposal." Stella laughed.

"He won't make the first move anymore. What happened to the fellow who convinced me to marry him? Where did he go? Was it truly only eight years ago?"

"Hard to believe," Stella said. "A lot happens in eight years."

Even harder to believe was the fact that the both of them were going to have babies, Mary thought. She was digging walking onions for a salad when Arnie stopped at the house and she came up from the garden to meet him.

Claude stepped from the chicken shed to stand with Mary.

"Stella's had the baby," Arnie said, putting out his hand for Claude to shake and reaching into his shirt pocket with his other hand, pulled out a cigar. "Thank goodness the war's over and there's no more shortage of these."

"Congrats to you both." Claude sniffed along the length of the cigar before dropping it into his chest pocket.

"It's a boy," Arnie said. "We're calling him Nelson. After one of Stella's people."

"How's Stella? When can I see her? Can I go into the hospital? When will she be home?" Mary wondered why she hadn't thought to find these things out earlier. "How much did he weigh? What colour is his hair? She'll be so glad to be able to see her feet again."

Arnie laughed and handed Mary a note. "Stella was right. You do want to know all those things. I'd never even think of asking."

Claude nodded agreement as Mary snatched the notepaper and scanned her friend's handwriting. "Six and half pounds," she read aloud. "That's a good size. Smaller than A. J. Brown hair. Of course. They all have brown hair, don't they?" She rubbed her tummy as her own baby kicked. "When you see Stella, tell her this

Junior here sends his or her regards. Is she feeling alright, Arnie? Any complications?"

"Mom and baby are doing fine. They'll stay in for a couple more days Stella said. Just to make sure everybody is healthy and eating. And pooping," he added. "And then they'll be home. You're allowed to visit. You can come tonight with me when I go, if you like."

"I would like that a lot, Arnie. Thank you. What time should I be ready?"

"I'll pick you up at seven o'clock." He turned to walk down the pathway to the road.

"I'll be waiting." Mary and Claude waved. "It won't be long until it's our turn, Claude. A little over four more months," Mary said.

"I don't know about you, but I've a ton of things to get done between now and then. Better get at the fencing right now." Claude leaned in toward her cheek and didn't touch it as he made a kissing sound. Then he was gone off to work.

"Claude, I was thinking, it would be a nice outing for us – just the two of us – to go driving in the wagon on Sunday," Mary said. "Like old times."

"It's supposed to rain Sunday," he said, not looking up from his bible.

"We don't melt in the rain. Come on. Say yes. It'd be fun to go out on a tour around the neighbourhood. See how people's crops are coming along." She smiled.

He didn't look at her. "Hard on the horses. And on the guy who has to brush them down afterward."

"You never seemed to mind in the early days."

"I'm older now."

"Not so young and foolish," Mary teased. "It used to be fun to look into the yards as we went past, imagine what the folk were doing that they mightn't want us to know."

"Things change, Mary. I haven't got that kind of time anymore. Mother needs me home."

"Mother needs to let you spend time with your wife."

Claude looked up from his reading. "I have responsibility, Mary. Animals to care for. There's always things left undone because time runs out. This place doesn't run itself. I can't be out jaunting about like a carefree young buck anymore."

"It sounds like you're turning into the grumpy crotchety man you said you were never going to be. You even asked me one time to tell you if I thought you'd gone down that road. And I'm telling you now. You are getting there."

"What would you have me do?"

"Take some time to be with your wife. What have I to look forward to? If you're this way now, you certainly won't have time to spend with a new baby. Maybe I should never have gotten pregnant."

"That's for God to decide." Claude rapped his index finger on the bible page. "Maybe you should spend time reading the bible. Get some guidance from the good book."

"Maybe so," Mary said. "I have plenty of free time to read since you and I have no time together anymore." She folded her arms under her chest letting them rest lightly on the baby.

"That's a better attitude," Claude said, missing Mary's raised eyebrow. "Idleness is the devil's playground. I know you'll be pleasantly surprised at the wisdom to be found here." He tapped the book again. "Just pick it up and begin reading. Wherever the book opens is a good place."

Mary nodded her head and let her mind wander into the world of baby garments. Mother was an accomplished knitter and had offered to teach her some new stitches; it seemed now would be the right time to learn a new skill.

As the pregnancy had progressed into its third trimester, Mary felt awkward and too rejected to be flaunting her sexuality in the face of Claude's increasing aloofness. "I give up," she confessed to Stella. "No more throwing myself at him." She quit trying and she sensed Claude's relief. He'd adopted a solicitous, attentive kindness toward Liz, and Mary noticed him now treating her the same way. Well. Physical contact these days was more brotherly than husbandly. Mary bided her time, as she knew not what more she could do to make a change.

When the baby comes things will be different.

# Chapter 14

**Brassica oleracea** – cabbage – **A standby cure for all manner of family ills.**

**Strip out the central rib then gently beat the leaf to soften, and place in bra cups for mastitis or engorged breasts.**

**From The Complete Medicinal Herbal by Penelope Ody, Key Porter Books Ltd. (Pub) 1993**

On June 21st, 1948, at Saint Joseph's Hospital in Peterborough, Mary and Claude Johnston became the parents of a boy, whom they named Edward.

"A far cry from the strawberry patch," Mother said, when she and Stella first arrived for a visit. Claude and Mother Elizabeth got to Mary's hospital room soon after, having run errands first.

They stood – Mary, Claude, Stella, Sadie and Elizabeth – in the hospital hallway, outside the nursery room, peering through the long, wide window at the new baby. "I can't stand here too long," Mary whispered to Stella, wishing she could sit somewhere, anywhere. She leaned on Claude's arm, wondering if her uterus was going to fall out. Did that ever happen? How many stitches were there? How long would this heavy, swollen, soreness last? How would she ever carry a baby around in her arms, when she wasn't sure her legs would keep her upright for one more minute?

Animal births, especially an experienced cow giving birth, seemed so much more eloquent and beautiful than her own experience. Did the unfortunate nurse have teeth marks on her hand or had Mary only imagined biting it? That had to be just a bad dream. Edward's birth was nothing like the myth she'd carried and embellished in her head since she'd first heard her birth story from Mother. No wonder Mother cleaned it up. No blood. No screams. No swear words to be ashamed by.

Claude's mother wore the beatific smile she normally wore on Sunday mornings at church when she returned to the family pew after receiving Holy Communion. Stella, grinning, stood on Mary's other side and Mary took part of her weight from Claude's arm, leaned herself half on him and half onto Stella.

"He's a beauty," Stella whispered.

"A fine strong boy to carry on the family name," Liz said. "We'll make him into a minister."

"A farmer, I think, Mother. He'll have the land and stock given him." Claude squeezed Mary's elbow.

"He has the Johnston mouth. And the long fingers of an organist. Music can soothe the soul of a man of the cloth. Give him moments of peace between the tumultuosity of leading his flock."

"Working with God's beasts is where he belongs, Mother. A simple life. Hard work. Tending nature." Claude's grip on Mary's elbow tightened.

"A farmer?" Sadie said. "He's young yet to be making such plans for a wee babe."

"There's not enough young men picking up Jesus' cross these days. Always wanting the easy life but someone's got to swim bravely through the waters of sorrow. Pull the drowning souls safely ashore. Your father and I always hoped …" Liz gazed longingly into the nursery.

"A priest?" Sadie said. "You might just as well plan for him to be a banker or a lawyer. Either of those will set him up with enough money to raise a family and to look after his parents in their old age. That's got to be thought about."

"A man can't know the ways of the Lord on an empty stomach. Feeding the flock comes first. He's meant to grow into a farmer," Claude said with a slight frown at Sadie.

"I've been thinking our young Nelson might turn out to be a circus performer," Stella offered, with a long, slow wink at Mary. "The way he wraps himself in his blankets during the night he could even be an escape artist."

Mary rubbed her arm where the strength of Claude's grip still remained. "We'll grow the boy to make up his own mind what he'll be," she said.

She heard Stella's quiet sigh beside her. "Good luck, my friend."

"Well, Mother. Time to get home for chores." Claude turned away from the window. "Let Mary and the babe get their rest." He looked pointedly at Stella and Sadie. "Mother and I will bring the car around." He leaned in to Mary, brushed her cheek with his lips. "You'll be home soon."

"You're right. Mary needs her rest. Come on, girl. Back to your room. Here, lean on Stella and I. You must be ready for a lie-down," Sadie said.

Stella and Sadie helped Mary shuffle to the bathroom first and into her room and then into bed where they sat on either side of her. "Sounds like I have my work cut out saving the baby from growing up too soon," Mary said.

"Yes. Liz seems quite determined that life must not be enjoyed, but lived according to hardship, and grief. That's the Irish in her." Mother patted Mary's shoulder.

"Wily ways, Mary." Stella's eyes were tear-filled. "You'll never fight her outright, I don't think, but you'll need to stay strong. Not let Claude get pulled in under her influence. You must use every wily way you know of. And then some."

Sadie gazed out the bedroom door toward the nursery as if she could still see her first grandson down the hall. "I could come." She hesitated, as she chose her words. "I could come to live with you.

Help with the new baby. And with Elizabeth. Maybe she needs a friend. At least it would be less time you'd have to spend with her. I could do some housework and some cleaning. Amy and Jacob don't need me with them anymore. They'll never have children."

Mary and Stella's eyes met over the bed. This was new. Instead of less people there would be a new baby and Mother. And Mother Liz still.

After Mother and Stella left, Mary lay in her bed considering options, and realized that Mother's moving in would solve more than one problem. It would mean Mary could go back to work at Fynch's one day each week when the time was right. She would tell Claude she'd need the car and he would agree. Mother could baby sit Edward and keep Elizabeth busy at the same time. And Claude too for that matter. Mary enjoyed mulling this new idea. She'd wait a bit. A few months. Give everyone time to adjust to the baby; get mother moved in 'to visit' right away, and then she'd talk to Mr. Fynch. She'd make arrangements with Mother. And Claude. And Elizabeth. Stella surely would approve.

# Chapter 15

### "Whom the Lord loveth, He chasteneth."

"We'll close up the shop early today, Mary," Mr. Fynch poked his head through the opening in the wall between the shop proper and the dispensary where he and Mary mixed the teas and creams, simples and tinctures. "Seems as if all the folk are healthy today." The bell on the shop door had rung only twice all morning.

"I'll drop Mrs. Burnie's foot salve in to her on my way home, and that'll take care of her," Mary said. She'd make a stop at Wilson's Store on her way past for some of the cinnamon that had arrived on last night's train.

Straight from India, cinnamon was a luxury, but today was Claude's birthday, and Mary could use some of the windfall apples to make the apple and cinnamon rolls that he loved. Brown sugar and flour. She went over the recipe ingredients in her head.

It was thirteen years ago that they'd begun celebrating birthdays together. The first birthday spent together as a married couple had been Claude's. They'd lived in Peterborough then, and Mary had hurried home from Fynch's, her thoughts on her list: candles; cinnamon rolls; change my dress.

Once home, Claude ushered her into the shop, shut the door behind them and turned the little white and black sign to read CLOSED. "Closed for business," Claude murmured against her lips. "But you and me, we've got some business that needs to be handled."

Mary pressed against him, her arms reaching to encircle his neck, moving down to clasp his shoulders, stopping there to steady herself as his hands moved gently and roughly with welcome familiarity on her back … moving, holding, kneading.

"Come into the office, Mrs. Johnston." He took her hand, his eyes holding hers and he pulled her into his office where all else was forgotten. "It's been so long," Claude murmured into her neck.

"Mmmm. Hours."

The setting sun cast red glows across the sofa where they'd lain after making love, whispering and planning, limbs entwined, lazing. Later, slipping into their roles as housewife and welding shop owner, Mary prepared a supper of stew and bread, while Claude stayed in his workshop to tend the fire and set up his orders for the morrow. When Mary passed the shop on her way to the garden for salad greens, she waved at Claude. He stepped through the doorway, pulled her into a hug, kissed the top of her head, tapped her bottom, sent her giggling, on her way.

Mary knew that scene would not be repeated this birthday. Since his sixth birthday in June, Edward no longer took an afternoon nap. And, now that both Mrs. Murphy and Mrs. Johnston lived with them, there were very few episodes of love making – spontaneous or not – in the house at all. Every three or four months, early in the morning, Claude would let it be known that he was ready for intimacy. Mary wondered sometimes if she should just tell him no, but she hesitated to shun their only physical contact, knowing, if she could choose, she would increase, rather than decrease their times together. Claude was always very polite, thanking her afterward as if she was a stranger he'd used to perform the act. Like she was his hairdresser or the young boy who polished his shoes. "Thank you, Mary. I do appreciate your accommodating me like this."

What was the correct answer to such a comment? You're welcome? Come again? Mary wasn't sure and so would nod, wisely she hoped, and restrain her tears until Claude washed himself and dressed and clomped downstairs, leaving her alone to ponder what had just transpired. She thought of what she could do to fix the situation, running over scenarios and conversations she and Claude might have. They did need to talk over their circumstances, but,

Mary knew, men don't talk about relationships. How many times had she heard that? So, she chose not to talk about it with him afraid that it could become an argument and possibly worsen the situation.

Mary knew that after a morning tryst, she would be treated to a trip into town, often without Liz, where Claude would do some errands and she would sit in the truck waiting for him to finish so they could stop for lunch at the local restaurant. A somewhat friendlier atmosphere would prevail for one or two days following their daybreak exertions.

Stella and Mary had heard the older women talk about young couples running into trouble maintaining intimacy when the newness of marriage wore off and the babies started to come. It would be a relief to talk to Stella about this whole mess, but Mary knew it would anger Claude to think they talked about him. It wasn't right to share that sort of personal information, she knew, though there were other women in the neighbourhood who talked freely about their personal affairs. More reason not to do so herself, Mary thought.

"We can't even be called young anymore," Mary said to Stella over tea. "We'll both turn thirty-five this year. It seems we should celebrate the milestone somehow. But I don't feel a lot like celebrating these days."

"Are you too tired?"

Mary shook her head. "Things have changed somehow." What did a person tell her best friend? It felt wrong to discuss Claude's shortcomings – if they were shortcomings. It could be that there was nothing wrong with him at all. Maybe he was normal and there was something wrong with her.

"Don't let it worry you," Stella said, a gleaming twinkle in her eye and a grin beginning on her lips. "Nature will find a way to keep itself…" She searched for a tasteful word as Mary shifted her weight from cheek to cheek on the chair.

"Interested," Mary blurted, at the same time as Stella tripped over the word 'propagating'. They both laughed, Mary uncomfortably and Stella with a knowing nod. "You've got to keep that spark lit. So much of life seems to want to douse it, but don't let it."

On the morning of Claude's birthday, Mary had lain in bed beside Claude's huge warmth and rubbed her socked feet against his legs to get her blood circulating. In his sleep, he ran his hand over her top hip, sending heat down her leg, and a plan formed in Mary's mind of how she'd visit her husband in his workshop; invite him into the back office and offer herself to him there. Like in the romantic days when they were first married. It was time to take back her marriage.

Mother's routine was to walk with Edward to visit Amy on Thursday afternoons, and Liz usually napped, so Mary was sure she would find Claude alone in his shop, and she'd have to take her chance that she could convince him to make love to her. He was still a man after all. He'd enjoyed her physical comfort at one time more than just every few months. In their early days she was sure they'd spent more time in bed than out of it. Why not now? In the afternoon?

Early afternoon was not overly busy in the shop and the barn chores weren't begun until late afternoon. They'd turn the sign to CLOSED and assure their privacy by pushing the chair under the doorknob. 'Closed for Business'. Mary hoped she could stir his memory.

This morning, when Mr. Fynch moved to close the apothecary shop early, Mary felt her guardian angel smiling on her and she decided that today, Claude's thirty-fifth birthday, was the perfect time. She'd wave Mother and Edward goodbye, and tell Liz that she and Claude would do the books in the shop while Liz napped. She smiled as she thought of Claude's surprised reaction. He'd be pleased. She'd let this part of their marriage lag for too long; Stella often said so, warning her since Edward was born that it was the woman's duty to keep her husband interested. Keep the spark ignited, Stella called it. How time flew. Thirteen years already. Well, Claude would know what to do. Just like riding a bike. She'd wear the blue dress – the one that clung to her waist and enhanced her curves which were certainly more plentiful now than when they were newly married. More curves. Was she too curvy? She'd caught him noticing the dress last Sunday at church. Was he liking the added inches too? The changes wrought since Edward's birth? He didn't ever tell her she was attractive anymore. So much had changed. Too much.

There was no one in sight when Mary arrived home from work. Of course, they wouldn't expect her home so early. She set straight to work at the kitchen counter, glad of Liz's absence, mixing the biscuit dough and stirring the sticky, sugary sauce on top of the stove. The exotic aroma of cinnamon melting into the butter and corn syrup mixture made her mouth water. She heated the sauce on the stovetop before pouring it into the muffin tins, then she added a teaspoon of chopped walnuts for each sticky bun, before setting the doughy biscuits into the sauce, and put the whole dish into the oven.

While the buns baked, Mary whisked into their bedroom to change into her blue dress, fairly dancing with the thought of the pleasant encounter she and her husband would soon have. She could see signs of his busyness through the window and was glad to note no horses tied at the hitching posts. She twirled, her dress swishing and flowing lightly, prettily, about her ankles.

Warm buns in hand, Mary stepped out the kitchen door into the mid-afternoon sun. As she strode to the welding shop fragrant cinnamon wafted through the towel she'd wrapped over her creation. The back door was propped open, and she could smell the fire Claude used to bend and shape the pieces of metal, no matter the outside temperature. He was inside, his huge form lumbering to and fro, and she saw him straighten his back, then rub his hands against the thick leather apron he wore to protect himself from the sparks of cherry red, molten, metal which could burn right through his trousers, leaving a nasty welt that took weeks to completely disappear.

He smiled and Mary smiled back, surprised that he could see her from that angle, until she realized that he was speaking to someone, agreeing, nodding his head, and laughing. She'd supposed he was alone in the workshop. If he was serving a customer, maybe they would not stay long.

They usually don't, Mary thought, and continued down the walkway to the open door. She saw Claude bring a cup to his mouth. In his other hand, he held a chocolate-covered morsel. "Why are you having cake?" she blurted from the doorway, wishing she could control the screech in her voice, but the words were already said. Liz sat across from Claude under the window, feeding Edward milk and cake.

Her husband, her mother-in-law, her son – all looked at Mary with questions in their eyes: Why are you home so early? Why are you wearing your Sunday dress? What is on the plate?

"I brought you your favourite. Cinnamon rolls," Mary said, shoving them toward Claude. "With walnuts." He stuffed the cake into his mouth to free his hand while he set his cup on the tea tray and gamely chose a sticky cinnamon bun from the plate. "Happy Birthday," Mary said.

Liz pursed her lips then seemed to remember her manners and smiled. "Come in, my dear. Claude, get Mary a chair, would you? You will join us for tea?" She lifted the pot and filled a cup with steaming tea for Mary, dropping in one lump of sugar, the perfectly accommodating hostess showing off her years of experience. "There, and try some of my coffee cake with chocolate streusel. I made it fresh this morning. And you've brought cinnamon buns too. How lovely. Thank you. This is a real birthday celebration. Your mom walked over to see Amy for the afternoon. Edward decided to stay home to share birthday cake with his dad and me."

Mary smiled, hiding her disappointment. Her heart beat slowed to a dull throb.

"Mama." Edward extended his hands to Mary, and she welcomed his warm, firm, wriggly body on to her lap. His breath smelled of milk and Liz's coffeecake as he nuzzled into her neck. "I played in the dirt pile," he told her. He rubbed a dirty hand across her cheek. "I made a fort for the ants."

Mary noticed Liz and Claude looking over the account book as they sipped and ate. She chose a cinnamon bun from her offering and shared it with Edward, aware that his hands dirtied her blue dress with each touch. "It's time for our walk, Nana," Edward demanded.

Liz's eyes beseeched Mary. "Would you please take him, Mary? We normally go down to the bridge and back."

Claude shrugged his shoulders, silently endorsing his mother's request.

"Edward, you be a big boy and show your mommy the way to the bridge. That'll give me and Daddy time to get these accounts straightened out."

"You go ahead, Liz. You take Edward for his walk as you normally do. I'll give Claude a hand with the books. That's why I came home early. I wanted to help him with the bookkeeping." Mary kept her voice light as she gave Edward a gentle push toward his grandmother. "Run along, sweetie. Go with Nana."

"Mary, you are so kind, but no, I insist that you take Edward today. You've worked all morning at Fynch's. You need some time outside. Leave Claude and me here to do this boring paperwork."

Liz patted Edward's head and kissed his chubby cheek. "Big boy. Show your mama the way." Liz directed him back to his mother.

Mary took her son's sticky wee hand. She tried to catch Claude's eye, to give him a hint of what he was passing up. He had no idea what he was missing. Maybe he'd rather do books with his mother. How can I refuse? I might as well have stayed working for Mr. Fynch today if I've just come home to be ordered about by my mother-in-law. Mary turned, flounced, her ankles tickled by the lovely blue dress that looked so good on her. She checked to see if Claude noticed, but he and Liz were both frowning, engrossed by their work, and Mary couldn't think of what she could say that wouldn't sound boorish. Tightening her grip on Edward's hand they left, by the same door she'd so recently entered with her plateful of warm, sticky buns.

This would be another defeat to share with Stella and to laugh about over tea. Did all women have this much trouble in their love lives? Somehow Mary was sure her case was not common. She'd heard the women at church complaining because their husbands wanted sex more than they did. Why was Claude so different from the rest? Even Stella let drop that she and Arnie ….

Mary turned her thoughts to Edward and the beautiful day and his high happy voice. Today she could think of nothing more within her power that she could do to lure Claude back, away from his mother and into his wife's arms. For now, she would enjoy Edward's youthful energy and trust that the guardian angel who seemed such a friend earlier today hid another trick up her sleeve because Mary was plum out of ideas.

Edward had inherited some of Claude's endearing traits. He held her hand every chance he got, like Claude used to do; Mary thought his large, round, blue eyes might contain answers to the big universal questions. Claude used to make her feel hopeful in that same way.

Edward led his mother down the road toward the bridge. "See Mama? That's the creek." He pointed, stopping in the middle of the bridge. "Be very careful near the water."

Mary could hear Liz's warning echo in Edward's voice. He almost sounded like the Mothers but that couldn't be. She tugged a little too roughly by his hand, and led him off the bridge to the path that would take them down the bank to the water.

Edward held fast to her hand pulling her back toward the bridge. "No, we're not allowed," he cried. "That hurts my hand."

"Come on." Mary loosed her grip slightly. "We won't tell Nana because she'll be worried, but if I'm with you, it's okay to go down to the water. Come on." His knees were dirty, and Mary removed his shoes and socks to bathe his feet and legs in the cold, clear water. She took off her shoes and stockings too, then they threw stones as far as they could throw.

"Mom! My stone went all the way to the other side of the creek."

With squeals of delight mother and son waded into the water which was just six inches deep at this time of year. In the middle of the creek, they marveled as the sun shone on the constantly moving water, causing reflections of sunlight.

"It's like twinkling stars, Mommy. In the daytime."

"Twinkle, twinkle, little star. How I wonder what you are." Mother and son sang to the water.

"Underneath the bridge so high." Mary sang.

"Like a diamond not in the sky," Edward laughed.

"Twinkle, twinkle, little star. How we wonder what you are." They finished together grinning at their improvisations.

"We can't tell Nana we went in the water," Edward instructed his mother.

"It'll be our secret," Mary said. July 1952. My son is six beautiful years old and I am so lucky. Sun sparkles. Daytime stars. Tadpoles. The thwarted rendezvous with Claude was mostly forgotten as Mary's toes grasped the muddy bottom of the creek bed. "Thank you, God," she breathed. "Thank you for Edward, and sunshine and blue skies. Thank you," she whispered, "for summer, and towering trees and reflections."

Edward squealed as he reached for a short stick that came floating toward him on the current. He held it in his plump hand, slapping at the water to splash droplets. "Ouch, bad kitty," he yelled. He thrust the stick at the slender furry body rubbing against his leg. Where had it come from? The sleek animal snarled as it latched onto his leg and already blood dripped and covered its tanned length from knee to ankle. The kitten-sized creature curled itself around Edward's leg. Mary reached for its furry neck as she would any small cat, but this vicious creature was no domesticated pet and instinctively she pulled her arm back.

"A fisher!" she hissed as its small, brown, shiny eyes burned into hers.

"Mama! Help me!"

Mary grabbed a rock from the creek bed and pounded on the fisher's spiky-haired head, using Edward's slick wet leg as a guide. The boy wobbled and fell into the water, forcing him to let go of the stick to use his hands to keep his head above water. The fisher pulled its fangs from Edward's limb, still snarling, then the animal was gone, his long bushy tail the last bit of him to disappear. He left five long gashes along each side of Edward's thin leg, and blood dripping in his wake.

Mary gathered her son into her arms and carried him out of the creek up the path to the road, calling for help as she hurried. "Help! Claude! Mother! Liz! Help! Come quick!" So much blood. She laid Edward on the bank, still calling as her hands sought the knot of her sweater, folded it into a wodge of material to push hard against the bleeding wounds. She pulled her stockings from her shoe where she'd so happily left them before climbing down to the water, and she pulled the nylon mesh up over Edward's foot and thin leg to keep the sweater in place. It was still bleeding. Not spurting. She peered around. What caused the fisher to attack? She'd seen one only once before, a sleek slender body, a flash of shiny, reddish black fur, and long bushy tail scurrying away from the woodpile, but never had she seen one in the water; nor never heard of anyone being bitten. It must have been a mother defending her baby or maybe it was a youngster frightened by Edward's stick or his voice. No sign of the animal now. She eased the pressure on the leg wounds. The bleeding had lessened.

Edward watched her closely, fearfully. "We should not go in the dangerous water." His lips were dry, cracking.

Mary lifted her son into her arms. "Come on. We're going home." Tears. Shaking hands. Weak legs. Mary wondered if she would make it. Knew she must. "Claude! Mother!" She must be careful to not let Edward feel her panic. Oh God! Don't let him die! Memories of horrors she'd seen at Fynch's Apothecary rushed to mind. Infections, horrible scars. Severed limbs. Simple causes like a rusty nail resulting in death. And Claude's father. She mustn't think of that. Just move quickly. Get the doctor. Save the boy. In an emergency time was the enemy. She moved as fast as her burden and her bare feet allowed, her blue dress billowing in brilliant sky-coloured puffs of movement as she hurried toward home and help.

Claude and Liz came running to meet her in the lane way.

Mary stopped crying their names. Their voices were so loud around her; they mixed with the sound of the fisher's vicious snorts and her own animal snarls as if they still fought, beast and Mother over the leg of the child.

Edward clung to his mother when Liz would have taken him, cradling his head into Mary's chest. She kissed him over and over. Sobs came forth now from her, and shivers, shaking her whole body, and she accepted a shawl from Sadie, who was out of breath from running the last leg of her journey home from visiting Amy. Sadie wrapped Edward and Mary together in the shawl.

"Get us to the doctor. Get the car. Edward's leg – we were attacked. Get us to the doctor." Mary said, surprised that her voice sounded so calm. "It was a fisher. In the creek. Can't you hear me? Why don't you hurry? Claude. The wagon. No. The car."

And finally Claude was moving; he put his arm around her shoulders, guided her to the car; his big hands fumbled with the car door handle. He helped Mary into the back seat with Edward bundled against her chest. The car started first try and then they were chugging – Claude and Mary and Edward – down the road toward Peterborough.

"God speed," Sadie called after them.

"We'll pray for you," Liz added.

Mary checked the thin leg again. "I'm afraid. I'm afraid of infection, Claude. These gashes are nasty."

Claude concentrated on driving. "I'm giving her all the gas I can. Not long now. I just hope the Doctor is home."

And he was.

Doc Martin knew Mary well from her work at Fynch's Apothecary. "Don't see fisher bites often. Never seen one myself. Must have been a sharp-toothed little critter." He readied a syringe to administer the antibiotic. "Infection's a serious danger right now. Complete bed rest until we're sure there's no infection present. I'll let you know when he can get up. You won't be doing the boy any favours if'n you let him up walking. You hear me, son? No walking 'til I say so!"

Edward didn't answer; focused on the approaching needle.

"Has he had a tetanus shot?"

Mary shook her head.

"You'll need to lave the wound with this mixture I'm going to prepare for you." The doctor reached a squirt bottle from the shelf. "It's going to take some stitching, Edward. The creature made a mighty mess. But we can fix you up, young fellow. Good as new."

The familiar scent of iodine comforted Mary as the doctor worked on the leg. She stroked Edward's forehead. Claude watched, silent, frowning, arms crossed over his chest. She saw his fingers keeping count. Of the stitches, she wondered? Hail Marys? He took no notice of her watching him and she turned back to Edward and the doctor.

"I'll come by," Doc Martin said. "Tomorrow morning and we'll go over the maintenance of this wound. It's fortunate you know your way around medical terms and procedures. This will take some care."

Mary nodded. "I see that."


Edward lay on the parlour sofa for two weeks under doctor's orders.

"He should be up walking," Liz complained. "Build up his strength."

"Doc Martin said he mustn't move the leg," Mary said. "For fear of sending infection coursing through him. He's weak from losing all that blood."

Claude listened from the doorway, turning his head from Mary to Sadie to his mother.

"If the doctor said not to move him, then we let the boy lie," Sadie said.

"They should never have been in the creek," Liz blurted. "You had no business in the creek. Boys have drowned there. It's not safe."

Mary didn't answer. She set down the wash cloth she'd used for Edward's sponge bath on the table next to Claude's reading chair.

"It was an accident, Liz," Sadie said.

"An unnecessary accident," Liz insisted. "The creek is too dangerous for boys."

"That's enough," Claude said. "Mother." He held out his hand. "My bible." He pointed to the book on the table.

Liz carried it to him.

Mary picked up the washcloth and set it in the enamel basin.

"Come to the kitchen and I'll make us all some nice tea." Sadie took Liz's arm and pulled her along. "What's done is done."


Mary sat at Edward's side in the rocker, knitting an afghan using wool leftover from previous projects. With her hands occupied she let her mind roam, remembering the long nights spent nursing him, in the same rocking chair. As a baby he'd been hungry, an eager nurser, Stella called him then, and with his small tummy filled to satisfaction, he'd fall asleep in her arms. In those days, Claude often sat in the room with her, on the sofa and when Edward was in a deep sleep Claude would lift him, and carry him gently to his bed, kiss his head, tuck him in. Mary wished she could have Claude beside her now on the sofa, have his strong, quiet presence there, but he went each day to the workshop, and to the barn, thinking, she supposed, that Edward was well cared for. Claude had more than enough work, she knew. He said so every chance he got and she in turn encouraged him to lessen his load, to rent out some of the fields or to take in less welding. Even as she spoke she wondered what he would ever do if he had spare time. He came to check on Edward when he came into the house for lunch or for supper, but those were quick visits. Check-ins.

148

Mary wished she could hold Edward now, nurse him, comfort him in her arms, but the doctor shook his head no.

"Complete bed rest." His instructions were clear. "Bed pan, sponge baths, talk to him constantly. Keep him thinking and aware of the people around him, but he needs to lie still."

Though Edward barely responded, Mary did as the doctor said. She wanted so much that he know his mother was watching over him.

"You can't die on me. You can't leave me … us. Don't leave me to take the blame for being in the creek." She knew it was wrong to speak to a child this way. When the Mothers or Claude came to check on the boy, Mary sat quietly. She knit. She rocked. She watched. There were no words she could share with them. She had led her son – Claude's son and the Mothers' grandson – into danger. She had caused this; it was her fault; she encouraged him to play in the forbidden creek, and her sin – her contradiction of Liz's rules – reaped a most cruel reward. A boy hovering at the door of darkness. A boy who might be crippled for life. Or minus one leg. If he survived.

The accusations weren't spoken again, but Mary heard them clearly, in the silence of her husband's visits and in the carefully polite inquiries from Liz. And the praying. She would have heard them even when Claude and Liz were out of the room, but as soon as she was alone with her son she forced herself to override the guilt.

When they were alone she talked to him all the time.

"Edward. Edward, please come back to me – to us – come back whole and we'll start over."

"We'll go for the mail every day, and we'll learn where the fishers live so we can stay miles away from them. Your dad and some of the men have been hunting them, killing them, scaring them off because there's been other sightings. They're nasty creatures, those fishers. They're dirty fighters and dangerous around the livestock too." She'd stroke Edward's face where his soft hair lay damp on his skin.

"The sweating is a good sign," the doctor said. "Shows the boy is fighting off the infection."

Edward's recovery seemed slow to Mary, but Doctor Martin was pleased with his steady progress. Mary read aloud to Edward as he rested, taking down from the parlour shelf one of Claude's childhood readers: Try and Trust by Horatio Alger Junior. Edward lay on the couch in the parlour, not allowed to move, but with his eyes open and alert. Mary thought he looked almost as healthy and robust as before the fisher attack and often paused in a story knowing he would beg her to continue. His sweet voice soothed her; reassured her. At least he could talk.

They wouldn't know if he would walk again for two more weeks.

By that time, there'd be enough tomatoes ripe to make chilli relish. The Mothers began the fall cleaning, working around Mary and Edward when it was time to clean the parlour.

Finally, Doctor Martin announced there was no permanent damage, and Edward should be allowed off the sofa. Grinning, Edward stood for a moment looking at his mother and at the door, until, his balance improving with each step, he walked out of the parlour and down the hall to his bedroom. Mary watched, curious to know what he would do first.

The Mothers observed from the kitchen doorway, Sadie with a grin that left no doubt of her relief, Liz with a frown. Was she looking for a limp, a defect, something to hold over Mary's head for the rest of her life?

Doctor Martin nodded his head as the boy walked. "I knew he'd be fine," he said. "With the good care he received. You make a fine nurse, Mary."

Mary rose from her rocking chair, set down her knitting, and escorted the doctor to the front door, thanking him. When he'd gone she traveled down the hallway, peeped into Edward's bedroom and smiled at his pleased face. He was sitting on his bed, just sitting. Mary continued through the house, relieved and disoriented at the same time. She stepped into the room she shared with Claude. The curtains were still shut, to keep out the morning sunlight. Had they been pulled open at all since the accident? She dragged them across the window. Her blue dress lay abandoned where she remembered tossing it four weeks ago. It might belong to someone else. Edward's dirty handprints on the sky blue fabric were a reminder of the time before the fisher attack. She scooped it up. The blood might never come out.

Was it still her room? Her home? This house hadn't ever welcomed her wholeheartedly, hadn't felt like home to her, since they'd moved in, and now especially it felt foreign and stiff and closed. It seemed there was no place for her in the bedroom that she'd been so quick to disown for the parlour. She stuck her head into her mother's room trying to regain some familiarity – to establish ownership. While caring for Edward full-time, she had forgotten the needs of the house, turned away from it, and it felt that the house had turned away from her too. She opened the door to the summer kitchen and smelled the sharp scents of the changing season. Her legs were weak and unsteady after the weeks of inactivity.

At the door, her rubber boots languished under a thin coating of dust. She pulled them on and stepped outside. From Claude's shop window came the sound of metal clanging against metal, and from the shop chimney, a steady torrent of grey smoke billowed.

Rubber legs carried her across the yard and into the shop where she stood, staring into the fire's red, orange, and blue flames that licked the walls of the fire pit. The bottom of the pit was a deep mass of throbbing coals. She wanted to burn something, to purge the numbness and the fear she'd held in check since the fisher attacked her son. Seeing Edward walk only served to remind her that she was at the mercy of powers greater than herself.

Her blue dress? Mary searched her mind for the item that would burn away the guilt and fear that held onto her shoulders and her feet, keeping her heavy when she should have felt happy, when she should have been thanking God. She would hit at Him if He were standing here with her. She gazed unsmiling into the fire, her face red with a heat that didn't warm her heart.

Claude finished shaping the hinge he was working on, then with the tongs, held it in the trough of water to quickly cool it. The hiss reminded Mary of the pancakes she'd made on the morning before the fisher attack. She laughed out loud, startling herself and Claude. Would their lives from here on consist of before the fisher attack and after the fisher attack? Before Mary almost got Edward killed?

"He can walk." She felt the sobs begin somewhere deep inside. Following so soon after her crazed outburst of laughter, Claude didn't realize at first that she was crying. "He's as good as new." She repeated Doctor Martin's words as they'd watched Edward walk across the parlour floor. "He's not steady yet, still slightly weak and wobbly, but the doc says he'll be back to normal in no time. Days."

Claude approached Mary, set her blue dress on his work table, took her in his arms, let his chin rest on the top of her hair.

"My hair's not too clean," she said.

"It doesn't matter." He rubbed his chin back and forth over the top of her head, and they stood in the shop clinging onto each other. "We survived," he said. "We all survived."

Mary's face was wet with tears that mixed with the soot on Claude's apron. "I almost killed our son."

"No, don't think that. It wasn't like that. A wild animal attacked him and you saved his life."

"We shouldn't have been in the creek."

"You can't protect him from everything. Boys have got to explore."

"Your mother said we shouldn't have been in the creek. She taught Edward that, but I said it was okay."

"You saved our boy. It was you who fought the beast off. One of them killed twenty-one of Arnie and Stella's chickens. We've got some boys out hunting them now to scare them off, because we can't have them so close to the houses. Don't know what they're good for anyway."

Mary could bring that day back as clearly as if she held a still photograph in her heart. She and Claude had stood by the fire, talking, making up for the weeks when there'd been only worry between them and nothing to say. They stood in the shop, Claude in his thick coveralls, she, her hair in need of washing, in a brown housedress. Now with the huge worry lifted from her shoulders, she needed to talk about all that had festered inside these past months. Or was it years?

"Claude, there's too many people in this house."

"Be careful, Mary. In what you say. And how you say it."

But the need to talk was on her. "We need privacy. You and I. I feel like I'm your mother's daughter, and sometimes like your daughter, too. As if you and she are the parents and I have to behave, do as you say or I'll be punished."

"You know that's not how it is." Claude made to turn away and back to his work, but she held him facing her.

"It is so like that. I talk to her as an adult but she's got this way of not hearing what I say and I can't get through to her. She won't listen."

Claude shook his head. "She's my mother, Mary. What do you expect me to do?"

"It has to change. We need to have a marriage separate from her. And separate from my mother too. I know they live here, but we must make a place of our own. Where we can be private.

"We need to, Claude. You, me, and Edward. I think we three could move upstairs. Take over the two bedrooms up there and get the Mothers settled downstairs. Save them using the stairs and let us have time alone as a family."

"You're talking of a big expense. We'd have to put in a kitchen. And a bathroom. It won't work, Mary."

"We can still eat together. Cook together. But we need a private place of our own, to sit and talk and read and sleep. We need our own time together as a family."

"Easier said than done," Claude said. "Mother and Dad shared this home and that bedroom since she first came here in 1918. And I was born two years later in that same room. She'll never agree."

"If we said we were building on a bedroom for ourselves downstairs, maybe Liz would want it for herself and we could generously give in. Let her have it."

"That will never work," Claude said.

Mary thought he was likely right. "Let's talk about it anyway. Get started on it. If she doesn't want the new room, then we'll have it ourselves and work out a way for privacy somehow. We haven't been husband and wife really since we came here. It's important."

Sure enough, soon after Claude and Arnie began to build the new bedroom, Liz and Sadie approached Mary and Claude at supper one evening with the idea that perhaps both Mothers should sleep on the main floor, Liz in the new room and Sadie in what was now Edward's room. "Then you, and Claude, and Edward could take over the whole upstairs. Mary beamed at Claude over their mashed potatoes. Liz nodded at Sadie who winked back at her and gave her the thumbs up sign.

When the new bedroom was complete, Arnie and Claude, following the Mothers' instructions, rearranged reading chairs, and beds, and dressers to their proper spots in their proper rooms. Edward was given the task of carrying his books and setting his toys neatly on the shelves Arnie constructed in a corner of Edward's new room. "I'm sleeping in Nana's room now." Edward shouted out his bedroom window to Nelson and Arnie Junior. "I'm away up here! I can see your house from my new bedroom! Come on up."

By afternoon the sheets and pillows were laundered and switched and after a few tries Liz's room was arranged to her liking.

"We'll hang the new curtains next," Sadie instructed Arnie.

She and Liz stood watching as Arnie and Claude installed the rod and threaded the curtains. "There," Liz treated them all to a rare smile. "It's all ready to be lived in."

There were a few times in the months after the moves that Mary or Claude awoke in the night to find Liz wandering about their room, fingering items on the dresser, rummaging blindly through a drawer. "Enough to keep a person slightly unsettled," Mary said to Stella. "But not enough that one could call her a nuisance. Or unmanageably intrusive. Not out loud anyway. Just a little bit annoying." She and Stella agreed over tea that this would likely occur until the end of Liz's days, since she'd spent over fifty years sleeping in what was now Mary and Claude's bedroom.

"Is it weird for Claude sleeping in his parents' bedroom?" Stella asked.

"He hasn't said, and I'm afraid to ask. It's weird for me, as if there are ghosts, but I just try to ignore them. No use opening a can of worms like that right now, eh?"

They both laughed.

All in all, Mary was well pleased at how smoothly the building of the new addition and the moves within the household were managed. An added bonus was that building the addition together seemed to have brought Claude and Arnie closer.


During Edward's recuperation, Mr. Fynch had come regularly to the house, but Mary held only a vague recollection of those visits. "When Edward has recuperated and life gets back to normal," Mr. Fynch said, "you must return to work for as many days a week as you can manage. I need the help. You need to get away."

When Edward was running and yelling as well as any other six year old boy, Mary returned to work at the apothecary. "Liz is happy to have me out of her hair. She'd take over even more of the house if that were possible."

Stella and Mary resumed their habit of morning tea times together, visiting at each other's houses, on the days Mary didn't work, sometimes including the Mothers, and they often walked over to have tea with Amy. "We need to stick together us women folk. Help each other out. Share the joys and the tough times."

"But not too much sharing," Stella laughed.

"Right," Mary agreed. "Things are pretty good at home these days. Liz and Sadie spend most of their day in the kitchen over cups of tea and freshly baked goodies. Cookies and squares and cakes. There's always something fresh in the jar and a hot pot of tea ready. I got what I wanted. Privacy upstairs. Now Claude and I can have a conversation just the two of us."

"Hope you're having more than that," Stella said.

"Stella!"

"Oooo. That's not sounding promising. Need a little help?"

Mary shook her head.

"Advice?"

"Nooo. Everything's fine. It is," Mary said. "I've made a bit of a sitting area upstairs in the hallway. Just a table and a lamp and a chair. A place to read, away from the rest of them. It's nice. And I'm sure that as soon as I'm not so tired we'll get back to normal in the bedroom too."

# Chapter 16

Homey noises from the kitchen filtered upstairs as Mary turned a page. She was settled in her new reading area in the hallway, taking a short break before she had to leave for work at Fynch's. Liz and Sadie were engaged in one of their never-ending discussions about cooking, Mary supposed, as they waited for Liz's cake to rise. Claude was in the shop and Edward was out playing in the yard with Nelson, from next door.

Liz insisted the boys play outside, though it meant getting out the rain slickers and rubber boots.

"They could play puzzles in the porch," Mary said.

Liz shook her head. "They're not made of sugar, Mary. They won't melt in the rain."

You don't want your clean floor messed, Mary wanted to say. He's been so sick. He almost died. But she didn't. The Doctor assured her that Edward was fine and not in a weakened state at all. He was coming by shortly for another look at Edward's gait. Mary knew she must stop being afraid of what could happen to her precious boy. God saved him, maybe had great plans for the boy, and Mary must let him be normal, healthy, and mud-streaked. She must let him be that.

"It won't hurt him to toughen up," Liz said.

Sadie, Liz, Claude and Edward all looked at Mary, and she knew they were right. He shouldn't be babied. Still, that didn't make it any easier to let him go out. He's my baby, her heart cried, as she pecked him lightly on the forehead. "Have fun," she told him. "Come in if you get chilled or wet or ..."

Edward was gone out the door, shouting hello to Nelson.

It made Mary feel better that she could look out and see the boys from her reading chair. They sure won't have trouble staying warm with all that running. She watched as they sped from one side of the driveway to the other. Their shouts carried on the chilly fall air. I hope they won't get too wet. It's rained quite a lot.

Mary turned back to her book. She'd decided to plant an herb garden and was having her first look at a book from Stella. "A house-warming gift," Stella said, "though I realize you've lived here seven years already." She'd ordered it specially from Great Britain for Mary: A Modern Herbal by Mrs. M. Grieve F.R.H.S. The book listed medicinal, culinary, cosmetic and economic properties, cultivation and folklore of herbs, grasses, fungi, shrubs and trees with all their modern scientific uses. "The only herbal you'll ever need," Stella said.

"It'll take a whole shelf on the bookcase with all that information in it," Mary said, fascinated and ready to crack it open immediately.

Mary planned to allow herself some time each day to research the different herbs hoping to find some less common useful ones to plant in her new herb garden. Mother was in full agreement with Mary's plan, while Liz had her own opinion.

"A frivolous waste of time and money. You could be growing vegetables that people could eat."

"It's a thing of beauty," Sadie said. "We all need beauty for inspiration. "And a herb garden is useful too. There's herbs for teas and for medicine – even for dyeing if you've got the inclination."

"Mmmph. Beauty. Inspiration. Give me a warm kitchen and the smell of chocolate cake baking. That's enough inspiration for anyone."

"That's right, dear," Sadie said easily. "You'll have to bake the chocolate cakes around here to give Mary time to look after her garden. Weed it. Plant it."

Mary realized again that having both of their mothers under one roof presented advantages.

As Mrs. Johnston baked her delicious chocolate coffee cake on that grey, rainy, fall afternoon, six-year olds Edward Johnston and Nelson Jenkins played in full view of the house, in the water that rushed under the laneway and through the culvert. They threw sticks in the ditch on one side of the lane then ran across to watch them come bobbing out the other side.

The adults never knew which of the boys fell in first. Or had they gone in together? Did the fast water sweep them into the culvert? Did one boy jump in trying to save the other? There was no way to tell for sure. Just the tracks where size three rubber boots slid down the muddy bank dragging soil and stones into the rushing water. And two sons.

Claude, welding in his shop, heard Arnie's shout from the laneway. By the time Claude got outside, tongs in hand, Arnie had pulled the boys out of the ditch, and held them upside down, feet in the air to force the water out of their lungs. With one boy under each arm he ran toward the shop, and toward Claude, shouting; he set them on the ground when he got to Claude and the two men blew air into the boys' lungs over and over.

Mary heard the shouting, looked up from her book and checked her watch. Half past. Nice. Lots of time to prepare for work. She glanced out to check on the boys, expecting to see them at their game, running from side to side of the culvert. They weren't there. Instead, the boys were laid flat on the ground, with Arnie and Claude breathing air into their boys' mouths, waiting, breathing again.

"Oh, God! Oh God! No! You can't do this! Not again!" She skittered down the stairs, ran through the living room, the kitchen. "Call the doctor," she cried and ran past the Mothers, repeating her prayer. "No, please, God, NO!" Outside Stella had arrived.

"How long?" Stella asked. "How long have you been breathing for them?"

"I don't know," Arnie said. "A long time. A lot of breaths." He put his mouth to Nelson's again, and Claude breathed into Edward's mouth. The boys' chests rose as air filled their lungs. And fell as it was exhaled.

Mary and Stella could do nothing except watch. The Mothers stood silently together holding each other up. As the men breathed into the boys, the women breathed in rhythm with them.

"I saw you from our window. It has been well over ten minutes." Stella put her hand on Arnie's arm. "It's too long for them not to breathe."

Mary checked her watch. Twenty minutes since she'd run down the stairs from her reading nook.

The men continued to breathe into the boys.

Doctor Martin arrived with an umbrella. "How long has it been?"

"More than twenty minutes," Mary answered. "It's not too long is it, Doc? Tell them to keep on, Doc."

The Doctor checked each boy's pulse in turn. "I'm sorry, Mary. I'm sorry, Stella. Arnie. Claude. Mrs. Johnston. Mrs. Murphy. Doc brushed each person's arm or shoulder as he said their name, then he smoothed the boys' soaked hair. "I'm so sorry."

"Ooohhh." Mary exhaled all that was in her, leaving no air with which to plead that they continue. Surely the next breath ...

Stella pried Arnie's fingers from Nelson's sleeve, hooked her arm into his and tugged him away from Nelson. "It's been too long. They won't breathe again on their own." Was she speaking to convince herself? Arnie pulled away from her and breathed into Nelson's mouth again.

Stella stood with her arms crossed; she pulled away when Doc patted her arm. "No. This can't be. Not my Nelson. Why weren't you watching them?" She looked first at Mary, then at the mothers. "Why wasn't anyone watching these children?"

"Stella, it was an accident. They were old enough, strong enough. They've played in the ditch thousands of times." The doctor held his hand on her arm. "It's nobody's fault. It was an accident."

Arnie listened to Nelson's chest. "Nothing. There's nothing. What can we do, Doctor?" His tears ran freely.

Mary knelt on the wet grass beside her still boy moaning, sobbing, kissing his face and praying his name, getting wet with tears and rain and ditch water. It could not be too late to save them.

"Two at the same time? How could You? How could You dare, after just saving him? You sure must want Edward badly to come after him twice. How can I live? Please God. How?"

Claude and Arnie lifted their sons, cradling heads, bums; the women tucked in their boys' arms, their sopping wet, lifeless arms.

Claude and Arnie carried the boys into the house, with Mary and Stella walking beside them. Claude stumbled as he travelled, silent but for huge gasps of air, half cry, half-beastly moans. The walk took forever and then they were inside and Mary reached out her arms to take Edward.

She waited, with her boy in her arms, while Sadie spread a clean white sheet over the table, then Mary laid him down gently, and waited with his head in both her hands, while Sadie brought clean towels to use as cushions.

Across the room Stella stood, holding her boy. When the sheet was smoothed down and towels set in place, she laid Nelson next to Edward, and with unsteady fingers both mothers unbuttoned their boys' jackets, their shirts, their jeans. Mary kissed Edward's neck, his elbows, his chest, and his small white feet, one after another. She covered him with another sheet. Used a warm facecloth to wash the boys' faces. Sadie towelled their wet hair, brought a comb from her room, and Stella combed and smoothed their locks.

Liz walked around and around the table twisting her hands together, stopping to pat Edward's head and his feet, then circling again.

Doc Martin used the Johnston's phone to call the undertaker. "There's been an accident, Joe, at the Johnston place ... get here as quick as you can ... can you come? It's the two boys, Joe. The Johnston boy and the young Jenkins boy – Nelson ... yes, Joe, yes it is ... they're drowned, Joe. The two boys, Joe. I'm sorry to report. I'll expect you right away, Joe. I'll stay here ... I'm at the Johnston's place now, Joe. I'll stay here until you come."

There were no words after Doc Martin hung the phone back in place, just quiet water noises and footsteps. Washing, combing, kissing, wordless, painful breaths, warm tears falling onto ribby chests, a hand placed on a neighbour's arm for a moment. Eyes, when they met across the table, were quickly lowered, averted, too much pain evident to be spoken of or shared just yet.

The washing stopped; the room was quiet. The boys, dressed in their Sunday suits, lay peacefully as if asleep, on the table, stretched side by side. Around them stood Stella, Mary, Arnie, Claude, Amy, Jacob, Sadie and Liz and the doctor.

"We'll pray," Claude directed. "Let us bow our heads."

One by one they all did as he asked.

Mary reached for Edward's hand and saw that Stella held Nelson's hand in hers across the table. Prayers won't help. She squeezed her eyes shut, as Claude's voice droned familiar words.

"Our Father, who art in heaven."

Liz's voice joined his. "Hallow-ed be thy name."

"Amen," Mary said loudly after the last line.

"Amen," she said again, and moved away from the table, pulling her mother with her.

# Chapter 17

**Rosmarinus Officinalis** – Antiseptic, digestive, mouthwash. Strewing herb carried by judges to protect from contagion. 'Tis also strewn over graves and burnt in chambers of the sick to defend against morbid effluvia. Refreshes the memory, comforts the brain. Symbol of fidelity and remembrance.

Where Rosemary flourishes the woman rules; spirit made from essential oil and wine will renovate paralyzed limbs if rubbed in with brisk friction. Increases flow of milk. Stimulates growth of hair, kidneys, medicine for gout in hands and feet. Garland put around head remedies stuffiness, rekindles lost energy, relieves hysterical depression. Remedy for chilblains and bee stings.

"Crying. There was no end to the crying." Mary and MaryArlene sat in the library at Sunny Acres. "I cleaned him and dressed him in that outfit you see there in the picture." Mary stroked the cracked photograph. "And we laid him – Edward and Nelson both – laid them on the kitchen table, while we waited for Joe, the undertaker to arrive. And later Claude and Arnie made the pine boxes. They weren't big. Not half full-grown yet. I thought we'd have the wake at home but Sadie and Liz, well, everyone except me, wanted to have it in town at the funeral home – make a big fuss – put it in the newspaper too. All the neighbours knew already anyway, they were coming to the door that same evening as it happened."

"You could always count on your neighbours in those days. Didn't matter even if you didn't like them so much, if there was a need, like when the boys drowned, the neighbours came."

"I wish ..." MaryArlene said.

Mary waited. What did MaryArlene wish? But the moment passed.

"You'd have fit into that community. You'd have fit right in. It's too bad you couldn't have stayed on there, but times change. People change," Mary said, and she patted her daughter's hand. "You've heard this all before, dear. Why don't you stop me raving on about the old days?"

"I want to know it all, Mother," MaryArlene said. "I wish I'd lived in the old days. Simpler times they were. When you could count on your friends."

"True. But there were troubles, don't fool yourself thinking we didn't suffer." Mary wondered sometimes if she'd raised MaryArlene wrong. To be wishing too much for what she couldn't have. Claude often questioned her, on what she was teaching her daughter. But they both agreed that despite any of the troubles in the family, they'd raised a good daughter in MaryArlene.

"Tell me the rest of what happened. Did the neighbours come to the funeral parlour too?"

"Stella stayed on when the men went out to tend to the livestock and she only went home to change when Claude came in. No. That's wrong. It's so hard to remember everything just right. Claude and Arnie went over to Jenkins' to do the chores and then Stella and I went with them to tell the other children. The Jenkins had the twins ... and there was Arnie Junior ... Jake and Amy must have taken care of the twins ... oh dear ... I don't remember exactly ..." Mary twisted a thread of the red quilt. "Stella was back later that evening and she marched right past Elizabeth who'd stationed herself at the door. I was the one Stella came to see, and she let herself in to the parlour where I was sitting in the dusk, waiting. We just sat together, mostly quiet, but she talked a bit about herself and her twin girls. There just wasn't much to say. And a lot of folk stopped in to pay their respects. Brought food and cards and memories. I hardly cried at all. Then." Mary paused and MaryArlene stroked her thin legs through the red quilt.

"Later, Stella and I got to laughing. Probably from being overwrought, but I'll never forget that. Everything was funny ... for a little while. We made each other laugh though we neither of us felt like it. Crazy. After a while Arnie came in, and Claude and the Mothers, and we all sat together, with the memories of our boys all we could think about. And talk about. Our dead boys. Claude was broken. I think that's when it happened to him, sitting there in that room full of grief, and not a thing we could do to change circumstances. It's like one of those bad dreams that you keep hoping you'll wake up from and it just will not end. Ever."

Mary paused for breath as she stared into the past. "And then we all went together to town. Took the wagon 'cause it was the only thing big enough to fit us all. Drove into town to McNabb's Funeral Parlour. Past all the houses and the apothecary and the people. It didn't feel real. How could that be real?"

"Claude said how it was always the wagon. Me and Claude in the wagon, travelling together."

We sure went down a lot of roads. Mary wasn't sure if she'd said that out loud. MaryArlene sat still, waiting for her to continue.

"Everything was changed after that. Suppers, breakfast ... so quiet. Me, Claude, Sadie and Elizabeth ... we didn't have anything to say; Sadie shrunk the table by taking out the center leaves. We would all four of us sit at it; we could reach anything we needed; there was no need to speak." Mary shook her head. "So we didn't."

MaryArlene hugged her mom. "And you planted the herb garden in the spring. That was good."

"Yes." Mary nodded. "The herb garden. Is there any tea left, Stella?"

MaryArlene rubbed Mary's arm. "I've kept you talking too long, mom. You sit and rest and I'll go find us some tea. And I'll find Stella too."

Mary watched her leave. She was a good girl and she'd have probably done better at managing all the complications that rose up in Mary's lifetime than Mary had. Kids these days got more help learning how to get through life's troubles. "I did the best I knew how," Mary said. "The best I could with the cards I was dealt."

Stella and she had met every morning, usually in Stella's kitchen and worked together. They made jam using Stella's plums; they dug Mary's potatoes. On rainy mornings they sewed, repaired coveralls, darned socks, knit new ones. As they worked, they planned the herb garden, developing between them an intricate maze of stakes and strings and greenery and beauty. At lunchtime they'd part, going home to feed and tend to what remained of their families.

On the days Mr. Fynch didn't need her to work at the apothecary, Mary went to her garden again in the afternoon, digging and hoeing the black pallet of earth, turning over memories of Edward as she turned over the rich black soil of her garden, sweating in the cool fall air, making a straight edge around the new herb plot. She saw it as it would look, imagining the plants in their full maturity. She'd taken clippings from the two Buxus shrubs that framed the front walkway, liking the fact that anyone who entered or left the house passed between the shrubs. Most people touched them and she thought that left bits of the visitor's essence, a homeopathic distillation of well wishes and memories. The clippings from these shrubs she carefully planted in a straight outline around the edge of the plot.

In one row she planted a packet of johnny jump up seeds – Violas it said, on the package – thinking as she did so, how like a johnny jump up Claude Johnston turned out to be. So many times she'd thought she understood him fully, only to have him jump out of the convenient portion in her mind where she'd placed him, and take up some new idea. Or an old one, she thought, seeing him sitting with the bible resting on his knees, his glasses pushed tightly to his face, crushing his eyelashes. They should call them johnny jump outs, she thought. How could one ever know where they'd land next in their efforts to reseed themselves?

In the spring, across from the violas, she would plant borage from seed. Smells and beauty and memories were what Mary would plant in her garden. She decided to name the patch of borage plants after Edward. "Borage for my boy, my sweet brave boy." Mary pondered the passage in A Modern Herbal. "Borage comforteth the heart, purgeth melancholy, quieteth the phrenticke and lunaticke person."

Mother was glad to go with her, back to the Murphy farm, to thin the patch of Egyptian Onions in Mother's old vegetable garden, where Jacob and Amy provided shovels and a pail for transporting their finds. What began as a square boxy outline, Mary soon realized would need to be an L-shape to accommodate the onions she would always call walking onions, who refused to be contained.

She snipped a cutting of sage from Mother's garden, and Arnie donated a root from his mother's Hansa Rose. She'd promised to exchange with him a piece of a lovage plant she'd salvaged from an untended herb garden Liz knew of in the back corner of the Johnston yard.

There she felt very lucky to find the lovage and some lily of the valley, both overgrown with weeds, but still looking quite healthy. It was helpful to have so many of the planned plantings available this late in the fall. It kept her busy digging, kept her thinking, planning. She would have to wait for the borage seeds which must be planted in spring, and a beebalm plant, which she was quite sure she could get a piece of from Mr. Fynch, who also was a gardener. "I only dabble in the garden," he insisted, but Mary learned much from her boss, who over their working time together, had become a close friend.

Mrs. Grieve's Herbal talked about Gallium, also called Lady's Bedstraw, and Mary remembered seeing the plant in her neighbour's garden on Water Street. On one of her trips into Peterborough she visited the old neighbourhood and asked for a cutting. The lavender seeds she would buy from Town's Store to plant in the spring when the ground warmed. She hoped it wasn't too cold in the area for lavender, but a few of the local gardeners were bragging of success with it, so Mary decided to take a chance.

And there, a garden. If only the rest of life could be so easy to plan and implement.

Eventually, she and Stella agreed, they could make 'knots' in the herb garden using the dark green of the box shrubs and the grey green of the lavender. There was a diagram in one of the horticultural magazines of an English Knot Garden and Mary could see this taking shape in her own yard. Its symmetry would be pleasing to look down on from her bedroom window.

It was easiest to see the whole image if she surveyed the plot from inside, from the window upstairs. She could examine from above what from below seemed a chaotic confusion of sticks and stakes and tiny green bits, and see the shape develop. Mary envisioned the garden as it would look when she was finished creating it. A rich, deep green hedge of boxwood shrubs, eighteen inches high and one foot wide, perfectly trimmed, would run around the outside of the L-shaped bed. There would be hedging of lavender around each of the garden sections to keep them separate from one another.

The oncoming winter meant Mary must garden during the rainy season, which she did, but there were days when it was too cold to be outside. On a frigid Tuesday morning in November, Mary and Stella sat over cups of tea with their plans laid on the kitchen table in front of them.

"I wonder, Mary, if we've left enough room between the plants," Stella said, frowning at the pages of drawings. "They say we need 24 inches between sages and we've done that but we haven't really left a pathway, have we?"

"No pathway," Mary considered. "No pathway. The beebalm will be pushing itself over into the sage. That's you, I figure. You're the beebalm. I'm the sage. Funny eh? If Edward is the borage and Nelson is the basil, they need their parents there with them too."

Stella shook her head. "OK. I hadn't really thought of it that way, I must admit. Not at all. But it's interesting to say the least."

"Is it too flakey?" Mary raised her eyebrows, willing Stella to understand.

"It is different. Will we need to name it something? The People Plot? Gardens of the People? Or keep this to ourselves?" Stella pulled the sheaf of papers closer to her. "That's what these notes are about. Borage comforteth the phrenticke ..." she read.

"I know what we can do! Bring our tea to the parlour. I'll get the 'bible'; you bring our plans."

The parlour held memories of the boys' last journey. Here the parents had waited to go to the funeral home. The room had been unused since then. Liz and Sadie kept it clean, and dust-free, easy now that there were no young boys to race across its wood plank floor. No one to call 'I'm the King of the Castle' as he stood on a pile of cushions from the plump sofa, daring his friend Nelson to dethrone him.

In the empty centre area Stella laid the page of borage on the floor. "We'll map it out right here in the parlour." Mary gathered green strips of quilting fabric for the box shrubs; three red cushions became beebalm. "Here's some violas in this magazine. Think Liz will mind if we rip out these pages for our plan?"

"Of course she will." Stella tore the pages out at a nod of Mary's head. "Perfect."

Pots of Christmas cactus placed strategically in chaotic order denoted the walking onions and a floor lamp stood in as the lovage. "It's the right height."

The two women stood back surveying their work. "Gosh, we're good."

"Or utter fools."

"That's the most fun I've had since ..." Mary didn't finish her thought. Liz and Sadie stood at the parlour doorway looking in at the younger women's creation, hands on their hips.

"What's this?" Liz's face was flushed. "You're rearranging my parlour?"

Sadie watched Mary, question marks in her stance, and said nothing.

"Oh. We … uh … we're mapping out the garden. See, here's the lovage." Mary lifted the lamp. And …"

Liz shook her head. "Like a couple of five-year-olds, you two are."

Sadie nodded her head. "We need a couple of young hearts in this house again. Come on, Liz. I bet that cake is ready to be checked again."

Mary and Stella held back their laughter until the older women were gone. "Oh dear. In trouble again," Mary said. "Oops."

They left the room as it was and went to the kitchen to refill their teacups and spend some time with the Mothers before Stella left to make lunch at home. Mary revisited the parlour garden at the end of the day, when the Mothers were gone to bed.

Outside, she lined the paths with stones and was pleased at how well the grey contrasted against the rich loam Claude brought in the loader for her from the barnyard – a dark mixture of soil and manure and trampled golden straw. It rained every day; her feet were wet and cold. She shovelled; she carried dirt; she wept, and at night she closed her eyes as soon as her head was laid on the pillow. Sleep came quickly with only a few minutes to think, to wish, again, that she'd insisted the boys play inside.


Mary awoke, found herself sitting in her wheelchair, with the faded red quilt that Mother sewed almost a lifetime ago, tucked around her legs. So long ago. MaryArlene must have taken advantage of my snoring and snuck on out of here. Mary snickered to herself. Can't blame her not wanting to be stuck here with a batty old woman like me. I remember having to work to stay awake lots of times at home when Mother and Liz were going on and on about things.

The Mothers had sewn plenty of quilts, mostly for the church, in their spare time, when Edward was no longer there to be fussed over. They spent their mornings cleaning and in the afternoons there was the quilting.

Mother made a red quilt for Mary, and one for Stella too. "I need to keep my hands busy," she said, and Mary understood well the need to do and to be busy. Her shoulders, legs and back ached with the hard gardening work she set for herself, and her hands grew callused and rough.

The season changed from fall to winter; the Mothers quilted and baked and cleaned. Then it was spring, and Mary hurried to her garden to turn over the soil. It was heavy clay, wet and black. Following the map she and Stella had drawn, in the center of the plot, Mary planted borage from a pail full of self-seeded baby plants that Mr. Fynch had dug from his patch. Mary's tears fell on the rough, bristly, cactus-like, hairy leaves.

"Borage, the herb of courage," she recited, from Mrs. Grieve's Herbal, as she thrust her work-reddened hands into the soil, forming a series of holes in the garden. She pushed her fingers deep into the pail, reaching under to cup in her hands the root of the borage plant, gathering with it as large a quantity of soil as she could manage. Mr. Fynch and Mrs. Grieve both, insisted that borage intensely disliked being transplanted, that a gardener should plant borage from seed. Carefully, Mary lifted a borage plant from the pail and set it gently into one of the prepared holes.

She knelt at the row sifting the black soil through her fingers until it was ground as fine as sugar. Dark black sugar. From her pocket, Mary withdrew scissors and the envelope of Edward's hair that she'd saved. She nipped one lock into short pieces and sprinkled the precious blonde hair of her dead son into the hole, then sprinkled a handful of soil over it. She shoveled in more earth, tamping it with the palms of her hands until the plant stood secure in its new place.

Mary repeated her actions, scooping more plant from the pail with both hands, soil dripping as she raised the treasure to the sky. She held it high, gazed toward heaven, her lips moving soundlessly, then in a graceful sweep she lowered her arms. Her eyes followed the plant, as she bent over, and settled the borage into its final resting-space, adding more snippets of hair, then moved the surrounding earth in around the plant to secure it. All the while, her lips moved in silent benediction – a prayer to the God she resented for taking her son, even as she pleaded with Him to watch over the boy.

When the pail was empty, Mary dampened the plants and soil, giving each one a careful measure from the aged watering can she'd found in the shed, left there by Claude's father perhaps. She stood back from her work and surveyed the plantings.

"It's good," she whispered. "I've made it good for my boy."

Mary plucked at the red quilt that kept her arthritic knees warm. Even after all this passage of time, the memories returned with stark clarity.

"Hi Mum!" MaryArlene planted a kiss on each of Mary's cheeks. "You're looking perky today."

Mary squinted at her daughter. Watching MaryArlene pass through the ages of her life helped Mary to keep Edward's memory alive. MaryArlene, born two years after Edward's death, was always eight years younger than the age he would be. Should be.

"You should have a new quilt, Mom. That old thing is ragged."

Mary smoothed its worn, soft, almost pink cloth. "Your grandmother made this for me many years ago. It helps me remember."

"Yes. Yes. The memories. How about I get us some tea? A nice cup of tea."

"You sound like your grandmother. Or Stella. Always getting tea. Your grandmother made this quilt before you were born."

"To keep her hands busy after Edward died right, mum?"

"That's right. She was the quilter of the family. Your grandmother Johnson made chocolate cakes and oatmeal cookies to no end; Stella and I took up herb gardening; grandmother Murphy was the quilter. We all reinvented our lives."

"The house would have been quiet," MaryArlene encouraged.

"It was. I didn't want to be in the house much. Edward was buried in the cemetery beside the church and I could walk there in five minutes. I spent a lot of time in that cemetery."

"It's a beautiful spot."

"And I always made sure there was some sort of flowers there. Borage usually, but for early spring I planted daffs. And mums for the fall. Looked nice against the white marble marker."

"I know, mum. It's time for us to take a drive out there again. Bring some flowers for the grave."

Mary nodded. "On the way back home, I'd stop in to Stella's, have a cup of tea. We spent hours talking."

"Strange that she wasn't able to talk about Nelson after he died." MaryArlene stroked Mary's grey hair, brushed it back from her face.

"But she wanted to talk, so that was OK by me. We made garden plans, and she always knew the latest goings on at the church. We were all on a party line and Stella listened in to everyone's phone calls."

"That's one thing I would have hated," MaryArlene said.

"Oh, everybody did it. You just learned not to give out private information over the phone. And it was handy for getting certain stories passed on. But we did have to be careful." Mary plucked at her red quilt, memories floating in her head. "Stella seemed to need to keep things light, so we did. Talking to her was the only conversation available some days."

She could see Stella, standing at the kitchen stove, as they waited for the kettle to boil, and nattering about everything and anything the whole time. "Life has some long silent times, so when the conversation comes along you sure appreciate it. No matter if it's all fluff. Long silences," Mary repeated, but MaryArlene wasn't there, leaving Mary alone with her memories of the past.

At first, Mary remembered, she had wanted to talk of nothing but Edward, and aside from Sadie, there weren't many who would indulge her need. Stella talked about everything except the boys. Stella got afraid in the silence, Mary thought. So she'd let her talk on and on. And Stella did pass on good gossip that she heard over the telephone line. That's how they'd found out about the affair going on between Joe, the undertaker, and Beatrice, who lived on the next road over. Party lines kept things interesting in the day.

It was nice to visit back and forth, the two couples, have each other over for dinner. "We should have made more time for visiting and that sort of thing. But we never were able to be close friends – all four of us at one time. On again – off again. Ebb and flow." Mary said, forgetting that she was alone. "Not the way we might have. Maybe that was my fault." Mary shrugged. "Mistakes were made all the way around. Hard to explain exactly what went wrong and when. Life is hard." Talking to myself again, she thought. Hope no one noticed. She looked around, to see for sure that no one was listening.

Mother and Liz took full and complete charge of the kitchen, and it was not well received when the Jenkins were invited for dinner. Partly because Stella blamed Liz for Nelson's death. And the children. There were three hungry healthy Jenkin children. There wasn't much love lost between Arnie and Claude even then. Though they'd been through their hardest of times together.

I wonder if things would have been different if I'd insisted they be better friends.

Mary picked at the scab, which had formed again on her cheek, worrying it until she got a corner up; she pulled it quickly off. MaryArlene would come back in and scold her, but it was too late now. It wasn't as if she worried about disfiguring herself, she thought. Advancing age looked after that well enough. Sometimes at the sight of herself in the dresser mirror, she wondered who the man was staring back at her.

If I was to make an herb garden now – a small one along the same lines as the original – who would I put in it? Would I still plant myself as the sage?

Mary reached for the note pad in her bedside table. Everyone I planted in my first garden is dead, except me, and Stella, and we're not far from it. Aren't you a bundle of good cheer? She stuck her tongue out at herself in the mirror. Crazy old lady, who looks like a man, blood dripping down one cheek. Not much use planting dead people, I suppose.

An article in the latest issue of Women's World listed the different herbs and their meanings. Sage had caught Mary's eye. "Domestic virtue," she read and snorted. "Good health, long life, wisdom. Three out of four's not bad."

At the end of the article, the author showed a garden plan for the prayer of St. Francis using herbs. Gardeners praising the Lord. Mary thought it unlikely to catch on. I could be wrong as usual. Prayer gardening may become the latest fad, but who would ever understand the garden unless it was explained to them? Maybe there are already gardens planted out there that are rooted in St. Francis' words. Surely more people than just Mary Johnson have read the article. Maybe that explains the statues I've seen, of St. Francis, in people's gardens, cement birds perched on his hands and shoulders. I must ask MaryArlene if we can go out again for a Sunday drive soon.

If they can plant their St. Francis gardens, why shouldn't I plant my own version of an herb garden? No one but me needs to know what it means. Mary wiped at the trickle of blood on her cheek.

"Stella!" Mary called, and she wheeled out of her room and down the hall in search of her friend. Is that her sitting in front of the television? Sleeping. Pshaw. "Stella!" she shouted, patting her friend's arm none too gently, startling Stella out of a semi-dozing state. "We are going to plant ourselves a garden. I have a plan."

"I knew you'd want to do it," Stella said. "You just need to be left alone to make up your own mind." They rolled together down the hall toward the new greenhouse.

"I love that new building smell," Stella said, taking a deep breath.

"Not for long," Mary said. "These places all smell the same: piss, shit and heat."

"Don't forget the smoking room," Stella said. "Reminds me of when I used to go to bingo."

Frenchie blocked their way into the greenhouse. "Excuse me," Stella said. "We're coming through."

"Bossy bitch," he snarled. "You'll have to get past me first."

Stella engaged the brake on her wheelchair to keep her still, and shoved against his armrests to roll him out of the way. Frenchie flipped the brake on his chair, and stuck out his tongue, grinning at her.

"You gotta be the most frustrating," Stella began, but she stopped when Mary shook her head.

Mary maneuvered her wheelchair as close to Frenchie as she could get and signalled to Stella to pull in on his other side. "How are you today, Frenchie?" Mary smiled sweetly. "Is that a new shirt?"

Frenchie let go of the brake and stroked his blue plaid, flannel shirtsleeve. "My son sent it. He's with the navy. In Halifax."

Mary dove in, pulled off his brake, and Stella yanked back on his armrests, shoving him close to the wall. She and Mary rolled on past him, smiling and waving.

"Stupid old bitches," he called after them, his hand still caressing the soft flannel plaid sleeve of his new shirt.

Inside the greenhouse, Mary inhaled the dark, damp scent of earth, and she turned toward a pile of soil on a table, built the right height for a wheelchair to roll up to. A young man worked transferring the soil into square, green boxes.

"Good morning ladies. I hope you're gardeners?" He wiped his hands on a towel before approaching. "I could use some help potting up these poinsettias." He waved his hand in a broad sweep, and the two women found themselves looking at a poinsettias-covered table that was partially hidden by the pile of soil. A smaller pile of gravel, sat on another table.

"That's the most brilliant red," Mary said. "It's just like a postcard … or a calendar."

"Better than that," he answered. "They're real."

"What can we do?"

He positioned them side by side in front of the gravel pile, and in front of each of them he set a wooden box containing a healthy potted poinsettia. "Layer the box with five centimetres of gravel. That'll make them heavy enough that they won't fall over," he said. "The box is plastic-lined, so there won't be any leakage. When you've got one done, I'll take it away to the cart, and give you another to do. I hope to have this batch ready today, so they can be out on the tables in time for supper."

The three of them set to work. Mary considered how many years it was since her hands worked with black soil. More years than she was prepared to calculate just now. Her fingers plunged into its crumbly softness, and she found herself kneading it, clenching it, to see if it would clump. It didn't.

"This is fine soil. Perfect for making an herb garden. Too good maybe." As her hands worked with the poinsettias, her mind pondered the possibilities of her new garden.

"You've gardened before," the young man said.

Mary noticed he didn't fill every space with unnecessary chatter, and he was respectful. A young fellow could do much worse than to be respectful, especially in a home full of people older than himself.

"What's your name, son?"

"Christopher." He rubbed his chin on his shoulder. "Chris is good enough."

"That's a big name to live up to," Stella said.

Chris shrugged. "Kind of a lot of responsibility to put on a little baby, but I got the name on account of I was born on Christmas Day. This'll be my twenty-fifth. Quarter of a century this December." He seemed about to go on, but stopped.

He was likely going to make some smart comment about getting old, Mary thought, appreciating that he dropped his eyes when he saw her watching him. Slightly embarrassed. Mmph. A nice boy. Must have a good mother. Raised him right.

"You won't be needing a wheelchair or a cane anytime soon," Mary said. "A twenty-fifth birthday calls for some kind of celebration. Any plans?"

"Oh yeah. My girlfriend is throwing a party. Her parents are away, in Cuba, so we invited a few friends over. No money so it's potluck."

Mary nodded. Young people certainly lived differently these days. At twenty-three, she'd been married. Maybe even pregnant? She could count back, but what did it matter?

"If you feed your guests too much, some of them will just get sick faster," Stella said. "Messier."

"They won't get so drunk on a full stomach as on empty," Mary said, remembering a Christmas dinner spent with Jacob and Amy shortly after Claude's death.

Christopher laughed. "Yeah. Marjorie – that's my girlfriend – told me who I've got to watch and take outside if I think they're looking a bit green. Mostly it's a pretty quiet group." He put two more pots in front of Mary and Stella. "You ladies got any rowdiness planned for the next few weeks? You'll be stuffing down the chocolates, I suppose?"

Mary laughed at Stella's passionate reply. "No chocolate for Mary."

"I want to plant an herb garden," Mary blurted.

No use wasting time on small talk. He may be just twenty-five, but my clock is running down fast. "An herb garden," she repeated.

"I've never done much indoor gardening, but at one time, my thumbs were green." She held up her two hands for examination and was surprised as usual to see the dark brown spots, the protruding veins, and the wrinkled skin. It was comfortably familiar though, to see how in their short time in the greenhouse, dirt had worked itself under her nails.

"Here's where you two are hiding." MaryArlene set the two mugs she was carrying between her mom and Stella. "You can have this cup of tea if you like, Stella. Do you take cream and sugar?"

"I guess we all should have been wearing gloves," Christopher said.

Mary and Stella's eyes met and crinkled at each other. He noticed and grinned too. Each woman reached forward and patted his hands at the same time. "Bare hands are good, dear."

"I'm Mary's daughter, MaryArlene. I've heard about this Horticulture Therapy programme. It's quite new, isn't it? Seems like a good idea."

"Yes," Christopher said. "We were just discussing your mother's garden plans. What sort of herbs will you be growing, Mary?"

"I'll want a sage for sure, and borage. Maybe some basil and some pansies. I'll do some research before deciding on the others. I'd want my own place for planting. Wouldn't want anyone else poking around in it."

"There's going to be a spot for people who want to grow plants in pots. House plants. But you want something larger?" He led them all to the back of the greenhouse. "There's these contraptions." He showed them a three-foot square by eighteen inches deep, planting box that could be rotated for access on all sides.

"That's perfect! It's exactly what I need. Me and Stella will have this one. This box please."

"You're lucky you came early. I'll put your name on it, and after the poinsettias are potted up, that'll be my next job – to get your box ready for planting. I'll be here Mondays, Wednesdays and Fridays.

That's all the funding we were able to get for now. Nine AM 'til four PM," he added. "Eighteen hours a week."

"Let's get back to those poinsettias right away," Mary commanded.

"Slave driver," Stella mumbled but followed her friend's order. "This'll be better than fighting with the geezers in the hallways."

Christopher cocked his head but made no response.

After lunch, Mary opened A Modern Herbal by Mrs. M. Grieve, the huge tome she'd spent so many hours poring over, in the dismal days after Edward's death.

She sat in her wheelchair, clutching the book to her chest, a little afraid to delve into its memory-laden pages with the marginalia written in her large, clear, schoolgirl penmanship. In front of her, the dresser mirror reflected an aged woman with grey hair that stuck out in tufts around her head. Reading glasses hung around her neck on a bright red shoelace. The eyes peering at her squinted, then the wrinkled face broke into laughter. "Looks like you can still wear the drama queen crown, my friend."

Reaching into her pocket, Mary found lipstick and applied a liberal coat to her thin lips. She worked a brush over her grey hair, succeeding only in rearranging the jutting tufts rather than controlling them. She acknowledged her efforts with an approving nod at herself in the mirror. "It's probably a blessing that my eyesight's fading." Taking a deep breath she laid a pillow in her lap to bring the book to a comfortable reading level.

Mary thumbed through the pages, letting them stop where they would. "Borage," she murmured and put on her glasses to scan the familiar entry. "Of course."

Her vein-lined right hand worked its way into the back cover of the herbal; she felt the brown envelope taped there so many years ago on a chilly fall day.

1952. Inside the legal-size, brown envelope, was the original garden plan she developed over that long, snowy winter with Stella. And Mrs. Grieves. She'd updated the plan over the years as she'd made changes, recording additions to and deletions from the garden. She'd created a new sketch whenever the previous one became too messy to read. In the large envelope were smaller envelopes in which she'd saved seeds from some of the herbs. Would they be viable? Basil, 1953. Borage 1953. Both packets, when shaken, gave off the satisfying sound of well-preserved seeds. Not too fresh, but they might grow. Worth a try anyway, just for the heck of it. There were dill seeds and radish too. I'll need a list. A plan. Who to include. Who to exclude. "And what herbs shall they be?" She spoke to the woman in the mirror. "It's so long since I've gardened maybe I've lost my touch. Should I wait until spring?" She waggled her eyebrows at herself in the mirror.

I could be dead by then.

Mary drew four lines down her page, making five columns with headings: Name, Plant, Ailment, Treatment, and Result. She numbered down the side of the page from one to eight. Eight will be enough to start with. Number one. Edward – borage. It's not an herb garden without borage, even if I can't help him. She left the Ailment, Treatment and Result columns blank. Now, what about Stella? What does she need? Mary chewed on her pen.

Mary spent the afternoon plotting her garden, reading about the individual herbs in Mrs. Grieve's bible to decide their suitability. Just like God she thought, as she chose the eight people she would include, and pondered her ability to help them. It was easier when I gardened for a lark. Now, I'm almost afraid to be planting this garden. Flower Power. Have I gone completely off my rocker?

She recalled Claude as he lay dying, on the parlour room sofa, under her care. She found the photograph taken for their twenty-fifth wedding anniversary. 1964. Even in this one, Claude seemed to look right at her, questioning her. Why Mary? Why can't you just let things be? In their fortieth anniversary picture, both their heads were topped with thick grey hair. 1979. They'd worn corsages made by Mary: one pink Hansa rose with two sprigs of borage, and, to symbolize MaryArlene – asparagus clippings. Claude refused her request to visit the cemetery that day.

Mary stuck her fingers into her ears and squinched her eyes shut, but she could not block out his look, nor his questions. "Why do you always have to bring up the past? You can't bring him back." Claude seemed to get over Edward's death so much better and quicker than she had. Or Arnie.

Her book, her papers and pen tumbled from her lap to the floor. Mary checked that the brake was on before placing one foot at a time flat onto the floor and lifted herself out of the wheelchair. She lowered herself to her knees to retrieve her accouterments.

It was a long time since she'd gotten out of the wheelchair under her own steam. I shouldn't be letting myself stay in that dang chair all day, all the time. Before I know it, I'll have completely forgotten how to walk or crawl. Maybe I should be a rue plant rather than a sage. No. Too negative. Starting today, I will make myself get more exercise. I'll get out of this chair and walk. All this talk about fixing other people's ailments. What I'll do is plant myself in that herb plot and loosen up these creaky joints. No reason I can't benefit too. Maybe I should just plant sage and borage and the heck with the others.

She considered the sage plant, its supple stems that with age grew woody and gnarled and twisted. Would it be possible to soften the stiff wooden branches?

"Mary!" Cathy's voice startled her thoughts away from the garden. "Code six in Mary's room."

"Is there a fire?" Mary turned to greet Cathy with a smile but before she could utter another word, she felt each of her arms taken in a strong firm grasp.

"Did you fall out of your chair, Mary?"

"No. I was getting my pen. And my papers."

"Are you hurt?"

"No. I just got out to get my things."

"We're going to lift you, Mary. On the count of three. One, two, three." Mary felt herself borne up in strong arms and in a moment she was seated in her wheelchair.

"There. Safe and sound again," Cathy said, patting her patient's knee in what Mary supposed was meant to be a comforting manner. "Now, tell me how you happened to fall out of your chair."

"I didn't fall out of my chair. I was …"

Cathy squatted in front of Mary, clasping the aged hand in her own firm, unwrinkled, un-veined ones. "Your skin is so wonderfully soft, Mary," she said. "Look at my red chapped messes. They feel as rough as pineapples. How do you keep yours so smooth?" Cathy didn't wait for Mary's reply. "You mustn't get out of your wheelchair, Mary. Not without help. It's too dangerous." She fluttered her eyelashes and widened her eyes. "We don't want you to fall and hurt yourself, now do we?"

Mary pulled her right hand free to gesture at the pen and paper on the floor. "I wanted …"

"I'll get those for you. Just ring your buzzer to call the staff if you drop something. You can't be climbing out of your wheelchair. It's too dangerous. It could roll away on you. Or over top of you."

"They're trying to keep us in our wheelchairs, stop us using our own two feet," Mary complained to Stella later, as they sat at their poinsettia-decorated table in the dining room, waiting for supper. "As soon as I moved in here, they put me in this thing. Said it was for my own good, so I don't fall and get hurt, but it keeps me from being independent.

"I don't usually make New Years resolutions, but I've got one for this year, and it's to build strength in my legs and arms so I can walk on my own again."

Stella shook her head, "You be careful, Mary. I heard if they catch you out one time too many they'll start tying you in the chair."

Christopher whistled as he examined Mary's plan for the herb garden. "I can get you a sage plant," he said. "And Rosemary, lemon thyme ... I'll ask around. Nasturtium. Best to start that from seed."

As he named the plants Mary imagined them all growing happily together. Of course, the nasturtium will need to be planted around the edges and it will have to be kept clipped back from the other plants. Nasturtium is a wanton grower. Mary giggled to herself. That's why I chose it for MaryArlene. An annual. Won't ever self-sow. It has to be planted from seed every year and babied along until it gets a good root system growing. Exactly like my MaryArlene.

Mary closed her bedroom door, put the brake on her wheelchair, and carefully placed both her feet on the floor. Using the bedpost for balance, she stood and gazed around the room at this new angle, then took four steps along the bed until she reached the dresser. With her added height, Mary could see that there was dust on the top of the tall boy and the television.

"They think I don't see up there. I won't tell them either. It matters not." She rummaged in her top drawer for an old blouse she could wear over her sweater to keep the dirt off when she was gardening in the greenhouse. She lowered herself onto the bed and shoved her right arm, then the left, into the sleeves of the blouse.

"Flabby. Skinny. I'm a mess. How do you like me now, Claude? Liz? Mother? I've got one comment for you all: at least I'm still kicking.

"Ha! And one more thing. I might look a mess – not disputing that – but at least I held on to my self respect. I didn't just give it away. While you all were busy selling your pies and your quilts to the church I did ... well ... I did my gardening I guess."

She caught her eye in the mirror. "Who am I fooling? I'm no better than the rest of you, am I? Was I? I'm still living anyway. Wouldn't you think at this age I'd be over the angst issues? Do I have to live until I get it all figured out? Is that what this old age is for? You all got yourselves all set right with the world, with God, so you got to check out? But me, I'm not ready yet? Not wise enough?" Mary shook her head.

"I don't know. I do not know any of the answers to any of the questions and it's a waste of time thinking about this stuff. I may be a fool – I know I am – but ... God or Claude or whoever you are, prolonging this life until I make sense of it. If that's what you've planned you're going to have to lay it all out for me in a logical sequence. Put your cards all out neatly on the table with an explanation cause I don't get it. I don't understand it. I don't know what's going on. If the key is for old Mary Johnston to understand the meaning of life, before I'm allowed to move on, I'm going to need some help. And in the meanwhile you can find me in the greenhouse."

Mary dragged her hairbrush over her scalp, the soft bristles reminding her of MaryArlene's consideration for her physical comfort. "She a good girl, that one. A thoughtful girl. Maybe she won't have to live as long as me."

Mary grinned into the mirror at herself. "I hope I don't have to live forever, but at the rate I'm going ... Gawd!"

Rising from the bed, Mary walked slowly back to her wheelchair. Already her legs were weak. "It's like learning to walk all over again." It took a few moments to regain her breath, but she waited, knowing it would come.


Mary rolled out of her room and down the hall to the greenhouse where Christopher, shirtsleeves rolled up, was planting marigold seeds into cell packs.

"Good morning. Your plants arrived this morning." Together they admired Mary's newly arrived plants.

"You don't know how good this feels." Mary wiped a strand of hair out of her eye leaving two streaks of dirt along her eyebrow. "This greenhouse, the smell, the plants. I feel like my chest will burst."

She dug a hole in the center of the rich, dark, damp soil of the planter box that Christopher had readied for her garden. She read the label – sage officinalis – and slipped it into her pocket. There'll be no need for labels in this garden. I know my plants.

The sage was just one stick – eight inches high. "The roots are healthy." Christopher scraped his thumbnail across the woody bark to reveal green underneath the brown. "Two buds here." He pointed to the barely visible knobs developing near the base of the twig. "Before we know it, there'll be leaves." He nodded, satisfied.

Mary settled the sage plant into the hole and pushed soil around its roots and woody stem. She caught her breath. It was exciting to be gardening again, to think about growing things. Oh. How did I let gardening slip away from me? She dug four holes around the sage, leaving enough room for the plants to stretch and grow. A fine healthy bay leaf plant - Laurus nobilis – went into one hole and the label she stashed in her pocket. Spreading its roots and tamping them into the soil she said, "There, Frenchie. A noble plant for you. We'll use its leaves and berries in an ungent for your rheumy joints. Should help your memory loss too. One hopes. I wonder if there isn't a plant to soften up your crabbiness." She laughed at herself.

The rosemary plant went in next. "Happiness to the living and peace to the dead," Mary quoted from Mrs. Grieves Herbal. "Rosmarinus officinalis."

"Some herbs don't transplant well," Christopher advised, noticing the rosemary's lack of needles. "A week or so will maybe make the difference."

Just the same, Mary thought, I'd better stop in and see Ruth tonight. She ran her hand along the stem and four more rosemary needles fell to the soil. "You are not looking so good."

Lemon thyme and rue 'Curly Girl' were placed on either side slightly in front of the sage. Along both sides of the planter, Mary dragged her finger in the soil, and spaced borage seeds along one side and nasturtium seeds along the other.

"You'll have plenty of bright, strong colours in this garden when they're all blooming," Christopher complimented.

Mary just smiled. She'd planted borage for Edward, whom she'd vowed to include in every garden she ever made, while the bright orange, red, and yellow nasturtium flowers represented MaryArlene. Flamboyant, useful, cheerful, and clean. A large likeable plant in most ways. Nasturtium leaves were peppery on the tongue, Mary remembered, from gardens past. A bit pushy as they liked to take up every inch of available space, but all in all, delightful plants to grow and to eat. They were easy to care for and the round dark seeds, about twice the size of peppercorns, could be pickled. There's got to be some sort of moral in that, Mary thought. Here I go already – thinking like that again. I have to be careful what I say out loud. I wonder if nasturtiums grown in a greenhouse will still emit sparks at dusk?

She'd been with Claude the first evening she noticed the phenomenon, and they assumed they were seeing fireflies, but on closer observation became sure the actual flowers were sparking. Mary found no mention of the cause in Mrs. Grieves Herbal and later Mr. Fynch explained it was due to nasturtium's high phosphoric acid content. He also told her the flower was considered by some to be a powerful natural antibiotic and that a certain German scientist claimed that nasturtiums possessed aphrodisiac virtue. Hence, it was given the name, 'flower of love'. The glory of herbs, Mary thought. I think the German idea was right.

How could anyone not be carried off completely into this world of fantastic natural wonder? If there was a God, Mary knew, He existed in the garden. Arnie used to enjoy her plant lore as had Stella. Claude ... hadn't. Well at first he actually seemed interested and he was, to the extent of his own ability to understand. Claude's mind worked in fact and tangibility and common sense. He kept his shop neat and tidy, and threw out what was no longer useful. He had adopted his mother's way of thinking and so with Liz's attitude that the garden was a waste of time, he'd .... Mary looked up from her box of plants.

"Christopher, you got any ideas of fertilizer? I won't be able to get manure quite as freely as I used to." Mary grinned wryly, thanked Claude silently for the reminder.

"We've used slow release already in the soil," Chris said. "Should be OK for a month or so. I'm starting a chart to record fert' dates and planting dates and such. Tracking."

"I should show you my diary records of garden plans from way back when," Mary said. "I used to like to know what plants worked where."

"What time frame are we talking?"

"1956 and onward … until 1990 or so, I guess. That's when I let up on the gardening – when Claude died. I've got some seeds still from the early gardens too. I planted some of the borage to see if they'll grow."

"Borage seed from 1956? That's like thirty years before I was even born."

"Hard to imagine isn't it?" Mary liked how his perspective worked. "You're making me remember things I thought I'd long forgotten."

How much do I want to remember? So many things she thought she'd left buried in that garden when she'd left the farm for the last time. Stella helped. Stella was there for her at the end when Claude's time was over. As Mary had been there for her when Arnie died. So many deaths. So many memories.


Mother had been certain that Claude's problem was grief. "Pure and simple grief," she said more than once.

Over tea Mary and Stella had drawn their own conclusions.

"He never really came back from the war, I don't think," Mary said.

"I wonder what exactly happened over there."

"Not sure," Mary said, massaging the handle of the bone china cup. "He doesn't say much. It's more than the war. I think coming back to the farm … we had no choice … but it wasn't good. He needed to be away from his parents, not living with them."

Stella nodded. "For sure. You couldn't do any differently though. The war was the start. And then the old man dying. That was just plain old bad luck that."

"Yeah. And Liz milked it." Mary shook her head. "Not fair. Not fair. Not fair. Talk about something else. This is too depressing."

"I just can't believe there isn't something we can do to change things."

"Well," Mary said. "I could just disappear. Fake my own death. Or his."

"Right. That's why we keep ourselves busy. So we don't kill our husbands."

They both laughed.

"And our mother-in-laws. Who says Claude has to be the surrogate husband? That's just wrong."

"Guilt. Religious fanaticism. Call it what you want."

"Of course, that's it. And he's afraid. Of what'll happen after. You know after … he dies. I think maybe that's the thing that happened over in France. During the war. Arnie doesn't seem to have been so affected as Claude."

Stella nodded. "Different personalities maybe. Arnie is not as serious as Claude so that helps. He saw a lot of guys die over there on the boats. Lost good friends."

"I know. Claude's maybe just a sour puss. He probably inherited that from his mother's side. Dour and depressed. Mrs. Doom and Gloom. That's what Mother calls her. She thinks it's funny and it is, but scary too."

Mary didn't bring up the boys drowning. Stella, quick to discuss Claude's shortcomings, and Arnie's too, had a huge blind spot when it came to admitting that she couldn't talk about her dead son. Neither could Claude, Mary knew. It made him angry and so she avoided that topic with her best friend and her husband. Arnie had a better perspective.

The Claude that Mary promised to love, honour and obey, went missing on or about November 1956. Rare glimpses of the young man Claude used to be, kept Mary cautiously hopeful, but for the most part, Claude might as well have drowned that day with Edward and Nelson.

Along the front edge of the planter, Mary laid the Woolly Thyme. No association with anyone – yet. "Woolly Thyme is a funny one," she said to no one. "You swear you've got it in the perfect spot, and suddenly it dies on you."

Mary decided to wait to see how the plant did for a while, before giving it a name. Today it looked pretty scraggly.

I should talk to Stella about getting us in for a haircut this week. We could both use a spruce-up.

Christopher showed her how to work the overhead watering system. "You reach up, and pull down the hose-head, flick this here switch on the nozzle and, voila, you've got water! Easy peasy."

She gave each of the plants a drink and soaked the two lines of seeds. Mary leaned back in her chair to admire her work. Like God on the seventh day. Her stomach growled. Mary steered her wheelchair to the door, assuring Christopher on her way past, that she would be back tomorrow to tend the plants. "And I'll bring Stella too."

In the dining room, Susan served them thick cream of mushroom soup. "Where's Ruth?" Mary said. "Not like her to miss a meal."

"Said she wasn't feeling good when she woke up this morning, poor woman." Susan shook her head. "Her hair is still coming out in clumps."

A long buried, familiar dread nagged Mary's stomach. "Silly old coot," Mary said. "She'd better not die on us." She tried to smile, wished she could laugh it off, and assured herself there couldn't possibly be any significance at all to Ruth's illness and the sickly rosemary plant and her own wish to ease Ruth's unease. Still. Her stomach twisted. Do something.

At Mary's insistence, she and Stella rolled down the hall to Ruth's room after lunch with cookies, wrapped in serviettes, stashed in their pockets. Ruth never refused cookies.

"Mary. Stella." Ruth's voice was weak. She lay flat in bed, the sheet rising and falling jerkily as she worked to breathe. "Set those in my drawer," she directed when they made their cookie offering. "I'm not hungry now."

Mary placed her hand on Ruth's forehead, caressed its porcelain smoothness. Too cool.

"I think I'm finally going to get out of here," Ruth said, her dry lips sticking to each other, flecks of white at the corners moving with each word. "It's about time."

"No, don't go." Mary held her hand against Ruth's forehead. "We're planning a beach party for you. You don't want to miss Stella in shorts."

Ruth coughed and the spirit disappeared from her eyes for a moment.

Mary held her eyes. Struggled to find the words that would keep her with them. "We finally have a greenhouse. You've got to stick around and plant a garden."

"No more gardens. I'll be back with my Rosemary soon." Ruth smiled and closed her eyes.

Mary kept her hand on Ruth's brow. Felt her withdrawal. No struggle, just a mild, peaceful, welcome leaving.

"That must have been her daughter's name, eh, Mary?" Stella asked. "I never knew her name before. It's not a good sign when they start talking about reuniting with them that's pre-deceased. Gives me the creeps kind of."

"Yeah. Well she's checking out if I know anything." Mary pulled the sheet up around Ruth's chin and smoothed the extra blanket over her feet. She opened the drawer of the bedside table and removed the cookies they had put there. "No use wasting these." She handed one to Stella and kept two for herself. Raised one to her mouth.

They munched the cookies and watched their friend sleep, her mouth opening and shutting with each breath, until Cathy came in and shooed them out.

In the morning, on her way to the dining room, Mary stopped by Ruth's room. The plastic-covered mattress glowed stark white in the morning sunshine; family photographs had been taken down. The bedside table was bare, wiped clean.

Cathy laid a hand on Mary's shoulder. "Ruth left us in the night," she said. "She was ready to go. The new aide, Becky, was with her at the end. Ruth liked Becky."

"I wasn't ready for her to go," Mary said. She shrugged Cathy's hand from her shoulder.

"She was a dear soul," Cathy said, stroking Mary's shoulders. "Always a smile and a compliment, unless she couldn't find her slippers." She chuckled, leaned down to check under the bed. "Guess they got everything," she said.

"I better get you down to breakfast or you'll miss your morning tea. Can't have that." She pushed Mary out into the hall, came around in front of the wheelchair and reached into her pocket.

"Ruth thought you would enjoy having this." She handed Mary the stained glass artwork Ruth's granddaughter had hung in the window the day Ruth arrived at Sunny Acres.

Mary stared at the bright colours remembering Ruth's smile as she told stories about her granddaughter. In the centre was a brilliant blue, star-shaped flower with a hummingbird flying toward it, needle beak pointed at the middle of the flower. Borage.

"She was looking forward to a reunion with her daughter, Rosemary," Cathy said. "It was her time."

A reunion. Would Ruth's daughter recognize her mother? Would they have anything in common in that new world?

"Morning, mum.

"What are you doing here so early?"

"I thought you'd like some fresh croissants from the market." MaryArlene stroked her mum's hair.

"One of our residents, Ruth, left us in the night. Your mom's friend," Cathy swung her arm at the emptied room.

Mary saw Cathy nodding her head at MaryArlene. "Thanks for coming," Cathy whispered.

"Oh dear. I'm so sorry." MaryArlene kissed Mary's forehead. "Come on, we'll go to the dining room and share these yummies with Stella. Does she know about Ruth?"

"No," Cathy said.

"I always," Mary said. "No. Liz, Claude's mother, always said, 'You're too busy. Better let me do the cooking. Gotta keep myself useful anyway.' So what could I say? It sounded perfectly reasonable, but it was my kitchen, and my husband and my son. I enjoyed making our meals and darning the socks. But when Liz said that she might as well do that job to free me up for more important things it seemed, once again, perfectly reasonable. And Mother went along with it, helping her push me away from a task that I enjoyed. I wasn't allowed to look after my family. She took over everything."

Again, Cathy and MaryArlene looked at each other over Mary's head. "She has many memories. Clear as if they happened yesterday."

"Oh yes. She surely does that." MaryArlene pushed the wheelchair toward the dining room. "You are thinking about my grandmothers?"

"They would never admit it," Mary said. "But that's how it went. The two mothers took over running my household bit by bit, rearranging the kitchen cupboard and the linen closet and the preserves. My whole home was how they wanted it. Hardly a bit of me in it at all. I'd sit a picture on the mantle and next thing I knew it'd be shoved away in a drawer someplace. That's why I never would live with my children. Wouldn't put that burden on them."

"You wouldn't be a burden you know, Mum. I'd love to have you live with me. But this is a wonderful home you've got here. Comfy. Lots of people your own age."

"If I ever dared to mention that I liked and wanted the towels on the bottom shelf, it seemed, well, it seemed mean after Liz did all the work of taking the towels out, shaking them out, wiping the cupboard and refolding the towels. She was an expert at turning on the waterworks to make certain Claude and Mother would feel sorry for her. How could a daughter-in-law continue that discussion without being seen as ungrateful?"

Mary sighed. "Regret is a waste of time."

"Here we are," MaryArlene announced. "Oh look! Stella saved your place. What a sweetie. Morning, Stella. Hope you have room for a croissant."

"Frenchie says Ruth died in the night," Stella said. "She was ready to go. We knew it yesterday after lunch didn't we, Mary? That Ruth wasn't good. Who's next, I wonder?" Stella bit into her croissant. "Did Mary tell you we're making a garden?"

"A herb garden," MaryArlene said. "I got to meet Christopher the other day when I was in. Remember? He seems a nice young fellow."

"Yes. Yes. He seems awful young to be done school doesn't he? But he's twenty-five. When I was twenty-five..."

Mary was pleased to see MaryArlene slather strawberry jam onto the croissant in thick gobs.

"It's like when we would open up a fresh jar of preserves and sit at the kitchen table at the farm." Stella laughed.

'I miss those days," Mary said. "When we'd leave the mothers to do the housework."

"And we found other things to occupy ourselves. Gardening and weeding mostly. On rainy days we made plans for the herb garden. We made trips into the town library to research plants. The good old days."

Mary chomped another jammy bite. "They weren't all good days."

Stella nodded. "Liz. She could test a person's patience."

"You'd be telling me to get myself something else to do, something else to think about or I'd make myself crazy. She kept pushing at me. Trying to take over my life it felt like. And she couldn't understand why I didn't fall on my knees giving thanks for her interference."

Obsession. The word repeated in her head. "You were right, Stella," she said. "I practically moved out to my garden. Weeding. Yanking out that damn lily of the valley." Mary laughed out loud. "It's threatening to take over the whole herb garden."

"What did you say, mum?" MaryArlene and Stella were looking at her.

"These croissants are very good," Mary said, taking another bite. A gob of jam landed on her bib. She tried to pick it up in her fingers. "That lily of the valley …"

Mary shut her eyes remembering. When she and Stella chose the herbs for the first herb garden, Mary picked lily of the valley to represent Liz. Lily of the valley's lacy, frilled, delicate bells of pure white, hung from scapes which eventually spread themselves over the whole garden in the spring with a sweet and lingering scent. The first year Mary wondered if the plant would survive. By the second year, it was healthy and brilliant green in spring with a few lovely scapes of dangling bells. By the third season Mary realized that lily of the valley was going to be troublesome. By that time, it seemed that with each slice of her spade into the rich humus of her herb plot, she found herself slicing into lily of the valley roots that were invisible on the surface of the garden but spreading their insidious, pure white, fleshy appendages underground.

Research into the plant brought her to realize that a creeping, sly, invasive thug flourished in her once peaceful plot.

"Mary, you've tracked sand onto my freshly washed floor." Liz would scold. "Mary. Did you hear Father Byers say, 'Children today have lost their respect for authority?'

"Mary. Are you sure you want to shorten that skirt? It already shows all of your ankle!"

"Mum. Let me wipe that jam off your chin." Mary felt MaryArlene's gentle hands on her face bringing her back to the present, but she was in her herb garden too, back on the farm, digging. Each time her shovel cut into the roots of the lily of the valley, it didn't weaken the plant but rather it seemed she was pruning it and rejuvenating the plant, and Mary knew she must battle in earnest against the foe which sought to over-run her herb plot and her home.

"You're right, Liz. The skirt should be even shorter. Just below the knee, Liz.

"Children are meant to question, Liz. However will they learn if they're not allowed to ask?

"Floors were made for walking on, Liz."

Mary and Stella had giggled over their cups of tea as Stella encouraged Mary to push on with her gardening. "You've got it coming real good, Mary. But you should yank out that lily of the valley. Every last piece of it."

Mary dug and yanked and perspired and swore. She carted a whole wheel-barrow load of the slender white roots to the laneway where she spread them on the gravel ruts in the hot baking sun, standing over them as she whispered, "Bake in Sunshine, Wither with Heat, Squashed, Trampled, Death, Defeat." She felt a miniscule twinge of conscience as she looked up toward the house. There sat her mother and Liz in the white wicker rockers on the front porch.

Liz wore a brilliant white bib apron tied neatly at the waist. Her lime green dress with tiny white flowers cascaded demurely to her ankles that were often swollen from their miles of hard work. She kept her curly white hair trimmed short. Watching her from the garden, Mary saw that her mother-in-law was an old woman. Her head's perpetual nodding motion made her seem to be always in agreement with what she heard or read.

Beside Liz, sat Sadie. Mother's head fell forward and a rush of tenderness flooded over Mary as she realized her mother too was fading. "My own dear Mother is getting near to the end of her life. The woman who raised me, who changed my diapers and worried over my schooling is old. The grandmother who cared as best she knew how for her rambunctious grandson." A wave of grief washed over Mary's heart. She gulped for air, struggled to lift her head above the pain of her losses, past and future.

On the porch, in the wicker chair, a breeze lifted Sadie's white hair. Her mouth gaped open, and she snorted as she slept.

Mary looked up into the cloudless blue sky. Who will watch over me asleep on the porch when my hair is snow white, my ankles swollen, and I'm no longer able to lift a shovel? Where is my promise of the future? Fury raised her foot and stomped it down onto the white snake-like roots. She mashed them with her boots and with the shovel, into the cement-hard clay, not stopping until they were a pulpy, stringy, slimy green damp mess, unidentifiable to anyone but herself.

With a snort worthy of a drunken sot, Liz awoke and made to stand, but called out in panic. "My back. I can't straighten my back."

Leaning all of her bony weight on Mary, Liz made the pain-filled trek from the front porch into the house with Sadie following behind. Liz wasted no breath talking or complaining, merely groaned with each movement.

Mary had seen and heard pain over the years when she helped Father calve cows and she recognized the eloquence of mooing that came from deep within, from the center of the beast, traveling every joint, every vertebra, and every muscle. Liz's groans spoke of the same depth of pain.

When they reached her bedroom off the kitchen, Sadie and Mary helped Liz, drenched in sweat, to lay on the bed. They removed her shoes and socks, and dried her off as best they could without moving her unnecessarily. Liz bore it all, watched with huge brown eyes that sometimes drooped shut, and other times sprang wide open as spasms of pain overtook her. Covering her with a clean, white sheet, and a light wool blanket, Mary told Liz and Sadie that she would go phone for the doctor.

Sadie nodded and turned back to watch as Liz dozed.

After a mostly silent examination, Doctor Martin asked how the injury had occurred.

"I was fine at lunch," Liz said. "Mary and Claude both left to work in the shop and in the garden and Sadie and I got busy doing the dishes. That's when the pain started. We'd been working fifteen minutes maybe."

Mary reached with the towel to wipe sweat from Liz's brow.

"It started as a twinge in my side under my ribs. Right there." She winced as the doctor touched the spot. "I kept on working. Got the dishes done and the floor swept. I knew I must have a wee rest, so I came out on the porch thinking I'd feel better in a bit.

"I just closed my eyes for a minute. It was even hurting to sit. The breathing hurts. And, when I tried to get up, the pain was too bad, and I couldn't stand it. Like someone was stomping on my back. On my ribs. Everywhere. Breaking all my bones at once."

Be careful what you wish for, Mary thought, catching a glimpse of herself and her anger at the lily of the valley on the driveway.

"There's nothing broken here, Mrs. Johnston, as far as I can figure, but you'll have to stay lying down awhile."

"Don't imagine you'll have any trouble keeping her in bed for a few days. Bed rest and liniment." Doctor Martin looked kindly at Mary.

"I'll stop in to Fynch's on my way past. Tell him what to prepare for you. Rub it on three to four times a day. You'll be good as new in no time, Mrs. Johnston." He turned to Mary. "What age is your mother?"

"Mother-in-law," Mary said. "She's closing in on 65 years."


Mary and Claude sat out on the front porch after their evening meal.

Just the two of us, like it used to be. Before … Mary stopped the thought.

They sat facing west toward the full glory of the sun's blazing journey behind the tree line. Pink and rose and golden grey, the trees stood dark against the impossible beauty of the sun's exit.

Claude squinted; Mary recognized his thinking pose and waited until he spoke.

"What is that damp spot there where the wagons pass?" he asked.

"I pulled all the lily of the valley out of the garden today," Mary answered.

Claude doesn't know I ripped every lily of the valley out by the roots and all the while wished … again she stopped her thought.

"I hope I'll have time tomorrow to check it over – the garden – make sure I got it all out. The stuff is like quack grass," she said. "Just one little root and you've got it forever. I wish I'd known that before I planted it."

"Mmph," he answered.

"It's nice. Just the two us. Like it used to be."

The sun was fully set. As they sat in the dusk Claude reached for her hand. He rubbed his thumb over her palm, her wrist, wriggled it into her buttoned cuff. Gently he tugged each finger in turn, cupped his fingers into hers. The silent ask.

It was at least three months since they'd made love. Mary wished she'd changed out of her soiled work dress, perspiration stained and scented from her work in the garden; her teeth felt like they wore sweaters.

"It is nice … out here … alone," Claude voice was an unfamiliar whisper in her ear.

She murmured agreement. "Uhuhmmmmmmm." Almost a song.

Claude nuzzled her neck, bunted her ear with his nose. Can we? Should we? Do you want to? Please?

Did she want to? Yes, of course. But … it had been so long. Maybe they'd fallen too far apart, lost the necessary closeness. Not necessary for Claude obviously. He seems quite willing to take up where we left off. How long has it been?

Was it just months? Or was it years? Mary wasn't sure. How long had they lived here? In this … place. Mary thought it was about seven years. How long since Edward died? One year and two months and three days ago. There's nothing wrong with my memory. I just remember the important things. The important thing.

Everyone said how well she'd picked herself up after Edward's death. She did the laundry, the gardening, shovelled when it snowed, made lunch for Claude and for the Mothers, smiled when she was spoken to, and often she heard, "You've done so well, so remarkably well to get yourself going since Edward's accident."

That is what they said. They didn't see that it mattered not to Mary if she washed the floor or left it dirty, if she made a batch of red apple jelly or did not make a batch of wriggling red jelly. What worth was there in life? The only thing that captured her full attention was the herb garden, especially her courageous borage plants. There, Edward came alive again. Nothing else mattered.

She rubbed the hairy, cucumber-scented leaves of the borage at every stage of development – their tender green tips in the spring, and in July, their bristly rough stalks. Best of all, she appreciated the star shape of the brilliant blue flowers with their black stamens, that jutted abruptly from the center of the flat, spread-eagled flower petals.

People assured her that time would heal her sorrow and that the memory of her lost loved one would fade, but Mary knew her memories of Edward were strengthening as time passed. The bright blue of the borage flower was the exact hue of a summer sky and the colour of Edward's eyes. The hollow grey bristled stems reminded her of his straight thin legs and the day the fisher ripped into his innocent flesh.

He spoke to her while she worked in the herb garden. He put his soft hand into hers. His was cool, slim, and delicate, and Mary loved the time she spent caressing its precious slightness. Gently. She mustn't hurt him.

"I'm fine, Mom." Edward's voice was boyish and full of energy. "Don't worry about me." It was enough to make a mother cry. Over the months he'd been gone, she imagined he grew as a boy should; he was now seven years old. When would his voice start to change?

Claude halted nuzzling, but still held Mary's hand. "You're going away from me, Mary." His voice held urgency and hurt. "I don't know how to keep you here."

Mary squeezed his hand in sympathy. He's right. I'm not with him anymore these days, not the way I should be. I don't know how to change it. Or even if I care to change it. It might be a relief to land somewhere instead of drifting in this limbo between Edward and no Edward.

Sometimes it seemed she could slip away permanently. Close her eyes and not wake up. She'd considered stepping off the sidewalk into the path of an oncoming team of horses or popping an unknown mushroom into her mouth to end this hovering between two worlds.

But it wouldn't be right. Edward said so. "Father needs you now. And Gramma too. All of them." He made Mary remember the promise she'd made to her father to take care of Mother as long as was needed. Edward would know if she broke her promise, if she killed herself. Let herself go, Mary corrected. It wouldn't be fair to Claude either. He worked so hard to make a life for them – to keep them in flour and meat, and she'd promised to stick by him.

That's what she'd said in her vows, and vows weren't meant to be taken lightly.

"I'll try to stay, Claude," she answered. The night seemed to be happening in slow motion. It was never like this when the Mothers sat with them on the porch. When the Mothers were here, they did most of the talking, so Mary hardly participated at all. It was easy to float, to drift in and out of the conversation. Tonight however, it was just Mary and Claude here on the porch. She reached her fingers to twine with his warm ones. She closed her eyes and felt his whole presence beside her. It might be nice to … . Rub legs … . She freed her thumb and circled it in his palm, pleased when he returned the pressure.

He reached down and lifted her legs to rest on his where he massaged the soles of her feet. He used to massage her feet in their early days, before Edward was born. His hands didn't move from her feet; she remembered that feeling. Anticipated the familiar sensation of his light touch on her calves, behind her knees. It had been so long since she'd felt her man's touch.

"Mum? Mum." MaryArlene stroked Mary's shoulder. "Let's go to the greenhouse. See how your garden grows."

"Don't you want the rest of your croissant?" Stella reached for the croissant but Mary quickly slipped it into her mouth.

"Good jam," Mary said.

"I made it myself," MaryArlene said. "Used your recipe. Remember when you taught me to make jam all those years ago?"

"Not so long ago that I can't remember," Mary said. "I remember it all."

MaryArlene kissed the top of her mum's head. "Stay with me, Mum. Sometimes I swear you're miles away."

Not miles so much as years. Mary squeezed her daughter's hand. Poor MaryArlene. She'd always been a sweet girl. Poor MaryArlene.

# Chapter 18

**Borage** – Borago Officinalis – Cures weak conditions of the heart. The fresh plant has a cucumber-like odour and hairy, bristly stems with heart-breaking blue flowers. The leaves eaten raw do engender good blood. Borage strengthens neighbouring plants against insects and disease.

The Flower of Courage carried by King Basel whenever he led his troops to invade a country. 'To give the men courage'. They'd chop the leaves into their drinks. It might have been the whiskey that made them brave, but you didn't argue with King Basel from the sound of him.

"Father Byers was into the shop today," Claude said. "I repaired his fireplace tongs. He said he could use some help with altar flowers, if you've ever got any extras."

"I might have," Mary answered. "I thought of throwing all the extra seeds that people keep giving me into one long row and see what comes up."

"Want me to run the plow through? It's still out. Give you more room for planting."

Claude plowed a long wide row and Mary planted her extra seeds in it. Within days, little bits of green poked through the black soil – thin grassy thread-like stems – assurances of cosmos and larkspur and marigolds, all annuals that would bloom in one season, then die. She'd keep seeds of these ones, Mary reminded herself, the same way she collected and dried and saved the borage seeds each year. Make a note on her calendar.

"These round ones look like hollyhocks. If so, you'll be waiting two seasons for a flower but they're worth the wait. Too soon to tell though. Maybe they'll be money plant – silver dollars," Stella said, as she and Mary did a walk-about admiring the garden.

"Father Byers asked if I'd bring some flowers in for the altar. Hope these grow into something that won't be an embarrassment."

"At the least, you'll have calendula. I see some of the lily of the valley has returned. Hard to get rid of it completely."

"Yes, it is," Mary said. "Every time I dig it up Liz gets sick. Odd isn't it?"

It seemed silly to say it out loud, but Mary knew that the two times she dug up the lily of the valley, bent on eradicating it from her garden, Liz had taken ill and almost died. It made no sense, but there it was, plain as day, to Mary anyway. For this year, Mary devised a new plan. There was a spot on the property, that Claude called the back forty – the perfect spot, Mary decided, to allow the lily of the valley free run. She would dig it out and eliminate it from the herb plot. The plant had again snaked its white fleshy roots throughout her garden plot and removing it would take days – even weeks. The johnny jump ups were full of the sharp pointed leaves of the Lily. The sage was holding its own for now, but Mary noticed green tips poking through that shouldn't be there. They couldn't be left or the sage would succumb. Lily must be removed.

Mary planned to work one section at a time, digging out the good plants, the sage, the borage, the johnny jump ups, and replanting them after she was sure not one single root of the pestilential lily of the valley remained. Edward, Mary and Claude. Borage, sage and johnny jump ups. Those were the ones who belonged. Lily of the valley was an intruder and this was her last summer in Mary's garden.

"How are your other people? In the garden?"

When Mary didn't answer, Stella continued. "Because I'm curious. How are we doing, Mary? Me and Arnie? In your garden?"

Mary's answer was slow and thoughtful. "It might be time to add onto my garden. Keeps me from fighting with the Mothers when I spend time out here – out of the house. Not fighting exactly, just nattering. But it keeps us away from each other when I'm busy out here."

"We've all got our troubles. You're not alone."

What troubles did Stella have? Her house brimmed full of children. Lovely children. Except of course, Nelson, but Stella seemed to be getting over his death just fine. It almost seemed to bring their family closer together, Mary thought. When she and Claude visited for supper or for tea the house felt comfortable. Stella always seemed happy and content. She rarely ever mentioned Nelson. And Arnie was so easy going.

Stella laughed. "Is the biddy Liz trying to push us out of the garden too?"

"You guys are safe. For now." Mary disliked how foolish the conversation sounded. Still. Why did the lily of the valley not bother the bee balm, or the walking onion? Just coincidence? Maybe.

"I like being a bee balm. I looked it up – Monarda Didyma. Refreshing. Tall. Easy care. A nice showy herb and a change from the everyday tastes of oregano, sage or parsley. A little sweetness for the palate. Beebalm is …"

"I'm familiar with beebalm. It's what the natives used to make Oswego tea," Mary said. She considered Stella's words. Is there a message here? A warning? Is she teasing me? Mary wished sometimes for another friend to talk to, but there was no one. Who else could understand anyway? Just Edward.

"Monarda's a strong grower," Stella said.

"Can be." Mary clenched her hands. "In the right conditions."

"It's a plant to be reckoned with, but well worth the time it takes to cultivate. The garden needs colour and verve. Excitement. Beebalm's got that for sure. And the deep red colour looks good against the purple johny jump ups."

"Last night," Mary said. "I was reading about sweet woodruff. That's a lovely plant." Could be Arnie. "Useful to treat earache and diarrhoea. I'll be on the lookout for some." 'Be cheerful and rejoice in life,' she'd read from the Herbal. Sweet woodruff. That was Arnie. Light hearted. Undemanding. Helpful. Fun. But he is already a walking onion. Why now does he want to be a sweet woodruff? And parsley would be perfect as Stella. But she's already beebalm. Are the plants thinking for themselves?

"This is a wonderful mature sage plant." Stella was bent over, rubbing its leaves, sending the scent of poultry dressing over to Mary.

"Sage. That's me," Mary said. "How do I look?"

"You could take a cutting from the old girl and start a new plant. Give her a make-over," Stella laughed.

"That's exactly what she needs." Mary reached to touched her long straggly sun-streaked hair that she'd tied into a ponytail before stepping outside. "Any baby plants growing?"

Stella found a small one rooted near the older thick woody stem. They cleared an area of all the plants and roots above and below ground, and started the fresh, green sage plant there.

"She'll look sick for a week or so. I must be sure to give her a drink every day and she'll take off. Sage is a good hardy plant. Anyway, I'll leave her parent plant here until we're sure the new one is rooted."

With Stella's help, over the following weeks, Mary was able to get the garden cleared of the troublesome lily of the valley. They dug up the boxwood shrubs growing as an outline along the edges of the garden and they pulled out every piece of the intrusive lily of the valley before replanting the boxwoods.

Stella argued against transplanting the lily of the valley roots to the back forty, but Mary insisted and they trundled the wheelbarrow back to the fence line where they planted them in the rocky soil.

Stella said, "We don't need to water these weedy things. They'll grow anywhere. Anyway it's going to rain."

Sweaty and tired from their hours of labour, the two women retired to Liz's kitchen, bringing borage leaves and flowers to add to their drinks.

"Fruits of our labour," Mary sipped her drink gratefully. "A make-over," she said. "We did it to the sage. I might need a make-over. Got any suggestions?"

Stella's knowing look caused Mary to blush. "Things getting boring in the bedroom? Two herb gardeners like us ought to be able to spice things up a bit. Let's see, variety. That's what we need, something different – out of the ordinary, so Claude thinks he's got a new woman." She grinned and whispered. "We could just make a switch, you know?"

Mary shook her head. "A switch?"

"Once they've gone to bed, you and I could exchange beds for the night."

"You and I ...?" Mary shook her head again. "You and I ..." Mary felt a little tremor, saw Stella grinning – finally caught her meaning. "Exchange husbands, you mean? Stella!"

"What were you thinking?" Stella raised her eyebrows. "Mary!"

Mary imagined Stella slipping into bed beside Claude. He'd roll over, let his long warm body rest beside hers a minute, after which he'd probably roll back over and go to sleep. She imagined herself entering Stella's room. Lying beside Arnie. Imagined his body asleep beside hers ... awakening ...

"Claude likely wouldn't even wake up," Mary said.

"I could make sure he woke up." Stella said. "And we'd see what would happen after the awakening."

Mary couldn't answer. Was she serious? She processed shadowy images of her bedroom, with a candle glowing on the night table. Its flame flickered against two bodies exploring warm skin; a knee slid from knee to inner thigh, resting there while hands journeyed over bodies freed from cumbersome clothing.

Mary couldn't stop the blush that coloured her face or the warmth that surged intimately through her.

"Arnie might enjoy a stranger visiting him in the night." Stella chuckled. "They wouldn't know what hit them. Neither of them."

"They would kill us," Mary said. "Or something."

"Probably or something first, before they kill us," Stella said. Her cheeks were flushed.

Mary didn't know how to imagine herself in bed with Arnie. Didn't trust herself to allow that thought in, knew it was too late. The thought was planted. Oh Stella. What have you started?

"Here, let me help you do your hair up on top of your head," Stella said. "Since you've finally got it to a length you can put it up, why not take advantage? When Claude gets in the mood, he can let it down. Men like to do that. At least Arnie does. And we'd better quit this talk of switching husbands. Too dangerous." She smiled.

"Yes. We mustn't think such thoughts."


With Liz remaining bedridden, Sadie read to her in the evenings until both were tired allowing Mary and Claude time on the porch together without the Mothers. Again Mary's legs found their way onto Claude's knees where he massaged her feet, worked his hand up one leg to her knee, then up the other. He moved his chair closer, and brought his head to hers.

"This is nice," she said.

"Reminds me of the old days," Claude said. "Remember when we were first christening the little house on Water Street?"

His memory stirred under her foot.

Claude reached for her chin and drew her toward him. They kissed, his fingers large and warm on her bare neck. "Mmmm," he breathed, and let his fingers wander her face, outline her ear. He patted her hair where Stella had pulled it tightly away from her neck, caressed the unfamiliar bareness and followed it up to the loose bun perched on top of her head. She imagined Arnie and Stella sitting on their porch, Arnie's fingers discovering in Stella's ears the tiny earrings borrowed from Mary, and his fingers traveling along Stella's neck to loosen her hair.

Mary didn't stop the smile from reaching her lips when Claude brought his hands to her face. He pulled back. "What's funny, Mary?"

"Not funny. Just nice," she answered. "You like my hair pulled up like this?" She directed his hands to her legs and he walked his fingers from her knees to her feet, where he kneaded and massaged each toe in turn.

"It is nice out here alone," Mary said, pushing away the thought of his mother lying in bed, sick, withered, listening for their voices. She put her hand over his, stroked the bristly hair on his fingers. Wanting to make love with Claude was more memory than reality.

Don't think so much.

She relaxed against him. Let her muscles mould into his chest, nuzzled her hair along his neck.

"Feels good," Claude whispered. "Good."

"Mmmmm." She slipped her hand under his shirt remembering ... other times. Her fingers found his waist, walked his ribs one by one ... so warm ... so familiar ... their breath mingled ... kisses wet ... warm ... too wet ... Mary turned her face away, made herself stay close to him. She moved her fingers inside his shirt ... too wet and warm ... she blocked the picture of Edward lying wet and cold, on the ground, Claude over top of him, breathing into his mouth, breathing wet warm kisses of life past frozen wet lips ... Oh God, not now. She pushed the image away and kept her hands light, roaming, as Claude sighed into her hair, his breath warm against her neck. She held herself still as he touched familiar places. She made herself react in the proper manner ... a sigh ... a thrust ... stroking ... moving ... felt tears slide from her eyes, knew Claude was carried on his own momentum, could continue without her involvement, using her body, leaving her mind, her heart, to wander in the past that remained present always.

"Oh, Mary. Mary." Claude stroked her hair. She looked into his face, once so dear, now the catalyst of memories that tugged at her heart, that kept her son near, even as they reminded her of how far away he stayed.

"Mary." Claude cupped her knee in his hand, and continued up her leg. "You want to see my workshop?" he asked, his hopeful grin a reminder of the years-old expression from their newly married days. She'd found him so beautiful in those days. The workshop. How she'd tingled to that suggestion, been so open to him.

Mary forced her thoughts back to the porch. She needed the warmth and the comfort of Claude. Father slipped into her memory. "Reality is where we must live our lives, girl. It's too easy to get caught up, to let the mind go traipsing down imaginary paths. It's easy to get lost, to get confused, to think of dreams as reality." She pulled herself away from her father's voice. It was her and Claude, here, on the porch. Now. Tonight. Making love with Claude had always been special. Wonderful. Claude, the man she loved, was here. Now. And even better: the Mothers were not here.

"Your workshop," Mary murmured. "It's so long since I've heard an offer like that." She felt Claude's comfortable, familiar arm resting on her shoulders, rubbing, while his other hand fondled her knee. She smiled against his neck, made sure he felt her lips curve. Couldn't kiss his mouth right yet, she knew that, but she let the pressure of her socked foot answer for her. "A visit to your workshop. Mmm. That'd be fine."

He stood, pulled her up with him, held her hand, desire in his gentle touches. He was her Claude still. They were whole still; she could walk beside him in sock feet that remembered dancing and joy, and she hoped that would be enough because it was all she could salvage just now.

# Chapter 19

**"Giants often trip and fall, but worms don't because they dig and crawl." Lessons learned in the garden.**

The wide row of seeds that Mary planted beside the herb garden produced brilliant colours – oranges, yellows with great dark centers, and pure white daisies as well as red poppies and blue larkspur, pink cosmos and orange calendula. She cut a basket full and brought them into the kitchen. The memory of last night's lovemaking, fresh on her skin, paused her hands as she trimmed the stems then plunged them into an inch of just-boiled water to force them to stay open and to suck water into the stem. Right away she added cool water to the glass and keeping the cut ends under water filled a vase with the flowers' vibrant beauty.

"They look good, Mary," Sadie said. "You have any extras to bring to the church for the altar?"

Mary nodded. "Yes. Of course. There's plenty where these came from." She took the empty basket from the table and slipping her scissors into her apron pocket she returned to the row of flowers to cut a supply for the altar.

She arrived at the church with her contribution just as Father Byers waved goodbye to the last of the dedicated ladies who attended early morning Mass.

"Mary Johnston. Come in to the vestry with your welcome load." He held the door, and she stepped ahead of him into a room scented with candle wax and lemon furniture polish. A long clean countertop ran from wall to wall at one end of the room with cupboards underneath it. Half of the opposite wall was lined with chairs and the other half was taken up with an arched doorway wide enough to accommodate three full-grown men side by side.

The other two walls were full-length closets, filled with vestments for the different religious feast days. A self-supporting full-length mirror stood in one corner near the door.

Father Byers opened a cupboard door under the counter and squatted in front of it, rummaging among vases of various sizes and colours.

"You want a big one, Mary?" Father Byers' muffled voice found its way out of the cupboard. She put her basket down and squatted beside him, recognizing some of the vases she often admired from the Johnston pew in the center of the church during Mass.

Now here she was, Mary Johnston, posing as a flower arranger in God's house. 'How dare you presume to be worthy?' the small voice in her head asked. 'You don't pray. Not really. It's all pretence. You don't even know how. Why are you here when so many of the other parishioners' flowers are more beautiful than yours?'

"Probably white would show off the colours best, do you think?" Father Byers held out a round, thick, milk-glass bowl with a frog insert and rummaged again, coming up with the bowl's identical mate and frog. "What about it, Mary? These will look splendid, one on either side of the altar."

Father Byers stood and Mary followed him through the huge arched doorway into the familiar church, and they stood in the house of worship discussing the height of the arrangements, and their distance from the altar as if this was an everyday occurrence.

"Breathe," Mary reminded herself, as she looked out into the church at the pew where she and Claude, and the Mothers sat each Sunday morning at ten-thirty Mass. There was the pew Jacob and Amy sat in – the Murphy family pew. Sometimes Mother went there automatically – years of habit, Mary supposed – and she'd keep an eye on her during Mass, recognizing her lapse of memory. This was the church where she and Claude were wed. They had buried Mary's father from here. And here Edward came for his last journey.

"These colours will show up well against the altar cloth. It is white for the next four weeks," Father Byers explained. He led her back into the vestry. "Anything I've forgotten? There's water." He pointed to the sink. "Scissors." He opened a drawer.

"Just pull the door shut behind you when you leave. We never lock it. Thank you for bringing your flowers, Mary. The Lord notices and appreciates every gesture large and small." Father Byers gave Mary one last smile and left her to arrange her flowers in solitude.


At church on Sunday, the congregation sat in their pews waiting for Mass to begin. Mary's attention was drawn to the altar, and the flowers, and from there to the doors at the left side of the altar. Through the carved ornamentation in the doors, she could see shadows moving past on the other side and imagined Father Byers and the altar boys preparing for Mass. She was quite sure that it was a confessable sin to think about holy men dressing, and she turned toward Claude to distract herself.

He sat, staring straight ahead with his hands resting on his knees. Those huge hands that could shape a piece of hot iron into a horseshoe as easily as they could pull a hairpin from the bun atop her head.

Mary turned slightly to catch sight of Stella and Arnie sitting in their regular pew across the aisle. The children fidgeted. Arnie stared straight ahead. As Mary watched, he brought his hand to his face and smoothed the eyebrow over his left eye. His fingers were long and clean; his skin weathered. Mary thought it might be soft. He wore gloves when he worked, training the Clydesdales. Mary sensed Stella watching her. Their eyes met, and Stella raised her brow. Mary blushed; wished she hadn't; Stella winked.

"Aren't those your flowers?" Stella asked, after church was let out. "They're lovely." She and Mary waited until the church was empty before they climbed the altar steps to check the water in the vases. Father Byers followed them, his ankle-length sutane swishing as he walked.

"I've been receiving accolades for the beautiful flowers." He squeezed Mary's hand as he spoke. "Do they need water? I topped up the container last night."

"Mm. No, they're fine." His hand was soft and warm on Mary's – a hand not used to hard work. She thought her hand next to his must feel like tree bark against his skin. Still he held on, willing her to raise her eyes to his.

"Mary, I wonder. Would you consider visiting two of the parishioners? It's not for housework. I want you to know that right off. It's for company. Emerelda is eighty-two, and she'd benefit if you could stop in, say once a week and read to her for an hour or so. The other is Robbie McDonald, whom you have likely met from working at Fynch's. He likes to do crossword puzzles, but his eyesight is failing and he has difficulty reading the clues. I know you're busy, Mary, but it occurred to me that you have experience with the elderly, and I could sure use the help."

If you could draw kindness, Mary thought Father Byers' face would be the model. Maybe it would be good to get away from the Mothers for a few more hours a week. But this visiting plan smells. Was it cooked up by Claude and Father Byers to give me something new to think about? Appealing – yes. But .... When had he and Claude spoken? And what exactly was the planned outcome?

Mary and Stella followed Father Byers to the vestry where he wrote out the two names for Mary and drew a simple map of the locations of the two houses she was to visit. "I'll be seeing them this week, Mary, if you'd like to come with me for a first visit?"

She nodded. It would be best to have a formal introduction.

"And, perhaps, I could visit with Mrs. Johnston. What do you think? How would she take to having the priest make a regular call to see her while her daughter-in-law is off on church business?"

So that's the reason. Did Claude put him up to this? She looked at Stella to see her reaction. Stella was nodding her head at Mary and Father Byers.

"My mother is living with us too. Sadie Murphy," Mary said. "The last person to visit from the church was Mrs. Perkins who came to welcome Mother when she first moved in with Claude and Liz and I. I think the Mothers will be very pleased to see you."

Mary knew the Mothers would insist that the house be cleaned, and that Liz would need Mary's help to bathe and to dress. She would expect Mary to wash and set her hair too. Extra work. But it will get me out of the house – a legitimate excuse. When did it begin, this need to justify the usefulness of how I spend my day?

"Let's try it, shall we?" Father Byers asked.

Mary nodded. "Yes, of course."


When Mary moved into Sunny Acres forty-five years later, she saw her long-gone friends Emerelda and Robbie McD. in the various faces she came to know. Mary would be drawn back to Emerelda's vinegar-scented kitchen, and the hours she'd spent there reading aloud from the weekly newspaper and describing the black and white photographs it contained. She had read to Emerelda accounts of the local boys enlisted in the Canadian army and posted as peacekeepers in Cyprus. It was dangerous over there, Mary and Emerelda decided, reading between the lines of the veiled comments of those who returned from missions involving the Turks and the Greeks. Mary supposed she should be thankful that she'd never see her Edward in a soldier's uniform heading off on a mission; the thought of him waving good bye made her cry.

Reading a sports story from the paper for Emerelda, Mary imagined Edward wearing the team colours, saw him scoring the winning goal, speeding down the ice, the home-town hero. He could have been an altar boy, or sung in the church choir, or taken the trophy at the county spelling bee. So many opportunities stolen.

It was healthy for me to visit Emerelda and to get some time away from home. Away from the Mothers and from Claude, Mary thought.

And I got to know Arnie better when we were driving together into town, alone. It was our boys who brought us together, and Stella, and the priest and Claude. While Claude didn't mind her taking the car to town to work at the Apothecary or visit the shut-ins, why not share a ride with Arnie? It made perfect sense, in fact it was Stella who suggested that Arnie drive Mary to Robbie McD.'s every second Monday, since he drove right by the door on his way to work with the horses. When she was done there, she would walk to Emerelda's home to have lunch with her, then read or sit in the garden or on the porch and play Scrabble, until Arnie was done work and would pick her up on his way home.

Mary and Arnie talked of their dead sons as they journeyed through the town.

"Stella doesn't hardly ever talk about Nelson," Arnie said. "Does she talk to you about him? About our sons?"

"No. Never. We rarely mention the boys. Not Stella and I. Not Claude and I either. But I think about Edward all the time."

"I wish you'd talk to me about them, Mary. I need to remember."

Mary had kept Edward with her, in the garden, and in her mind every day in the years since he'd died. She told Arnie how each morning she thought of what Edward would look like now and would he be starting school and would he be an altar boy or going off fishing with his friend Nelson. What sports would he play?

"It's like I've got my boy back, Mary. Thanks to you," Arnie said. They'd been driving together since the spring. "It's such a relief to talk about him. I wish … It's as if the rest of them have forgotten."

"I tell myself that it's too painful for Claude to dwell on thoughts of losing Edward. That's why he doesn't want to talk about him, I think. He can't because he blames himself. But I haven't lost him. He's here, right here with me every minute, every day. I talk to him and it is just how it should be. I'm so glad you understand. That we feel the same way, you and I. And I'm sorry that Claude and Stella don't keep the memory alive. Such a shame. The memories are my comfort."

Arnie jumped down from the wagon to help her on and off; he held her elbow; he patted her hand or brushed her arm to make a point as they talked. Their time together was short; it seemed he no sooner helped her onto the wagon than he was handing her off and promising to see her soon at the end of his workday. And hers.

Often, when he'd drop Mary back at the farm they'd find Stella there snipping herbs from the garden for supper and some lettuce or flowers for the table and in the house Mary might find a small bouquet on her table from Stella. There would be tea cups washed and set in the dish drainer to dry. Maybe the mothers had made tea for Father Byers, Mary told herself. Of course, that was why there were tea cups used when she was away.

It wasn't a complete surprise when Arnie began talking of him and Mary as  a couple. And yet … that couldn't be. It wasn't right. They were both married to other people. "You and I are meant to be together. We always have been. Your Claude's too busy shoeing horses to even look at you," Arnie said. "Otherwise you'd have a dozen children milling about your skirts. You're not happy at home or you'd be there instead of making sick calls on the folk in town while my wife fusses in your garden."

"Arnie," Mary said. "Maybe I've given you a wrong impression."

"A wrong impression. Well." He paused, looked off into the distance. "I'm honoured to be giving you a lift on this hot, still day. Here, have a drink of water." Arnie twisted off the lid and handed her his thermos.

Parched, after two hours of reading to Emerelda, Mary lifted the thermos to her lips and drank. Had she led him astray? Had Stella disclosed any confidences? Thirst slaked, she handed him the thermos, pulling her hand away from his when their skin touched.

He grinned at her, his eyes full of laughter. "Don't worry. I've no plans to force you into anything. I'm going right by your place on my way home, as usual, and I'm glad to give a neighbour a lift. Just offering you a drive." He raised his palms in submission. "And some food for thought." He grinned at her with raised eyebrows.

She gestured to him that he should drive, and with a slap of the reins they were on their way.

Arnie entertained her with a long story of how his laying hens increased their egg production by changes he orchestrated to the hours of daylight they received, and Mary was glad to sit and listen and laugh with no need of conversation from her.

People would talk. Were probably already talking.

Slippery slope. Well. What of it? What just happened here? Nothing exactly. Exactly nothing … and yet …

Mary leaned against the seat, tested its strength, felt her feet flat on the wagon's floor, heard Arnie's words, and his silences. Arnie reached to pat her hand. The horses hooves drummed as they travelled; the sun threw prism reflections from Emma Jean's windows. Mrs. Sketcher waved from the street; Mary waved back. A child's muffled voice reached Mary's ear, and a robin watched them drive past his nest in the red maple in front of Fynch's. I work tomorrow. At nine. Until noon. He said, I want to be with you. Really? In what way? She looked at Arnie, at his hands and his face. Oh dear Arnie. My leprechaun. My walking onion. A slippery slope.

In the driveway Arnie got down from the wagon to help her off. "You're a fine woman, Mary. I'd be pleased if you'd consider my offer of companionship when convenient. We could work out the details as we go along. I've thought more on this idea than you as we've been driving. I see it's a new consideration for you, so I'm just asking you to not say no until you've pondered it awhile." He inclined his head at her, shyly, before he leapt onto the wagon and clip-clopped away, before she could think of what to say.

But she knew, that had he moved in to kiss her, she'd have let him. In her own driveway! Mary laughed out loud. Preposterous!

Now, at Sunny Acres, the thought of Arnie Jenkins' gentle ways made Mary smile, as they had when they'd first tilted her world. He'd made a point of being convenient when Mary needed a ride, or a drink, or quiet understanding, and gradually their friendship had deepened.

Always thoughtful, Arnie's way with a story kept Mary laughing at his tales.

"Mary, you'd never believe so much foolishness would come to one simple man," he started as they drove past the cemetery. "I heard the shutter knocking against the house when I was just getting ready for bed."

Mary felt her lips curve wryly. Got caught naked outside, she thought.

"So I grabbed the first shirt I could feel there in the dark. Stella had been in bed for a while already. Out I went in my shorts and shirt with a couple of nails and a hammer.

"Got the shutter stopped banging anyways. But I don't know if Stella believed me.

"You'll have to see if she mentions it to you – me wearing her clothes. Wouldn't have been so bad, I suppose, except I'd lathered her face-cream all over me to keep the mosquitoes away. I thought it was bug repellent. She said she'll be watching me closely from now on."

Mary thought her life boring and ordinary, it being concerned with the mundanities of housework, the Apothecary, gardening, and visiting sick parishioners, but Arnie's reactions convinced her otherwise. He liked to hear about Mr. McD's crossword puzzles. "Maybe that's what I'll do when I'm retired and get some spare time. Do the crosswords. There's worse ways to spend a day."

Mary thought of Emerelda stroking her cat and listening while Mary read to her. It was both pleasant and peaceful to consider.

"Especially if the priest sends me a beautiful woman such as yourself to read to me. I might even pretend to be slightly blind." Arnie grinned.

When did Claude stop saying such things?

"Is that a new sweater, Mary?" Arnie asked.

"Oh. Yes."

"It's nice. Sky blue would you call it?"

She fingered the buttons. Claude's only comment had been that his mother said that colour of blue was more suitable knit into a sweater for a newborn baby boy. "There are so many blues and they're all my favourites," Mary said now to Arnie. "It was difficult to choose just one."

"How long does it take to make something like that?"

"I don't exactly know in terms of hours but it was most nights in the winter when the light wasn't good enough for reading. Mother helped me to decipher the pattern."

"Your mother is a dear soul. Claude's ... well. That is a woman I couldn't live with. I admire how well you manage."

"She has some good days," Mary said.

"I'm sure. We all do. Why doesn't Claude put her in her place? It's too bad ..." Arnie busied himself with the reins.

"What's too bad, Arnie?"

"I shouldn't say."

"Too late now, isn't it?"

"Claude's letting her have too much say, if you ask me. And you didn't. It's not my business."

"Oh, Arnie. You know you're right. I've tried telling him that. She had her marriage and raised her family. I know we're living in her home and that gives her some say, but it's like her and Claude are the parents and I'm their daughter."

Arnie shook his head. "An incorrigible one I hope? Badly behaved?"

"I do my best but you can imagine I'd much rather ... ."

"I'm sure," Arnie said. "We'd all rather." He took her hand in his.

Claude didn't mention her renewed friendship with Arnie, and Mary placated her conscience that there was no harm in her unrequited fantasies.

Even Stella in her own way encouraged her.

"A little fantasy never hurt a marriage," Stella advised.

"Sometimes I think about being with another man," Mary worried to her neighbour.

"So long as you don't act on it," Stella said. "Didn't Claude like your hair pinned up on top of your head?"

"Oh sure," Mary admitted. "I didn't mind it either. I pretended I was someone else. A foreigner in town for the day. And Claude was a knight on a white horse."

They giggled. "Good imagination." Stella said. "Once I pretended I was the school teacher and Arnie was one of my students."

"Stella! A schoolboy?"

"He was a senior student," Stella explained. "And he needed extra help with his lessons." She rubbed her hands together and grinned.

The next time Arnie picked her up in the wagon, Mary noted his gawky boyishness and blushed when she thought of Arnie and Stella together, playing teacher and student.

And she told Arnie it would be best if Claude drove her home after her parish visits from now on.

"Sure, Mary, but I'll miss our conversations."

At dinner that night, Mary asked Claude if he could pick her up the next day when she was done reading to Emerelda.

"Arnie busy tomorrow?" he asked, his cheeks flushed.

"I thought it would be nice if you'd pick me up from now on. I hope you don't mind? It's the same afternoons that Father Byers is here, so you can get away without having to leave the Mothers alone. It'll give us a chance for some time together."

"I suppose. What time should I be there?"

"If it's too much of an imposition I can drive myself." Maybe she'd made a mistake. Was it too late for them?

Mrs. Murphy dropped her spoon into her fruit cup. "I'm here! You two talk about me as if I'm invisible."

Mary rolled her eyes at Claude across the table. "I'm sorry, Mother. You're right, I wasn't thinking." She rose and came around to give her mom a hug.

Mr. Fynch and Mary had recently discussed new research that suggested the elderly needed more physical contact as their faculties deteriorated. Mary explained that hugging and touching were more in her father's realm than her mother's, even though Father's ways had seemed gruff. He'd been the one, Mary remembered, who patted her shoulders and stroked her hair. Things change.

She'd taken Mr. Fynch's advice and found Mother accepted her hugs readily, even contrived opportunities for Mary to lay hands on her. Combing Mother's hair, smoothing cream on her legs and arms and face, Mary felt like a mother herself. Again.

As Sadie's aging body became more like a helpless infant's, beneath Mary's soft touch, memories of Edward's baby years flooded through her. Mother's limbs became Edward's as Mary stroked, lifted, and loved her mother-child, laid their cheeks together, kissed her pale white skin.

Mother was so much easier to manage now that she was less independent and not trying to take over Mary's house or her marriage. She accepted what was offered and appreciated it with plentiful smiles and thank yous. Mary's time at home was measured by Mother's needs; massages were part of the daily routine as were teas and snacks. She lived around Mother's schedule, stayed up late reading to her. Father Byer's visits seemed to have worked a minor miracle on Sadie, rounding her coarse edges. Her voice softened, yet still she retained her watchful habit and Mary sensed that Mother knew more than she said. As always.

Had Mother observed how things had developed with Arnie? Mary thought it was good she'd asked Claude to start driving her. No use encouraging Arnie thinking down the wrong track. Or herself. There were always rumours flying around the country of marriages on the rocks because of wandering eyes. The memory of Mrs. Sketcher waving from her yard made Mary glad she'd chosen the higher path. Arnie and Stella were their best friends. Best friends were hard to replace and not to be taken for granted.

Claude spent his time from daybreak until dusk, in the shop forming metal into farm tools and household items. Ten to forty people might stop at his bench in a day so he knew most of the goings-on in the neighbourhood, and it would have been just a matter of time before a hint from a helpful customer caused old jealousies to surface. He enjoyed sharing the bits of news he garnered with Mary and the Mothers over supper.

Mary noticed Claude worked his father and the days of his youth into his conversation more frequently these days. Especially in the garden, Father's memory was often dredged up. Mary liked the solitude of her garden, liked to let nature's restfulness wash over her there, but when Claude came to spend time with her, the quiet was broken. "Father always said a weed should be pulled as soon as you see it, not to wait for weeding day," Claude would say bending to pull a huge dandelion from the pathway between the borage and the johnny jump ups.

Mary rose from the bench where she'd come after lunch for a five-minute nap that had turned into a half-hour reverie. "Gardens are for enjoyment too," she said. The buzzing bumblebees and colourful flowers were a diversion from Mother's diapers and from gardening tasks.

"The seventh day is for rest," Claude said.

"What does that mean?" Mary asked, still drowsy from the heat of the noon sun.

Claude stooped to pull another dandelion. "I'll help you weed," he said. His glance around the garden took in the grasses creeping over the edges and purslane that inched out into the pathways. Though all the agricultural papers and magazines called purslane a weed, Mary saw its red stems as a pleasant contrast to the overall green in the garden and she let it meander where it did no harm.

"Weeds get quickly out of control," Claude said.

Mary surveyed the garden she'd so recently admired and praised herself for, observing it through Claude's eyes now. There were cosmos in need of deadheading; the twitch grass should be dug out; the uneven edges needed freshening. It seemed slovenly, untended, unkempt. How had that happened? The blue of the borage was still heavenly but some of the plants had toppled and needed staking.

The boxwood hedge needs trimmed. Purslane is a weed.

Claude reached to pull out a borage plant leaning across the path.

"Don't you pull that! Here. Let me." Mary leaped to rescue the innocent plant. "I'll prop him against a stick."

Claude's face whitened. "It's a weed, Mary. A weed." Still, he stepped back and watched without argument as she leaned the borage against a twig. "I'm thinking, Mary. Maybe you need some help keeping the garden in order."


Mary spent Friday morning arranging her flowers for the altar, then walked across the field to deliver them. She stopped in to Amy's kitchen for a cup of tea, surprised at how quickly the morning had passed. Arnie drove by as she and Amy said their good-byes, and she accepted his offer of a lift home. As they neared Mary could see three mounds of greenery piled outside the boxwood hedge of her herb garden. She stood up in the wagon to see better, then jumped down without saying goodbye or thank you to Arnie and sprinted through the front yard to check on her plants. Tears pricked at her eyes, blurring the newly straight, neat lines of the paths.

"Where is my borage?" A pain-filled groan sprang from her soul as she stumbled through the garden from bed to bed. Her full and vibrant beebalm, reduced to half its previous size, stood, tidy and alone, the bare soil at its feet naked of all but the memory of Sweet Woodruff's shady cover. Sweet Woodruff huddled, clipped to fit into a six-inch square space.

"I'm sorry. I'm so sorry." Mary wept, repeating her apology to flower, to hedge, caressing the plants as her tears landed on their leaves. "Who has done this to you?"

The sage plant that she and Stella rooted in the spring had been pruned back hard, leaving just three short shoots. The old sage that she'd left to nurse the young one, was gone, separated and removed from its sucker.

The absence of johnny jump ups' cheerful deep purple and lilac faces struck a blow to her lower abdomen. Her stomach clenched in pain so she could hardly breathe. On weak legs she stumbled to the bench where she slumped, shaken, and afraid. How could the garden survive?

"Surprise!" Claude's pleasure was unmistakable through Mary's stunned perception. She removed his hands from her eyes, shrank away from his warm bulk standing behind her – aware of his complete unawareness of the travesty committed in her garden. She held his hands at her neck, stalling, while she worked to form an appropriate reaction.

How could he be so innocent of how important this garden was to her? Sobs broke through her attempt at control.

"Mary? Mary, what is it?" Claude came around in front of her, wiped her tears with his sleeve but fresh tears replaced them right away.

Mary couldn't stop, didn't care if she stopped. Her carefree, happy garden where she made all the decisions, where she communed with Edward and where her soul could bathe in beauty and hope, now was clipped and sorted, and weeded into a strict picture of a proper herb garden with not a weed or a stray plant in sight. Picture perfect. Damn the man. Or had it been Liz's idea?

"Mother and I thought you would appreciate some help to get your garden in order so I got Brenda to come in. She's home from Guelph for the summer. She said she can come every week for as long as you need her until school starts again. Don't you like it, Mary? Don't you like what she did?"

"I liked my garden. I liked my own place." Mary pushed him away, wishing she wouldn't, but not able to stop herself. "It's ruined. All my beautiful plants. It's awful."

Claude moved out of the garden and stood behind the box hedge, newly trimmed to knee height. "I'm sorry," he said. "I thought it was a good idea. I wish you wouldn't cry." He raised his hands and dropped them. Mary watched him leave, plod slowly, round-shouldered, to his workshop.

Mary sat on her bench aware of passing in and out of sleep as the sun moved overhead. The sweet grassy scent of the shortened Sweet Woodruff drifted into her breaths as the afternoon warmed. The sounds of the garden were as comforting as usual. A bee buzzed and nuzzled into tiny purple thyme flowers. A pale blue moth fluttered through the hairy leaves of the few borage plants left along the edge of the path. A hummingbird sipped from the red beebalm flowers. The beebalm would survive. As would the sage. Sage is a tough one. The plant to suffer the most was Johnny jump up, Claude's plant, though he knew not the significance of his removal. Or of the separation of the bee balm and the Sweet Woodruff. Arnie and Stella. Mary frowned to herself. It's imaginary, fanciful, not real, just a game. She tried to convince herself it wasn't important, but for so long she'd believed the plants' lives mirrored happenings in real life.

"He'll be back, in the fall for sure," Mary whispered, desperately looking for even one lone Johnny jump up. "He'll be back. Seeds will sprout, but what's to happen in the meantime?"

Tears squeezed from Mary's eyes and she let them run. She sat, knowing there was no one to whom she could turn. No one, not even Stella, understood how closely tied Mary felt to the life in this garden. All the plants depended on Mary's management of this chaos, this calamity. All is not lost. Mary knew she must tread carefully, must repair the damage to Claude's feelings. If only there was even one small johnny jump up somewhere. She searched the plot and found, hiding in the tall stalks of the newly trimmed bee balm plant, one purple-faced viola.

Relief had her on her knees touching its soft petals. The wee face of the flower peeked out at her from the thick surrounding stems. She must stop Brenda from coming back, must make it known that she, Mary, was the tender of the herb plot. The herb garden was her domain. This must be made clear to Claude, to Brenda, and to Liz. Mother understood. And she needed a plan to circumvent the damage done by the removal of the Johnny jump ups. If only there were a few more left growing.

# Chapter 20

**I know a cheery woman**

**And every time she calls**

**She leaves my carpet on the floor**

**My pictures on the walls.**

**She doesn't steal my silver**

**Or ask me for a loan**

**She doesn't use my fountain pen**

**She always brings her own.**

**But, show her in the garden**

**The treasures you have got**

**And if you turn your head away**

**She'll pinch the blooming lot!**

**Unknown**

Dread and foreboding coloured Mary's thoughts. She tried to convince herself that she imagined Claude building up his courage to talk to her. At breakfast he'd laid his fork down and opened his mouth three different times but no important words had spewed from him – not the ones she heard in her heart when she looked at his shuttered eyes and his folded arms.

As she read to Emerelda, Mary made mistakes, losing her place. He'd got so quiet. Why could he not just blurt it out? But, of course, that wasn't Claude's way.

Emerelda tugged on Mary's sleeve. "That's the third time, Mary. It's not a great book, is it?"

"Sorry," Mary apologized again.

"I see your husband's been picking you up these days."

Mary coloured. Even Emerelda noticed. She who was half-blind.

"The Mothers let him out of their clutches every so often."

"You still have both your mothers living with you?"

Mary nodded.

"Do you get any help?"

"There's just my brother Jacob who's on the home farm down the road. He's not much for helping." Emerelda waited for Mary to continue. "Mother's good-natured most of the time. But she's getting to be more and more of a handful with her arthritis and her sore joints. I try not to complain. She looked after me and my brother for a lot of years. And Claude's mother … is … a bit of a challenge. Always has been since her husband passed on."

Emerelda reached for Mary's hand. "I looked after my husband's mother. She lived twenty years longer than seemed useful. Such a waste. She was bored, lonely, and unhappy. I was tired. My husband, he couldn't do anything different. She needed to be looked after but …"

"That's the thing, isn't it? What else can we do?" Mary asked.

"Enjoy your health while you've got it," Emerelda instructed. "Take advantage of every minute you get alone with Claude. Nothing lasts forever. Not the good or the bad."

Emerelda patted Mary's hand. "There's Claude now. Way you go, dear. See you next day."

Claude grasped her hand tight as he helped her up into the wagon.

"Are things as serious as they look according to your face?" Mary asked.

"You have a way of reading me," Claude said. He was silent as he frowned at his hands for almost a full minute. "I need to be away awhile, Mary. To think. I feel like I don't belong here anymore."

"Why, Claude? Is it the garden? I promise you, I'll keep it weeded. I just need to do it myself."

"A little. The garden. Sadie. The Mothers. You're unhappy. I don't feel at home here anymore. I don't know what I'm doing. I've lost my purpose. I'm sorry, Mary." He stared straight ahead as he spoke, leaving no spaces for Mary to insert a word. "I know that you promised your father, in fact, I admire you for looking after Sadie the way you do. And Liz."

"You can't mean it, Claude. What are you saying? Where will you go?"

"I can get on with the corn harvest crew. They need another man. It'll be hard work and the long days will clear my head. I can save up some money. That might help - not to worry about money."

"We should talk it over," Mary said. "I deserve a say in this."

"I'm sorry, Mary. Tomorrow I'll go sign on. It's just a month."

"Would you talk to Father Byers first?"

"I need to do some thinking." Claude stared ahead. "All the plans we made, they've changed now. No children … no … " His upper teeth clamped his lower lip and held tight.

"Or talk to Arnie?"

Claude frowned hard. "Arnie is not the answer, Mary."

"You'll come back and we'll talk. We belong together."

A month away might make home look good. Maybe I could find more Johnny jump ups. Put Claude back into the garden. Bring him home to me. She ignored her heart telling her it was too late – that he was already gone.

Beside her, a muscle jumped in Claude's upper arm.

She could find a patch, transplant them. Stella often remarked at how the Johnny jump ups just never seemed to settle in reliably.

"Oh, Claude, what will I do without you for a whole month?" Mary asked, laying her hand on his leg.

He turned to her, determination in his unsmiling lips and his unreadable eyes. He was not prepared to back down. "I'll be gone for a month. At least a month. Depends on break downs and weather."

"When you get back, we should make plans to build on. We will make plans. Add another room along the back of the house like we've always meant to. We could get away by ourselves once in a while. The Mothers won't live forever."

"I keep thinking she might. They might," he answered. "They outlived Edward, why not you and I?"

"We can't spend our time trying to figure out who will die first. Maybe we'll all burn in a fire tomorrow night." Don't say things like that.

Mary thought of how she would fill the time when Claude was away. I could get the kitchen painted. Maybe Stella will come and help me. Or Arnie.

"We haven't been away together," Mary said. "Not for ever so long. The two of us should go away. Together. Get someone in to look after the Mothers." She looked at Claude. He hadn't said no yet. "Stella could keep an eye on things."

"Stella," Claude said in a voice Mary wasn't sure of.

Had they quarrelled? What would they have to quarrel about?

"I'm going to clear my head – to think," Claude said. "To figure out some changes. Maybe."

Mary didn't tell him there were no changes to be made. No choices. He'd work that out for himself. While he's gone I'll think up some jobs to keep him busy.

She kept her hand on his leg as he slapped the horses to start, and when they were well on their way, Claude covered her hand with his large, warm one. "I'm sorry, Mary. I know I'm not the easiest man to live with." Claude patted her hand.

Mary helped Claude pack a suitcase, with what she hoped was enough subdued meekness mixed with cheery optimistic comments concerning his return. "I'll ask Father Byers if there's any parishioners who could come in for a few mornings a week to look after Mother," she said. "It's crept up on us, on me, I guess. How much care she needs. So much more than before. She might be different with a stranger."

"Seems foolish, me going to Emerelda and Mr. McDonald, while asking for help with my own mother, but … "

Claude grunted.

Mary sniffed and smoothed the wrinkles from the green, checked, flannel shirt that Liz gave him last Christmas. He'd worn it just once since Christmas; Mary inhaled his scent as she held it against her cheek. She imagined she could feel his warmth, his solid chest, and she was unable to continue the casual chatter that she'd thought would ease his leaving. What if he doesn't come back?

That won't happen. But … Should I keep the shirt here? A memory held as insurance against his absence.

"Your mom gave you this shirt for Christmas," Mary said. "You should wear it. And tell her thanks."

Right after arriving home from church on Sunday morning, Claude set his suitcase in the hallway and turned to hug Mary. He held her, kissed her lightly on the lips, and set off walking down the road. He'd catch a ride with Clete and the others on the corn harvest crew. "I'll be back," he called.

Mary watched him walk away, keeping her hand up in the air in a motionless wave. When he was no longer visible, she turned to the house and stepped quickly along the front path, touching the box shrubs and the chrysanthemums that lolled voluptuously along its edges. She sat on the porch in the straight-backed chair that Claude constructed when they lived in their little house on Water Street and she wondered if she'd ever want to rise from that chair.

Arnie Jenkins pulled his wagon to a stop, leapt from his seat, and travelled the front path in three great strides. "You left church so quickly, we didn't get to ask if you and Claude would come for supper. Will you?"

Arnie looked fine in his white shirt, and pressed pants with matching vest. The white set off his tan and his deep blue eyes, that searched hers now with concern as he waited for her to speak.

"Mary!" Mrs. Murphy's frail voice called from the depths of the house, and Mary shrugged her shoulders at Arnie.

"I'll wait," he said, and he watched her walk into the house.

Mrs. Murphy was huddled on the floor, against the wall, almost under the bed. "Oh, Mary, I'm so muddle-headed. I can't get my stockings on, and now we'll be late for church."

"Don't worry, Mother." Mary stroked Sadie's white skin, which was chilly to touch. "How long have you been on the floor?"

"Not long. I had a little weak spell, so I've been resting here." Mrs. Murphy's grip on Mary's arm was anything but weak.

"I'll help you up," Mary said. "Can you raise yourself up to sit?"

Mrs. Murphy lay with her legs curled into her stomach. Mary could smell Mother's hair. How long since I washed it? My task for this afternoon.

"Put your arms around my neck, Mother. We'll both stand up slowly at the same time."

Mother seemed not to hear, but held on even tighter to Mary's arm, looking behind Mary. Mary felt his presence and smelled his cologne before he spoke.

"Good afternoon, Mrs. Murphy," Arnie said, loud enough that the sound penetrated through the old woman's failed hearing. "Have you hurt yourself at all?"

He gently felt her arms, one after the other, making sure that she could pull them out straight. He did the same with her legs, talking all the while, asking, "Can you feel this? Is it sore here?" until both her legs were straightened out; he helped her bend them again so she was sitting against the wall with her legs angled.

"I'll give you my arms and Mary will give you hers, and we'll get you up on those legs, Mrs. Murphy. Don't worry. You're in good, strong hands here."

Together, they up righted Mrs. Murphy, and walked her to the chair at the end of the bed. She dropped into it and sat gripping tight to the chair arms with her twisted fingers.

"I'll be alright here now," she told Mary. "You'd better go on to church without me. You and Claude."

Arnie tilted his head at Mary. "Church?" he mouthed.

"I'll bring you a cup of tea," Mary promised.

From the kitchen as she prepared a tray of tea, toast, and cheese, Mary heard Arnie's gentle voice raise in question and her mother's swift reply. "Mary is the only daughter I've ever needed, and as good a one as I could ever ask for."

What had Arnie asked? These days, praise for her daughter was Mother's oft repeated refrain to any conversation. Maybe he asked her about the weather; Mary laughed to herself.

She heard rummaging in the bedroom closet, and soon recognized the sound of Mother's slippers shuffling along the hallway accompanied by Arnie's heavier, hard-soled footsteps. "We're coming to have tea in the kitchen," Mother called in a happy voice.

Arnie's charm has found another lonely woman. Mary felt her heart soften. Tears threatened as she thought of Claude's grim face waving to her from the driveway. Mrs. Murphy held Arnie's arm as they walked, and she beamed at Mary.

"Mr. Jenkins says he can make some railing to put around my bedroom and down one side of the hallway. He'll do it right away. I asked him to come tomorrow."

Arnie nodded his agreement. "If that's what you want, Mrs. Johnston?"

"Call her Mary," Mrs. Murphy said. "Everyone does."

Mary answered Arnie's full-sized grin. "Yes, that's what they call me. You'll come tomorrow? I was going to ask Stella if she'd help me paint while Claude's away helping with the corn harvest.

"Away?" Arnie raised his eyebrows, but made no comment as Mary busied herself serving the tea. "I'll come as early as I can. Stella will come too."

He and Mary walked through the house, he with his measuring tape, and she with paper and pencil recording the measurements as he called them out.

"I've done this before," Arnie explained. "For my own parents when they ran into trouble getting around."

Sure that Mrs. Murphy was safely sipping tea in the kitchen and couldn't see them, he took Mary's hand in his and turned her to him. "I promised you never to force myself on you, Mary, but you've got my heart. I'm glad to worship you from afar, but the closer I can get, the happier I am. Can you…?" Arnie stopped. He turned back to his measuring tape. "I'm sorry, Mary. It's not a good time for you is it? I shouldn't be saying these things to you."

"Now for the sides of the toilet here," Arnie suggested, "I think a wooden frame would work for support." He showed Mary how she could help her mother step into the bathtub without concern for falling. "I'll make up a contraption so she can sit higher in the bath. It's hard on tired, worn bones to get up and down," he said.

They returned to the kitchen and found the plate in front of Mrs. Murphy cleared of every crumb of toast as well as all the cookies that Mary had laid out. "Sure nothing wrong with your appetite, is there, Mrs. Murphy? How about I pick you two ladies up in time for supper tonight?" Arnie asked. "And Liz? She'll come too?"

Mary nodded her agreement almost sure Mother was going to clap her hands in glee. "Liz will come too. She stayed behind at church to help set up for the noon tea. One of the ladies promised to drive her home after they've finished. Thank you for everything, Arnie," Mary said, as she walked him to the door. "I do appreciate your help." She smiled at him, hoping it showed her appreciation, but worried that she should comment on his earlier plea.

Her face felt warm as she searched for the right words to tell him. Maybe she'd consider … she couldn't say that … her face warmed even more.

Arnie laid his hand on her shoulder. "You'd do me a favour if you'd disregard what I said earlier." His apology seemed earnest. "I'm sorry for that. But we will need to talk, you and I, later, about why Claude has left you here alone with the Mothers. How long is he gone?"

"A month." Mary tried to smile. "He's away for a month, Arnie."

He left, turning at the walkway to remind her, "I'll be back about five o'clock."

As if I would forget.

"Sometimes a life seems to go on and on, doesn't it, Mary?" Mrs. Murphy agreed to Mary's suggestion of a sponge bath and to washing her hair. "You should be off with your husband making babies. Instead, you're stuck home with me. I'm sorry."

It must be my day for apologies. Mary briskly towelled Mother's wet hair. I'm sorry too, but a lot of good it does me. She thought she should feel cross at Claude's abandonment, but to the contrary it seemed as though a month of holidays stretched ahead. A lovely holiday, full of painting and gardening and looking after Mother and Liz. And less cooking and cleaning and laundering. Mary tried to overrule the tiny hope that Arnie would offer to resume driving her to her visits with Emerelda and Robbie McDonald. She knew she need only ask.

She blushed into the mirror. Will I give in to Arnie? Will I suggest a rendezvous late one evening after the Mothers are asleep? This is something I wish I could talk to Stella about. Lusting after your best friend's husband is not something, though, that can be comfortably discussed.

"I think that's enough scrubbing, Mary."

"Oops. Sorry, Mom."

Another apology.


"Will you give me a hand with the vegetables?" Stella asked, after she'd greeted her guests and hung their sweaters in the hall closet. "Arnie, maybe you could show Sadie and Liz the doilies that your mother made for us, while Mary and I get the last minute things ready for dinner?" She took Mary's arm and practically dragged her through the swinging door and into the kitchen.

"What's the story on Claude?" Stella asked, as soon as she and Mary were alone.

"He's gone with the corn harvest crew."

Stella waited with her hands on her hips.

"For a month."

"Did we not promise to tell each other the truth?"

"I don't exactly know the truth," Mary answered. "He said he'd be back in a month."

"Has he got the seven-year itch?" Stella wondered. "You don't know what's got Claude so out of sorts?"

"Maybe," Mary said, with a twinge of guilt, almost adding, 'I might have it too. And Arnie. Maybe it's an epidemic.' She giggled, thinking she sounded out of control as she heard herself. She took a deep breath and straightened her shoulders.

The door swung open into the kitchen, and Arnie entered. "Drinks?" He shrugged at Stella. "Can I offer you something?" he asked Mary. She giggled again and blushed.

"We'll have drinks with dinner," Stella said. "Tell the Mothers we're almost ready, and keep them busy. Mary and I are talking." She waved him out of the kitchen. "It's private."

"Just trying to be helpful." Arnie shrugged again and left the room empty-handed, leaving the door swinging back and forth in his wake.

"I think that's enough pickles, Mary." Stella patted her hand "We'll talk some more later. Claude will come back." Stella rolled her eyes. "Men," she said.

Mary nodded, not sure what to say, or if she might cry.


In the morning, Mary awoke earlier than usual, and spent extra time in the bathroom combing her hair and pinching her cheeks. She experimented with piling her shoulder-length, dark blonde hair on top of her head, securing it with bobby pins. What will Stella think? Does she suspect anything? Anyway, it is reasonable, and necessary, to have my hair up and out of the way for painting.

What kind of woman seduces her friend's husband? It's Arnie who has seduced me. So why don't I just tell him no? Claude will come back, and everything will be back to normal. But if Arnie and I start something, things will never be the same again.

Mary dabbed scented cream behind her ears and on her wrists. I'll stop it before it goes too far. Just a little flirtation, and that's all it can ever be. The neighbours will all be watching my every move, and there's Mother, and Stella, and Liz. Arnie knows that too. A harmless flirtation, she assured herself as she stepped out of the bathroom, biting her lips to bring on more depth of colour.

"Mary." Mother called from her bedroom. "Mr. Jenkins is coming today to put on my railing."

"That's right. Good thing you reminded me. I might have forgotten. I'll just go put the water on for tea, and I'll be right in to help you dress."

Nicely nonchalant, Mary. Her heart beat quicker than usual and she wondered how Arnie was feeling this morning. Will he hurry to get here before Stella or will the two of them come together? Are they sitting over coffee right now talking about me – the poor soul whose husband has left her in the lurch with two aging mothers to care for?

Mother sat on the bed waiting, when Mary got to her room. "With the railing, I won't be so nervous of falling," Mother said.

"No," Mary answered. That's why Arnie's coming over here. For Mother's sake, not to make love to me.

In the mirror, Mary observed her red cheeks and her hair piled proudly atop her head. Quite the get-up for a woman who plans to paint all day. Still, she was pleased that her faded blue shirt was the shade of blue that turned her eyes to smoking, smouldering weapons.

Arnie and Stella arrived together, their wagon loaded with railing Arnie had fashioned from scrap lumber.

"You and Claude ever plan to have more children?" Stella asked, once they were set up painting the kitchen.

"It's complicated," Mary said. "He's changed."

"And you haven't?" Stella asked.

As they painted Mary and Stella discussed how living with Liz and Sadie crimped Mary and Claude's marriage until Mary felt she was back living with her parents again. Liz Johnston guarded anxiously her role as parent and matriarch and mistress of the household, so that Mary felt herself being pushed out.

"Slowly and kindly," she explained to Stella. "But the woman is not giving in until she's got me and Claude both, totally under her thumb.

"It is strange to think like this. I know it, but it is as if an actual lily of the valley has taken up residence in the marriage. On the surface, Liz is so very helpful. Who could refuse her offer to do all the cooking?"

Stella murmured agreement.

"And she can be a charming woman. You'll rarely catch an unkind word cross her lips. She is intelligent and handy. She helps Claude with his bookkeeping and applies poultices to his chest when he gets that racking cough."

"She sounds like she's everything a wife should be," Stella said. "Well, almost … "

"Exactly," Mary said. "He doesn't need me around. In fact, I'm a bit of a second thought most of the time. And we hardly ever make love anymore."

"Mmmph. Sounds like Liz has planted herself right in the middle of you two. And with no intention of budging."

"You know it," Mary said. "I feel so ungrateful and guilty but it's like Liz's roots intrude into every area she can reach, under-mining plants that should be well established by now. It's like she's strangling us. Just like what happens in the herb garden. It's a bit scary, really."

"Lily of the valley is certainly one of those plants that takes over." Stella put her hands around Mary's throat gently. "Moving and writhing in the dark understory of the marriage like a den of albino snakes. Sounds like a bad movie." Stella shook her head. "A crazy and fantastic bad movie. That you can't stop watching."

"At first I was thinking it was Edward's death that caused the distance between us and truly, that is probably where we got off track. But it's gotten bigger than that."

"Go on," Stella said.

Recently, Mary explained, she was noticing all the problems that living with her mother-in-law wrought on the household.

"And of course there's my mum. She's a dear; she really is. I love her, but … it's too much. There's too many of us here. And there's one missing…"

"Edward," Stella said.

"You know how that is," Mary said, wondering if she was right to bring up Nelson, remembering Arnie's complaint of Stella's unwillingness to talk about the drownings.

Too late now.

"She is kind," Mary said. "But so forceful. So definite. She says things with a gentle, little smile, even a giggle. How could anyone refuse such a dear, kind lady anything?"

Stella drew a circle of paint onto the wall, slapped in two eyes, a nose and a mouth. "Take that!" She swiped the face with a brush full of paint. "And that!" More paint.

Mary laughed. "It amazes me at how close I came to reality with those plants in the garden. The lily of the valley has pushed the johnny jump ups right out of the garden. It's impossible, but it's happened. With some help from Brenda."

"Who's Brenda?"

"Claude hired Brenda Perry to do some weeding and she yanked out all the johnny jump ups that the lily of the valley hadn't smothered or choked."

"Oh he did tell me that," Stella said.

Mary nodded.

"And you're the sage? The wise woman?"

Again Mary nodded and snickered. "When lily of the valley threatened to overtake the sage, I dug myself up and moved to a safer place in the garden." She shook her head, thinking again of the parallels in her life and her garden. "And when the Mothers threaten to overrun my life, I do the same thing. She moved into the house, and I moved out to the garden. She started doing all the cooking, and I started volunteering at the church. She took over all my husband's spare time, and I...."

Mary stopped herself as Arnie's face came to her mind.

"Did you get yourself another fellow to replace your husband? Is that why Claude's gone off in a snit? I thought you were looking proud of yourself lately." Stella squinted her eyes.

Mary felt the colour rise in her cheeks.

"Why, Mary Johnston! I believe you've gotten yourself a beau!" Stella regarded Mary with a mixture of emotions moving over her face.

Was it awe? Envy? Worry?

"Does Claude know? Who is it, Mary? Anyone I know? What's he like? What about Claude?"

Another look Mary couldn't read crossed Stella's face.

"You're blushing," Stella whispered. "Don't worry. Your secret is safe with me. If Claude said he'd be back, he will be."

That's exactly what I'm worried about, Mary thought, as she returned Stella's hug. A picture of a lone johnny jump up peering out from behind bee balm stalks came to mind.

"It's not like that. I don't have a boyfriend, but I kind of wish I did. Claude's gone because of the Mothers. I think. Things aren't good between us right now," Mary said.

Stella frowned, concentrated on painting.

"Claude's gone away. To think. He says."

Stella didn't answer; she looked up to watch Mary think about her next words.

"I didn't know … I knew he wasn't happy, but I didn't know he needed to get away. And so quickly. He's gone on the corn harvest with Cletus and his crew."

"Sometimes working is the best medicine. Physical exhaustion, mindless work. It can be good therapy," Stella said.

"Mmm. Yes. I suppose. That's what Claude said too."

"Can you manage?"

"Of course. There is quite a lot to do here with the Mothers needing more care every day, but yes, I can manage. Thank God Arnie is putting in those railings. I won't have to watch Sadie so closely and I hope Liz will get into the habit of using the rail too. She's an independent one, that woman."

"I knew they were trouble. You can't get rid of them? No sisters who could take them? Even just for a little holiday?"

Mary shook her head. "There's nobody. Besides, I promised my dad and Claude promised too. Liz really has no other place to go."

"You've got to get a sitter. You and Claude have got to go away together. Arnie and I could come over here for a night. The kids could go to their friends; they're old enough; and you and Claude could have our house. It would be like a honeymoon."

Mary shook her head.

"I insist," Stella continued. "There's not many couples around our age. We need to help each other."

"Mary," Mrs. Murphy called, and Mary left Stella painting in the kitchen to answer the call. Mrs. Murphy and Arnie stood in the bedroom admiring the sturdy new railing. "Will we shellac it now, Mary?"

"I think it will be better if Stella and I paint it the same colour as the walls. It'll blend in better."

Mrs. Murphy used her cane to thump happily out of the room and down the hall to the kitchen to see the progress being made there.

Arnie and Mary eyed each other from their separate corners.

"This can't go any further," Mary whispered. "It's not right."

"I know." Arnie stepped toward her, his foot pushing the door shut as he pulled her to him. "It's not right that we can't be together. We'll talk about this later. When we're alone. Tonight." He held her chin so she was forced to look at him. "I'll come to your porch at midnight."

"No, Arnie. Don't come tonight."

"I'm coming. Just to talk. That's all. We need some time alone to figure something out."

He opened the door and explained that tomorrow he planned to nail more railing all the way down the hall. "Tell me where you want it in the kitchen. The more railing we put up, the easier it will be for Liz and Sadie to get around safely, and the less worry for you that she'll fall." He winked at Mary as they neared the kitchen.

"Tonight," he mouthed silently.

She shook her head. "No."

"Are you sure?"

She nodded slowly. "Not tonight."

Arnie and Stella left with the promise to return for more of the same tomorrow.

# Chapter 21

**Black-eyed Susan** – Rudbeckia hirta – One of the most loved wildflowers, golden-orange daisies, brown centres. The plant and root have both been used by North American native tribes to treat a wide range of ailments from worms in children to snakebites and earaches.

I once loved brown-eyed Susan

But my love for her is dead,

For I found a bachelor's button,

In brown-eyed Susan's bed!

**Bachelor's Button** – A clarifying flower. An aid in finding things that were previously hidden.


Mary closed her eyes, thankful for her exhaustion. In what seemed just short minutes of sleep, she heard knocking at the door, then Sadie's horrified call. "Mary, we've slept late! Arnie and Stella are here!" With plenty of laughter and teasing, tea and breakfast were soon underway and Arnie put himself to work attaching handrails along the hallway, just like yesterday.

Mary and Stella got themselves back to painting in the kitchen and talking about the Mothers again.

"I don't quite know how you stand it. Don't know how you stand either of the Mothers to be honest. Claude says ..." Stella paused in her painting.

"Edward's death ... made big changes. We haven't ... you know ... we haven't ... things haven't been the same in the bedroom since he died," Mary said.

Stella didn't answer.

"I'm not sure when it all changed. Having the Mothers living with us ... that's not great for sure, but it's not the whole problem."

"I've wondered about that. Claude mentioned once he felt ... well ... restrained." Stella gave a little smile.

"Claude talked to you about it? It must be bothering him more than I realized." Mary stepped back to admire her work. "This is a great colour. It's kind of ... buttery. I like the freshness of new paint."

"Good choice," Stella agreed. "Arnie's been wanting to paint our place. I'm not enthused, I must admit. Seems like too much effort. And here you are doing it and Claude not even here to help you."

"Claude's just not involved in the household anymore. His mother ... You know, Stella, I've got to tell you ... that woman is driving me nuts."

"You'll never be nuts, Mary."

"You know what I mean. She butts in to everything! I just want to kill her ... not really but you know. We can't move the fence because Claude Senior built it. We can't eat salmon because that was his favourite. I'm thinking .... It's been long enough now. And Claude never tells her to smarten up. Whatever Mother wants. I swear, Stella, some days the woman's life is in danger!"

"You're funny, Mary. You who are so correct and kind. I can't imagine you doing anyone in. I'd better be careful what I say to you anymore."

Mary grinned and waved her paint brush. "Do you think it's menopause or something hormonal?"

"No. I think it's your dang mother-in-law interfering in your marriage. And it sounds like Claude isn't being any help either."

"You know what's funny, in a not funny way, is that Amy and I went through this exact same discussion one time about her mother-in-law – my mother – and now Sadie is here living with us and she's no problem whatsoever. But Liz …"

"Mary. I've seen Sadie in action and the woman is a dear, but she can also be a great big pain in the ass. I know she's your mom."

"Yeah. You're right. They're both horrible. There. I said it."

"Feel better?"

"No. I don't. I don't think there's anything to be done about the whole mess. And now Claude's gone away and left me here in the middle of it all." Mary slapped paint at the wall. "The whole situation is awful. I wish I was the one who was gone to do the corn harvest."

"Oh Mary. I'm so sorry. Let's not talk about this. It's too hard on you." Stella patted Mary's shoulder.

"I need to. Now that we've started I really need to." Mary wiped her eyes with her hand wishing she wouldn't cry. It made her nose red, but it was too late to worry about that. More tears ran down her face.

"I've known for a while things haven't been right here."

"What do you mean?"

"Claude's let me know sometimes just in the things he says. Or doesn't say." Stella concentrated on stirring the paint.

"I haven't seen you over here too much. Guess I didn't really notice because I've been so busy trying to keep my own problems under control. Have you and Claude been talking things over?"

Stella nodded. "A few times."

Mary remained quiet, digesting this new information.

"You've talked about our home life? Our personal business?" She could feel her stomach rejecting her breakfast; she swallowed to keep it down. "What goes on here?" She swallowed again.

"We've been talking … a few … conversations. He's trying to … he's worried about all the time you and Arnie spend together."

"And you? Are you worried about me and Arnie?" Mary heard her voice rise. What was this really about? Did Stella and Claude know just how far Mary's mind travelled on that frightening road? Nothing had happened. But she knew that to deny would be to admit that she considered, maybe was still considering, doing what she so wanted to deny right now, right here.

She wished Arnie was here to stand beside her. To tell her what to say. And knew right then, that things had gone too far. They had both erred. And it was her fault for allowing it, encouraging it, not stopping it, before it got to this point. What now?

She let the tears roll down her cheeks without wiping at them. Knew they were going to flow until they were spent. Maybe she'd never stop crying. Would she lose her lifelong friend?

Mary kept painting; saw that Stella was doing the same. "We've been through so much together. Lost our sons together," Mary said.

"I know," Stella said. "We've been friends and neighbours almost all our lives, you, me, Claude, Arnie. Went to school together. I tried to tell Claude that. Tried to tell him to wait it out, that things would get better, but nothing doing, he needed to make a change. It seemed like going off for the harvest was a kind of safe thing to do rather than …" Stella's voice was hardly a whisper. She stopped talking. Got busy painting. Got busy not looking at Mary.

"Rather than what?" Breakfast churned again.

"Just … Claude wanted to …"

"Stella Jenkins! Did you seduce my husband?" Mary hoped Arnie wasn't able to hear them and yet, maybe he needed to. Why would she keep this secret? Stella and Claude? How could he? How could she?

A small voice in her head warned her to be careful. This could change everything. She needed to think, to understand, before she did or said anything else.

Stella's face was wet with tears now too. "We didn't know how to tell you. And Arnie. I'm so sorry, Mary."

"Sorry! You're sorry? Oh my God! You are my best friend. I thought you were my best friend. What have you done with my husband? What do you expect me to say?" Mary forced herself to dip the brush into the pail, to brush paint onto the wall. Smoothly. The creamy yellow tone, the smell of paint, the sound of Stella breathing, sobbing, waiting. Waiting for what? For Mary to give her blessing ... what?

Her brush coloured the wall in quick strokes. Paint dripped onto the wooden floor. Stella and Claude. "How far did you go?"

Arnie appeared in the doorway. Mary knew Stella couldn't see him. Willed him to stay back, to stay out of it until Mary knew what she thought, what she felt, and how she planned to react. Shook her head slightly at him. Liked that he stood where he was. Arnie. Well, this was too new. And yet ...

"I don't know what to say, Stella. I have to think. Maybe it's good that Claude is out of the picture right now." Suspicion made her look at Stella. "Have you made arrangements to meet? To get together while he's gone?"

Stella hung her head.

"You have!" Mary thought about pouring the pail of paint over her lifelong friend. Knew she'd be the one who'd have to clean it up. Too bad they were in her house. She laughed out loud.

Stella watched her. Watched Mary laugh and saw the laughter change to weeping again.

"I hardly believe this conversation. My best friend. My husband. Does Arnie know?" Mary felt her voice rise again. Recognized how close to hysteria she was.

Arnie stood in the doorway, waiting, listening. She nodded at him to come in and he came. To her. Directly. First. Hardly looked at Stella. Came into the room, stood beside Mary, without touching her, though she could feel him tall, steady, strong at her right side, slightly behind her.

"You and Claude?" His voice was low as he spoke to his wife.

Stella nodded.

"How long, Stella? How long have you and Claude been …?"

No answer.

"How could you?"

Mary watched him. Did he know about this before today? Had he known about this before making his move on her?

"How long has this been going on?" Mary hardly recognized her voice. It might have come from some other poor misguided woman just discovering her husband and her best friend have been sneaking about behind her back. Oh my God. This is happening to me. The paint can beckoned. Stella's tired face was ugly in its pain. Don't waste the paint. She dipped her brush into the can. Continued to cover the wall. How did I not know?

Arnie shook his head. "You need to leave now. Go home. Leave us to think. Have you and Claude made plans to be together?"

Stella nodded.

He turned away. "I can't look at you right now." He waited as she put her brush down.

She reached her hand out to him, but didn't touch him. "You've been so quiet, so distant," she pleaded. "I needed …"

He stood beside Mary. Put his hand on Mary's arm. "You've done enough damage for now. Go. Leave us."

"I'm sorry. Me and Claude. We're both sorry." Stella turned away.

Alone, Mary and Arnie stood looking at each other.

"I had no idea of this. Though I knew Claude was unhappy. Did he talk to you at all? About anything?"

Arnie shook his head. "I didn't know. I should have known." He put his face into his hands, stood there shielded from her.

"It's my fault," Mary said. "I let it happen."

"It's not at all." Arnie rubbed her back, pulled her to him, let her resist, held her steady, without letting her pull away, until she relaxed against him.

He was so tall and strong. She'd needed someone to lean on and here he was, where he belonged. The tears kept coming and Mary felt his shirt dampen under her wet face as he held her without moving. Just held on and she held back. "Now what will we do?"

"We'll not do anything just yet," Arnie said. "We need to think and this is too big a decision to make without thinking it through completely. There's the children .... And the parents." She could almost hear him calculating all that they needed to consider. He held her closer. "Maybe this is all for the best," he murmured into her hair.

"Maybe this is our chance at happiness – to do what we should have done all those years ago."

What will the neighbours think? Stella's abandoned brush dripped butter-tinted paint onto the floor boards. Complicated. Isn't this just lovely? Isn't this lovely? She said it aloud. "Isn't this just lovely?" Louder. "Isn't this just lovely?" And she laughed like a crazy woman.

Betrayal. By her husband and her best friend at the same time. There wasn't much reason to laugh. But maybe, it was a good thing. Maybe this was God's way. Too much hardship. Too much work. A life of too few laughs and too few loving words. Claude's choice was made. Why wouldn't she make some choices of her own?

Mary let her hands feel Arnie's warmth. He'd been there for her for so long when she needed a good friend, a hand. It was Arnie who understood how she felt about Edward and her garden. He appreciated her subtle humour; he let her sit quietly when she was overwhelmed with looking after her mother and Claude's mother. Why was she left to look after Liz? That should be Claude's responsibility. And now she was left to deal with this revelation from Stella. If Claude chose to hide his head and his shame in work again was she obligated to clean up his mess? What would Father Byers and the church ladies think? Anger welled behind Mary's tears. Guilt wasn't going to force her hand. Where was God when Claude and Stella were groping each other? Pulling off each others' clothing? Clasping to each other while their spouses struggled to maintain marriages. Mary's tears dried in the heat of her anger. Who did Claude think he was anyway? And how did friends like Stella justify jumping into bed with the neighbour's husband? How long did Stella suppose she could make a fool of Mary? And Arnie? Laughing with Claude behind her back. Behind both their backs. Pulling the wool over their eyes.

Mary felt Arnie's breath on her cheek, felt his lips search for hers, let her eyes stay closed, reached her mouth to meet his, and let their lips brush together. His lips were soft. Dry. Warm. Restful against her lips. Quiet, comfortable, safe lips. His arms around her were safe arms. A safe quiet place while her head swam with ugly thoughts of betrayal, worry, fear. What happens next? What happens when Claude returns home? How could he have left her to deal with this travesty on her own? His travesty. How dare he?

Tears began again. And sobs. Arnie's arms stayed warm and strong around her. Oh God. She wished for this and now it was here. Bigger than she had ever imagined. Now what? Had she caused this with her wishing? Was she to blame for this shift in her life? Caused her husband to have an affair so that she could be with the man she'd been in love with since … How long had it been?

Mary pushed the thought away. She hadn't done anything to help Claude and Stella get together. They made their own choices and now she was obliged to make decisions based on their errors in judgment. This was not her fault. She held on to Arnie for another minute. First – think, then – action. For now – one foot ahead at a time.

How long had they stood here like this? Mary opened her eyes. Took in the mess of the unfinished painting. Saw Mother standing in the doorway watching them. Felt the dampness of Arnie's shirt. Smelled the soap he'd used this morning. Wanted to taste his lips again. Time for that later. She gave him one last squeeze as she pulled herself away from him and took a step back.

He kept his hands on her shoulders, until he too, noticed Sadie in the doorway. He patted Mary's shoulders and turned to Sadie. "Better get back to work. There's plenty to be done here in the next few weeks or so and I intend to be doing it." He looked at Mary. Held her eyes and she saw the things he hadn't formed words around yet. Stay strong. More.

"Come with me, Sadie, and help me with the height for this railing." She gladly followed him, after a long questioning look at Mary.

Mary turned back to her painting. It was 9:20 AM. The day was barely begun. So much was already over.

# Chapter 22

**A chef who makes potato salad without onion has no soul.**

**Much virtue in herbs, little in men.**

**Benjamin Franklin in Poor Richard's Almanac**

"I heard your conversation this morning," Sadie said at supper.

Liz grunted and filled her mouth with mashed potatoes.

"Stella and Claude?" Sadie continued. "I wondered. He's been so gloomy of late. Out of sorts. You want to be careful what happens next."

"What?" Liz said. "What about Claude?"

"Nothing," Mary said. She shook her head at Sadie.

"Stella and Claude have been stepping out together. Not something to be proud of."

Mary frowned.

Liz looked from one to the other. "Not my boy. Not without good reason."

"With all his bible talk. They say them folks is the worst."

"Stop it, Mother!"

"I won't stop! I knew there was something not right about that man. And now I've heard it. Right from the horse's mouth this morning. That woman. Calling herself a friend. She … That Stella stood right here in this kitchen and said she and Claude was … have been …" Sadie pointed to where Stella's brush had dripped paint on the floor.

Liz squinted at Sadie and Mary.

"And all the time him making judgments on the rest of us. That's not something I'm going to be quiet about."

"You'll have to stop for now. You don't want to make things worse so we'll let it rest. I need time to think and you need to let me decide what's to be said and what's to be done," Mary said.

Sadie opened her mouth and shut it again. "Mmph."

"You should have been home more. Tending the home fires," Liz said.

Mary took a huge bite of meat.

Liz scraped her chair on the floor as she stood. She glared at them both then left the table. Her footsteps tapped steadily on the wooden floor, down the hallway. The door to her room opened, closed quietly and the hall was silent.

"I'm so mad, I could spit," Sadie said.

Mother hadn't been this het up since … Mary wasn't sure how long it had been since Mother was so het up about anything, but it was kind of invigorating to see her angry. Spitting nails, Father would have called it. And at someone else besides Mary. Nice to have her on my side, Mary acknowledged. "Let's not talk about this in front of Liz. She didn't know. And it isn't her fault. So, let's just let it sit awhile and I'll figure out what's to be done next."

"There's some things I've been wanting to tell that woman ever since I came here. You just watch I don't let loose on her one day real soon."

"I'm asking you, Mother, for my sake, to keep your thoughts to yourself for the time being. I want to get my head clear and I can't do that if I've got to baby-sit your tongue, now can I? No hasty decisions. No words that'll come back to bite our bums."

"And that dear Arnie Jenkins," Mother said. "If he isn't just one of the nicest men in this countryside ..."

"That's true, Mother."

"And, Mary, even with my failing eyesight, I'd say that dear Arnie Jenkins has got that rugged sort of handsomeness. Like a movie star."

"Arnie Jenkins is easy to look at."

After reading a chapter of Atlas Shrugged, by Ayn Rand to Mother, they listed once again the outstanding attributes of Arnie Jenkins, including thoughtfulness and common sense as well as good carpentry skills, and the deepest, bluest eyes. Mary reflected that this was the first time she could remember her and Mother agreeing so wholeheartedly on anything. That Mrs. Murphy would just as wholeheartedly disapprove of the tryst planned for later this evening, Mary chose to deny for the time being.

After the day's work of painting, it was wonderful to lounge in the bath with a sachet of lemon balm leaves collected from her herb garden during the summer. Mary sank into the warm, scented water until just her head poked out. On the edge of the tub she'd set a beeswax candle to flicker.

Mary had never been in the house without Claude overnight until this corn harvest adventure he'd taken himself on. She had never bathed herself for any other man. She lifted her legs one at a time and lathered them with languorous strokes, feeling an electrical twinge when her knee accidentally brushed her breast.

The nipple hardened. When the other hardened, it was intentional. She sat up to soap her arms, held her lathered breasts, one in each hand, enjoying their weight and the curves of pale soft skin. Their tips of puckered tawny pink, stiffened beneath her fingers, slippery and sensitive. Mary rinsed in the scented warm bath.

She pulled the plug and used her wash cloth to wipe down the sides of the tub as the water swirled away. The candle flickered; the tongue of flame sent unfamiliar shadows against the walls of the bathroom. Her shadow was a stranger with hair piled atop its head and long legs distorted by the angle of light. She'd quickly dry in the warm night air, she decided, and disdained the towel, to tiptoe naked from the bathroom, aware of a draft brushing over her steamy, wet skin. She hoped the Mothers would sleep soundly after their long day, with no nocturnal visits to the kitchen for drinks. Blessed be the deaf. Shielding the candle from the draft she enjoyed the prickling feel of her skin as it dried.

She checked her watch. Plenty of time. Mary patted great puffs of powder on her neck, shoulders, and legs, turning her skin into a silky, scented mass of tingling nerves. When Arnie arrives I'm afraid I shall jump him like an animal in heat. As she tidied her bedroom and stretched fresh sheets on the bed she allowed no excuse for her actions, knowing always that she was in full control. She slid a loose linen dress over her bare skin, blew out the candle and felt her way in the darkness to the kitchen where, by the light of the full moon, she prepared a pot of tea and a plate of cookies. She pressed herself against the counter as she waited for the kettle to boil.

Mary wondered what sort of night Claude was having on the road. Did he feel any inkling of what was about to transpire this night? Had she? It was as if another woman owned her body – a woman who chose to dress and prepare herself for Arnie's coming as Mary, in her normal frame of mind, would never allow. She didn't want to think too much. Knew she might think herself out of this act. Wondered how she could dare carry this through to completion? How could she not? Why would she not?

Still there was a sense of separation from the woman who clearly observed the possibilities arising from this night. For this one evening, Mary told herself, she would set aside her commitment to Claude.

At ten minutes to midnight, Mary sat in Claude's chair on the front porch with the tea tray on the table beside her. On the other side of the table an empty chair waited. The moon flooded the front porch. Mary walked around the house seeking an area of darkness and found the east side less exposed, shaded by a tall Canadian White Pine. She pulled the two chairs into its shadows, set them side by side, and brought the table and the tea things around as well. She waited, standing, on the front porch, at the railing, in the moonlight, aware of the silhouette she presented in her long clinging dress. She held her fingers to her lips and beckoned Arnie to follow as she moved around the porch into the shadows.

"Come." Mary said nothing more.

Arnie groaned lightly and reached for her. They kissed, slowly and long. He loosened the pins from her hair and it tumbled around her shoulders and into his hands. He buried his face in her damp mane. An ache of tenderness began in Mary's chest, travelled the length of her body, and she knew the richness of feeling outweighed the chance they took. This one night and these precious moments were all she would think of. She would not consider right now if the night would ever be repeated.


As the sky lightened, Mary and Arnie whispered their good-byes against each other's lips.

"Until tomorrow," Arnie said.

"No. Not tomorrow. I need to think. We all need to think."

Arnie walked backward, away from her, for as long as he could see her, then turned around and loped toward home – to Stella, to the life he couldn't leave, unable, he had said tonight, to perceive how he could stay.

She held her dress closed over her belly, as the chilly air lit on her flesh where Arnie's hands seemed still to caress her.

"I will remember you forever," Mary whispered to his unhearing, disappearing shadow.

When Arnie was out of sight, Mary carried the tea things into the kitchen. Nothing on the tray had been eaten or drunk, though they'd spent four hours together. One lone teacup rested on the kitchen counter. Which mother had been up? Liz? Sadie? When? What did she hear? What did she see? Anything? Everything?

In the bedroom Mary removed her dress, held it to her face and inhaled its fragrance. The fragrance of memory. Of love making. The bed beckoned, and she snuggled into the wrinkled sheets caressing the dress against her face, tucking it along the length of her body.

Mary's last request of Arnie was that for her sake he must stay with Stella and that Mary must convince Claude to return to her. This night could never be repeated. They couldn't be together. It was impossible. And yet … the dress folded its arms around her and finally Mary shut her grit-filled eyes and slept.

"It can't happen again, Arnie." Mary shoved her spade deep into the patch of walking onions. "It's what happens when we let dreams come true. People get hurt." She pulled on the long, slimed stems of the onions. With the coming of fall had come numerous killing frosts and the onions, while still edible, had strengthened in taste and scent. They brought tears to Mary's eyes as she tried to bring order to their disorderly growth. The frost turned the stems to mush, thus the bulblets that grew on the tops of the stems were falling onto the ground in a wanton disarray that Mary normally found endearing. This fall, and particularly today, they refused to do as she wanted. "Why can't you behave yourselves and stay where I ask? I am the gardener and you are just the onions!" Was she truly reduced to yelling at her onions? Taking out her frustration against defenceless plants? "I'll fix you. I'll yank you all out. Maybe plant something more well-behaved like lavender or periwinkle or  …"

"If your nose offends you, cut it off," was one of Liz's favourite quotes.

"I too can cut off the things that offend me. This morning I am offended by walking onions. Too many complications." She'd told Arnie he shouldn't come to the house this morning. And she'd warned him last night, though he was not in agreement, that they couldn't repeat their lovemaking.

Mary's arms, her heart, her whole body ached to run to him for comfort.

Mother. Claude. Liz. What was her responsibility to them? What would the people in town say if they knew the goings on in this household? What would Mr. Fynch think? Would she ever dare tell them that Claude and Stella were lovers first? Did that matter one iota? Would they even believe her? The priest would surely shake his head in disappointment. What a mess! And Claude gone off on the corn harvest.

She jammed the spade into another riotous clump of onions. Damn Claude! Sweat and tears. How often must she spend her days in this garden crying of a broken heart? She'd cried in the garden more times than she could count. Over her father, and her son, and now her husband. It wasn't all Claude's fault. Just this one huge situation, right here, right now, was Claude's fault. And it was one heck of a big problem.

Does he get to ruin my life? Mary's face warmed at the thought of making love with Arnie. She would harbour no regret in that regard at all. He wanted to return, she knew that, and knew that she wanted him too which was why, this morning, she'd come to the garden.

The borage plants were bare of flowers; the basil was black and mushy since the first frost; sage looked perky still; there were a few lovage leaves that could be used in a stew or a soup. There was still no sign of renewal of the pansy population. Did that mean Claude wouldn't come back either?

The monarda ... "I should yank you out and toss you to the deer," Mary threatened. Stella ... best friend ... right! Friends like that ... who needs enemies? What kind of friend have you been? She sliced her spade into the centre of the plant.

And yet, how could she judge Stella when truly, she and Arnie might just have easily have been the ones to first commit ....

adultery? Damn that guilty conscience that notices even the slightest imperfection. What a horrid word … adultery!

Stella's black curly mop of hair peaked around the Hansa rose, like a giant crow.

Mary jumped out of her thoughts. "Haven't you done enough damage already?" Mary wanted to chase her from the garden whacking her head with the shovel.

"I came to see if there's any hope of talking this out. I'm a stupid idiot. I know that. You know that. Mary, I'm so sorry."

"I'm sure you are. Sorry that you got caught. Sorry that Claude left you to handle the mess."

"Well, yeah, I am mad at him. But more mad at me. And at what a stupid awful person I am." Stella stood, hands at her side, hair obviously uncombed, and it was just as obvious that she'd spent a night of little sleep and many tears.

Tough luck. You deserve it. Mary thought back on her night with Arnie. Perhaps no one in the neighbourhood had slept last night.

"Too bad for you, Stella. Now get the hell out of my garden! I've nothing to say to you right now."

"Mary, we're friends."

"That's what I thought too. Before you jumped into bed with my husband." She wished she could cover the ears of the borage plants.

"Arnie told me. Told me he's leaving. That he loves you and that me and him are finished. I had no idea, Mary. He's a good man."

Mary dug into the onion patch again. Arnie leaving his marriage? For her? For goodness sake! What was he thinking? Not much. Now things were just out of control. Did he think things were fixed with words? She remembered hearing that males lost brain capacity when having sex. Was it possibly true? Seemed so in this case. Arnie Jenkins seemed so sensible, so normal, so able to consider this from its many angles. Well, he'd sure just made things one whole heck of a lot worse. Geesh! Now what? What more could possibly go wrong? Mary knew she shouldn't even think that thought.

Arnie's head showed from behind the lovage plant. Was the whole damn family coming for a consultation? "What do you people want from me?" Mary wished she could just be dead. This was too hard and she didn't even know what she wanted. Yet. It was so tempting to chase them both out with the shovel at their backs. Now would the kids be coming over too?

What a bunch of fools we all are. Mary contemplated Stella and Arnie both so apparently in pain, heartfelt, but of their own doing. "Don't be looking to me to fix your problems or to tell you it's OK that you've been messing around with the neighbours. It is not OK! You're playing with peoples' lives here. Mine, in particular!" She shook her finger at them both. "Now, stop it!"

She suddenly knew exactly what must happen next.

"Let's not talk anymore of sorry or of leaving your marriage." She glared at Arnie. "We're none of us leaving. We've been friends and neighbours for the best part of forty years. So, now, what we're going to do is to forget this business ever happened. We will not say one more word about it. Not to the Mothers, or to Claude, or to anyone at all. Agreed?"

Stella and Arnie stared dumbfounded at her.

"There's no choice here, folks. I've got two Mothers to look after and you both have children and obligations too. No, sir, what's been said these past few days, what's been done, we'll just forget it ever happened and so will everyone else."

Mary shoved the spade deep into the soil. "These onions are going to the compost heap. No use having them around any more."

Mary tended her garden, and cared for the Mothers. She did her church visits, welcoming the long walks to town that left her physically drained, though her mind churned with memories and worries.

She knew she wasn't the only one left off-balance by recent events.

Mary heard the Mothers as they came up the walkway, heard them on the porch. No time to get away so she slipped into the pantry. Why couldn't they stay shopping for hours and hours at a time like normal women? Oh no, they got their necessities and then they'd hurry home to make sure she'd not done any of the work in the kitchen. God forbid that Mary should make the home her own. She knew that wasn't fair or right but that's how it felt sometimes. That's one thing she and Stella agreed on. The only thing it seemed … well except for Claude. And Arnie. Oh God. Could she just for one short while quit thinking about the whole mess? What should she do?

"The nerve of that Stella Jenkins! As if she didn't come from the same neighbourhood. She puts on airs that one does."

"It's not over yet. I know it. There's no more of them visiting back and forth anymore."

"Claude should never have gone off on the corn harvest crew. Did he think they needed the money?"

"I can't imagine that but maybe."

China clinked against china. "Let's have a cup shall we, before we put these things away."

Mother's slow footsteps neared the pantry. "I think Stella has been eyeing your Claude since the very start. Never satisfied that one. And my poor Mary, hard worker that she is, wouldn't ever suspect. And why should she? Her best friend and her husband. If that doesn't just take the cake."

"Well something's happened that's sure. Claude wouldn't be one to look outside the marriage if there wasn't a reason. Maybe Mary's been …."

"Don't even put words to that thought. My Mary would never look at another man."

Mother opened the pantry door.

"Things haven't been right since Edward and Nelson drowned."

"Mary! We didn't realize you were here."

"Oh, you're home," Mary said, looking up from the cook book she'd grabbed.

"Cup of tea?" Liz asked.

"We were just talking about seeing Stella in town."

"I heard you."

"She wasn't real friendly. Mary, tell us would you please, what's going on? She's your best friend."

"Friends aren't easy to come by."

"Oh Mother, I can't talk about it right yet. We'll get things worked out, I'm sure."

"Is Arnie coming over today? It's nice to have a man around the house especially with Claude gone. I'm going to make my famous chocolate cake for Arnie for lunch. He's got a good appetite."

"Doesn't Stella mind him being over here so much?"

"She might, but I ...." Mary chewed her bottom lip. She felt tears welling. "I'll take my tea out to the garden. Spend some time with my weeds." She tried to smile. "And, yes, Arnie said he would be over this morning."

"He's sure doing a good job putting the railing up. Whatever's happened with you and Stella we'll pull through it. This too shall pass. That's what Father Byers was telling me on his last home visit."

Mary rolled her eyes. Thought of what Stella would have to say about this conversation. She'd probably get a good laugh out of it, even now. Even though it was about her. Strange. She is still my best friend. Oh God.

What will Edward think?

She pulled her sweater tighter around her shoulders. What time would Arnie arrive? It was nice to have a man around the house. Especially since he took an interest in the goings on without thinking he needed to manage everything. Claude going away made more sense now, knowing his mind was occupied with other things. Distracted one could say. How did he dare?

"Still, I miss him terribly," Mary told Edward as she sat on the rock, warm from the morning sun. "And I miss Stella too. Will it be possible to get things back to the way they were? I'm so mad at the two of them. Maybe they don't want things back to normal." Arnie sure wasn't eager to have Claude return. Well. "We can't just toss two families into upheaval. That's not right. Edward, what do I do?"

Mary was tempted to yank out the beebalm as she'd done with the walking onions. Was Stella in the marriage because Mary had planted her in the garden? Too crazy and yet ... Arnie – the walking onion – had planted himself here, but Mary planted the beebalm – Stella. And Claude got himself pulled out by hiring the gardener. Crazy? Maybe. "Edward, I wish you'd talk to me today. I need some comfort."

Edward had aged nicely. He'd be seven years old and no longer sported knobby knees, but he retained his cauliflower ears, and soft blue eyes that sometimes turned as dark as the stamens of the star-shaped borage flower.

"I don't understand how you could betray my father like that," he said to her now, standing just far enough from her so she couldn't pull him to her and nestle him in her arms to warm away his questions with hugs and kisses. His arms hung straight at his sides, and steadily he watched her, awaiting a reply.

Each day as she'd transplanted and dug, weeded and gathered, Mary argued her case. Sometimes eloquently, other times begging forgiveness, she flung weeds away from her, jabbed the shovel into the earth, relished the quick shot of pain that travelled her arm and jarred her shoulder, like the recoil from Claude's shotgun. The easy, undemanding refuge of Arnie's embrace as they'd watched the night sky and talked, rested on the edge of Mary's mind, a comfort and a burden.

In the evenings after they'd eaten their supper and the Mothers were in their rooms, Mary, exhausted from her exertions in the garden, pulled on the dress she'd worn during her night with Arnie and fell quickly asleep as soon as she was in bed. The fragrant memory of their time together permeated her dreams and Arnie was again with her, warm and large, enveloping her from behind, kissing her hair, her neck, her ears, arousing her to ever higher heights. In her sleep, she pressed herself against him, wanting the lovemaking to continue, willing the night never to end. "My love, I'm so glad you've come back."

"I couldn't leave you. You are my life," her lover answered, as he turned her to face him.

Mary gasped, powerless to stop the tears streaming onto her pillow and the sobs that shook her shoulders as Claude hugged her close to his heart. Stroking her arms and down her back, he whispered into her neck. "I'm so sorry," he said. "I'm so sorry. I love you. I missed you. Just being away for that short time made me realize how much we have together. I will never leave you. Never."

Wails of grief arose from a place she did not recognize.

Spent and more exhausted than when she'd first lain down, Mary rested in Claude's arms, holding the dress from her night with Arnie, its fragrance more imaginary than real now. Had it been three weeks ago already? The ache in her soul was still raw and it surprised her to feel warm arousal as she pressed against Claude. Their lovemaking this time, was slow and tender. Mary rubbed her cheek the whole time against the wrinkled damp dress and sighed luxuriously as she and Claude, exploring with their hands, their tongues, their skin, made love again. It could have been the beginning of their life together – before Edward, before Liz, before Mother's arrival.

Before Arnie.

# Chapter 23

**Rose** – Rosa – No flower has stirred the imagination and passions of poets and romantics quite like the rose. The rose is a symbol of love and women, and of compassion, friendship and honour, and as Charlemagne decreed, it ought to grow in every garden.

**Parsley** grows for the wicked and not for the just. The wickedness of parsley could be nullified only by planting it on Good Friday under a rising moon.

**Weed** – any plant that is growing in the wrong place.

"We're here!"

Mary groaned and rolled out of Claude's tight embrace. How long had she slept? Not long enough. She grabbed her housecoat and fumbled down the hallway. The mothers had been up a while. Tea was made and bowls set out for breakfast. Four bowls. Mother had heard Claude. Mary blushed and hoped they hadn't made much noise.

From hooded eyes she glanced at Arnie. She could still taste the blood of biting him. Could hear his groan still against her mouth. Felt a stir of embarrassment. Arnie had not been a dream.

Arnie frowned, "I didn't get much sleep last night. Trouble with a cow calving."

He winced when Stella touched his cheek. "She got me in the lip."

"Maybe you'd better have some of Mrs. Murphy's tea," Stella offered him. "You don't look so good."

"Claude will be out in a minute," Mary said, as nonchalantly as she could muster, wondering if she looked as nervous as Arnie. "I didn't get much sleep either." How will we proceed as normal? Can we? She poured herself a cup of tea.

"I dug you up a sucker from my mother's rose." Arnie handed her a plastic wrapped thorny stem. "I thought you might like it. She's a climber, yellow and fragrant."

"Thank you," Mary said. A rose from Arnie. Arnie's rose, I'll call it. Let it climb all over the house, anywhere it wants.

Claude entered the kitchen fully dressed and stood behind Mary, hugging her and resting his chin on her shoulder. "I got home very early this morning. We rode all night." He kissed her lightly on the ear.

Mary blushed.

Arnie choked on his hot tea, sputtered it across the table.

Mrs. Murphy handed a napkin to Stella. "Your husband needs a hand there." She looked at Mary and Claude standing together.

Without warning Mary's stomach twisted. She ran to the bathroom, retched into the toilet, nothing came up.

Mother followed, and when Mary stopped heaving, Mother put two soda biscuits into her hand. "Eat these, and keep a couple beside your bed for the next few months." She left on slippered feet.

Mary crushed the crackers, intent on flinging them at the mirror, but another flutter in her abdomen made her lay a piece of biscuit on her tongue, allowing it to melt before she swallowed. "Isn't this just lovely," she said, applying another wedge to her tongue. "I look like the wrath of God. I'm a mess. She shuffled into the bedroom and lay on the bed where memories of last night, and the confusion of the past month, and questions about the future, braided themselves about the main unknown.

Whose baby is this?

"Mine," she whispered.

Had they spoken, Arnie and Stella, about Arnie's indiscretion? Did she want Stella to know?

Of course not. Stella does not know and Stella will not know. That was obvious from their conversation yesterday in the garden. Arnie and Stella had come over together to talk to Mary as she'd dug the potatoes.

"Last year I didn't get these dug until early December and I promised myself never to leave them that long again," Mary had said.

Arnie rolled the wheelbarrow along the row and signalled to Stella to continue rolling it as he bent to retrieve the potatoes and set them into the barrow. "I assume this is the plan." He bent for another handful of spuds.

"Yes. I'll let them dry a bit so the dirt'll fall off them," Mary said. "It's a great crop this year."

"Mary. I know you want to act as if nothing has happened," Stella said. "And I know you don't want to have this conversation over and over. So we want you to know that's exactly what we want too. We talked it over, me and Arnie. We're so thankful you can ... I'm so sorry ... we're so lucky ... we know that. I know that." Stella shoved the wheelbarrow hard to get it past a huge clod of earth. Potatoes rolled out and onto the ground in front of Arnie. "Oh, I'm sorry. I'm such a klutz." She stooped to pick them up.

Mary continued to dig. "It's the only thing I can do. Any of us can do, I think. We say nothing to Claude. Well, you need to talk to him at some point. I told Liz and Sadie it was all a misunderstanding. So you, Stella, have one quick conversation with Claude and then ... it's all back to normal."

"Whatever the hell normal is." Arnie spread the potatoes gently in the bottom of the wheelbarrow. "Don't worry, Mary. We'll hold up our end of the bargain, and we know you will too. It's for the best.

That's what we all of us need to remember." He reached his hand out to help Stella up. "Friends till the end," he said.

They worked in the cool fall air until the potatoes were all dug, and by the time the job was finished their cheeks were red from exertion.

"We've all earned a cup of tea," Mary said. "I'm sure the mothers have been watching us from the kitchen window, so let's go in and show them how this is going to work. It won't be long until Claude gets back, so let's get some practice acting normal." She stretched her arms behind her back. "I can't remember how long it's been since I lied to my mother."

Mary forced herself to go back into the kitchen.

"What brings you two here so early in the morning?" Claude held his tea with both hands. All seemed normal.

"Get the corn all harvested?" Arnie asked, looking at Mary.

"Yup. Hurried the job so I could get to my wife quicker." Claude reached for Mary's hand.

Stella examined the contents of her mug.

Mary moved away from Claude. He continued to look at Stella and Arnie waiting for their answer.

"We have been giving Mary a hand with getting the hand rails put up for Liz and Sadie," Arnie said.

Stella nodded. "And Mary and I thought it was time we painted the kitchen." She looked around the room seeming to notice for the first time how much remained undone.

"I didn't know you would be back today," Mary said. "Would you rather we put off the painting? And the railings?"

"Do I need to leave?" Stella asked, looking from Mary to Claude to Arnie, and back to Mary again.

Arnie said. "I'm sure Mary can use the help."

Claude looked from one to the next at the people around his kitchen table.

Were they all suddenly become strangers? Mary pulled her housecoat tighter around her and reached for her tea. Proceed as you mean to continue. Whose wisdom was that? It was good advice anyway. Her stomach flopped. She couldn't remember what she'd eaten yesterday. She couldn't remember any food past breakfast. What did they say about people in love? That they lost their appetite? I can't be in love with Arnie. I can't. I refuse. She wished she could reach over, stroke his hair, touch his lip where she'd so recently bit him. God! Proceed as I mean to continue. How was that? How do I continue?

"I can't paint in this garb," Mary said. I'll go put on some work clothes while you catch up on things over tea. How was the weather, Claude, while you were away?"


The week whizzed by with Mary and Stella painting mostly in silence, while Arnie and Claude sanded and nailed the remaining railing in strategic places around the house. Mary was careful not to find herself alone with Arnie and noticed that Mother had the same mission.

She knows, Mary thought, and she understood that Mother would help keep them apart. "It will be easier that way," Mary told herself, surprised at how satisfied she felt.

Although Claude didn't yet know about the baby, plans for the future filled their talk in the evenings. As they walked through the herb garden, he admired her work or sometimes brought her into the shop to show her the latest piece of ironwork he'd created.

"I thought I could sell some of these at the market," he said, showing Mary a weathervane crafted in the shape of a horse.

"It's practical, and it looks nice." Mary agreed that they would sell. She and Mother were working on a pattern for sewing quilted curtains to insulate windows against winter winds. "We can share a table at the market," she offered.

"We'll leave Mother at home with Liz. Maybe ask Arnie or Stella to come over to check on them so we don't have to rush back."

Stella was only too glad to be helpful, and reiterated her offer of exchanging houses with Mary and Claude overnight to give them a break from the Mothers. "It'll be like a honeymoon for all of us," Stella laughed.

"It would be just uncomfortable," Mary said. "I don't think it's a good idea, Stella. Let's forget it. For now anyway."

"That's what Arnie said too." Stella shrugged. "Anyway, I let him know it's up to you. If you want a night away with Claude we'll switch houses for the night and that's that."

It was an interesting exercise of the mind, to ponder how that would transpire, to exchange beds with Stella and Arnie for a night. She'd have to tidy the house; set a dish of rose petals on the dresser. Would she drape the dress over the chair on her side of the bed? She could still catch the lingering scent of love as she held it to her face, and decided no. There were many reasons not to leave reminders out. It had been a one night only occasion, not to be repeated. She patted her tummy; it still was flat and firm, but not for long. Should she tell Claude tonight about the baby? He'd be happy.

Claude shared news of his own with Mary. "I want to build an addition to the back of the house – looking to the east. We'll have our bedroom there and a bathroom. It'll give us a nice new place of our own away from the Mothers but close enough. We'll share the kitchen and sitting room. Maybe you could set up your quilting in our old bedroom upstairs. Have a private place for yourself."

Mary closed her eyes to envision the changes as he spoke. Their new bedroom would be accessed through a hallway that Claude wanted to build where the porch was now.

The porch where …

"I won't have to touch the big pine tree. I'll go east of it," Claude explained.

Arnie's rose would be saved, and in fact, would climb on the wall of their new bedroom, beside the window. As she and Claude lay in bed, Mary pulled Claude's hand to her belly. "You can't feel anything yet," she said. "But will there be room in the new bedroom for a small cradle?"

The knowledge of the pregnancy hastened Claude's work on the addition and he enlisted Arnie's help. They framed the two rooms and the hallway, trying not to disrupt Mary's schedule of caring for the Mothers, tending the garden, working at the Apothecary, and visiting her shut-ins. She planned her day so she could be home to serve lunch to the two men, trying to ignore the knowledge that either Claude or Arnie could be the father of her growing baby.

"She's settled," she heard Claude tell Arnie one day over their sandwich lunch at the kitchen table. She was glad not to be facing them, stayed rooted in the pantry purposely, giving herself time to control her ire at his choice of the term used for a cow confirmed pregnant. "Three months and six more to go." She heard the grin in Claude's voice as he continued. "Happened the night I got back from working the corn with Cletus she says." She turned in time to see him beat his fists against his chest. She wanted to hit him.

"Cat got your tongue, Arnie?" Claude asked. Mary carried an apple pie in each hand. She placed them carefully onto the counter before turning to look at the two men at her table.

Arnie raised his eyebrows at Claude, before looking down at his plate of potato salad and ham sandwich. "Congratulations to you both," he said, with a grimaced smile, and Mary was put in mind of a time on the wagon when he'd been going to tell something about a neighbour but stopped himself. "There's a time," he said that day, "when a man should keep silent."

Mary watched the men's progress, encouraging them to hurry in order to beat the snow which was being forecast often on CBC radio these days. She knew Arnie kept silent about their time together. She could sense his discomfort over Claude's proprietariness, with the heightened sensitivity she had first noticed when pregnant with Edward.

The baby grew well, pushing against her tummy, arms and legs jutting here and there attracting Claude's attention as it became more active.

"It must be a boy," he told her. "He's so strong. Forceful."

Claude liked to kneel on the floor at her feet and sing lullabies to her growing stomach as she alternately praised herself for saving their marriage and berated her stupidity at risking the marriage for one too short night of passion.

"It's a perfect tree, Mary." Mother's teacup rattled against its china saucer as she set it down.

Mary carried Mother's breakfast to the table. A slice of toasted cinnamon raisin bread. Hardly enough to keep a cricket alive, she thought. She brought her own bowl of oatmeal porridge and cream topped with slices of banana. They sat, each chewing their food, watching the flashing tree lights take their turns at accenting the glittery decorations. Tinsel twisted and glinted in the light; while plentiful balls reflected the greens and reds and yellows and blues of the lights.

"It's the gaudiest one ever. As soon as Claude saw Arnie and Stella's tree he made sure ours was twice as big and with more stuff on it. What's he trying to prove?"

Mary rubbed her hand over her bulging stomach. Next Christmas there'd be a baby on her knee.

Mother didn't answer. "Are you having them here for dinner?"

"Yes, we are." Mary looked full at her. "They're coming. And we're going to their home for dinner tomorrow. Just like we have every year. And it'll be fine. I got a nice warm sweater for Stella and Arnie needs a new hammer. Claude made a crokinole board for the children, so that's the gifts looked after."

Mother squinted and lifted her teacup slopping tea as her hand shook. Her nodding head made it difficult to raise the cup accurately to her lips.

Mary told herself Mother was agreeing. She knew it was right to treat the neighbours just like always at Christmas. She'd help repair the rift, and things would continue on.

So long as nothing is said out loud, Mary thought. Nothing more. No accusations, no confessions, no admitting of guilt. Everything must continue as normal. Better than normal. So far, so good. Weren't she and Claude expecting a baby in a few short months? A baby that couldn't ever take the place of dear Edward but who could truly help to fill the holes left in the hearts of those who had loved him.

This baby could mend the marriage torn apart by guilt. This baby could ease the two grandmothers through their final years and maybe help them all forget that awful day when they'd let Edward out of their sight and lost him forever. This baby could give Mary a reason to keep on keeping on. Whether conceived on the front porch or in her marriage bed, this baby was meant to be.

"You're old to be having a baby," Sadie said.

"So you've mentioned before," Mary said. "I think this baby is part of God's plan." She gazed skyward and instructed the God who she wasn't sure listened to her anymore. Let the dear child look like me, Lord, and save this family anymore grief for a while. Please.

To Sadie she said, "We'll have a merry Christmas in this household or we'll die trying."

Spring came and with it a burst of new energy. Sadie and Liz cautioned Mary that it was natural to want to get everything done when birthing time approached.

"When you're so big you should spend your time resting," Sadie said.

Liz agreed, and the two of them did their best to make sure Mary sat in the parlour with her feet up on the footstool. Mary snuck outside at every chance, to spend extra time in the garden talking to Edward about the new baby.

"He or she will never take your place in my heart." She spoke to the bright green shoots of the borage plants, impatient for their sky blue flowers. "You'll be a sort of guardian angel to this child." As she weeded she wondered whether he knew if the child-to-be was his full sibling or just a half brother or sister. "I couldn't stop myself, Edward." She hated how desperate she sounded defending her actions.

"A woman can't go on day after boring day without trying to make changes for the better. Of course, with my luck that means stirring up more trouble. I guess it was wrong. I know it was wrong, but it was almost like some sort of a dare from the universe. Here Mary, take a chance. Live a little!

"I said no at first. You heard me. I resisted a long time, but something happened. The rules didn't seem so important. I'd followed the rules all along – to the letter. It got me a son in the grave, a houseful of mothers, and a long-faced husband, and then a husband gone to work with the harvest crew and ..." Mary stopped herself talking to Edward about Stella and Claude's affair. "It felt like I didn't have much left to lose."

There was plenty of work to be done in the herb garden, but Mary's bulk made digging and bending difficult. Though she and Stella vowed to maintain their friendship, Stella used her own pregnancy to excuse herself from their regular activities and Mary found herself alone often. She missed their easy friendship, and though she knew she could count on Stella and Arnie to help in an emergency, there was no going back to the way they'd been before. Lines had been crossed. Mary wasn't sure she could ever build a new friendship with anyone else.

"I'm alone now," she told Edward. "Not what I'd have chosen had I known the results but it's too late and you know me. No use crying over spilt milk. Enough tears have been cried in this garden.

"I've got to think about me and the new baby now. About what I need and what the baby needs. I must take care of this baby." She patted her almost full-grown tummy.

Mary hoed the rows, considered what should be put into the empty spaces left by her elimination of the monarda and the walking onions. Those two plants had taken a lot of space in her garden and a lot of her energy. In their absence, she could grow plants that would be more manageable. "Crazy, but true." She'd consulted Mrs. Grieves Herbal and was leaning toward parsley, sweet woodruff and lavender. A personality makeover she thought. The lavender would stand in for Jacob and Amy, while parsley and sweet woodruff could be Stella and Arnie respectively. Not that those two really needed to be in the garden anymore, but there was a quote she'd heard once about keeping your friends close and your enemies closer. Maybe if she made Stella and Arnie more controllable and manageable as plants, she might be successful at mending their differences as friends too. Arnie was already represented by the yellow rose he'd brought over last fall, immediately after the goings-on that had changed everything, but there was room in the herb bed and Mary wanted him there too. For old time's sake, she thought.

The parsley, slow to start, would need to be thinned once the seedlings sprouted, and then there'd be nothing to do but wait until late summer when she could harvest and dry the leaves. Parsley needs little or no care. That's how I'll deal with Stella as well. Take what I need from her and otherwise leave her to her own devices.

Sweet woodruff, also known as Lady's bedstraw, was a slow grower. Mrs. Grieves' Herbal said, "The dried herb may be kept among linens, like lavender, to preserve it from insects. In the Middle Ages it used to be hung and strewed in churches, and on St. Barnabus Day and St. Peter's Day, bunches of Buxus, Woodruff, lavender and roses found a place there. It was also used for stuffing beds." Stuffing beds. Well, you did that good. Although, technically not precise, I like the universe's humour – excellent word play. Mary grinned at herself, wondering if she should look into a different sort of hobby, one that would take her out among people. But ... she reasoned ... I already do visit the shut ins. And I see enough people at the Apothecary. I'm too big right now to be running about town much anyway.

They'd be good additions to the herb garden and useful too. The box shrubs were growing nicely. Keeping things boxed in, as they should, Mary said to herself. Under control. I need that.

She took herself to Town's General Store, in search of seeds. Mr. Towns offered her cuttings from his garden of a parsley plant that he said came back every year. He'd been growing it since 1942.

"It's not supposed to be perennial, I know that," he said, shaking his head, "But I'm not gonna argue with anything that wants to think it's a perennial. Saves me waiting for seeds to sprout. Parsley is one of the slower ones you know. I'll dig you up a bit."

Mary picked fresh green lacy leaves from the parsley plant on the morning she felt her labour pains begin, placing the leaves into the cotton bag she'd brought for that purpose. "And I'll tell you something, Stella," she whispered to the parsley plant, "I noticed it hasn't hurt your marriage either." Mary plucked another handful of the crisp curled leaves. "Guilt is keeping Arnie close to home at nights, isn't it? I took what was extra, what he offered me, just like I'm taking off these extra leaves from you. The plant will grow back even stronger, bushier." Mary brushed the parsley plant as she would a child's head. "A bit of pruning is what you and Arnie needed. I'm glad to be of service."

She moved to the Sweet Woodruff plant. "Today we find out if this huge lump is a boy or a girl. I'm sure we're both hoping he or she looks a lot like me." Mary watched the butterflies dipping into the early flowers. "I don't ever regret what we did ... wish we could continue on as a matter of fact .... But it's better this way. And we both know that."

"You shouldn't be hearing this, Edward," she said, turning to the borage plants. "I'm doing my best to put the past behind me, but memory is strange. I think all is forgotten and suddenly there it is back again. And I don't really want to forget the best night of my life anyway. I need to keep it tucked away, like a baby tooth, or Father's tobacco pouch. It's the only way I can make sense of things anymore. Spending the night with Arnie was like wearing my Sunday dress on a Tuesday. I can't do it all the time but my God that one time...." Mary leaned back and raised her face to the sun.

"That one time," she repeated smiling. "Just once. Seems a waste of good love."

# Chapter 24

**Nasturtium** – The name means 'nose twister'. Used to treat infections. Rich in Vitamin C. Promotes appetite in men. Makes women secretive. Secret sexual liaisons sometimes occur in mixed company. Do not let your guests out of your sight.

Mary rocked back and forth in her wheelchair humming "Yellow Rose of Texas" and stared unseeing out the window. Edward was a man now. He had stayed with her all this time – aging, developing a paunch and grey hair. His nose was red and grown large like his father's. His voice was deep and kind, though he'd matured into a man who didn't speak unnecessarily.

He's grown up to look just like his dad, Mary thought, but he wore business clothes, usually dress pants and a button-down shirt, and cologne. His father never used scent, while Arnie splashed or sprayed it on every morning. Today is Edward's birthday.

"How's it feel turning fifty-eight today, Edward?" she asked the boy who'd followed her all these years. "Happy Birthday. How do you like your mother now? All lumpy and misshapen. But still feisty. Never lost that. It's probably just as well that you died when you did.

"I didn't think so at the time, but looking back, I can see the sense of it. They say things happen for a reason, and to be honest, son, if you'd lived to be a teenager your father would have made your life hell. The way he got so cross and cranky.

"I still can't figure it out – what happened to turn him mean like that. Maybe it was in his genes all along. His father was a cranky old bastard too. But I don't have to tell you this stuff. You likely know more than I do. Do you know what set him off?"

Mary rocked in her wheelchair. When did Claude change? Was it as sudden as she remembered or was memory playing tricks on her? False memory syndrome as MaryArlene called it.

"That's not how it happened, Mom," she'd said, when Mary recounted the day that Stella came to the house to tell them Arnie was sick. As Mary remembered it, Stella had been crying. "My poor Arnie. He's not going to last the night. The doctor says his heart's giving out and there's nothing to be done. I thought if anyone was able to cure him, Mary, it would be you."

Mary hurried to the garden, her snippers and collecting basket in hand. Little MaryArlene followed close behind, her blue eyes filled with tears. "Poor Uncle Arnie, you have to make him better."

Convallaria Magalis, came to Mary's mind. It worked the last time that Arnie's heart acted up, but if he'd been taking the tinctures as instructed, Mary wondered why he was having troubles now. Maybe he'd reached the end of his life, though he wasn't much after fifty.

Mary cut leaves from the mints, lemon and peppermint, and snipped raspberry leaves into the basket too. She'd get some of the rose hips from the cupboard in the pantry. Stella would have a long few days ahead of her as Arnie would need someone to sit with him and to keep a close check on his reaction to the treatment. Might as well have plentiful pots of soothing tea for comfort. Back inside, Mary chose the largest specimens of rose hips from the jar in the pantry and she tucked the bottle of powdered digitalis leaves into her basket.

She sent MaryArlene to collect a goodly bunch of yellow roses and together they arranged them in a vase to bring to the Jenkins' home. Mary, Claude and MaryArlene listened to Stella's account of the doctor's visit as they hurried toward the Jenkins' home and Arnie.

Stella's youngest son ran out to meet them. He took MaryArlene's hand. "I found tadpoles … bunches of them. In the creek."

MaryArlene would have followed her mother and Claude, but the boy held fast to her hand. "My mom said I should show you the tadpoles while the adults talk." He rolled his eyes.

MaryArlene handed her vase of roses to her dad. "Mom said to put them where Uncle Arnie can see them."

"You'll not go near the creek," Claude said.

The two children stayed outside on the porch to examine the bucket of swimmers while the adults trekked into the house.

Claude furrowed his brow. "We're bringing Arnie flowers?"

"A happy memory helps a patient feel better," Mary explained. "The rose came from his mother's garden; he told me that when he gave me the root. It's just a thought. Can't hurt. It might be all we're able to give him."

Arnie lay on the couch, unmoving but for his eyes that turned to gaze at each person as they spoke.

"Isn't it nice of Mary and Claude to come see you?" Stella said.

Mary held Arnie's hand while she felt for the pulse in his wrist. "Mary." Arnie licked his too dry lips.

"Would you get him some water, Claude, please?" Mary asked, holding Arnie's eyes with her own, assessing his state. His skin was pale, seemed thin.

"He's been trying to say something off and on," Stella said.

"You're going to get better," Mary instructed Arnie. "Don't try too hard to talk. Save your strength." She pinched his arm and watched his eyes widen in response.

"Hurts," he gasped.

"Where does it hurt?" Stella asked. "Is it your chest again?"

"My heart." Arnie watched Claude come in from the kitchen with a glass of water still carrying the roses. "Thanks, friend," he said. His sour breath told Mary what she didn't want to admit.

Stella wet his lips with spoonfuls of water. Mary motioned to Stella that they should talk in the kitchen. Claude took over spooning the water, and the two women left the room.

"I'm afraid the doctor is right, Stella. His heart is weak. Do you believe in miracles?" They stood without speaking until Stella moved toward Mary who held out her arms to her oldest friend.

"What will I do without him?" Stella moaned into Mary's shoulder.

"We'll look after you. It's what we do. We've always helped each other."

They rocked together, desolation thick in the air. In their silence they heard the men's voices from the living room.

"We'd better stop Arnie in case he feels the need to talk too much." Stella pulled herself away from Mary's comfort.

"Claude's not big on forgiveness," Mary admitted. Had Arnie confessed to Stella about their one night together? He wouldn't, Mary thought. There'd be no sense in telling. Even if he had, Stella had no right to judge.

MaryArlene came in to stand beside Claude as he spooned water for Arnie. She often came to spend the day at the Jenkins' home, to bake cookies with Stella or catch tadpoles with Jamie who was almost her same age. Most days, the two children kept company with Arnie in his woodworking shop where he built fine furniture. MaryArlene was showing promise in woodcarving as she worked on a duck that Arnie bragged was sure to be the best decoy ever, when he and the boys went out hunting in the fall.

Arnie's death would be difficult for MaryArlene. She and Jamie were often mistaken for brother and sister. MaryArlene's knees bowed as his did, and when she concentrated on a thing, she held her head at the same angle as Jamie did.

Some secrets are better kept secret, Mary assured herself. I'd best get in there with Claude and Arnie to make sure this one goes with Arnie to his grave.

"You've no worries there," Claude was saying. "Me and Mary will look after the family for you. Same as you would do for me."

Arnie and Mary joined eyes over Claude's head as he continued speaking.

"I always remember how you helped Mary and our family when I went away, and when I came back, you were right there helping. It's what neighbours are for – to hold a person up until they find their feet again. I'll never forget you did that for me."

Arnie and Mary's eyes stayed locked together, both glistening with tears. "I wish…" Arnie's voice was weak.

Stella crouched at her husband's side and took his hand. "The doctor said we need to let you get plenty of rest, so we'll take turns sitting with you – the children, me, Claude and Mary. But you have to promise me that you'll sleep when you feel tired, no matter who is here."

Arnie nodded at her. "Tired." He shut his eyes, and Stella tucked his hand underneath the covers.

"I'll give him some of this mixture, but truly, Stella, I can't give you a guarantee. He's not good." Mary hated the sadness her words caused. "Of course, we can always hope. There have been miracles and we'll definitely be praying for one and I'll do all I can. I'm giving him a very small dose. We'll wait twelve hours to see how it acts on him. We'll have to watch closely in case he has an adverse reaction."

Claude stood and Mary saw how he had aged over the years. His hair was more grey than brown. His shirt, tucked tightly into belted pants, accentuated his round belly. His shoulders were still broad, but today he wasn't standing as straight as usual, and his neck displayed the rough, reddened slack of middle age.

Mary raised her eyebrows at him. "Will we go home?"

With a slight nod, he adjusted his waistband; Mary buttoned her sweater; Claude blew his nose on a handkerchief he found in his pant's pocket – familiar, comfortable, unremarkable signals of understanding, and they both turned to the door, toward home.

"Thank you for coming," Stella said, hugging Mary first, before she moved to hug Claude.

"We'll stop in again tonight," Claude said. "Take the early night watch so you can get some sleep."

"Hang out the red quilt if you think his condition changes for the worse," Mary said. "I'll keep an eye out for it."

The red quilt... Mary had hung hers out a number of times in the past: When her labour pains for MaryArlene had begun; the morning her mother hadn't awoken; and once when she had started weeping over a broken piece of Sadie's china and couldn't stop. The red quilt had lain on the rocker and sometimes it was wrapped around shoulders against the draft. It was a friend to Mary – her security blanket she called it, her comfort. When she walked past it on her way to hang out the clothes or to collect salad greens from the garden, she laid her hand on the quilt, to see again images of her and Stella and the Mothers stitching with the other church ladies during the year of the quilts. She and Stella had each received one that year.

Mary rested her head against the headrest of the wheelchair. The one great advantage of the wheelchair was that she had time to sit and think. That was a pleasant, un-planned-for luxury of old-age, that she'd wished for many times over the years. "Be careful what you wish for, Mary." So many people had said that to her so many times, yet as she sat here now in Sunny Acres, Mary thought that having wishes come true could be a very good thing.

But yes, one should be careful what one wished for.

Wishing on the moon had been a favourite of Mary's in her younger days. Stella made wishes in those days too.

Once, on a clear night, Mary and Claude lay outside on the quilt, star gazing, picking out Orion, the Ursas, the Dippers. That night Mary wished for a long life, happiness and wisdom. Should have been more specific, Mary thought. I should have requested more wisdom. To recognize what was right in front of me.

"It was a full moon." Mary remembered. "A beautiful full moon." In June ... we were still in the little house in Peterborough.

The first day of June had dawned sunny, then turned cloudy with no rain in the air. The world of the garden overflowed with brilliant greens, thick, heady, heavy scents, pulsing growth, and all the colours of spring – pink honeysuckle blossoms, Cardinal red tulips, white bleeding hearts and purple lilacs and sweet woodruff. Blue forget-me-nots and yellow tulips danced together across the garden, spilling onto the grass, overwhelming in their sheer joyous brilliance after the long wet, snowy drab layers of winter. Mary stood in the doorway, the sound of the radio fading as bird chirps and buzzing bees took over her ears.

They invited her out the door, to follow the path around the house, through the damp lush shady copse, over soft earth, under the plum trees and the apple trees. So much activity played in the garden in these late days of spring. Urgency sounded in the calls of bird mates. Mary could almost hear the hostas thrusting their way up through the warming soil. She watched a sparrow work to free a fallen seed from under last summer's Echinacea stand. Nature provided an abundance of food to the wildlife in spring before new growth covered it. The cleanup crew, Mary thought. I need to get myself out here cleaning up too. Yet, I'd rather strip off my clothing and roll against the earth, rub myself into the dampness of straw, and the smoothness of grass. How utterly decadent to lean and scratch bare shoulders against the welcoming rough bark of my basswood tree.

Fully clothed she lay in the bright sun on a pile of straw she'd shaken loose yesterday to spread over the strawberry plants as a mulch. She welcomed the warmth after the long winter, on muscles unused to spring's raking and digging and hoeing tasks. Just a quick rest, she thought. A few minutes of sunshine and cloud gazing. There was a fluffy white poodle and a roll of toilet paper in the sky's canvas.

Claude came around the fruit trees where she lay picking fantastic pictures from the sky. The rain last night had left the air heavy with moisture; spring scents filled Mary's head. The plants were messy, straggly, still carrying last year's debris. Mary could see the potential in their brown stems and firm green shoots. Claude stretched full length beside her. Yes he had used to do such things.

Mary remembered that same spring – a late evening scene. She'd followed the same path to the garden. Clouds passed over the full moon giving moments of clarity and times of muted dull glow to the night. Puddles muddied her shoes and she'd taken them off. How gloriously childish to disrobe my feet, to let my toes curl into the window of water, to splash mud all the way to my knees.

Mary smoothed the red quilt around her thighs, remembered her toes squishing mud. "Moon River," she sang, softly. "Wider than the miles ... I used to sing out loud in those days." She'd sung Moon River that night. Out of tune. And she'd laughed at herself. At her joy. She'd fallen silent, listening as the night creatures resumed their rightful places in the night air. The old yew tree creaked as the soft wind shifted its limbs, and in the marsh, frogs grunted their need. Down the lane a mother cow called to her bull calf and he answered with the long nasal tone his mother strained to hear.

Mary watched the past from her wheelchair, seeing herself twirl in the dim moonlight, and there was Claude standing on the porch, his hands on his hips. Her skirt hung awry on the fence post that led into the orchard. Her shoes – Oxfords – and yellow socks sat beside the puddle, and her blouse ... She could not see her blouse. Reached for the shovel to cover her nakedness, felt her whiteness looming.

What folly. What use to cover herself? What sense would that make? Mary stood, hands at her sides waiting. Claude also waited, watched. Man and wife. She, naked in the moonlight. Slowly he turned to the door. In the semi darkness he removed his flannel work shirt and hung it on the doorknob. He slipped his work pants down his thighs, past his knees, stepped out of them like a dancer, folded and set them neatly on the chair in front of his boots. His socks and underwear shed, and set aside, flashes of white thighs, long ribbons of legs and arms glimmered in the porch shadows.

He disappeared to leprechaun-like reappear from behind the rose bush. Lanky white legs free of cumbersome clothing, flicked and sliced. Mary's throat rumbled, sighed as his knees marched toward her. He circled, a wolf, predatory, his hands raised over his head humming, grinning, and the clouds uncovered the moon. Without effort Mary's hands drummed her thighs, a firm thumping; low intonations sang from her throat. There was no tune, just one note in time with the drumming and Claude's feet and his humming. They danced and sang in the emerging moonlight with the bullfrogs' accompaniment. The earth was powered with life, with energy, so that the frogs' songs and the whistling wind in the trees, and the lap of the water and Mary and Claude's movements, their noises, joined into one huge synergy of dance. They lay on the grass, holding hands, and watched as the northern lights came out to dance, the joyous colours laughing and cavorting in blissful joy at the beauty of the night.

A mighty fine night. Mary kept her eyes closed. Smiling.

Claude and she had held hands until they felt the night's chill, then they rose and ran into the house and into bed.

In the morning Mary very nearly convinced herself it was all a dream except she found her clothes neatly hung to dry in the kitchen; her shoes and socks waited on the porch beside the door. Mud streaks on her legs made her grin.

That was a night to remember. Claude grinned over his tea cup at her. "Thank you for last night."


"Mary, I'll tell you something if you promise never to breath a word of it," Stella said, as they chatted on the phone later that morning.

Mary nodded. "Go on."

"Arnie's sure got it in him." There was a smile in Stella's voice. "After the baby fell asleep last night ... we snuck outside really quiet.

Brought the quilt out and we just lay there on the grass in the backyard, looking up at the moon, Mary."

"Unhunh. And then what?"

"Just that, Mary. We just laid there. Held hands. Picked out all the stars either of us knew and it was just nice. Romantic. We saw the Northern Lights."

She sounded happy, Mary thought. Do I look happy too?

"Must have been the full moon, Stella, brought out his wild side. Claude caught something of the same fever too." Mary described some of their encounter, somewhat sheepishly admitting to their erotic moon dance.

"It was a full moon," Stella said, and over the phone Mary could hear the grin in her voice and her teacup tapping. "To the full moon."

"The full moon." Mary raised her cup to magic.


On the day that Arnie died, Mary went to the garden early to collect the peas that were ripening as fast as she could pick and jar them. With her huge bowl brimming, she was stopped on her way to the house by the sight of Arnie's rose.

In its eight years of life, the rose had climbed to the window of Mary and Claude's bedroom in the addition, and Mary trained it to grow around the window shutter. Occasionally a wayward stem broke free from the trellis, and Mary would catch it facing into the room. Sometimes she'd let a flower peek in for a week or more, enjoying a tiny thrill at the thought of Arnie's rose watching in her bedroom window. Sometimes she provided him with something worth looking in at.

Overnight, squirming black worms no thicker than a piece of baby's wool and not quite as long as Mary's pinkie fingernail, had stripped every leaf of the rose, leaving lacy, wispy veins on prickly, thick, green branches.

"Damn." Mary set down her bowl, sure, before she examined too far, that there'd be no more roses this year. She'd have to prune the rose back and spray it – spray it heavily with ... what was it that Arnie advised her to use? She'd written it down. Arnie. She glanced toward his house and saw Stella's red quilt flapping on the clothesline. Her stomach clenched.

"It's Arnie's time," she said to Claude. "I'll go over now. You come when you can." She kissed him and covered her head with a kerchief, then she rushed out the door to be with Stella. And Arnie. But he didn't need her, wouldn't again, ever.


When Mary moved to Sunny Acres, MaryArlene sewed a nametag on the inside corner of the worn red quilt, and wrote on it, in permanent marker: 'MARY JOHNSTON'. One strip especially had suffered sun-exposure as it sat on the rocker all those years, and the quilt's red brilliance had faded to brownish-pink. Sadie's neat blanket stitches had loosened through constant use and washings, and the repairs with strips of bias-cut binding to strengthen the edges had stayed a different shade, faded at their own rate – never quite the right colour.

It started off slow, Mary mused, as she sat in her wheelchair, the quilt draped over her knees, Mrs. Grieves Herbal open at the sage section. Who'd have thought that of all those ones from days past, Mary Johnston and Stella Jenkins would be left alive. Who'd have predicted it? She and Stella used to sit together over tea rhyming off the ones who'd died before them. Edward, Nelson, and Mary's father all passed when still quite young. Then Stella's parents, Mary's mother Sadie, Arnie, Mr. Fynch. Liz. Gone too. She'd lived too long. The dying had started slow but momentum picked up. "It's our Morbid Muster," Stella had said. "We know more dead people than live ones."

They'd laughed it off but the expression stuck in Mary's head. As she and Claude sat together of an evening they spoke less and less of their plans for the future, and more and more about those who had died. Arnie's passing put the fear of the Lord into Claude, who was still a good man, Mary knew that, but she had to keep reminding herself of his goodness.

She looked hard at him some days trying to recognize the fellow she'd married – who'd sat beside her on the wagon, slapping the horses' backs with his reins, laughing easily, making plans. The man who'd shyly asked if she'd come see his workshop rarely showed his face in the later years. Too much heartache.

Mary closed the book on her knees. A Modern Herbal – by Mrs. Grieves. Her bible. That's what Claude used to call it, and Stella too. You could read the herbal and make what you read mean almost anything you wanted. Just as  people did with the other bible. Mary remembered Liz using her deceased husband's King James version to prove her point many a time. Claude too, had been one of the best at making Mary feel inadequate by quoting from the Holy Book. Or one of the worst. Advancing age gave him the self-appointed right to judge whatever and whoever came across his path. He could find a passage to prove anybody wrong. And he went to extreme lengths to do just that.

It became his favourite evening past time as he and Mary sat by the fire. She would seek answers from Mrs. Grieves Herbal, while Claude, his spectacles freshly cleaned, settled down to prove how one or another of the neighbours was going straight to hell.

"D'ya see old Herbie Byer stookin' his straw this morning, Mary? He figured none of us would see him working the back fifty, but you don't put that sort of thing by the good Lord. Workin' on a Sunday. The seventh day was made for rest. Says so right here." Claude stabbed the textual proof and read, 'Thou Shalt Keep Holy The Sabbath Day.' Holy, Mary. It's God's law."

Mary thought about reminding Claude that the Lord also counselled, 'Judge not that ye not be judged,' but what did it matter? Claude's mind clasped certain truths; one of them was that the wisdom from the bible applied to other folk. He never said that out loud but … Their neighbours were in for a sound scolding tonight.

"It's not bad enough him workin' on a Sunday but I see he's letting that Ethel of his run wild. Off every Wednesday night into town at 7 o'clock. She's headin' into the bingo hall, she is. Gambling." Claude spit the word out in the tone other men saved for swear words.

What will he think of me? Mary often found her mind wandering over that thought as she watched out her window at Sunny Acres Residence. I hope I don't have to meet up with him when I die. He'll kill me. "You'll already be dead, you senile fool." Had she said that out loud? She listened but no one came into her room to see what she was on about, and now that she'd strayed into the rut of thinking about Claude she couldn't seem to wrench free.

These days her mind veered down avenues she'd rather not travel. Time enough for dealing with judgement day when I get there, she tried to tell it, but once started there were no brakes, no control to this careering mind of hers. The only stops allowed were when she got to some thought she didn't care to dwell on.

Always there was a lengthy stop at why there was no photograph of Claude, her husband of fifty-one years, who'd provided her with a comfortable home and wholesome food and serviceable, sturdy clothing. What kind of ungrateful woman didn't keep a picture of her deceased husband on her night table? Even give him a kiss maybe before falling off to sleep?

Mary knew she couldn't have a picture of Claude anywhere in sight. She'd tried, after he'd died, to have their wedding picture on a white, crocheted doily, on the night stand, by the bed, right next to the bible he used to read every night. He'd watched her, from the ornate brass frame, eyes all squinty, slitty. She tried to tell herself it was the sun but she couldn't get comfortable in the room with him staring at her like that. No matter where she stood, or where she sat, those eyes followed her. And he talked to her too.

'You're not gonna wear that dress are ya, Mary? Ya look just like one of them old cows heading off to the bingo hall. A Jessabelle.' She swore that's what he was thinking. Well so what was the harm that she learned to enjoy a game of bingo on a Wednesday night? Coming home with Stella, her dress stinking of cigarette smoke, she knew he'd be shaking his head and writing down her sins on the tablet. Sure, probably God put him in charge of her conscience, her admittance into heaven. Him and his mother.

Mary tried talking to the priest about it. "Ah, Mary," he'd said, and Mary had trouble remembering it was the priest she was speaking to and not her husband; they sounded so much alike. "You know that Claude - God rest his soul - is in heaven praying for you, wanting only the best for you. A fine woman like yourself." Father Byers' quick glance took in her dark brown, calf-length dress with approval. "Surely, you've nothing to feel guilty about. A God-fearing woman like yourself. Make a proper examination of conscience and you'll find that your mind will be put to rest."

Stella laughed for a long time when Mary repeated the conversation. "Examination of your conscience. Don't let that frustrated, muddled up priest make you feel guilty. Put the pictures of Claude face down in the dresser drawer where they won't bother you. That's the solution for that problem."

And it was. Pretty much. She'd made him stop watching her, but she still worried what she'd ever say to him when they met up again. If there was one thing that Mary knew about Claude Johnston it was that he was not a forgiving man. She pulled her sweater closer around her shoulders and fastened all the buttons before shoving her hands back underneath the faded red quilt. But how much did he know about what happened before he died? Did the dead automatically become privy to all knowledge? Could they read minds? See into the past?

The red quilts for Mary and Stella had been the last ones that Mary's mother, Sadie Murphy, designed and worked on. It was lucky, Mary thought, that she'd been able to keep hers – that it didn't get raffled off or sold to raise money for one of those projects the church ladies kept themselves busy at.

I suppose if I threw the damn, worn rag out, it would take a lot of the guilt with it, Mary told herself, fighting again a battle she never won. In fact, the guilt quilt served to bring not only sadness, but pleasure too, especially when her memories were of Arnie.

How could just one night still cause such conflict? Was it her married status that brought her such guilt? Or that he was the husband of her best and dearest friend? Surely the daughter spawned during their single night of lovemaking, served to remind both herself and Arnie of their sensuous marathon. Perhaps they'd never again spoken of it, never again allowed themselves to be alone together, because they knew that there'd be no stopping their physical need if ever an opportunity arose.

Mary wondered that Stella never commented on the lapse in Mary and Arnie's friendship. Did Claude ever wonder at the unexpected passion that brought Mary out of a sound sleep? Did Stella wonder the same of Arnie?

During her involvement in the community, Mary realized she wasn't the only woman with a secret. It kept her occupied gazing around the church or in the market, making up stories of who was hiding what from whom. She even dared – but only once – to guess aloud that a fellow quilter was off her stitching that day and was there something she wanted to share to make her feel better?

The secrets were well kept, and she grew to know they were more titillating locked away – to be summoned in quiet, solitary moments to polish, to savour, to taste, to relive while sitting in an old rocker or a wheelchair with a faded red quilt tucked around one's knees.

She smiled thinking about Sadie, who for years had bragged about her perfect teeth. "People say I've got the straightest, whitest teeth of anyone," Sadie Murphy told Mary for just as long as she could remember. "Not one cavity. Not even a chip out of one of them!"

In 1970, when Mary was 49 years old, and Sadie Murphy was 85, Mary and Claude heard Mother calling in the night. They'd gone to her, and found her sitting on the toilet unable to get up. With one of them on either side, her arms slung over their necks, they'd supported her weight and helped her return to bed.

Two clear pictures stayed with Mary from that night: mother, toothless on the toilet, and her pink-gummed teeth – tops and bottoms – slightly yellowed but perfect, sitting askew and water-covered in their blue porcelain dish on the night table.

Why lie about that? And, what else did Mother lie about? People lived with untold truths. She delved into what they said to compare their outward appearances with what she knew was true.

It became a game, a quest. What and how much were they hiding? How far could people be pushed? How much could she learn before they snapped their mouths shut, aware of having given away too much, and conscious that to deny what they'd admitted would only confirm Mary's suspicion that more squirmed and writhed beneath the surface, pulsing and throbbing with the need to be exposed.

What had Colleen Cronie meant when she'd said "I tell my husband I take knitting class every second Tuesday. Better start showing some results." Colleen had ordered a knitted, newborn-sized, sweater from Sadie. Mary asked a few questions, and soon Colleen, with encouraging nods and murmurs from Mary, was telling about her visits with her daughter's illegitimate son every second Tuesday.

Her fellow human beings needed to confess those private thoughts and foibles and to be accepted regardless of the content of their disclosures. She studied the faces of the confessors as they told their secrets: their hatred of a child; an abortion disguised as a miscarriage; unrequited wishes. Even the smallest confession, such as a book borrowed from the library and never returned, relieved the teller, and Mary envied the visible effects of their unburdening. Their frowns smoothed; their shoulders relaxed; their bodies let go of their defences.

Mary never divulged confidences, although the opportunity presented itself regularly. In her heart was carried the greatest secret of all. To tell would destroy her husband, her daughter, and her best friend, so Mary kept the secret safely wrapped in her red quilt. She whispered her longing to Arnie's rose when she was alone in the garden, and she relived the secret in dreams as real as the event itself.

Mary sat in her wheelchair gazing out the window, past the parking lot, over the road and across the river into the trees and up into the sky beyond. What a wide view she had since the fir tree had been murdered. As wide a view in this realm as she had over the days gone by.

This time of her life, filled with aches and memories, meant a person could sit staring at nothing and wander for hours over the landscapes of the past. Today Mary's mind latched onto Stella's anger that day so long ago... More anger than was warranted, it seemed now from Mary's vantage point of thirty-seven years hence.

"I always feel so much better after talking to you," Stella had said, over a cup of tea in Mary's kitchen. "You must come to bingo with me. How about it?"

"Claude wouldn't think much of that."

"The old geezer! Do him good to sit home alone one night. What's he got on you that you sit here wasting your life away? As if you're his serving woman. He tells you what to do, and you jump. How high, Claude? Would you like your tea now, Claude? Tell the old bugger to fix his own tea. You and me are going to bingo and that's the last of it."

They went to bingo, and that night Mary slithered into bed much later than usual, sure that Claude was awake as she crept in, though he made no indication. She was careful not to let her cold feet touch his tempting warmth. The next morning he was his usual, morose self. She couldn't tell if he was angry or just quiet. There were no dirty dishes in the sink, so Mary knew he hadn't eaten while she'd been gone. He'd sniffed the air as she passed and Mary noticed the smell of smoke in her hair and on her clothes and she hurried through her morning chores to bathe and wash her hair.

Claude had been polite to Stella when he came upon her and Mary on the back porch later in the morning.

"Join us for tea, Claude," Mary invited, and he sat, waiting with Stella, who'd stopped in unexpectedly while Mary slipped into the house to get him a cup and to refill the cookie plate.

Mary was sure that Claude and Stella spoke while she fussed in the kitchen, but when she'd come back, they were turned away from each other suddenly finding the landscape all absorbing, and Mary's conversation dropped around them like the prickly chestnuts landing around the tree on the lawn.

"Stella's quite the bingo player," Mary said. Thud.

"Claude's been working on a new style of weather vane." Plonk.

"It's a beautiful fall day." She threw that one out to anyone. Kerplunk.

Now, Mary thought, patting the faded red quilt, I prefer the silence, but that day there was a need for conversation; it seemed wrong, antisocial, to sit with two other people, and none of us speaking. She gazed out the window, let her mind soar over the memory before zooming in close to poke and sort and examine. Like a still life, she saw the three of them. Claude, in his work clothes, sat in the lawn chair he'd welded from piping left over from a job, with its snugly-fitted green and white striped cushion that Mary had made. He looked comfortable at first glance, but ignored the tea she set in front of him. He didn't take even one sip. He was quiet, except for his tapping foot. The still life came alive. Claude's foot tap, tap, tapping on the wooden porch was quick, staccato, like a woodpecker. Or a rooster.

"That's a lovely new dress you've on," Mary had said to Stella. "And a hat too. Aren't you the stylish one?'

Stella blushed, looked at Claude, looked away at the chestnut tree.

Claude's foot tapped. He cleared his throat. He unbuttoned the top button of his work shirt. He wore a clean work shirt.

"Is Emerelda sick this morning?" Stella asked.

Claude frowned at Stella. His foot stopped tapping. "Mary just got a phone call, Stella. Fifteen minutes, maybe half an hour ago." He cleared his throat again. "Emerelda died this morning."

"Oh." Stella said. "I ... oh ... I see." She laughed a nervous, un-Stella-like laugh. "I'll need to fix the flowers then, for the altar. You'll miss her, Mary. You'll miss visiting Emerelda. I'm so sorry." She adjusted her hat. "I don't know what to say."

"Yes," Claude said. "It will change our routine here at home." He looked toward his workshop.

"You're wondering about changing the pattern of the weather vanes, aren't you? Don't stay here making small talk with us girls if there's work you need to do. Stella's here. You go on out to your workshop."

Viewing the still life from her wheelchair at Sunny Acres, Mary saw that Stella was not herself. Her lipstick smeared the teacup and needed special scrubbing to remove. Stella almost never wore lipstick except to church on Sunday. Certainly she didn't wear lipstick to visit Mary for morning tea. And she wore a brand new, yellow, flowered dress, and a sun hat with a red ribbon. Mary had assumed that Stella stopped in on her way to church where it was her turn to prepare the flowers for the funeral service.

The still life became clearer. Stella hadn't known about the funeral yet or even that Emerelda was dead. It was too soon to be getting flowers in place.

"Well, well well," Mary said to no one at all. Her mouth dropped open as she zoomed in closer to the scene. Stella hadn't known Emerelda was dead and so she thought I'd be off visiting Emerelda, as I did every Wednesday morning.

Mary's attention turned again to Claude. A clean work shirt. His hair was combed, she saw, because he wasn't wearing the usual peaked cap. Were those clean jeans? Mary's mouth dropped wider. You son of a bitch.

"Mary! What are you doing in here all by yourself?" Cathy, hands on her hips, pulled Mary abruptly away from Claude and Stella and into her bedroom at Sunny Acres, where she sat, knees covered with her worn red quilt.

Mary looked at Cathy.

"Claude. He ..." Mary let her mouth stay open. "Stella ... Claude ... he put on a clean shirt. And they ..."

"Claude was your husband, Mary." Cathy explained loudly. "You and Claude were married ..." Cathy's eyes swept across the wall over Mary's headboard. "You were married for fifty-one years," Cathy smiled at her, squinted, and continued. "Claude was a blacksmith. That's like a kind of a welder, I think."

Mary followed Cathy's eyes to the wall, to the typed sheet taped over Mary's bed.

**Mary Johnston D.N.R.**

**Birthdate: June 25th, 1921**

**Husband: Claude (dec.) blacksmith**

**Married 51 years**

**Children: Edward (dec. infant)**

**MaryArlene: (psychotherapist) Born 1962**

**Grandchildren: no**

**Occupation: Mary did volunteer work for her church, housewife, gardener, worked at Fynch's Apothecary**

**Fav. Food: Rhubarb Pie and Chocolates**

Mary realized her mouth was still hanging open and she shut it. She smoothed the faded quilt over her knees. Today was not the day to tell Cathy about what she'd been thinking. Some secrets – most secrets - were best kept quiet.

Her eyes traveled again to the typed sheet over her bed.

**Husband: Claude (dec.) blacksmith**

# Chapter 25

## Heartsease – Viola tricolour (Johnny jump up)

**Old English favourite with charming small purple, lavender and yellow flowers. Was once a potent symbol of romance for courting couples. Used for dropsy, respiratory catarrh and skin eruptions. Flowers are edible and are said to encourage the eater to give compliments and surprise gifts.**

The Deathwatch, Stella called it.

Mary sat in a chair beside the daybed to eat her breakfast, while she read from the herbal and intermittently peeped over her glasses at Claude, lying prone on the bed. He watched her all the time it seemed and she'd grown able to allow it without anger. She went about her daily duties knowing he hadn't long to spend in this world and determined that he be comfortable during his last days. Mary wanted nothing more to feel guilty about.

She smoothed her skirt as she stood. She was still a tall woman, too thin as always, but strong; strong enough to handle a shovel and today the garden called to her. Today was a day of wind and birdcalls. Towhees spoke mating tweets from the oak tree not yet budded, and a pair of robins fussed over nest building. Mary intended to clean away the dandelions that threatened anarchy in the asparagus patch.

She looked about, dry-eyed, swallowing the lump that worked to surface. No use to maintain a garden that didn't serve her purpose. No need anymore to wonder if she was putting her time and efforts to good use. No need to work for the sake of work itself. Fresh vegetables could be got cheap at the market and the young folk selling there needed the money to live, so why should Mary grow them? The work was hard and the memories harder. Claude often told her she didn't need such a large garden, or that they could get someone in to help.

That wasn't the answer; the garden was Mary's world.

Where the Mothers had wielded their power in the kitchen, Mary's strength centered in her garden. Mary knew her hands could make or break a heart. And a life. She directed her mind onto good thoughts.

One lone Johnny jump up had been missed in last week's purge. They'd come back strong after the fiasco with the hired gardener (Mary tried but couldn't remember her name) and they'd seeded themselves all around the herb garden cozying up to the beebalm, the sage, the woodruff, and the parsley, but these last few years, there'd been a decline. Their stems were straggly, their leaves scrawny and this time, Mary had decided to clear them completely from the patch.

She stroked the purple face of the johnny jump up. How delicate its petals. How fine the wee stamens that protruded from its center. She pinched the flower from its stem with a quick twist; ground it between thumb and forefinger, easily crushing its tender soft velvet beauty into a damp purple stain on her palm. As easy as that.

Now, no more.

Mary stood, wiped her hands against her skirt, and trod back to the house.

Claude lay on the daybed in the fireplace room, breathing steadily but with a definite rattle that could not be ignored. Mary sat beside him watching him die. Like doing penance. His eyes had closed while she'd been out. All the years she'd spent blaming him for Edward's death when he'd never really been to blame. And she'd blamed him for them moving back to the farm, living under Liz's rule. Finally in the end what did it matter? What good had the blaming done? It couldn't bring Edward back, and Claude lived with enough guilt already.

His skin, pale at breakfast, was whiter now. A scant cup of tea – no milk – and two soggy bits of toast were all he'd eaten today. She patted his forehead with a clean white towel. It was little enough to do, though unnecessary. Claude had no sweat left in him. No sweat. No strength. Hardly enough breath. Was this the man who'd twirled her round the dance floor every Thursday night when he was courting her? Was this the man who'd dreamed of moving to town and making a fine living as an independent business owner? Was this the same man who'd loved her and then seemingly just as easily left her to fend for herself amongst the grief and chaos after Edward's death? Why had he turned so hard and distant when she needed him most? She wiped his brow again, touched her lips to his, willed him to look at her. See her pain. But his own journey drew all his effort.

She waited.

Claude's breathing stopped. Mary wiped his forehead again. Checked his carotid vein for a pulse. Nothing. Good. She sat beside him in the loud silence. How long he had held her to this place. How much pain had she carried over these floors? Now, with barely a whimper, finally, it was over.

Mary stretched her legs. Now she could wear slacks. And makeup. And jewellery. Now that Claude wasn't going to look up at her from his bible with that wide-eyed disapproving stare. Now she could go to bingo with Stella without guilt. No more evening meals to prepare and to serve and to sit through in silence, worried that tonight would be the night he'd make some accusation of a sin she'd committed. No more would she kneel at his insistence, to spend the night on the floor beside him, praying in front of the crucifix. No more of that.

Mary thought she might stop going to church now that those days were over. And she might just buy herself one of those new contraptions the women used nowadays to curl their eyelashes. MaryArlene had one. Give herself a lift. She would let Stella put some colour into her hair. MaryArlene would be happy that Mary could accept perfume and nail polish. There was no end to the things she would do.

The phone rang. Mary listened to the answering machine earn its keep. "You've reached Claude and Mary Johnston. We'll call you back when we receive your message." Beep.

"Hi, Mom. Dad. It's MaryArlene. Just checking to see how you're doing this morning. It's about 9:30. I've one more seminar and this conference is over. I should be on the road by 3 o'clock and at your place two and a half hours after that. Call me on my cell anytime after 3. Talk to you later today. I love you." Beep.

Stella knocked and let herself in through the kitchen door. "He's gone hasn't he? I knew it somehow." She put her hand on Mary's shoulder. "You did right by him, Mary." She stood beside Mary who stayed sitting next to Claude's still body.

"Aye. Not perfectly, but as right as I was able."

"He's been a hard man to live with. Arnie found that out earlier than you and I did, God bless his soul."

Mary nodded.

"Now you'll have a load off your shoulders."

"That I will," Mary said. "I've been here thinking all this time as I watched him die. Now what? What'll I do with my hands and my time and my ... self?" She held up her finger to stop Stella's answer.

"I thought, I'll just pick myself up and get doing normal things. You know ... church ... and gardening ... and I can visit with MaryArlene ... and when I think that ..." Mary left a tear to slide neatly down her cheek. "when I think that, I realize just how far from normal I've wandered."

Stella opened her mouth. Mary stopped her this time with a headshake. "It happened so slowly ... seemed so natural, so normal ... I'll just ... I don't know how I'll be with other people. I mean ... I don't ... I can't ... conversation ... and jokes ... I don't think I can ..."

"Shshshsh ..." Stella stroked Mary's head. "We'll get by. You'll get by. There. It's good to cry." They stood rocking against each other in the welcome silence after the long vigil of the deathwatch.

"I'll tell you a secret," Stella whispered, when Mary's breathing was more steady. "You and Claude were probably just as normal as any of the rest of us around here. There is no normal. Not as far as I've seen."

Mary chuckled into Stella's shoulder. "Claude and I ... normal?" She pulled away. "Claude and I ... you think we were normal. Hah!" She grinned, as a laugh began deep in her belly and spewed out in waves. "Normal!"

Stella laughed too and they were both laughing and crying.

"Shshsh." Stella held her arms around herself. "Shshsh. You'll wake the dead."

Mary tucked Claude's bible under his right hand. "He's taking that God-forsaken book with him, I tell you that. That's one thing I won't miss. Claude and his never ending preaching."

They stood together to watch him lie still.

"I came to see if you need a drink, Mary. Are you feeling dry?" The aide stopped at the window a looming bulk of dark against the sunshine. "You are so lucky to have this room with its lovely view. I could sit and stare out this window all day long."

"You don't know how right you are, dearie. What drinks are you offering this morning?"

# Chapter 26

**One of the healthiest ways to gamble is with a trowel and a package of seeds.**

Stella and Mary rolled their wheelchairs side by side on their way to the greenhouse until Frenchie, parked in the centre of the hall, blocked their progress. "You and I are the only sane ones left, you know," Stella said to Mary, rapping her plastic tea cup on Frenchie's knuckles when he laid his hand on her knee.

"Sane." Mary echoed. "You mean like normal? Are you sure?"

She could sense Claude in the background. "Making a new garden! At your age. It's foolishness. A complete waste of time."

Mary ignored him. He was dead. He couldn't be talking to her. She had every right to pretend she didn't hear him.

"We do the best we can," Stella said.

"Yeah. Well. That's not what Claude would say. Maybe he's right. The bingo's a waste of time. So's the gardening."

"Here we go," Stella sighed. "Soon you'll start on about your hair being too long or some other silly notion."

"Well it is," Mary said, stroking her tight grey bun. "Too long for a matron like me. And I should lower my hemlines at my age." She lifted her stockinged leg. "My calves are still shapely though."

"Of course they are." Stella rolled on down the hall. "You've beautiful legs. And your hair is a lovely shade of grey."

"You don't think..." Mary trailed off, thinking ahead, picking her words. "Claude will kill me when he sees me again. I know he will. He knows I ate meat on Friday instead of fish. And I used the good dishes."

"I get tired of your worrying. Isn't there a pill you can take for it?"

"I try to imagine what I'll say to him. How I'll explain all the things I did and am doing that I'm not supposed to do. I don't know how."

"Why can't you worry about normal stuff? Like what's for dinner or what to wear today?"

"You're right. What about you? Did you sleep good last night?"

"I had this dream," Stella said. "There was a group of children, and a baseball field, and a herd of vicious attacking rats. Every time one came near, I lifted him on the edge of my slipper and tossed him out of sight."

"Are you certain the rats were male?" Mary asked.

Stella shrugged. "Don't know. Do you think it matters?"

"It could mean that you see all men as rats, dangerous to children and that you would like to save the world by shooing them all away—making them all disappear."

"Jeepers, Mary. I thought it was a kind of funny, interesting dream. I don't want to change the world. Not at my age." Stella indicated Chris with a nod of her head. "How come he's so quiet? Girlfriend trouble?"

Chris looked up from his table and bit the end of his pen. "Could I interrupt you girls to ask some questions?" He waved his clipboard at them.

"Anything for you, Chris," Stella teased.

Chris read from his notes. "Has there been any change in your sleeping habits since you've been participating in the Horticultural Therapy Program?"

Stella shook her head. Mary grinned. "She's been dreaming about men—hairy, long-tailed men. Think it's significant?"

Chris looked up. "On a scale of one to five where five is most important, rate the following: "How important is this program to you?"

"Five," both women answered.

"Are they talking about cutbacks?" Mary asked. "Is this why you're asking us?"

"No. It's just an assessment." Chris didn't look up this time.

"Assessment," Mary repeated. "Of the programme?"

"The programme and the coordinator. Couldn't let anyone get too comfortable in their job."

"Are they giving you the boot?"

"More of a promotion really," Chris answered. "I'll be training the new therapist, Dawn. That will give you a chance to get used to her before I take over at the new home across town." He read from the questionnaire. "How important are the friendships you've made while participating in the programme?"

"Five!" both women shouted.

"You're our friend," Mary said. "You can't leave us now that we've got you trained."

"That's the problem with doing a good job. Promotion they call it. The Peter Principle I call it. They'll keep on promoting me until I reach my level of incompetence, where I'll stay until I retire."

"Sarcasm is horrible in one as young as you. I mean cynicism."

"He's jaded," Stella agreed. "Fresh out of university, you'd think a promotion would be exactly what he'd want."

"It is, I guess," Chris said. "But I like all the people here, and I've got such great plans for this place." He turned the pages of his clipboard so they could see a chart he'd drawn with seasonal activities written in for each month.

"You're too smart to spend your days with us," Mary patted Chris' arm. "You'll come back to visit."

"You're right. I do have to move on. I won't forget you ladies though. You taught me a lot of stuff." Chris hugged each of them in turn. "I'll have to come back just for your advice. Anyway, I'm here for another week. See you tomorrow."


After supper, Mary found her box of blank greeting cards and went through them all, searching for the most flowery one.

"Dear Chris," she began. A lump formed in her throat. Tears blurred the words, transporting her back to a rainy Saturday morning in 1967. If she didn't blink too much, her blurred vision gave almost the same view as through the rain-covered window of her kitchen back on the farm.

She'd sat across from Claude at breakfast, their cutlery clinking against the Corel dishware. The CBC Radio One announcer explained to his listeners that a group of scientists working with a research grant had isolated what they hoped was the bacteria responsible for stomach ulcers. "Bacteria," Mary said. "Unbelievable and yet it makes perfect sense. I wish I stayed on at school."

Claude peered over his newspaper.

"I should have stayed in school," Mary said.

He cocked his eyebrow at her, refolded his newspaper to the next page. "You were smart," he said. "The time wasn't right though – with the war and then the babies."

"I could have been a doctor."

"You wouldn't have ever been home," Claude said. "It was good how it was. We had a good life. Have a good life."

"But we never travelled. We never saved any lives."

"I think we saved Stella's life. And the mothers. I think we made their lives better."

"Yes." Mary listened to the radio as a caller asked could he start treating his ulcer then with an antibiotic.

"We don't all get to save the world, Mary."

"No. Still, I always wanted to go to Europe, to Germany, and study herbal medicine. See the mountains. I never did that."

"We didn't do everything we planned," Claude pushed away from the table. "Time to do some work."

Mary sat sipping her tea. Some days it was harder than others to get up from the table and do all the things on her list. All those things she should be doing. What was the point?

Mary blinked, and the tears faded along with the memory. I probably should have gone to school, learned medicine or Archaeology or something just to get out with other people, thinking new thoughts. I probably should do it right now and save myself from all this wondering. Could I?

Mary read her words so far:

"Dear Chris,". She bit her pen, then wrote.

"You've been a great friend, and I'll miss you terribly. We'll all miss your friendly, helpful attitude. Best of luck with your promotion. Please come see us often. We'll be in the greenhouse.

Live your dreams,

Love and Best Wishes,

Mary

"You'd think I'd be used to people leaving at my age," she said to Claude's picture that had reappeared on her dresser. "And he's not even dying. I have to stop being such a big baby. Maybe Chris's replacement will be even better than he is."

From his frame Claude squinted unsmiling as Mary put the card into its envelope, stuck out her tongue and sealed it.

She stuck her tongue out further at Claude for a few seconds, then rolled her wheelchair to the dresser and set his picture face down. Again.

Mary handed the card to Christopher with what she hoped was a gracious smile. "It's been great having you here. I hope you'll be back often to visit."

Christopher pulled her into a gentle hug. "I'll sure miss having you and Stella tune me in every day." He reached behind him and brought forward a plant wrapped in green cellophane.

"A mum." Mary laughed.

"Well you are a lot like my mum. I thought that would give you a bit of a kick."

"I know exactly where I'll put it too." Mary wheeled her chair around and rolled toward her garden box. "A white mum," she mused, "virginal. Glad it wasn't a lily."

"You don't like lilies?" inquired a young female voice.

Mary looked up to see a curly haired, brunette about Christopher's age peering into the herb garden. "Who are you?" Mary asked.

"Mary, this is Dawn, the new horticultural therapist. Dawn, I'd like you to meet Mary, our resident herbalist."

"Pleased to meet you." Dawn held out her hand to Mary, and when Mary reciprocated, laid her left hand on top of Mary's, sandwiching it between her own and lightly squeezing and patting it.

"I sense a story behind your dislike of lilies. Maybe you'll tell me one of these days."

"It's a long story," Mary said. "Took up most of my life."

"I hope to be here quite a while.I like your nasturtiums."

When Stella arrived in the greenhouse, Dawn and Mary were chatting about the merits of different herbal remedies.

"I'm sure everyone agrees by now that Echinacea, taken at the first sign of a sniffle or a sore throat is the perfect preventative cure. But," Dawn screwed up her face in distaste. "Wasn't there some sort of herbal cure I read about where you mix certain plant roots with mare's urine and take it as a tea? Prevents boils or some such thing?"

"Cure ya' or kill ya!" Mary grinned. "When I worked at Fynch's Apothecary, our policy was not to be too specific about the ingredients in our remedies. To make a long story short...." She stopped mid-sentence remembering, then continued. "Mr. Fynch's standard instructions were 'Mix this with a spoonful of sugar.'"

"Just like Mary Poppins, Just a spoonful of sugar helps the medicine go down...." Both Mary and Stella joined in, and Christopher applauded when the singing ended.

"I'm so embarrassed," Mary said to Stella over her stewed prunes the next morning. "Did you hear me saying 'to make a long story short'? Dawn didn't seem to mind, but I remember old ladies, and old men, starting off like that, and I'd be rolling my eyes, knowing I was in for an extra long, boring time of it."

Stella nodded. "Kind of makes it official when you hear yourself saying a thing like that. Makes us old people."

"Too late for redemption, I suppose," Mary said. "I might as well just go with it."

Dawn asked why Mary grew borage in her herb plot. "It's quite scraggly and messy."

"I know," Mary said. "I tell it to pull up its socks but the borage is a dear plant to me."

"I have a spider plant at home," Dawn said. "Always dropping leaves. Dripping water on my carpet. It's a keeper anyway."

Dawn encouraged Mary to keep the herbs contained in specific spots within her garden.

"Keep them under control. Well pruned," she suggested, and Mary found herself pleased with the neat and tidy demeanour of her herb plot. Keeping the sage plant trimmed back encouraged new shoots to develop. Tender lime green leaves sprouted from the herb's woody stem.

"Tell me more about your family," Dawn said, as they bent over the nasturtium plants in search of the round black seeds they had decided to try pickling.

"My family," Mary repeated. "We're all spread out now. I came over here to Canada after the war; left the rest of them in Switzerland."

"Switzerland! I've always wanted to see the Alps." Dawn's cheeks flushed.

"I couldn't bear to stay after I lost both my son and my husband in a freak accident..." Mary let her voice trail off. She brought her hand to her throat; fluttered her eyelids.

"A freak accident?" Dawn sighed. "The mountains must be so beautiful."

"Beautiful! Ha." Mary spat the word back at Dawn. "The mountains are my enemy! Nature's cruel joke played out upon unsuspecting innocents."

Dawn's eyes widened further.

"You don't want to hear an old woman rambling on. I'll leave you to your task." Mary turned her wheelchair around, winking at the sage plant as she did so.

"But, Mary, I do want to hear. And we're not done looking for seeds."

"Yes, you're right. I guess I forgot." Mary wheeled her chair back into place. "It's a long time since I pickled nasturtium seeds."

"Tell me a happy memory of the mountains. Do nasturtiums grow over in Switzerland?" Dawn asked. "Was it the right zone in mountain country?"

"We grew them as annuals," Mary answered. "Just the same as we do here. My Arnie loved 'em pickled. He called them tasty nasties."

"Was Arnie your husband?"

"Arnie was the love of my life." Mary closed her eyes, lost in the memories. "He gave me roses. Yellow roses. Such a romantic."

Dawn sighed appreciatively.

"He was a fine-looking man too. Dark shiny hair. Smiling blue eyes that lit up when he saw me. There's some people are just made to be together." Mary sighed at the memory. "I never went back to Switzerland once I came over here. Now my family is writing me letters asking me to go back."

"Wow! You should go." Dawn said.

"Yes. I suppose. There's a castle there still, in the family name and some cousins, nieces and nephews. Probably some I've never met. I've been gone so long." Mary paused, enjoying Dawn's unbridled interest. "I should go back," Mary said. "You're doing a good job of convincing me. Hire a nurse as a travelling companion and move back to the old homestead."

"Go off on an adventure," Dawn encouraged. "Maybe the fresh mountain air would do you good. You won't have any trouble finding a nurse to travel with you."

"It's not really possible at my age though."

"My grandmother travels everywhere," Dawn answered. "And she's old. Over eighty."

"I suppose I should," Mary said, as if it was possible. "Pull on my hiking boots … well maybe not that. I'd like to go back and see if the edelweiss still grows in my backyard garden. Visit my little monument to Arnie and Edward. So long ago but it seems like yesterday."

"I shoulda known you'd be in here," Stella said from the door. "I bin lookin' all over for you. You could have said where you were going."

"Good morning, Stella. Mary was just telling me about her time in Switzerland. Tell me, Mary, do the cows really wear bells around their necks?"

"Oh they do. Makes them easier to find behind the rocks and in the scrub. There was always the faint sound of cow bells off in the distance around home. I used to think it was their way of talking to each other. When my dad called the cows in for milking the sound would ring loud and clear."

"You were never in Switzerland," Stella said.

Mary didn't reply but stared off across the room.

"What are you doin' anyways?" Stella asked Dawn.

She set to the task of collecting nasturtium seeds with Dawn; after a while Mary stopped staring into space and joined them.

"I'm worried about you, Mary," Stella said, as they sat in Mary's room after supper. "You feeling okay?"

"Oh sure," Mary said. "Can't hardly walk. All my family's dead except MaryArlene who I see about once a month. Yeah, I'm just great. Peachy." She scowled. "Listen to me bitching. I've got about the best friend ever. That's something. You must get tired of listening to me."

Stella laughed. "A little bit."

"I know," Mary said. "Let's go make some fun. Raise a little hell."

"You're a dangerous best friend. Always were," Stella said. "Will we sneak outside and play Knock Down Ginger on the residents' windows?"

"That's always fun."

"That was a good one too when we thought of hanging all the paintings in the TV room upside down."

"They took my saran wrap away or we could cover a couple of toilets."

"That was one of our better ideas."

"Christine almost knocked herself out when she smacked her head with the whole telephone."

The women grinned at each other. "Yes. Tape the receiver to the hand set. Good one. We haven't played a good trick in a long time."

"I do like the clear tape. It has such possibilities." As Mary spoke she rummaged in her top dresser drawer and found, hidden in the sleeve of a sweater, a partly used roll of clear wide tape. She tucked it behind her back with a wink at Stella. "In case we think of a use for it." She wheeled her chair to the door and looked both ways down the hall. "Time for our evening roll, my dear?"

"After you." Stella motioned to Mary to lead. They peeked into the dining room. The chairs were all neatly shoved under the tables, place cards with names and dietary requirements sat in the centre of each table.

"They've got everything all set up for breakfast," Mary said, as she removed the tape from its hiding place. "So tidy and organized. Shall we make sure the cutlery doesn't get blown away?" She winced as the tape screeched coming off the roll, then she taped a setting of cutlery securely to the plastic tablecloth. "There you go." She read from the name card. "Mrs. E. Brown. Enjoy your diabetic prunes."

"Very neat."

Working quickly and keeping a wary watch on the doorways into the dining room, in ten minutes they had taped half of the cutlery into place.

"I'd love to finish this, but it's risky. If they catch us they'll undo all of our hard work."

"And we can't have that. Let's take another roll through the wing. See if there's any other maintenance we can do."

"Ah. Ah! Ah! There's what's his name. Mr. Wanna-come-in-my-room-and-play-with-my-magic-stick."

"He's dozing. When opportunity knocks…"

Mary and Stella stopped in front of the window.

"We won't need the tape. We can slide up on either side of him and perform the button-his-cuffs-to-the-arms-of-his-chair trick. We'll be gone before he knows what hit him."

Mary tapped the window and waved at the woman who'd just parked her car. "That's Jim Beasley's daughter. Wonder why she's here so late."

Stella waved out the window too. "Now, focus, Mary. We're on a mission."

"Right. Sorry. You take his left arm. I'll slide up on his right."

"Aren't we devils?" Stella said, as they started toward the unsuspecting fellow resident who snored into his shoulder.

When Mary buttoned his shirtsleeve around the wheelchair armrest, he snorted and rolled his head to his other shoulder.

Stella buttoned the sleeve on her side, and silently the two women rolled away down the hallway, its bright lights glinting in their pure, white hair.

"Tempting as it is to stay and watch the results of our handiwork, our giggles might give us away."

"We're so bad," Stella said. "You've corrupted me. I used to be such a good girl!"

"My mission is accomplished then. Besides, we've got nothing to lose." Mary scanned the area. "For tomorrow we die." She shook her fist above her head once, but quickly brought her arm down to rest and massaged her shoulder and neck. "I know better than to do that." She grimaced.

"I gotta ask at the desk for a pain pill. Hope this neck business isn't gonna start again. Divine retribution, Claude would say."

"Didn't you tell Dawn your husband's name was Arnie?" Stella squinted.

"No. I did not. I said," Mary whispered, "that Arnie was the love of my life. And he was." She looked up into the ceiling lights. "How do you like that, Claude Johnston?" As if he could hear her. As if he would listen if he could.

"Although ... Claude made some fine moves in his younger days. He just turned sour when he got to be mature. Didn't believe in feeding his mind. No fertilizer. Except he read the Bible. No outside interests." She laughed without humour. "Except for the one."

"Mary!"

"Well it's true. You can't just keep on taking out and never putting back in." She pulled at a thread on her quilt. "I never told anyone. I didn't want to admit it."

"Yeah. Well. I think … Let's not talk about it."

"Oh no. You're not getting off that easy. Anyway, we've done enough pranking for one night. I will tell you," Mary said. "I couldn't ever feel the same for him after that. For Claude. My best friend. My two best friends. Or so I thought." It felt wrong to say it out loud.

Stella shook her head. "Not much of a friend."

"No."

Stella watched Mary rub her arm. "You need your pain pill. Come on. We're going to the nurses' station and look after that arm." She tugged Mary's sleeve. "C'mon, girl." Stella pulled Mary's sleeve again, and this time Mary turned her wheelchair toward the reception desk.

"I need a pain pill," she said to the girl working the desk. "I wrenched my arm in the dining room and I'll never get to sleep tonight without something."

"OK, Mary. I'll ask the nurse to put one on for you when she makes her rounds."

"Thank you," Mary said. She turned to face Stella. "I realized something today. You were at my house on the day that Emerelda died."

"You think too much," Stella said.

"But you didn't know she had died. You didn't know I had stayed home that day. And you came, and you let me serve you tea and cookies, not realizing that you weren't there to see me at all. I served tea and cookies to my husband and you. And you would have choked to death on a peanut sitting there on my porch in your perfect yellow sundress, and your pretty yellow hat with the perky flowers on it. And I did the Heimlich on you. Saved your life."

Stella cleared her throat.

"Claude stood beside me. Wasn't I the silly fool?" Mary put her hand over her eyes. "Choked on a peanut. So ..." Mary stopped talking.

Stella sat still and quiet.

"I oughta tape your arms to the chair," Mary said.


Stella was in the dining room waiting for breakfast with the other early birds, and she waved Mary over impatiently.

"He can't figure it out," Stella whispered, pointing at a bald man who sat at his place picking ineffectively at his utensils.

"Ah, I forgot." Mary rubbed her hands together. "Time to reap what we taped. I'm surprised it wasn't discovered earlier."

Their enjoyment was short-lived as, when the server was pouring coffee into Mary's cup, Cathy bent over Mary; her B earrings brushed Mary's cheek.

"Mr. Beasley passed on this morning. I knew you'd want to know right away. They just phoned from the hospital to say he didn't make it through the night. It's often the way." She patted Mary's shoulder in sympathy.

"I knew it," Mary told Stella. "I knew last night there was something wrong. Now he's dead—croaked, kicked the bucket."

"Headed for boot hill," Stella said. "No good for nothin' now but parking a bicycle!"

"Damn," Mary said.

"Shit," Stella said.

Takes the fun out of gardening, Mary thought. She rolled into the greenhouse. "Mr. Beasley?" She rubbed the brown leaves of the basil plant. "This plant was quite fine yesterday. It's not fair." She tugged lightly on the basil's woody stem and with little resistance the plant let go of its hold on the earth and came out into her hand.

Dawn watched her pull out the dead herb. "Bad luck, Mary. I'm sorry."

"Doubly bad luck," Mary said. The basil plant had not had a chance.

# Chapter 27

Mary looked over her herb plot. The sage plant sprawled untidily, having taken advantage of recent deaths to spread slovenly over the vacant adjacent soil.

"Time to cut you back," Mary, said, and with her snippers she clipped the long woody branches back until just one short brown stem remained.

One little snip and this sage could be laid to rest for good, she thought. No more wondering if I should or I shouldn't. No more aches and pains either, just one big, long sleep. Like Mr. Beasley. And Claude. And Arnie. And Edward.

She tugged gently on the sage plant. Its roots held firm in the dark soil. I shouldn't, Mary thought. The pain in her shoulder throbbed. It had moved overnight; this morning she felt it over her left ribs too.

A muscle twinge? Or a heart attack?

She yanked on the sage plant, bracing her feet on the floor and using both arms. Pain shot along her left arm. The plant held firm, and Mary pulled, harder, ignoring the discomfort in her shoulder, pain's grip on her arm, and the metal bands around her chest.

The roots snapped and broke with quiet underground releases, and still Mary pulled with all she had. The tiny branch came free of the earth, bringing with it a twisted brown mass of roots.

Rich, dark, damp earth sprayed in a four foot arc around the herb bed and onto Mary.

She lurched backward; her feet lifted from the floor; her chair toppled, leaving her suspended, feet pointing at the ceiling, her hands clamped to the stem of sage, its dirt sprinkled all about her.

"Are you trying to bury yourself, Mary?" Dawn teased.

Mary didn't answer.

THE END

Made in the USA
Charleston, SC
03 November 2011